WHS McIntyre is a partner in Scotland's oldest law firm Russel + Aitken, specialising in criminal defence. William has been instructed in many interesting and high-profile cases over the years and now turns fact into fiction with his string of legal thrillers, *The Best Defence* Series, featuring defence lawyer Robbie Munro. William is married with four sons.

By the same author

Present Tense
Good News, Bad News

LAST WILL

A Best Defence Mystery

William McIntyre

SANDSTONEPRESS
HIGHLAND | SCOTLAND

Published in Great Britain by
Sandstone Press Ltd
Dochcarty Road
Dingwall
Ross-shire
IV15 9UG
Scotland

www.sandstonepress.com

The publisher acknowledges support from
Creative Scotland towards publication of this volume.

ISBN 978-1-910985-85-4
ISBNe 978-1-910985-86-1

Cover design by Jason Anscombe at Raw Shock
Typeset by Iolaire Typography Ltd, Newtonmore.
Printed and bound by Totem, Poland

To my sons: Scott, Craig, Gordon & Andrew
Providers of so much material

ACKNOWLEDGEMENTS

With thanks to friends and colleagues:

Angela Barrett - Russel + Aitken
Morag Fraser - Fraser Shepherd, and
Brian Travers - Marshall Wilson Law Group Ltd
For their expert advice on adoption law and procedure;
some of which I listened to.

And to John Mulholland for his advice on the fashion
world; none of which I listened to.

1

'Are you sure you want to go through with this, Robbie?'

Barry Munn was a five-fruits-a-day man. Grapes were his favourite, preferably squashed, fermented and poured from a bottle. Barry might not have been Scotland's foremost family lawyer. He might not even have been the best in West Lothian. But he was the best family lawyer in the room and the only family lawyer I knew who owed me a favour.

'Because if you do . . . ' Barry continued, hands clasped on the desk in front of him, peering at me through large puffy eyes that had seen the insides of a million wine glasses, 'you have some very big problems.'

'Like what?'

'First of all there's the whole man thing.'

'What do you mean?'

'Well, you're a man.'

Even my finely tuned legal mind could take no issue with that statement.

'And the courts don't just hand out residence orders for wee girls to men like they're—'

'Sweeties?'

'Not the best analogy,' Barry said, 'but accurate enough.'

'What about the DNA report?'

'No one is disputing that you're the girl's father.'

'Her name is Tina.'

'Okay, okay, no one denies that you are Tina's father. It's just that a residence order is not all about genetics. The court will decide who has custody based solely on what is in the best interests of the child.'

'But—'

Barry unclasped a hand and showed me the palm of it. 'You remember my drink-driving case?'

I remembered it all right. Remembered how the Crown had botched up the breathalyser printout and how Barry had taken a miraculous walk from what would have been his second conviction and an automatic three-year ban. The good thing about a bad reputation was that Barry thought I'd somehow contrived the whole affair and was now forever in my debt – or at least until his next Section 5 allegation came tootling along.

Barry sat forward, arms crossed on the desk. 'Remember you told me how the evidence was stacked against me? How difficult a case it was going to be and how you had to apprise me fully of all the options available? Well, that's what I'm doing to you now, so shut up and let me apprise.'

Hands behind my head, I studied the yellow damp-spot in the far corner of the swirly white Artex ceiling.

'Right,' Barry said, 'I've already mentioned the gender difficulty. Add to that your restricted accommodation, lack of experience when it comes to caring for children, oh, and the business you run single-handedly.'

I wasn't sure how Grace-Mary, my secretary/commander-in-chief, would have taken that last remark. 'My dad says he'll help out with Tina.'

'Please, don't make it worse.' Barry waited until I had leaned back in my chair again and resumed the staring

2

at the ceiling position. 'What about your single status? Would the child ... would Tina have any female role model in her life?'

'Not immediately, no, but I haven't completely discounted the prospect of forming a meaningful relationship with a woman sometime in the, hopefully, not too distant future. I'm not planning on taking holy orders if that's what you're suggesting.'

'There's no need to be like that,' Barry said.

We both knew I was behaving like a punter. I just couldn't help it. 'Sorry. Look, I can buy a bigger place, that's not a problem, well, not too much of a problem. I might have to cut down on a few of life's luxuries for a while, like food, but what child-rearing experience am I supposed to have? What experience does any parent have in raising a child until the first one comes along? And, anyway, it'll be easier for me. Tina's not a baby. She's four years old. There are no bottles or nappies to worry about. My dad was a single parent and he raised me and Malky, didn't he? Sort of.'

Barry's smile was more of a grimace. 'These are good points. Most of them. I'm just trying to point out certain weaknesses in your case. That's my job. Will you let me finish?'

'There's more?'

'Yes. You're unreliable.'

Was I hearing him correctly?

This time Barry showed me the palms of both hands. 'I'm only stating the facts as I see them.'

'Unreliable? In what way am I unreliable? Name one.'

Eyes wide, Barry puffed his cheeks and blew out, the expression on his chubby little face that of a DJ who's just been put on the spot to pick his favourite desert island disc.

3

'You're hopeless at timekeeping,' he said at last. 'Don't look at the clock. What time is it?' I hesitated for a split second. 'See? You don't even wear a watch. You were well over ten minutes late for this meeting. You were supposed to be here at one fifteen and didn't roll in until closer to half past. I mean, you were only across the road at the court. It stops for lunch at one. It's a five-minute stroll at the most.'

I had him on that one. 'Not my fault. Blame Paul. We're in a trial together and you know what his cross is like. He practically regresses witnesses back to their earliest childhood memories. Sheriff Dalrymple is just as bad, letting him prattle on. So, you see—'

'So nothing, Robbie. Don't you see? You can't say to a four-year-old, sorry I'm late and there's no food on the table, but it's all my colleague's fault, he really needs to sharpen up his cross-examination technique. Tina will depend on you and frankly...'

'Frankly what?'

'Frankly, you're not... wholly dependable.'

'So you're saying I'm wasting my time?'

Barry shrugged.

I checked the clock on the wall. One fifty. I was due back in court in ten minutes. I stood. 'I better get going. Wouldn't want to be late.'

Barry came around the side of his desk and met me as I walked to the door. 'Listen, Robbie. I've spoken to Tina's grandmother, personally. Mrs Reynolds is a lovely woman with an even lovelier big house in Oban.'

I knew that already. I'd met Vera Reynolds on a number of occasions during the time I'd been going out with her daughter Zoë – a relationship that ended when the latter had emigrated to Australia taking a piece of my heart with her. Little had I known that she was not only setting off to make a new life for herself, but incubating one at the same time. After Zoë's untimely death, Tina had been brought to Scotland to live with her Aunt Chloe, while my application to be declared her father and for a residence order was considered by the court. Chloe had three young children of her own so Tina had been loaned out to her maternal grandmother who was now keen to make the move permanent. For the last few weeks I'd been travelling west every weekend, and despite our contrary views on what was best for the wee girl, Vera Reynolds was always perfectly pleasant to me, and Tina got on exceptionally well with her.

'What's more, she's retired and can spend all her time looking after Tina,' Barry reminded me.

I knew he was talking sense. I just didn't want to hear it.

'Why is it they call you the child-snatcher again?' I asked.

'They don't,' Barry said. 'The angry ex-spouse of a former client did. Once. I wish I'd never mentioned it.'

'Well, you've told me all the negatives. I want you to start throwing a few positives at Mrs Reynolds' lawyer.'

'Like?'

'Like? What am I paying you for?'

'You're not.'

'Oh, that's how it is, is it? Well, it seems to me that you've got your driving licence, but I'm short one daughter.'

'Robbie, I'll ask you again. Is this really what you want?'

Why was he even asking? 'Of course it is. Tina is my daughter. We're a family and we should be together.' I grabbed the door handle, ready to walk out. 'If you don't think you can help, maybe I should—'

'Okay, okay.' Barry's podgy hand stopped the door opening. 'You know how I said I'd spoken to Mrs Reynolds? I've spoken to her lawyer too. This morning. They're not going to be difficult.'

'You mean, I'm getting Tina?'

'No ... not exactly. But—'

'But what?'

'I've managed to arrange a trial run. You can have Tina for one month.'

'That's great. And then?'

'And then we see how it goes.'

'It'll go fine.'

'You're remembering that the court has ordered a Bar report?'

'I'll be on my best behaviour at all times.'

'Sheriff Brechin has appointed Vikki Stark to do it.'

'What's she like?'

'Extremely competent, unfortunately,' Barry said. 'There'll be no pulling the fleece over her limpid pools. She's a former Edinburgh City Council lawyer, now working in-house for an adoption agency and a member of the local Children's Panel. You know what Bert Brechin thinks about civil actions. Unless he's locking somebody up, the law's no fun. So far as he's concerned, whatever Vikki says will go.'

'Fine by me.'

'And if all goes well and the report is a good one, then Mrs Reynolds will depart the field. Without opposition from her and faced with a good report, even Bert Brechin can't refuse to grant a residence order in your favour.'

'Barry ...'

'You're not going to hug me, are you?' he said, taking a step back.

I took one of his hands and shook it. 'Thanks. I knew you'd do the business.'

'And you really feel that you're up to the task?'

I threw my shoulders back and straightened my jacket with a tug on the lapels. 'Raring to go.'

'Good,' he said. 'You can pick Tina up ten o'clock, Saturday morning.'

I did a quick mental calculation. 'This Saturday? But it's Thursday today.'

'Well done,' Barry said, ushering me out of the door. 'Maybe you don't know the time, but at least you know what day of the week it is.'

2

I sailed through the rest of that Thursday afternoon in a daze, barely noticing Paul Sharp's relentlessly pernickety cross-examination, Sheriff Brechin's guilty verdict or the ten-mile drive from court to my office. Even the sight of two unpleasantly familiar shapes, one little, one extremely large, through the frosted glass of my waiting room door couldn't dispel my happiness.

I slipped into reception where Grace-Mary was posting some legal aid receipts. 'What does Jake Turpie want?' I asked sotto voce.

My secretary didn't drag her gaze from the computer monitor. 'What does he always want?'

It couldn't be the rent. Yes, it was late. It was always late, but on this occasion not sufficiently late to merit a personal visit from my landlord.

'If he's not here for the rent, then your guess is as good as mine,' Grace-Mary said. 'Mr Turpie wasn't in a particularly talkative mood when he came in.'

No surprise there. Jake was never much of a talker. Not unless he was extorting money, and even then he was a firm believer that actions spoke louder than words. He must have heard my voice because the waiting room door opened and he came out, marched past reception and into my office uninvited. I followed, arriving in time to see

Jake take a seat. Deek came in after me. He looked at the chair next to his boss, assessed the logistics of fitting his immense frame into it and opted to stand.

'This eejit got himself involved in a frack-arse last week,' Jake said.

Deek remained impassive. Frankenstein without the Botox injections. There was a new injury on his craggy face: a cut to the forehead, held together by a couple of grubby steri-strips. It sliced through his left eyebrow and continued onto his cheek where it tailed off and disappeared into the depths of his stubble. By the looks of things only the overhang of his Neanderthal brow had saved the big man from losing an eye.

'What happened?' seemed the obvious question.

'I sent him through to Glasgow on business last Thursday. He met an old acquaintance, they went to the pub, had an argument and Deek ended up with a face like yon.'

'This old acquaintance – anybody I know?' Whoever he was, the person who could inflict such an injury on Deek Pudney shot immediately into my top five of people I never wanted to meet in a dark alley.

'Marty Sneddon.'

I thought hard. The only Marty Sneddon I could come up with had worked in Jake's scrapyard a year or so back before being caught stealing parts and selling them for drink. Jake, not a stickler for the ACAS disciplinary guidelines, had summarily dismissed Marty along with several of his teeth.

'Not the Marty Sneddon who used to work for you?'

Jake nodded.

'Marty the alky did that to Deek? When's the funeral?' I asked, only half-jokingly.

9

'Marty's up in court on Monday. Deek isn't wanting to make a big deal about it. That right, Deek?'

The big man stared straight ahead.

'So,' Jake said, 'I want you to go along to court with Marty on Monday, tell the judge there's no hard feelings and maybe get Marty off with a fine or something. I mean, what's done is done. Right?' It was a magnanimous side to Jake I'd never seen before. 'Good. That's sorted then.' He stood.

'There's only one problem,' I said. 'I won't be able to make it on Monday.'

Jake frowned, screwing up his eyes as though I'd started speaking in a foreign tongue.

'My daughter's coming to stay,' I said.

'How did you get yourself a wean?'

'The usual way, and I need to look after her on Monday, so I can't go charging through to Glasgow Sheriff Court on short notice. There are plenty of other lawyers who'll take on Marty's case.'

Jake thought about that for a nano-second. 'Naw, you sort it for him.'

Why was he so keen for me to 'sort it' for the man who'd carved a slice out of his minder's face?

Apparently satisfied that he'd put the necessary arrangements in place, Jake patted his knees, put his hands on the arms of the chair and hoisted himself to his feet. At that signal Deek walked past him to the door and opened it.

'Sorry, Jake,' I said, 'but I'm not going. I'll get Joanna to deal with it. You remember Joanna, don't you?' If not, he was my only heterosexual male client who didn't. 'She's worked with me before.'

Jake stopped at the doorway and stood there in Deek's shadow.

'Don't worry,' I said to his back. 'Joanna knows what she's doing. Everything'll be fine.'

Jake thought about it for a minute, then turned to give me a look that would have frightened a ghost. 'It better be,' he said. 'Seriously. It better be.'

3

Friday morning and I was feeling pretty pleased with myself. The Crown Office and Procurator Fiscal Service was no place for a person with a mind of their own, and former PF depute Joanna Jordan, freed once more from the ties that bind, was freelancing as a defence agent. It had been Thursday evening, as I passed on the instructions for Marty Sneddon's bail undertaking, that I'd come up with a great idea: now Joanna was lined up not just for Marty's appearance on Monday, but for a whole month's locum work at Munro & Co.

The only court case in my diary that happy day was a trial and it had been adjourned at the intermediate diet. I had nothing to do but deal with paperwork and set things up so that Joanna could hit the ground running.

'Of course you know it's a trap.' All in all Grace-Mary had taken the news that I was going to be having some time off to bond with my daughter remarkably well, though she did harbour certain concerns. She set two wire baskets of incoming mail down on the desk in front of me. They were colour-coded. Yellow: urgent. Red: screamingly urgent. 'Or are you too stupid to realise it?' she added, herself seemingly leaning towards that latter point of view. 'You're like one of those big woolly mammoths, happily lumbering towards a big bunch of juicy bananas, not noticing that some cavemen have dug a big hole and covered it with branches and leaves.'

I came around the desk, pulled out a chair and pressed my secretary down onto it. 'It's okay. Barry Munn spoke to the other lawyer. Tina's grandmother is not going to be difficult about things. You've got to remember it was Zoë's last wish that Tina came to live with me.'

'And you've got to remember that your opponent is a woman, that her lawyer is a woman and that in a custody battle anything goes.'

'Sexist and cynical?' I said. 'Nice.'

Grace-Mary took off her spectacles and let them dangle on their gold chain. 'This is serious, Robbie. A wee girl's future is at stake. Do you really believe that Mrs Reynolds has had some kind of road to Damascus experience? Or that your boozy lawyer has persuaded her lawyer to change her client's mind? Barry Munn,' she snorted. 'They'll run so many rings round him he'll think he's the Olympic flag. Can't you see that you're both being manipulated? Vera Reynolds is setting you up to fail. In twenty-four hours Tina will be on your doorstep, and what preparations have you made?'

Other than investing in a couple of packets of Tina's favourite BN biscuits, the answer was not a lot.

'For one thing, where's the girl going to sleep?'

'I'll borrow my dad's camp bed,' I said. 'I'll put it in my bedroom or in the living room and rig up a sort of temporary tent with some sheets. Kids love that kind of thing . . . don't they?'

Grace-Mary closed her eyes, meditated a while and then without another word, got up and left the room. Ten minutes later she was back, coat on.

'I'm going out for a couple of hours,' she said. 'If you're

looking for the petty cash it's in my purse.' She bent over my desk and on a legal notepad jotted down a long list of items, starting with underwear and ending with something called Calpol. She ripped the sheet from the pad and folded it carefully. 'And I'll be taking this.' Grace-Mary lifted my cellphone from the desk and dropped it and the folded paper into her handbag. 'Your daughter is going to need your undivided attention. Don't worry, I'll let Joanna know if anything urgent crops up.' She snapped her handbag shut. 'Oh, and if you can think of anything else Tina might need ... a Calor Gas stove to cook her dinner on ... some extra guy-ropes ... be sure to give me a call.'

4

'What are you doing here?'

'And a good day to you, Grace-Mary,' I said.

Wednesday morning I'd dropped into the office on the pretence of giving my locum the low-down on some upcoming cases, but in reality to make sure that everything was running smoothly in my absence. It seemed everything was – alarmingly so. Grace-Mary and Joanna were in reception carrying out a file check, entering court dates and bring-backs into a colour-coded electronic ledger.

'Where's Tina?' Joanna asked. 'Did you not bring her to see us?'

'Her Gramps dropped her off at nursery this morning to give me a chance to tidy the house and do some laundry. That girl goes through some amount of clothes.'

'Get used to it,' Grace-Mary said. 'That's not going to change as she gets older. Unlike men, women don't go through life relying on only a couple of changes of clothes.'

I was going to protest until I considered my own wardrobe: suit for work, jeans and some casual shirts for not-work.

'What's with the suit, anyway?' Joanna asked. 'You look like you're ready to start back.'

'Just thought I'd swing by and see how things were going. I've got some time before I have to collect Tina, so if anything's needing done, clients needing seen . . . '

'We're managing fine, thanks.' Grace-Mary came from around her PC, leaned against the edge of the reception desk and studied me closely. 'So you're coping all right with fatherhood?'

Coping? I was doing more than just coping. The last few days had been the longest, most difficult and happiest of my life.

'Hanging by a tack,' I said, laughing. 'No, really, everything's going fine.'

Grace-Mary didn't look too convinced. 'And how is the wee lamb handling her new surroundings?'

The answer to my secretary's question was that the wee lamb was great. The best. I couldn't believe how quickly she'd settled in. She'd lost her mother only three months ago, been transported across from the other side of the world, first to live with her aunt, then with her grandmother and now with a father she'd only recently discovered she had. And yet she seemed to be taking it all in her size three stride.

'How are the sleeping arrangements working out?' Joanna asked, smirking. 'Grace-Mary told me about them. Sounds exciting.'

I had to admit that, sleeping-wise, everything had not gone according to plan. At least not to my plan. As predicted, Tina had thought the camp bed set-up great fun. Such fun, in fact, that after the first night she'd let me try it out and from then on she and her menagerie of soft toys had moved into my double bed. 'I'm looking for somewhere bigger,' I said. Until then sleeping on a camp bed was a price worth paying.

'So what are your plans for the rest of the day?' Joanna asked.

'Like I say,' I swivelled the computer screen to face me. 'I can help out here for a while if there's anything needing done.'

Grace-Mary turned the screen around again. 'There's not.'

'In which case, after I collect Tina from nursery we're going to Sandy's for lunch and from there it will be the swing-park or maybe that new indoor play area, depending what the weather's like.' I reached out and lifted the corner of a file. 'Anything happening that I should know about?'

Grace-Mary slammed her hand down, pinning the file of papers to the desk. 'Everything's just fine. Isn't that right, Joanna?'

The phone rang. Grace-Mary went across the room to answer it, giving me a chance to talk shop with Joanna. 'How did the bail undertaking for Marty Sneddon go on Monday?'

She winced. 'Not so good, I'm afraid. From what you told me I thought it was going to be a summary complaint. You know, plead guilty, slap on the wrist and home again.'

'It wasn't?'

'You never told me that Deek Pudney had been badly injured. They put Sneddon on a petition for assault to severe injury and permanent disfigurement. I had to wait all day for the case to call.'

It wasn't exactly what Jake had been hoping for. Still, it couldn't be helped. But there was more bad news.

'And it turned out that Marty had a previous for assault on indictment. It was years ago, but enough for him to be remanded under section 23D. He's up for full committal next week.'

'Does Jake know?'

'Not sure. He hasn't been back in touch.'

17

'He has now,' Grace-Mary said, holding the receiver out to me, hand clamped over the mouthpiece.

'Tell him I'm not here.'

'You tell him.'

I went over and took the receiver thrust at me. 'Jake, how's it going?'

Rather surprisingly, it was going fine. I'd expected a rant on the subject of Marty Sneddon's incarceration, but he never mentioned a word about it. Even when he asked if he could come and see me about something urgent and I told him I was very busy, he didn't seem to mind. We left things on the basis that I'd do my best to catch up with him sometime over the next few days.

'What did he want?' Grace-Mary asked.

'I don't know,' I said. 'I'll phone him later. I've got his number on my mobile. By the way, where is it?'

'Perfectly safe,' Grace-Mary said, patting the big black handbag that hung over the back of her chair.

'Yes, but it would be equally safe with me, where it's supposed to be,' I said.

Grace-Mary thought about it and then said, 'No, you'd just answer it or do something stupid like actually call Jake Turpie. The man's a nuisance and you've got a daughter to look after.' She climbed out of her seat, went over to one of the cabinets and pulled out a file. When she returned to her desk she stared up at me as though surprised I was still there. 'Was there anything else?'

'Well, while I'm here I thought I could just take a swatch at a few files, maybe—'

'Joanna,' Grace-Mary said. 'Show him to the door. And, Robbie, the next time you drop in, bring your wee girl with you or don't bother coming at all.'

5

'Mr Munro, I wonder, could I have a word?'

Nursery places weren't easy to come by, so it was with some difficulty and at a price that I'd managed to find Tina a berth Monday, Wednesday and Friday mornings at The Little Ships Nursery, situated within a newly refurbished building in a wynd just off the High Street.

A seascape mural with blue sky, white-sailed boats, plenty of seagulls and a hooped lighthouse, stretched the length of the reception area, from the main door right down to the rows of coat racks, where each peg was identified by a different nautical symbol or sea creature. Tina's was an anchor. She'd wanted the smiley starfish.

'Mr Munro!' I identified the source of the voice floating above the heads of the other parents who'd come to collect offspring as being that of Mrs Fitzsimmons, boss, or maybe that should have been captain, of The Little Ships Nursery. Her age and attire set her apart from the other childcare staff, who were generally a lot younger and wore powder-blue tracksuit bottoms and sweatshirts embroidered with little yacht motifs, rather than fetching, aquamarine trouser suits. Mrs Fitzsimmons took me by the upper arm and steered me away from the crowd. By the grim look on her face I thought I might be headed for the brig.

'There's been an . . . an incident.' Mrs Fitzsimmons

stroked her red, white and navy-blue silk neck scarf.

I looked around. There was no sign of my daughter amongst the kids who were wandering through to the changing room to be stuffed into coats and have black gym shoes exchanged for outdoor footwear. Where was she? I had the sudden feeling that someone had opened my mouth and tipped the contents of an ice bucket down my throat. I tried to speak, but the only sound I could emit was a croaky, 'Tina . . . ?'

'Tina's fine, but I'm afraid she's been involved in a slight contretemps with another child,' said Mrs Fitzsimmons.

I took a deep breath and released. Tina was fine. A contretemps I felt sure I could deal with.

'Zack,' Mrs Fitzsimmons continued, 'is quite a demanding child and one, it's true, with certain . . . proprietorial issues, however—'

'Proprietorial issues?'

'Difficulty sharing,' she clarified.

The other parents and children were starting to drift past and away, waving to the blue-clad helpers standing guard either side of the front door as they went.

'Where's Tina?' I asked flatly.

'I've told you, Tina's fine.'

'Yes, but where is she?'

Mrs F took a step closer to me. 'Zack and Tina didn't see eye to eye over the counting bricks.'

Was that all? 'Oh well,' I said. 'Worse things happen at sea, I suppose.' Only I found that amusing.

'There was a fight.'

I could see where this was going and whether it was the relief of knowing that Tina was all right – whatever – I was prepared to be magnanimous. 'Boys will be boys. I know you'll have taken the appropriate action and I assure you there'll be no complaint from me. I'll buy Tina some ice cream and—'

'Actually, not so much a fight as an assault,' Mrs Fitzsimmons continued.

I could feel a surge of anger. If that little brat had hurt my daughter . . .

'Tina punched Zack. Twice. Apparently her Gramps refers to it as the old one-two.'

Over to my left an unhappy-looking woman, holding the hand of an even more unhappy-looking boy, exited through the heavy swing doors from the main play area. They were escorted by one of the nursery helpers who held a white tissue clamped to the boy's nose.

'Zack?' I asked. 'Big for his age, isn't he?'

Mrs Fitzsimmons signalled to another helper who disappeared through the swing doors, reappearing momentarily with Tina stomping along behind her, head bowed, arms stiff at her side.

'We've had a talk, Tina and I,' Mrs Fitzsimmons said, once Tina had drawn up alongside. 'It won't happen again. Will it, Tina?' My daughter didn't twitch a muscle. 'Mr Munro, if Tina is to remain here at The Little Ships she's going to have to learn that violence is never the answer. Perhaps you could pass that message to her *Gramps*.'

Tina mumbled something.

I hunkered down. 'What's that, honey?'

'He wanted all the bricks to himself, but we're supposed to share.'

It should have been a proud moment for me. My daughter's first plea-in-mitigation, and to an assault charge at that; however, I could sense her words of excuse were having about as much effect on the nursery manager as mine tended to have on Sheriff Brechin.

21

'I know,' I said, 'but you can't go hitting people. It's not nice.'

'He's not nice!' Tina shouted.

Mrs Fitzsimmons clapped her hands together. 'All right then. I'll leave you two to have a chat and . . . ' she patted Tina on the head, 'I'll see this young lady back here on Friday.'

Tina pulled her head away and did an excellent impression of one of her grandfather's trademark grunts. I hurriedly got her inside a puffy pink anorak and we left, skirting the genetically modified Zack and his mother on the road out, and arriving a few minutes later at Sandy's café, where my dad had already captured his favourite corner table. Tina ran over and gave him a hug.

'Tina! Come here quickly!' Sandy yelled. 'See what I make for your lunch.' Tina released the old man from her stranglehold and ran to the counter where the café owner was waiting.

'Don't forget our bacon rolls!' I called after her.

My dad penned an answer into his crossword, folded his newspaper and set it down on the table with an air of satisfaction. I'd always struggled with crosswords – the proper kind, the cryptic ones. He always made them seem so easy.

'How long did that take you?' I asked, studying the white squares filled with neatly printed letters.

'About two cups of tea,' he said, taking a final slurp from the big china mug that Sandy kept especially for him.

'I don't think I could even get one clue in that time. Burn em in boxes for instance? What kind of clue is that?' I asked.

'A tricky one,' he said. 'But they usually are. You just

22

have to solve it piece by piece. Don't start at the beginning, that's too obvious. What kind of boxes do you put stuff into?'

'Cardboard?'

'Crates. Put em into crates and you've got cremates. I thought your legally trained mind would have worked that out. It's all perfectly logical –unlike wearing a suit when you're about to have lunch with Tina. What's wrong? I do hope everything's okay at work. You know I hate to think of all those criminals being sent to the jail if you're not there to hold their hands.'

'Everything's fine at the office, thanks,' I said. 'Wish I could say the same for the nursery.'

'Problem?'

'Zack.'

'Oh, him. The bully. What's he up to now?'

'Crying a little and bleeding a lot. Seems like someone gave Tina a few boxing lessons.'

He put down his mug and shrugged. 'A girl has to be able to look out for herself these days. It's not safe out there.'

'Dad, this is not the mean streets of East LA. She's at nursery school. She goes there to colour in and make art out of cornflake packets, not to dispense her own brand of justice.'

My dad snorted. 'Have you seen the size of that Zack kid? I'll bet there's not too many forks in his family tree. He's like a gorilla.' He paused to take another drink of tea. 'Make anyone believe in evolution, that Zack would. What do you want Tina to do when he starts throwing his weight about? Scream and run away like a—'

'Wee girl?'

Tina arrived at the table carrying a big white plate.

'See what Sandy made me.' She tilted the plate at us. Spaghetti hoops hair, ketchup eyes, a fried egg nose and a big curved sausage smile all threatened to slide off and onto the floor.

My dad rescued the plate and set it down on the table. I removed Tina's coat and while she was grabbing her fork and knife, managed to stuff a paper napkin into the neck of her T-shirt.

Sandy came over with a plate of four bacon rolls, nodded down at Tina's lunch and took a grip of my shoulder. 'You want I knock you up one of those instead, Robbie?'

'There's only us, here, Sandy,' I said. 'You can go easy on the accent. You're sounding more like Robert de Niro every day and, thanks to her trainer here, the Munro family has already got its own Raging Bull.' I jerked a thumb at my dad and Tina in turn.

'What's this?' Sandy asked. 'Has Tina not been playing nice with the other kids?'

'She's just been sticking up for herself,' my dad said. 'Isn't that right, sweetheart?'

Tina was too busy carrying out a blunt dissection of Mr Food-Face to answer.

'A boy was annoying her,' I said. 'He wasn't sharing.'

Tina looked up from her surgery. 'He wouldn't let me play with the bricks and he said I talked funny.'

Though she'd picked up her mum's Scots accent, every now and again there was a distinct Aussie twang to my daughter's voice.

Sandy knelt down by her side. 'Don't worry, Tina. People, they say that I talk funny too.'

'That's because you do talk funny,' my dad said. 'Now, would the pair of you leave the girl in peace to eat her lunch?'

Sandy ruffled Tina's hair and shuffled off, I presumed to serve some new customers because I heard the bell above the door tinkle. I'd just taken a bite of a bacon roll and was poised for another when I realised that my dad was sitting immobile, staring over my left shoulder. I turned to see Jake Turpie standing a few feet away.

'What do you want?' my dad growled at him.

Ignoring my dad's words of welcome, Jake came over and stood by our table. 'This her, Robbie? This your new daughter?' he asked, as though I'd had an old one and traded her in for the latest model.

'I said what do you want, Turpie?' My dad threatened to stand. Still chewing, I shoved the plate of rolls at him hoping he'd take one and shut up.

'I'm here to ask a favour—'

'Robbie's got no time for favours,' my dad said, taking advantage of the silence caused by my mouthful of bacon roll. 'He's got a wean to look after.' He snatched a bacon roll from the plate and ripped a chunk out of it like it was Jake's head from his shoulders.

'And to give him this.' Jake produced an envelope and handed it to me. 'For you to buy your wee lassie something nice.'

I spirited the envelope away inside my jacket pocket. Jake took a few steps back. I stood.

Tina looked up. 'Where you going, Dad?' she asked through a clown's mouth of spaghetti sauce.

'He's abandoning you,' my dad said.

'He'll be back in a minute, pet,' Jake said.

Taking the napkin out of the neck of Tina's T-shirt and wiping my mouth with it, I followed Jake out of range of my dad. Almost.

'With some folk, money talks. With your dad, it gives

25

orders.' I heard the old man grumble to Tina. It was okay for him and his police pension.

'I need you to come with me, I've a job for you,' Jake said.

I would have protested but for the warm feel of the envelope nestling in my inside breast pocket, next to my heart. 'What kind of message?'

'I'll tell you all about it on the way.'

I turned to see my daughter, head down and shovelling spaghetti hoops like a stoker feeding a furnace, while her grandfather glowered at me, moustache rigid in disapproval.

Jake strolled to the counter and slapped down a ten pound note. 'Get the wean some ice cream when she's finished,' he said to Sandy. 'Extra sprinkles.' He gave me a shove in the small of the back. 'Come on. Deek's out there on the zigzags.'

6

Deek Pudney was waiting directly outside Sandy's in a dented white Ford Transit van that had never seen a soapy chamois since the day it had rolled off the assembly line.

I climbed in through the passenger door. Jake went around the other side and gave Deek a shove.

'Move over. I'm driving. Robbie's in a hurry,' he said. The big man budged along into the middle, his bulk squashing against me, keeping my right arm pinned to my side. Jake took a pair of black leather driving gloves from the top of the dashboard where they'd been lying amidst a gathering of Mars Bar wrappers, crumpled fish-supper papers and a half-drunk bottle of Irn Bru. He stretched the gloves across his hands, knuckles poking through the holes in the back, and leaned forward to look at me past the massive obstruction that sat between us. 'Don't worry, this'll only take ten minutes.'

By all scientifically recognised standards of measurement, Jake's estimation of time was way out. It must have been forty minutes later that we neared our destination, a farmhouse somewhere to the south of Livingston, near the village of East Riggburn. This was West Lothian at its deepest and darkest, and our slow journey, full of bends and B roads, gave my landlord the opportunity to set out my remit in detail.

I knew Jake operated an, on-the-face-of-it, legitimate used car business. What I didn't know was precisely why; though it probably had something to do with offsetting those genuine receipts against the cash payments he received via his much larger scrap-dealing operation. As he went on to explain, he'd sold a vehicle to a farmer who was now way behind in instalments. Getting money out of the average farmer was like growing orchids in a West Lothian winter, but credit ratings meant little to Jake and late-payers were a novelty thanks to his efficient credit control system. A credit control system that was sitting right next to me, squashing me against the interior of the nearside door.

Jake gave Deek a nudge. 'Which way next?'

Unfortunately, next was a sharp right turn. I'd been hoping for a left, the only manoeuvre that gave me a chance to breathe properly. Jake spun the wheel, Deek leaned into me and I thought I felt a rib crack.

'This Mrs Adams we're going to see,' Jake said, oblivious to my pain, 'she's some kind of lady farmer. I didn't want to send Deek 'cos I thought he might frighten her.' There was no 'might' about it, but wasn't frightening people into parting with money Deek's main purpose in life? 'If she called the cops, you can see how it would look, and I'm not wanting the big man getting himself into any more bother.'

So, there I had it. Displaying a so far unrevealed chivalrous side to his nature, Jake had decided on a softly-softly approach. Rather than send Deek to the door, I was instead to explain politely to the lady farmer all about the need to keep up payments, failing which further legal steps would be taken which would involve her in considerable additional inconvenience, embarrassment and expense. I was glad I was wearing my suit because it would make me more lawyerly-looking.

'Give it to her tight,' Jake said, as we trundled towards a red-brick farmhouse, along a rough track, fields either side, the only sign of life a bored-looking pony with a dirty canvas coat on its back, standing beside two hypothermic donkeys. 'Use all the big legal words. It was her who wanted to pay cash. I only done it as a favour. Cash is no good to JT Motors, I've still got to put it through the books.' By which I supposed he meant the set of books the Taxman was shown.

In a hail of gravel, he pulled our vehicle to a halt at the front of the building, where a red 4x4 SUV was parked. As arranged, we weren't going to visit mob-handed. I went to the door alone and knocked. No answer.

'She must be in – the car's here!' Jake yelled at me from the van, when there was still no response despite repeated knocks and a few loud rattles at the brass letter box. 'Try round the back!'

It was the route of least resistance just to do as I'd been told. The sooner I was done the better. I could imagine what my dad would be like when I got back home after having *abandoned* my child. Turning the corner of the house, I found a small area of garden ground sectioned off by a wooden trellis with a wrought-iron gate and a path leading up to a side door.

I'd only taken a couple of steps along the path when I noticed splintered wood sticking out from the frame and the door slightly ajar. 'Mrs Adams?' I called. 'I'm here about the car.'

I could have left it at that. I should have left it at that, gone back and told Jake she wasn't in, but he would never have listened. So, approaching the damaged door with caution, I gave it a push, not expecting it to fall open and hang suspended on its middle hinge; the only one of three that remained intact. As the top of the door toppled inwards and the bottom swung upwards and outwards at me, I jumped back, narrowly avoiding being hit by the door if not by the smell. The sweet, sickly smell that I'd thankfully encountered only a few times previously, and on those occasions insufficiently camouflaged even by the pine-fresh tang of mortuary disinfectant.

I clamped a hand across my face, pushed the collapsed door with the toe of my shoe and looked in to what at first sight seemed like a normal farmhouse kitchen. To my right a cream-enamel AGA range. Straight ahead an immense oak dresser, plates neatly lined up, mugs hanging from hooks, and, beside it, a cast-iron and porcelain double sink with a few pots and pans upside down on the draining board. Pride of place, dead centre of the room, was an enormous wooden table, and centre of that, and very dead indeed, was the body of a man, one arm outstretched, the other across his stomach, legs hanging over the edge of the table, milky eyes staring up at the squadron of flies that had scrambled, taken off and now hovered above him.

The cause of death was obvious. The man's throat was gashed wide open and the murder weapon, a black-handled carving knife, protruded from his chest. I stepped forward for a better look. The table top was stained black with dried blood, caked hard onto the wood. The hand dangling over one side of the table was swollen, the fingers stiff and black. Whoever he was, he'd been dead for quite some time.

I turned to leave, only to bump into Jake in the doorway, Deek at his back, towering over him.

'What's taking you ... ?' Jake asked, his voice trailing

off as first the smell hit him and then he saw past me to the corpse on the table.

'Better not come in,' I said.

Jake shoved me out of the way and marched right up to the table. I followed, trying to tell him that we needed first to leave and second to call the police.

'All right, all right, hold on a minute,' Jake said. 'I'm only having a look.' He peered down at the body, gloved hands in his pockets, tilting his head at an angle for a better glimpse at the man's face. 'No, that's definitely not her,' he said after a moment or two, then, glancing around, 'Where do you think she is?'

What was he talking about? He couldn't still be expecting me to continue with our mission. *Yes, Mrs Adams, I know there's a dead man on your kitchen table, but can I have a quick word about your instalment arrears?*

I took a grip of his arm. 'Let's go.'

He shook me off and waved Deek over. 'Look familiar?' Deek stared at the corpse for a moment and then shook his head.

Jake walked to the dresser. There was a twenty pound note and some loose change in a glazed-pottery fruit bowl. He took the money, shoved it in his pocket and started to look around, presumably in case there was any other cash lying about.

'Jake, we've got to get out of here. This is a crime scene. Start touching things and the cops could come up with some very funny ideas.'

I turned on a heel, hoping he'd follow. He didn't. He walked to a door in the far wall, opened it and stepped through. I went after him into a dark hallway leading to the front of the house, a flight of stairs immediately to my right.

'Seriously, Jake. We need to phone the police.' I reached into my pocket for my mobile and remembered Grace-Mary's big black handbag. No use asking Jake. He never carried one. Cellphones had solved more crimes than Sherlock Holmes. In Jake's uncertain world it was better to leave it safe in a drawer somewhere, like his own personal alibi.

A noise. Jake turned around. He heard it too. A whimper. At first I thought it must be a dog. Then I heard it again. It was definitely human and coming from upstairs.

'Wait here,' I said to Jake. From the kitchen I could hear the sound of footsteps and glanced back the way I'd come to see Deek strolling around, studying this and that like he might be thinking of buying the place. 'And tell that idiot to stand still and stop touching things!'

By the time I'd reached the middle landing, the initial whimpering and sobbing had increased to a wail, unmistakably that of a child. I turned the bend and saw a small face peering at me through the banisters on the top level. It was a small girl, lying on her stomach, blonde hair matted and greasy, face streaked black with grime and tears. She didn't look much older than Tina.

'What's your name?' I asked softly, taking the next step very slowly. The girl stopped crying, but didn't answer. 'My name's Robbie,' I said. 'What's yours?'

'Is that her?' Jake shouted from the hallway.

I looked around to see him at the foot of the stairs. 'No, it's not. Now shut up and find a phone.'

When I turned around again, the tear-stained face was gone. It wasn't difficult to work out where. There were four doors on the top level; three wide open, one firmly closed. I tiptoed over and knocked softly. 'Hello?' No response. I tried the handle, the door opened. Inside I encountered a different smell; not death this time, but the equally unpleasant aroma of stale urine and faeces. The room was small; a single bed, cheap wardrobe and chest of drawers the only furnishings. Empty crisp packets and biscuit wrappers were strewn across the threadbare carpet. A gnawed piece of orange cheese, hard around the edges, lay on a damp patch on the bed sheet beside a soft toy. On the floor across the other side of the bed I could see the corner of a duvet and, poking from beneath it, a shoe and part of a leg.

'Come out. It's okay, you're safe now,' I said. More sobs. 'I've got a wee girl. She's about the same age as you. Her name is Tina. What's yours?' I was giving it my best shot, but no amount of encouraging noises from me would tempt the child from her cocoon. I knelt down and gently tugged the foot that was sticking out. It withdrew sharply and she shifted, wedging herself under the bed.

'If you come out, we can go downstairs.' More sobbing, worse now. The girl began to squirm and drum her shoes on the floor. Talk of going downstairs wasn't helping. It should have been obvious to me from the crisps and biscuit wrappers that she'd been to the kitchen already. She knew what was down there.

'I've got a car,' I said. 'Let's go and see the police. Or how about you tell me the name of your teacher or ... ' My conversational repertoire was fast running out. What did you say to a starving child who'd been living in her own filth for several days with a dead body downstairs? It wasn't something they taught you at law school, or else I'd skipped the lecture.

I kept trying, but I might as well have been talking to the stuffed toy; some kind of bird, grubby-white with a long yellow beak, one wing hanging by a thread and, strangely, wearing a green waistcoat. It was no bigger than my hand. I picked it up. 'What's your birdie's name?' The frantic writhing and battering of feet on the floor slowed to a stop. A promising sign. 'I think he wants you. He's lonely up here by himself. He's sad and scared,' I said, pressing home my advantage. 'He must be hungry too. Why don't I take him and see if I can find him something to eat?'

I picked up the soft toy, made as though to walk out of the door and then turned to see the girl peeking over the top of the bed.

'Come on,' I said. 'Come with me and we'll find your birdie some food. We don't need to go into the kitchen. We can go outside where the donkeys are.'

Slowly the little girl unwrapped herself from the bedclothes and stood up. She was wearing a yellow dress, little white flowers embroidered around the hem. The garment was damp and stained and the source of much of the smell. In one dirty little hand she gripped a mobile phone.

'Can I see your phone?' I asked, reaching out. The girl looked like she was going to start wailing again. 'Please?'

She threw it onto the bed. I picked it up and pressed a few buttons, but the phone was as lifeless as the man on the kitchen table. I put it into my suit pocket. 'Come on.' I held out the stuffed toy to her. 'Let's go.'

Eyes fixed on the waistcoat-wearing bird, the girl raised an arm from her side in slow motion. She was only a few feet away.

'Come and get the birdie,' I said. She took a step forward, then another and another. 'That's it.' With a final step she took the toy from my hand, clasped it to her chest and squeezed it tightly.

'Hold my hand and we'll go downstairs,' I said, and

34

amazingly one little hand released its grip on the toy and an arm extended slowly in my direction.

'What's going on in here?' Jake Turpie marched into the room and glowered down at the child. 'Who's this?' he asked, as though wanting me to make formal introductions. We were joined by Deek who had to duck his head under the lintel to come in.

The wee girl stood there, looking up at the three of us, slack-jawed. Her grip on the stuffed toy weakened and she made a small whimpering sound. Before she could start wailing again I whisked her up into my arms and, her dirty little face pressed into my chest, carried her downstairs and as quickly as possible out of the house.

7

On 1st April 2013, the Scottish Government unified Scotland's eight territorial police forces into one state-controlled police service. The unification was supposed to be about efficiency and saving money. Many believed it had more to do with power and control. Easier for a Justice Secretary to give orders to one Top Cop than try and bully a room full of Chief Constables.

Whichever it was, the radical change had led to the closure of nearly one-third of the police stations in Scotland, along with three-quarters of control rooms. It meant that, without a phone, finding a policeman wasn't easy. To make matters worse, when I eventually did find a cop it turned out to be Detective Inspector Dougie Fleming. The years he'd spent training to be the world's most obnoxious individual had not been wasted.

'I don't buy any of this,' he said, leafing through his notebook for the umpteenth time. 'Why don't you have another go? Try the truth this time. It will make a nice change.'

'What is it you don't understand?' I asked. We were in an interview room at Livingston Police Station. The soundproofed walls were covered in a brown hessian material, our chairs, two either side of a plastic table, bolted to the floor. There was a camera in the corner of the ceiling and a DVD recording unit by the DI's right

36

hand. Both were switched off. Fleming preferred his notebook. He flicked through a few more pages, tapping the end of his pencil on the table. Perhaps if I humoured him he wouldn't insist on going through the whole thing again in minute detail, just so that he could try and pick up on any slight discrepancy.

I thought it would save time if I summarised. 'Earlier on today, I went with my client, Mr Jake Turpie, and his colleague, Derek Pudney, to the home of his customer, Mrs . . . sorry, I don't know her first name, Adams. The reason I was there was to warn her of possible court action in relation to an unpaid debt.'

'When did you start doing civil court work?' Fleming asked.

'And I take it Mr Turpie's got all the paperwork to prove that debt?' chipped in Fleming's sidekick, an extremely thin DC with lots of hair. It had been the skinny cop's first input to an interview that had lasted almost an hour. Before that I'd had a two-hour wait. Dougie Fleming liked his interviewees to marinate in worry for a while before he spoke to them. I'd spent the time reading through a stack of out-of-date *National Geographic*, and was now well up on, amongst other useful topics, the healing power of snake venom and crabs of the British shoreline.

'The side door was broken. I went in—'

'Uninvited?' the skinny cop asked.

I wasn't for being sidetracked. 'I went in, saw the dead guy on the table, heard crying from upstairs, found the girl and drove straight here.'

'I don't understand.' Fleming placed his stump of a pencil on the table between us. 'Why did you do that? Why not phone it in?' I didn't answer. I'd already explained that the farmhouse phone was out of order on account of it having been ripped from the wall. Fleming snorted. 'Strange how not one of the three of you possessed a mobile phone.' Fleming turned over a few pages. 'According to you, you'd left your mobile phone at home.'

'Not at home,' I said. 'At my office.'

'Not a very mobile mobile phone is it?' said DC Skinny.

Fleming turned to the last page of the pencil-written statement, took a pen from his breast pocket and slid both items across the table to me.

My turn to sigh. I slid the book and pen back at him and stood up.

'Sit down,' he said.

Skinny pointed at the chair.

'No, thanks,' I said. 'I'm leaving.'

The DC got up and blocked the door.

I turned to Fleming. 'If I'm being held against my will, I want to know why and to have a lawyer informed.'

'You are a lawyer. And why do you *think* you're being held?' Skinny said. He was really beginning to piss me off. 'This is a double homicide investigation and if we tell you to stay—'

'Double homicide?' I asked.

Fleming glowered at his colleague and then at me. 'Sit.'

I didn't.

'Please.'

I sat.

'Another body's been found,' Fleming said. 'A female. We think it's the householder.'

'Does that mean the dead guy isn't the householder?'

Fleming's little helper stepped forward and bent over, his face close to mine. 'You're here to answer questions, not ask them.'

'Yes, if you don't mind, I'll conduct the interview,'

Fleming said, and the DC withdrew to resume his position guarding the door.

Fleming continued. 'Obviously, we're at an early stage in our enquiries and don't want too much information leaking out at this time,' he said, glowering at his colleague as he squeezed out from behind the table. 'You can leave.' He jerked his head to the side, a signal for skinny cop to move away from the door. 'But we're keeping hold of your clients for the moment. Just until we check out their stories,' he said, stifling my protests. 'That may take some time – which is no bad thing. Better that than the pair of them spreading the word around every boozer in West Lothian.' He gestured with an open hand to the door. 'DC Grant will show you out, but I mean it, not one word of this to anyone, understand? Nobody.'

8

'Are you telling me you've gone and got yourself involved in a double murder?'

My dad was not at all happy at my prolonged absence and there'd been no danger of me getting away without a proper explanation for my extreme tardiness. I could have made something up, but that would only have brought on an interrogation far more robust than anything Dougie Fleming was capable of, so I'd told him everything.

'How do you do it, Robbie? How do you always manage to mess things up?' There was a chat show on the TV. The host was telling a famous actor how wonderful the famous actor was, even though the famous actor seemed to know how wonderful he was already. My dad pressed mute on the remote. 'Well?'

'It's not like that, Dad. I'm not involved. I didn't kill anyone. I'm a witness, that's all.'

'It's that man, Turpie, isn't it?'

'Not really . . . well . . . sort of.'

'No sort of about it.'

'He was there when I found the body.'

'I thought there was two folk dead?'

'There is. I only saw one and I'm not supposed to talk to anyone about them. Dougie Fleming wants to keep it top secret, so can we talk about something else? And keep your voice down.'

Through the living room wall I could hear Tina humming a tune to herself. She'd been in bed when I got home, and when I'd popped in to say goodnight I'd been suckered into a bedtime story. Since then she'd been up three times; first for a drink and a biscuit, then because she needed to brush her teeth again and finally for the toilet.

'That social worker was here earlier on,' my dad said after a period of silence. 'Vikki, she's called. It's not short for Victoria or anything. That's it. That's her name. Vikki. With two Ks.'

'She's not a social worker, Dad. She's a lawyer. What did she want?'

'To see you, of course, except you weren't here so I had to tell her you'd nipped out to the shops.'

'What's she like? Some dried-up old spinster with no kids who thinks she can go about telling everyone else how to bring up theirs?'

'No. She's young and a bit of a looker actually. We didn't discuss her marital status, but she seemed all right to me.'

'I like Vikki.' We both turned around to see Tina in her pyjamas, wide awake. I beckoned to her and she came over and sat beside me on the couch. 'Vikki smells like flowers.'

'Does she?' I said. 'Was she talking to you?'

Tina nodded vigorously.

'What about?'

'She asked if I liked living here and going to nursery and stuff.'

'And do you?'

Tina nodded again, smiling.

'What do you like best at nursery?'

'Painting.'

'And what sort of things do you like to paint?'

Tina thought for a moment, head to one side, then her face quivered, crumpled. She leaned away from me, planted her face into a cushion and started to cry. I picked her up, sat her on my knee and bounced her up and down. It only made things worse. When I tried to give her a hug, she broke away, ran over to the end of the couch and, head on the armrest, continued to break her heart.

My dad made to climb out of his armchair. I shook my head at him.

'What is it?' he whispered, lowering himself again. 'What's wrong?'

I didn't reply. Tina's tears flowed for a few more minutes and then stopped. She looked up and asked for a drink. When I came back from the kitchen with a glass of milk she was sitting on my dad's ankle, playing horsey and laughing as though nothing had happened.

'She does that,' I told my dad when, milk drunk, tucked up in bed and one very short bedtime story later, I returned to the living room. 'She misses her mum. Certain things jog her memory. It can be anything and it's usually around bedtime. One night I was reading her nursery rhymes, and when I got to Little Miss Muffet she was off into floods and completely inconsolable. I don't know what to do when it happens. You can't tell a four-year-old to pull herself together.'

'Malky was like that,' my dad said. 'After your mum died. You were too young to know what was going on. It takes time.' He switched off the TV. 'So, the murders. Who's dead? Anyone I know?'

'Doubt it. I saw one of them and had a pretty good look at his face.' That was a mental image I wasn't going to lose anytime soon. 'It was definitely nobody I recognised.'

'Why were you even there?'

42

'Jake wanted me to speak to the householder. She's a farmer and owes him money for a car. I think hers is the other body. It'll all be in the papers sooner or later.'

A car pulled up in the street outside. My front door opened and Malky poked his head into the living room. 'Where is she? Where's my niece?'

'In her bed where she should be,' my dad said.

'At this time? Why? Has she got work in the morning or something? Come on. Let the girl live a little.'

Ten seconds later he was giving my wide-awake daughter a piggyback around the room.

'Look what Uncle Malky got me!' Tina yelled, waving a Freddo bar above her head.

Great, that would mean a clean nightie after she'd smeared chocolate all down herself and then the whole rigmarole of teeth-brushing again, an activity Tina could spin out endlessly if the alternative was bed.

I tried to take the chocolate bar from her, but she was gripping it like a NRA member grips his semi-automatic.

'How about we play a game of something,' I said, hoping to distract her long enough to make the chocolate disappear.

'Don-i-moes!' Tina squealed.

Dominoes? I didn't know Tina could play dominoes.

My dad cleared his throat. 'I don't think you have any dominoes, do you, Robbie?'

I did. Somewhere.

'Gramps and me were playing don-i-moes today,' Tina said.

'Cup of tea, anyone?' my dad asked.

'I'll have a cup,' Malky said. 'Either that or a beer. You got any beer in, Robbie?'

I explained to Malky that I hadn't seen a beer or any other alcoholic beverage for a week and that there wasn't so much as a wine gum in the house in case Vikki the child welfare lawyer happened by and wanted to inspect the fridge or smell my breath.

'Me and Gramps went to a smelly shop,' Tina said.

'Tea it is, then.' For a big man with a bad knee my dad made the trip from living room to kitchen swiftly and nimbly enough.

'Gramps had special lemonade and I had cola and the man gave me three straws,' Tina continued. 'And we had crisps and—'

Malky laughed. He tickled Tina, who by this time had most of the wrapper off the Freddo bar. 'Are you trying to get your gramps into trouble?'

'Dad!' I shouted through to the kitchen. 'Did you take Tina to the Red Corner Bar after I left you at Sandy's?' But my question was drowned out by the sound of the kettle being filled with enough water to boil a missionary.

The phone rang. Saved by the bell, my dad popped back into the living room carrying the kettle. 'That'll be for you.'

He was right. It was Joanna.

'I'm at the police station. I wouldn't bother you, it's just that the cops couldn't get you on your mobile and they called me. They're wanting to arrest Jake Turpie,' she said.

'What for?'

'Murder. And he'd very much like a word.'

44

9

I wasn't sure what took the longest time, the video-recorded questioning of Jake by two detectives, or his pre- and post-interrogation rants at me in one of the interview rooms.

Afterwards, ears burning, I left him in the care of the custody sergeant, four bare walls and a plastic-coated mattress while I went off to sit in with Deek. I must have sat through hundreds of such interviews and it always amazed me that no matter how much you advised some clients to make no comment, they usually felt they had to have their say, not realising that, no matter how innocent they were, or how exculpatory they thought their answers, they were only helping the police to build a case against them. In the history of all police enquiries, I doubted if there had ever been a time when halfway through an interview a cop had stopped asking questions and said, 'Oh well then. In view of what you've told us, Mr Suspect, you're clearly innocent and are now free to go.' It just didn't happen. The cops might say they were only trying to help or just wanted to know the truth, but during a detention interview the only thing on a police officer's mind was convicting the person sitting in front of them, and nothing that person said could possibly help.

No such worries with Jake and Deek, however. Both

were past masters of the no-comment interview. Even then, it didn't stop the cops asking endless questions.

Once the formalities were over, I tried to catch a few words with Dougie Fleming. He must have known from the outset that he'd get nothing out of my clients because he'd left the interviews to a couple of his junior colleagues while he worked away in the background. If I had asked to speak with him, he'd have given me a body-swerve and sneaked out of the back door, so instead I waited at the front desk and caught him as he headed home after his long shift.

'They're staying put,' he said, anticipating my question as he came around the counter to where I was standing. 'So don't bother harping on about it. The decision's been made and now I'm officially off duty.'

'What evidence can you possibly have to keep them?' I asked, trotting after him to the front door.

'I don't need evidence. I have a reasonable suspicion. That'll do for now.'

'A reasonable suspicion? Based on what? Being at the murder scene this afternoon? Whoever the dead guy is, he wasn't killed today.'

'Really? Is that a special knowledge statement? Is there something you'd like to get off your chest, Mr Munro?'

'You've seen the body. It was way past its kill-by date.'

Fleming shrugged and pulled on a pair of polished, black leather gloves.

'And they were both with me.' I positioned myself between him and the big glass front door. 'How many murderers come to the police station with their lawyers direct from the crime scene? Do you see how unreasonably suspicious that is? You wouldn't even know about the murder if we hadn't reported it.'

Fleming tried to push past. 'If you don't mind. Some of us have got a home to go to.'

I'd loved to have ripped off one of those Gestapo gloves and slapped him about the face with it. 'So, tell me, what is your reasonable suspicion?'

Fleming smiled thinly, showing less porcelain than a doll's house tea set. 'It's like this. I'm a reasonable man and anything Jake Turpie does, I'm suspicious of. Good enough for you? Because it's good enough for me.' This time his attempt to shove me aside was successful. He pushed open the glass door. 'And the same goes for you. So just think yourself lucky you're not in beside them.'

10

I arrived home in the small hours of Thursday morning
to find Malky gone and Tina curled up on the couch
sound asleep, her wee chocolaty face poking out from
beneath the fleecy dressing gown that had been thrown
over her. Sitting in the armchair next to her, a partially
completed newspaper crossword across his lap, my dad
let rip a series of snores. He woke up when I gave him a
shove, snorted through his moustache and looked around
wide-eyed.

'Oh, it's you,' he said, composing himself. He folded
the newspaper then looked at his watch. 'What time do
you call this?'

Apology tendered, if not accepted, I offered to drive
him home.

'Don't bother, I'll call a taxi,' he said, prising himself
out of the chair. 'You just concentrate on putting that
bairn to her bed.'

'Dad, there's something urgent I've got to do in the
morning . . . '

'Turpie? Let him rot.'

'It's business. I can't turn it down. How else am I going
make enough to keep Tina in ballet pumps and tutus?'

But it was too late for an attempt at humour and,
anyway, ballet wasn't a subject open to discussion. My

dad was as yet undecided as to whether Tina would be the first woman to win The Open Championship or skipper Scotland to a World Cup final.

After a lot of persuasion, and mainly because he wanted to get to his bed, he agreed to take Tina home with him, but only once I'd promised to pick her up around lunchtime the next day.

And it was a promise I might have been able to keep if Dougie Fleming hadn't left instructions to drag out the arrest of my clients so that they weren't officially charged until after midnight and into Thursday, which in turn meant that the next lawful court day was Friday. I phoned the Procurator Fiscal's office first thing. As usual there was no one taking calls.

'I'm pretty sure Mr Ogilvie's not in.' The admin assistant stared innocently at me through the glass shield when, half an hour later, I arrived in person at the front desk.

I was pretty sure he was. Procurators Fiscal seldom made it the length of the courtroom. That was a job for the ranks of morale-deflated deputes, stuck on fixed-term contracts and easily got rid of at the first sign of initiative.

'Could you check and make sure?' I asked.

Apparently she couldn't.

I took a letter from my inside jacket pocket. 'I have a letter for him.'

The admin assistant flicked hair out of her face and pointed to the metal trough dug into the counter and under the sheet of glass between us.

'Love to, but can't,' I said. 'It's a witness citation. I have to give it to him personally.'

'You tried that trick the last time,' she said coldly

49

enough to send tendrils of frost creeping up the security glass. 'It didn't work then either.'

'Look, all I want to know is why he can't put the murder case through today. Could you at least pass the message on?'

'Thanks, Karen, I'll take over from here.' Hugh Ogilvie slithered from the shadows. Taking a step back to allow his admin assistant's exit stage right, he approached the counter and looked at me as though I'd dropped by to report a Bigfoot sighting. 'Murder? What are you talking about?'

'It's a legal term, Hugh. Look it up, it's in most of the good law books.'

He unlocked the security door and held it open for me. I came around the dark side of the counter and followed him through the open plan office to his glass-fronted room.

'I've not had a report of a murder,' he said, once he'd closed the door behind him. 'All deaths in the locality have to come across my desk.'

In which case he would have noticed it for his desk seemed unnaturally tidy. You could even see the surface, a highly polished wood laminate. The surface of mine was like gravity; you knew it had to exist, it was just that no one had ever seen it.

Ogilvie lifted his phone, pressed a button and waited. And waited. Now he knew how the rest of us felt. Eventually he slammed the receiver down and strode to the door. 'Who was on death-duty last night!'

Without looking up from her typing, the admin assistant sitting at a workstation a metre or so away mumbled something I didn't quite catch.

'Did he say anything about a murder?'

His assistant dragged herself out of her chair and walked into his office. Not looking at Ogilvie, she pulled open a desk drawer and removed a sheet of paper. Ogilvie snatched it from her. His curt 'thank you' was her cue to leave.

'Four deaths. No reports of anything suspicious,' Ogilvie said, letting the sheet of paper float to the desk. 'Is this some kind of joke? If you've wheedled your way in here on the pretence of a murder case, just so you can try and talk me into some kind of a soft plea for one of your—'

'I can assure you that Mr Turpie and his employee are both under arrest at this very moment for murder,' I said. 'If you're not going to release them, at least put them through court today. What's the point of keeping them banged up for another twenty-four hours?'

A smile crept across Ogilvie's face like mould on a Petri dish. 'Turpie? Jake Turpie?'

Ogilvie really did have no idea. There had been a murder on his doorstep and no one, it seemed, had bothered to mention it to the head of the local prosecuting authority.

'So you'll see,' I said, after filling him on a few details, 'there's not a scrap of evidence against them.'

The smile just wouldn't leave the PF's face. 'Apart, you mean, from being at the scene of the crime and their respective histories of extreme violence?'

'Don't give me that,' I said. 'Once the report lands on your desk I'm expecting a PF-release for both of them. An apology wouldn't go amiss either.'

Still smiling, Ogilvie went to the door again. 'Karen. Nip over to Costa's and fetch us a couple of coffees, will you?' He turned to me. 'Black, isn't it, Robbie?'

Ogilvie offering me coffee and using my first name?

'Two sugars,' I managed to get out.

He came over to me, pulled out a chair and patted the seat. 'This murder. Tell me some more about it.'

11

'I knew I should have locked you up too.' Dougie Fleming held open the door allowing entry to the inner sanctum of Livingston Police Office and led me down a corridor to his office. Compared to Hugh Ogilvie's, the DI's room looked like the aftermath of a bomb blast. Piles of paper were heaped in one corner, a toppled whiteboard with partially erased marker pen scribblings occupied another, and somewhere, under a pile of ring binders, coffee mugs and evidence bags, was a desk. Chuck in a desiccated umbrella plant and it could have been my own office during Grace-Mary's summer holidays.

Fleming stopped, turned and leaned against the edge of the desk. He stared me in the face, lips compressed, eyes narrowed, like a gorilla holding in a fart. 'After your little visit to the PF this morning, I've had him breathing down my neck wanting to know what's going on,' he said.

'What *is* going on?' I asked.

Fleming pushed himself away from his desk and stepped towards me. 'I distinctly remember telling you ... ' There were only the two of us present; nonetheless, Fleming poked a finger in my chest just in case I thought he might be addressing somebody else. 'Not to say a word about this to anyone.'

'But—'

'Anyone,' he repeated. 'I've got a tight unit working on

this case and now that I've been forced to tell Ogilvie, the whole world is going to know.'

'Isn't the PF the first person who's supposed to know about a suspicious death?'

'Not until my enquiries are finished he's not.'

'What's the big secret?'

'The big secret is that I've got two dead bodies and I don't know who they are.'

'I thought you told me you'd found the girl's mother?'

'I told you we'd found the body of a female.'

Fleming wandered over to his desk and squared a stack of blank A4 paper, tapping its edge on the desk.

I followed him. 'You've got absolutely nothing, have you? In that case, I want my clients released. If not, I demand to see them so that I can reassure them they'll be getting out soon and so that they know the only reason they are being kept in is because of your vindictiveness.'

'You're not seeing them.'

'Are you refusing your prisoners access to legal counsel? Do you mind if I make a note of that?'

Fleming peeled a sheet of paper from the wad in his hand and offered it to me. 'Note away. You spoke to them last night. A very lengthy chat as I recall and . . . ' Fleming picked up his phone and buzzed through to the custody suite. 'Billy, has either Turpie or the other one asked to speak to their lawyer?' Presumably Billy was the custody sergeant and equally presumably he replied in the negative. 'Didn't think so,' Fleming replaced the receiver. 'I think your clients' rights have all been adequately catered for, Mr Munro. They had the benefit of consulting with you last night before being interviewed. Now that they are officially suspects and under arrest, I'm sure you'll be permitted to speak to them tomorrow up at the Sheriff

Court. If not, you can visit them on remand as often as you like. The Scottish Prison Service is very accommodating that way.'

I'd had enough of his crap. 'I want to speak to the senior investigating officer.'

Fleming crushed the single sheet, straightened and thrust out his chins. 'I'm the deputy SIO.'

'Then I'd like to speak to your senior officer.'

He cleared his throat. 'I'm also acting SIO at the moment.'

How could he be SIO and deputy SIO? He'd have to make his own coffee. Suddenly, I understood. 'You're stalling. You don't want anyone else involved. Not the newspapers, not the PF and not your senior officers. You're trying to keep it under wraps for as long as possible, solve the case and take the credit. Chief Inspector here you come, and if that means fitting up a couple of innocent men, then—'

'Innocent?' Fleming sneered. 'Jake Turpie's many things, but innocent isn't one of them. I've spoken to Hugh Ogilvie. They're both going on a murder Petition. There's more chance of Voyager Two making a comeback than that pair getting bail. Which gives me plenty of time to nail them. And, trust me, I'll get them for something. If my investigations reveal that Jake Turpie has been breathing heavily I'll do him for stealing air.'

I was familiar with Dougie Fleming's recipe for crime investigations: take one suspect, add evidence from which guilt might be inferred, discard any that might suggest otherwise and present to the jury. Just like sculpting an elephant from a block of granite. Simply chip away all those pieces that don't look like an elephant.

'All you have is the two of them at the scene and then

attending at a police station to report the finding of a dead body. That's exercising their public duty, not a motive.'

Fleming yanked open an already full drawer and tried to stuff the wad of paper into it. 'It's enough of a motive for me.'

'And you don't even know who the dead people are yet. I take back what I said about you having nothing. You've got less than nothing, because I was there with Jake. In fact it was me who found the body. A body that had probably been dead for days.'

Fleming slammed the drawer closed, or tried to, because it jammed against the ream of paper. It must have been killing him. The knowledge that he had Jake and Deek under lock and key, and yet the two accused would spend no more than a week in custody before they'd have to be released due to lack of evidence. There was no way he could have them fully committed for trial on what little he had, no matter how thinly he stretched it.

'Anyway, it doesn't matter,' I said. 'This time next week they'll both be out. What's seven days inside to them? Won't make you look too clever, though. Big splash in the papers about two suspects being charged, only for them to be released, grounds no longer exist, a week later.'

Fleming pointed a finger at me. 'If you really want, I could let you speak to your clients – by banging you up in the same cell as them!'

Fleming was vindictive enough to do it too. Just not sufficiently stupid. He might have managed to persuade Ogilvie to prosecute Jake and Deek because of their criminal past and presence at the scene, but lock up the person, a lawyer, who'd reported the crime and rescued a starving child? That wouldn't look so good. He levelled an index finger once more at my chest.

'You're not going to start poking me again, are you?' I asked.

Fleming lowered his hand, his face fading slowly from puce to its more natural crimson hue. 'This is an ongoing enquiry. Until I know more about the victims and have had a chance to gather all the evidence, I'm not having you spreading rumours around. That means no phoning your pal at the *Gazette*.'

I wouldn't have to. As soon as Jake and Deek appeared at court the next day on a murder petition, Kaye Mitchell, editor of the local newspaper, would be all over the story.

'In fact I think I'll give the editor a call and warn her that . . . ' he fumbled in his pocket and then raked around his desk. 'Where's the number? I had it somewhere.' He cobbled together a smile. Alarm bells. 'Have you got the number on your mobile?'

'I have, but I don't have my phone with me.'

'Left it at home again, have you? Turpie's too smart to carry a phone around with him and that big clown he goes about with wouldn't know how to work one. But strange that you never seem to have one on you either.' Did the man never give up? 'Why's that then?'

'Because I'm supposed to be on leave. My phone's for business and I've left it at my office.'

Fleming grunted in disbelief. I knew he'd be dying to take a look at my phone, find out where it had been and who I'd been calling around the time of the murder, whenever that was supposed to have been. I had a good mind to ask Grace-Mary to hand the phone in, let him analyse it to his heart's content and then puzzle over why in the last few days the only calls made from it had been to a series of middle-aged women and the Linlithgow Bridge Club.

'If you want the phone, you're welcome to apply for a warrant.'

'Maybe I will,' Fleming said. 'My investigations have just started and I'm throwing the net wide on this one. Just watch out you don't swim into it.'

12

'You again?' was the warm welcome I received from Grace-Mary. She was putting on her raincoat. It was three o'clock.

'I need to speak to Joanna about something and, as you know, I don't have a phone at the moment,' I said.

Grace-Mary picked up a red nylon mail bag from the reception desk.

'Leaving so soon?' I asked.

'I'm taking the letters to the post office and then Joanna said I could go home early.'

'Did she indeed? Sounds like when the cat's away ...'

Joanna walked into reception 'Not cat,' she tutted, and stroked me under the chin, 'pussycat.' She laid a couple of mini-cassettes on the desk. 'I'll leave these here. You can make a start on them in the morning, Grace-Mary.'

'What's all this about letting the staff go home early?' I asked, once my secretary had left the building.

'I was at court most of the day. I've dictated some stuff since I came back which Grace-Mary will rattle through in no time. The woman types like a machine gun. And so, as there are no appointments left this afternoon, I thought I'd let her go home early.'

'Who's answering the phones?'

'I am. They're not exactly ringing off the hook. Stop looking at me like that. If I let Grace-Mary leave early on

59

slow days, then she won't complain if I ask her to stay late to finish off something important one evening.' It was a scenario I wouldn't have put money on, but Joanna was certain of her territory. 'It's called personnel management. I read a book about it. You know, it wouldn't do you any harm to praise Grace-Mary from time to time.'

'You mean patronise her?'

'No, I mean tell her when she's done a good job.'

'She always does a good job and she knows it. If I tell her I know it too, she'll want a pay rise.'

'That's plain mean.'

'No, that's financial management. I haven't read a book on it, but I have read my bank statement.'

'Well, read it again,' Joanna said. 'It's no worse now than it was before you went off. There's no need to keep checking up on us.'

'Why would you think I was checking up on you? And can I just say what a great job you're doing?'

Joanna elevated an eyebrow. 'Either tell me why you're here or go now, while you can still walk.'

'Jake Turpie and Deek Pudney have been charged with murder. They're appearing in court tomorrow. They'll both be 23D'd, so it'll just be a case of no plea or declaration, continued for further enquiries, bail refused.'

Scots law had adopted the European Convention on Human Rights in 1999 and the government had been trying to circumvent it ever since. The Convention had put paid to the old rule of no bail for murder accused, and so the Scottish Parliament had introduced section 23D of the Criminal Procedure Act to prevent any accused who had a prior conviction on indictment for a sexual, violent or drug-trafficking offence being granted bail unless there were exceptional circumstances. To date, Sheriff Albert

Brechin had never found anyone's circumstances remotely atypical far less exceptional.

'I think I can just about handle that,' Joanna said. 'Are you going to cut one of them out?'

Even though I couldn't see any conflict of interest, it wasn't worth the risk acting for two accused in a murder case, and, anyway, it wasn't like Jake would pay any more. He'd expect a two-for-one deal. If I cut Deek out to another lawyer then I could bill Jake privately, and his big, ugly co-accused would qualify for legal aid.

'Yes. Keep Jake. Give Deek to Paul Sharp. No need to bother him today. Let him know after court tomorrow and he can take it from there. Say I'll speak to him about the case soon.'

'And you think that Jake Turpie's going to be all right with me appearing? I told you he didn't even want me to speak to him when he was arrested. He insisted that I call you.'

'Tell him he's just going to have to get used to you.'

'Why's that, then?'

'Because, while there's no reason I can't prepare his defence, when it comes to the actual trial, I can't be in the courtroom and the witness room at the same time.'

'I don't understand.'

'It looks very much like I'll be defence witness numero uno. After all, I was there when the bodies were found.'

'Bodies?' As usual I heard Kaye Mitchell before I saw her. She thrust a parcel at me. It was gift-wrapped in blue paper featuring pictures of swaddled-babies and storks. 'Sorry about the paper.'

I took the parcel. An item of clothing I guessed. As a boy, at Christmas and birthdays I'd hated that soft squishy feel when what I'd really wanted was something hard with edges.

'Thanks.' I dropped the parcel onto the reception desk. It struck Joanna's mini-cassettes sending them skidding across the surface and onto the floor. Kaye went over, picked them up and studied them. 'Really? Tape? Haven't you heard of the digital age?'

'Thanks for the present, Kaye. I'm sure Tina will love it, but do you mind? I'm trying to have a confidential meeting with my business partner.'

'You never told me you were taking on a partner.' Kaye placed the cassettes on the desk again and stuck out a hand to Joanna. 'Congratulations . . . I think.'

Joanna looked from Kaye's outstretched hand to me.

'When I say partner, I mean colleague. Joanna's standing in for me while I look after Tina.'

'And where is the wee smasher?'

'Looking after her granddad. I should have collected her half an hour ago.'

Kaye sat down on the edge of the desk. Hints and the taking of them had never been one of her strong points. 'So, anyway, you were saying. Bodies? I take it we're talking dead ones?'

I remembered Dougie Fleming's threats. 'Sorry, I don't have the time right now. I'll need to get home. Joanna, would it be all right if you gave me a call later on after I've given Tina her tea?'

'Bodies?' Joanna said. 'Bodies, plural?'

It was half past four. The *Linlithgow Gazette* came out on a Friday and, this late on a Thursday afternoon, would have been put to bed long before now. Plus Jake and Deek would be appearing in court tomorrow afternoon and then the whole world would know.

'Is that it?' Kaye asked after I'd recounted my story. 'You don't even know who the murder victims are? What good is that to me? I need facts. What do you give me? Two unknown people are murdered somewhere out in the sticks at an address the main witness can't remember. Quick! Hold the front page.' She looked down at her notepad, shaking her head. 'Spell the names of the two suspects for me. At least I can get that right.'

Footsteps in the corridor. I thought it might be Grace-Mary, stricken with guilt and back from the post office, but it wasn't. It was Jake Turpie.

He looked at Joanna and Kaye in turn and then at me. 'I'm out.'

'Where's Deek?' I asked.

'In.'

'Kaye,' I said, 'you'd better make that just the one suspect.'

13

If I'd spoken to Jake in my office, afterwards I would have had to recount everything to Joanna and, no doubt, Kaye, before I could escape. My dad would be angry enough at the fact I'd been away this long, and so I decided it would be better if I took the conversation elsewhere. Joanna would be phoning me later and I could tell her the news then.

I suggested Sandy's café. Jake had other ideas.

'I've been choking for this,' he said, after necking most of a pint in one go. Taking my half-pint, I followed him to the far end of the Red Corner Bar where the patrons dispersed upon our arrival, like a slick of greasy water meeting a couple of drops of washing-up liquid.

Jake finished his drink and had ordered another before I'd joined him on the next bar stool.

'I'm glad to see all my work paid off,' I said. It would have been remiss of me not to have taken full credit, even though I suspected my chats with Hugh Ogilvie and DI Fleming had not been the real reason for Jake's release. I suspected the forces of darkness had other plans.

'What about Deek? Could you not get him out too?'

'One step at a time,' I said, as though I had a game plan. 'First thing is, you'll need to watch yourself.'

Jake's second pint arrived. He didn't give it time to settle before downing half of it. 'What do you mean?'

'They could be trying to give you some rope.'

'What's rope got to do with anything?'

I took a sip of lager shandy, the first alcohol to touch my lips in a long time. 'Enough rope so that you'll hang yourself.'

'I'll hang you if you don't tell me what you're talking about.'

'The cops will be thinking that if you and Deek murdered those folk—'

'What folk? I only saw one person and so did you.'

'I know, but there were two. The guy on the table and also a woman in the front room. I think she's the person you sold the car to. If she was in debt to you the cops will be thinking that gave you a motive.'

'If I killed people who owed me money, how would I get it back?' Jake sank the rest of the pint. 'And I could have taken the car back any time I wanted. I always get a spare key cut just in case.'

Back to the rope. 'They don't have enough and so they probably think that if you are out and about you'll maybe do something stupid.'

'Like what?'

'I don't know, but they'll definitely keep you under surveillance. Tap your phone calls, see who you meet up with, look for anything or anyone that might link you to the murder.'

Jake shouted up yet another drink. I'd barely drunk half of mine and that was enough. Being late home was one thing. If my dad smelt alcohol on my breath, there'd be hell to pay.

'So why have they kept Deek in?'

'There's a couple of reasons. They might have some evidence against him that we don't know about, or they're

65

lulling you into a false sense of security, expecting you to visit him in prison and then they'll record your conversations. Or it could be they think that keeping you apart will stop you concocting a defence while they continue their enquiries.'

'That's three reasons,' Jake said.

'And there could be more. Dougie Fleming's out to get you and he's not a man to let a little thing like your innocence get in the way. Any minor slip up, any wee mistake, and he'll find a way of using it against you.'

'What am I supposed to do?' Jake said, turning his attention to pint three.

'Keep away from Deek. Don't even book a visit. All it takes is for you to go see him and Fleming will plant a couple of undercover cops at the next table who'll swear blind that they heard the two of you discussing the murders. Once the bizzies have it in their heads that you're guilty, they don't care. Anything underhand they do is justified in their eyes.'

Jake mulled that over with his next gulp of beer. 'What if they do have other evidence against Deek?'

'Is that likely?'

Jake didn't answer, just wiped foam from his top lip with the back of his hand. 'Let me know what you need for Deek's legal aid. I can make up a wage slip or do a letter or something. Just tell me how much you want me to say I pay him.'

Did I want this? A murder case was interesting, but at legal aid rates a financial disaster. For one thing there would be tons of administration work that the Scottish Legal Aid Board wouldn't pay me to do and, for another, the Board expected the interviewing of witnesses to be done by unqualified personnel at unqualified rates. The kind of people who would agree to carry out investigations for that kind of money were the kind of people who couldn't be trusted to find their own backsides with the use of both hands and an Ordnance Survey map, far less find a defence to a murder charge.

With Jake Turpie breathing down my neck, the kind of work I'd be expected to put in to make sure his minder got off would be above and beyond. Add to that the fact that I was supposed to be on paternity leave and I could do without all the hassle.

'I can't take Deek's case on,' I said.

Jake looked at me, like he was a shrink examining his first nut-of-the-day. If drinking half-pints of lager shandy wasn't bad enough, now I was turning down work.

'I've got my daughter living with me. It's temporary. They don't think I can cope so I've taken a month's holiday to prove them wrong. There's a court-appointed lawyer checking up on me and doing a report. If it's bad, Tina goes to live with her grandmother. I need to be around. I don't have the time to spend on Deek's case. He'll need to find another lawyer.'

'You were going to act for me, weren't you?'

'I was, but I couldn't have acted for you both. Deek would have had to go to another lawyer, anyway.'

'And now he doesn't.'

I could have offered Joanna's services, but in the unlikely event that Jake thought a woman up to the job, I knew every time he couldn't get hold of her he'd be straight on to me to find out what was happening. Much better if Deek's case was dealt with by Paul Sharp, as previously planned.

'I've already got someone lined up for him,' I said.

'Then un-line them up. That man saved your life once.'

I hadn't forgotten. Or that on another occasion he'd tried to seriously damage me. 'I just think it's best all round if he goes to another lawyer. Someone who can give his case the attention it deserves. Obviously, I'll still be a witness if the case goes to court.'

Jake wasn't listening. 'Deek's important to me. He's a good worker. Knows a lot of things about my business.'

I was sure he did. Like where the bodies were buried – literally.

I finished my half-pint and climbed down from the bar stool. 'I'm sorry, Jake.'

'How much?'

'It's not about money,' I thought I heard myself say.

'I own your office.'

'Hold on a minute.' We'd shaken hands on that deal years ago. As long as I wanted, Jake had said. Just so long as I kept paying the rent. I really hoped that Grace-Mary had sent that cheque.

'You can have it,' he said.

'The office?'

'That's right. Legal aid and, if you get Deek off, the office is yours. I'll sign it straight over to you.'

The monthly rent was my biggest overhead by far. With the money I saved, I could afford not only to tell Grace-Mary 'good job' now and again, and cope with any resulting pay rise, but take on a reasonable mortgage for a new house for me and Tina.

'Let me think about it,' I said, though in truth I'd already made my decision.

Jake seemed to know that too. He took another long pull from his pint glass, pushed the tumbler away and jumped down from the bar stool. 'I'll see you at court.'

14

Tina had only been living with me for a matter of a few days, but already her grandfather had discerned the unmistakable signs of genius.

The pair of them were in the hallway waiting for me when I arrived home. My dad pushed Tina forward. She stood there, unusually quiet, head bowed, hands behind her back. At first I thought she'd misbehaved in some way, but even if she had, my dad would never have squealed. His standard conduct report on Tina was, 'as good as gold'.

'Go on then,' he said, giving Tina another gentle bump. 'Show your dad what you've done.'

Tina remained standing there, shaking with excitement. One more nudge of encouragement and she whipped a piece of paper from behind her back. It was wet and wrinkly. Rivers of poster paint meandered southwards to a soggy edge and began to drip onto the hall carpet.

I took the painting from her, studied it carefully and after a suitable period of admiration, asked, 'What is it?'

Tina had already mastered the hands on hips, head tilted to the side stance. 'It's you, silly.'

I looked at the picture again and came to the conclusion that I was the black square with an enormous pink blob balanced on top from which black spikes protruded. My arms and legs were sticks and my feet mostly toes.

'It's you putting all the baddies in jail!' Tina yelled.

Clearly, my dad had been explaining his son's role in the criminal justice system and putting his own slant on it.

'It's very nice,' I said. 'Let's put it up in the kitchen with all the others.'

Tina frowned.

'Look again,' my dad said.

I did. What had I missed? 'I've got lots of hair . . . ' I said. But that wasn't it. 'And look at all my fingers and toes.'

Standing behind his increasingly impatient grand-daughter, my dad was pointing his finger downwards and silently mouthing something.

What was the big deal? It was a painting. I had dozens of them, mainly houses with bright-yellow suns and flowers. Tina could knock one of those out in under five minutes and give herself a couple of coats of paint in the process.

'Isn't Tina really clever?' my dad said, pointedly.

They both stared at me expectantly. What did they want? True, I'd seen worse in the Tate Modern and a lot worse at the Joan Miro in Barcelona, but what did they expect me to do? Alert the National Gallery?

Then I saw it. Bottom left. Four letters. My daughter's name. Printing 'Tina' meant there was only one letter that could be transposed and she'd managed it. 'You've written your name!'

'Yes!' Tina screamed. She grabbed the painting from me and looked at the scrawl as though she could hardly believe it herself. I picked her up and pressed my face against hers.

She wriggled in my arms. 'You're all jaggy.'

'Writing her own name and she's not even at school yet,' my dad said.

I put Tina down. 'Keep this up and by the time you do go to school they'll want to make you the teacher.'

Tina looked worried. 'I can't do sums yet, though,' she said.

'Don't worry,' I said. 'Maybe next time Gramps takes you for a special lemonade, afterwards he'll take you to the special shop where they do sums about horses.'

Tina spun on her heel. 'Can we go, Gramps? I like horses.'

He took Tina by the hand. 'There's no such shop. It's just your dad being his usual hilarious self. Let's go and pin this up on the wall and then I'll make your tea. How does spaghetti on toast sound?'

Spaghetti it was, and off the two of them went, Tina yabbering excitedly about having written her name and my dad making it sound as though the Nobel Prize for Literature was waiting just around the corner.

I followed them. 'Dad . . . do you think . . . I have to work tomorrow and . . . could you look after Tina? Just in the morning. Possibly into the afternoon. But not late.'

No answer. Had he heard me above Tina's chatter?

On my return from a shower and change of clothes, Tina's dinner was already on the kitchen table. Some of it was on the plate. A lot of it was around her face. It is said that the hoplites of ancient Sparta wore crimson cloaks to disguise the blood. My daughter's red T-shirt was doing something similar with spaghetti-hoop sauce.

'Dad . . . ?'

'No.'

'Why not?'

He got up from his chair and took me aside. 'Listen, Robbie. I'd spend all day, every day, with the bairn, you

71

know that. But I'm just Grandpa. I'm supposed to flit in and out of her life, not be her dad.'

'I know, but—'

'But nothing. You need to spend more quality time with your daughter. If that Vikki shows up, what am I supposed to say this time? That you've gone to the shops? Again? You know what Tina is like, she'll crack under questioning. How's it going to look if you're too busy to watch your daughter when you're supposed to be on holiday, far less when you're working?'

'How did you manage?'

'I had your Aunt Elsie helping me, and, anyway, it was different back then, there wasn't a custody battle. I was the only show in town. Tina's got Vera Reynolds waiting to pounce—'

'I like Granny Vera,' Tina said, through a mouthful of spaghetti and toast. 'When are we going to see her?'

I ruffled her hair. 'Soon.' She swiped my hand away and continued munching. How much did she hear? More importantly, how much did she understand?

'It's only for the morning, Dad. I'll be back for lunch.'

'I've heard that line somewhere before.'

'Today was different.'

'And so will tomorrow be. I know you, Robbie.'

Tina finished the last mouthful, drank what was left of a glass of milk and jumped down from her seat. She took both our hands and looked up at us each in turn. 'Now what are we doing?'

'What do you want to do?' I asked.

'Paint more pictures.'

'No, I've put all the painting stuff away. Why don't we play a game of something instead,' my dad said.

'And then you'll need to get ready for bed,' I said. 'Remember, you've got nursery in the morning.'

At the mention of bed, Tina let go of my hand and began to drag my dad through to the living room. 'Don-i-moes.'

'One morning, Dad. That's all I'm asking,' I said, as Tina emptied the box of dominoes onto the coffee table. 'I'm seeing a man about getting a bigger house.'

'No, you're not. This is about Jake Turpie, isn't it?'

The three of us turned the dominoes over face down and Tina swirled them around the table, occasionally knocking one or two over the edge.

'In a way it is, but it's also about me saving enough money for a house. Really.'

The old man didn't reply, which I took as a good sign. We each selected our dominoes, my dad holding all seven in his hands while Tina and I stood ours up on the table like little black gravestones.

'I know you don't like Jake—'

'Gramps said this one is the currant bun and it goes first.' Tina said, holding up the double-six.

'Jake Turpie's a crook.'

'I make my money from crooks, Dad.'

'Is a crook the same as a baddie?' Tina asked.

My dad nodded. 'Yes, it is. And by the way you always seem to get the double-six, I think that you might be a wee crook too.'

He tried to tickle her. Tina pulled away from him. 'Will you send me to the jail then, Dad?'

'Don't be silly,' I said. 'You're not a crook and, anyway, wee girls don't go to jail. Grandpa's trying to be funny. He's just not very good at it, that's all.'

'He's sometimes good at being funny,' Tina said. She played the double-six. 'He told me to tell Vikki that you

73

were at the shop today. It was going to be a funny joke, but she didn't come.'

'See?' my dad said. 'You've even got the bairn prepared to tell lies for you.' He played the six-five.

I didn't have a six and only one five. I laid the five-two alongside. 'You know what else would be funny?' I said to Tina. 'If somehow I had enough money to buy a big house so that we could each have a bedroom and I wouldn't have to sleep in here on the camp bed.'

My dad was impervious. 'It's you to play, Tina.'

She thought about it for a while.

I took a peek at her hand. 'Do you want some help?'

My dad curled an arm around Tina's dominoes. 'You're the only one here in need of help,' he said.

'Come on, Dad. Just collect Toots from nursery, take her to your place for lunch and I'll pick her up the back of one. Three o'clock at the latest.'

'It's not happening. You've got a chance of a new life. You need to learn to prioritise the important things.'

'I'm trying to. Think what a difference it will make if I can tell the court that I'm moving to a bigger house.'

Tina played the double-two. 'Granny Vera has got a really big house.'

I looked at my dad. He was studying his hand carefully. 'See? Granny Vera's got a really big house. What have I got? A one-bedroom flat with dodgy plumbing. Come on, it's only for one morning.'

Eventually, he chose a domino. 'I'm sorry, Robbie. I know you mean well, probably, but acting for men like Jake Turpie isn't the way to go about it.' He placed the two-six onto Tina's double. 'And, by the way, you're chapping.'

15

'Walk me through it again.' Malky said.

'Right, Tina's at nursery just now. You know where that is?' He nodded. I'd already given my brother the address and directions to it by way of references to nearby pubs. 'Okay, so I took her there earlier this morning. You need to go back and collect her, at what time?'

'Twelve. Should we be synchronising our watches?'

'Shut up. I've told the nursery that you'll be collecting Tina. All you have to do is go in, sign the book and take her away. She likes to feed the ducks, so take a bag of bread with you.'

'Ducks. How am I supposed to find ducks?'

'It's not a problem. Just go down to the loch with bread and they'll find you.'

'Then what?'

'Give her a shot on the swings and then bring her back here and give her something to eat.' I led him through to the kitchen and pulled open some cupboard doors. 'Providing the ducks have left you any bread, make toast or roasted cheese and there's beans, spaghetti and sausages, super noodles, stuff like that, or you can make an omelette. No onions. Tina doesn't like onions. Not unless she can't see them. And no crisps or sweets, and only milk or water to drink, no sugary drinks. Got that?'

'No crisps, sweets or juice? Come on. Give the kid a break.'

'She's had too much sweet stuff lately, most of it from you, and sugary juice will rot her teeth.'

'She's got baby teeth. Who cares if they rot? They fall out by themselves anyway. She can look after the new ones when they come in.'

'Malky, listen to me. No sweets. If she eats her lunch and drinks her milk you can give her a biscuit. One biscuit.'

'When do I send her up the chimney to give it a sweep?'

'Stay focused, Malky. If she gets bored and I'm not back, put a DVD on or play a game or read a book. Do not under any circumstances answer the door. It will only be Dad or, nearly as bad, Vikki the lawyer who's doing a report on me. You got all that?'

'Nursery, ducks, lunch. No crisps, sweets, juice, female lawyers or elderly relatives. Possibly one biscuit. Yeah, I think I'm good to go. Any beer in the fridge?' He gave my cheek a friendly slap. 'Kidding.'

I went through to my room and took my suit jacket out of the wardrobe. By the time I'd returned, Malky's earlier cheery expression had changed to one bordering on terror. 'What happens if she needs to go to the toilet?'

'Just point her in the direction of the nearest loo and she'll take it from there,' I said. 'Just remember to take some toilet paper with you in case you're out and about and she has to go to the ladies.'

'And if it's a ...?' He blew a raspberry. 'There won't be any ... you know ... wiping involved, will there?'

'Unlikely.'

'How unlikely?'

'Extremely unlikely,' I said, but he didn't seem satisfied at my answer. 'Okay, yes, it is just possible that there could be some kind of bottom malfunction, but really it's not that big a deal. If you're worried, take a spare pair of undies with you.'

'I've only got the ones I'm wearing.'

'Not for you, for Tina.'

'You want me to carry kids' underwear about in my pocket?'

'Look, I've already told you it's not going to happen and if it does, well, what's the big problem? We're talking about a number two, not DEFCON 2.'

Malky sniffed several times and screwed up his face. 'Talking about number twos. Have you let one rip?'

I hadn't, but I knew what he meant. There was a very strong smell of ... well ... shit.

Sniffing like a bloodhound, Malky came closer. 'Yeah, it's definitely you,' he said, sniffing some more. 'I hope you've got a spare pair of undies with you, because I think you've filled the ones you're wearing.'

I backed away from him. He was right. The smell was coming from me. I removed my jacket. On the outside it seemed fine, but upon examination of the interior I could see, smeared across the lining, caked on hard, a substance which upon closer inspection was definitely the source of the smell.

'Forget to take extra toilet paper with you the last time you were out and about?' Malky asked.

At first I didn't understand how it could have got there and then it dawned on me. This was the suit I'd been wearing the day I'd rescued the little girl at the farm. I'd wrapped the jacket around her and she'd worn it in the car all the way to the police station. Before she'd been whisked away by the social services it had been exchanged for a fleecy blanket.

I found a black bin bag, folded the jacket and laid it

inside. 'Any chance of you dropping that off at the dry-cleaners on the way to collect Tina?'

'None whatsoever,' Malky replied.

By the time I was changed and ready to go, my brother was sitting in the living room with a cup of coffee and the newspaper.

'Don't be late for Tina,' I told him.

Malky didn't look up. 'Tell you what. I promise not to be late if you promise not to do poo-poos on your jacket again.'

16

Deek Pudney's first appearance was scheduled for noon but didn't call until after three. The wheels of justice grind slow. At Livingston Sheriff Court, even on a quiet day, they barely ground at all.

The sheriff had left the bench at the end of the summary custody cases to allow the courtroom to be cleared while Deek's petition was computer-linked between the PF's and Sheriff Clerk's offices. When I made my way up from the cells, clutching my client's recently served papers, Hugh Ogilvie was sitting in the well of the court, a single red file on the table in front of him. Ogilvie only attended court for the most high-profile of cases or to gloat. In this instance it was a bit of both. The charge was murder. Daisy Adams, proprietor of Sunnybrae Farm, had been at last identified as one of the victims. She'd been strangled by means of a ligature. Deek's other alleged victim's identity was meantime unknown. The latter had been struck with a knife or similar instrument. It was funny how the Crown always liked to hedge its bets on the weapon used, even when it was found sticking out of the victim's chest. The date of the crimes was vaguely stated as having taken place sometime during a seven-day period, ending on the 14th October, the date the bodies were found.

'Can we get this show on the road?' I asked the clerk. 'I've somewhere else to be.'

The clerk nodded to the bar officer who went off in search of the sheriff. 'Are you applying for bail?' she asked me.

'Bail?' Ogilvie laughed. 'Have you seen his client's previous?'

I waved the petition at Ogilvie. 'Almost as funny as your half-baked prosecution. You've got a nerve remanding my client. What have you got on him? Nothing. You don't even know the name of one of the victims, far less the date he was killed. This whole procedure is a disgrace. You've got nothing on Pudney that you haven't got against Jake Turpie or, for that matter, me. Why single him out, other than because you know bail is a non-starter and you'd like him off the streets?'

Ogilvie grunted and shuffled his papers. 'Perhaps you should read the summary of evidence before you start accusing the Crown of acting in bad faith.' The rest of his words were drowned out by a bellow of 'Court!' from the bar officer and we stood as Sheriff Albert Brechin swept onto the bench.

To become a sheriff you had to apply to the Judicial Appointments Board, recommending yourself for the job and stating reasons why you thought you'd be good at it. I could only assume that Bert Brechin had thought he'd make a good sheriff because he'd been so useless at everything else he'd tried. If I'd had my way, a burning desire to sit in judgement of others would have been a barrier to the job.

A few seconds later Deek appeared from the cells below, a G4S security officer either side, one male, one female, one old, one very young. It didn't look like either would be of much use if Deek decided he'd had enough and wanted to leave.

As it was, the hearing lasted only a couple of minutes, during which Deek was on his best behaviour. The case was formally continued for further enquiries and my client led off to start his seven-day lie-down. He'd be up again the same time next week. If the Crown was satisfied as to a sufficiency of evidence, he'd be fully committed for trial. If not, he'd be released.

I explained all this to Deek in the cells and he seemed neither up nor down at the prospect of a week's stay courtesy of Her Majesty. He probably thought it would be a nice break from being shouted at by Jake.

The case having called in private, as did all such matters in their initial stages, Deek's boss was sitting on one of the stone benches in the Civic Centre atrium waiting for me. He saw me coming down from the court and sauntered over to meet me at the foot of the stairs.

'What've they got on him?'

'They don't need much at this stage,' I said. 'It's enough for them that he was at the scene of the murder.'

'So was I and so was you. What else they got?'

Hugh Ogilvie had said something about the summary of evidence, a document stapled to the petition and usually compiled by the reporting police officer. It was supposed to give the accused early notice of the case against him. More often than not it contained what the cops hoped the evidence would be, rather than what it actually was.

'We'll know more this time next week,' I said, not mentioning that another thread of evidence the Crown had against Deek, apart from his mere presence at the crime scene, was what I'd told the cops in my witness statement about the debt due by Daisy Adams to Jake.

Although I hadn't said as much, Dougie Fleming would be well aware of Deek's role in Jake's credit control system.

'What now?' Jake asked.

'For now, I've told Deek that it's best if you don't go and visit him and he's asked that you send him up some money.'

'No problem. What's your plan?'

'I don't have one. Not yet. I'll need to see what the Crown has got first, but if it wasn't Deek who murdered those people, somebody else did.' Jake couldn't argue with that. 'And it will be down to us to find out who that person is. The cops will be too busy trying to link Deek to the murders to bother looking for other suspects.'

'What if Deek wasn't there when the murders were committed?'

'Alibi?'

'Yeah. Like you just said, if Deek didn't do it, somebody else did, and if Deek wasn't there when it happened, he must have been somewhere else.'

Which was all perfectly logical, I just didn't want Jake putting something together that wouldn't bear up to scrutiny.

'We'll need to do it right,' I told him. 'Nothing worse than a burst alibi, and I can't start looking into that side of things until I know when the murders happened. You saw the guy on the table. He'd been there a while. We need more information before we start lobbing alibi defences about.'

'I had one of the boys swing by the farm today,' Jake said.

'You what? Have you never heard the saying, the murderer always returns to the scene of the crime? That's the sort of thing the cops will be looking out for. They'll latch onto anything suspicious that can be traced back to you.'

'He only drove by. I told him not to stop.'

'What did he see?'

'The place is sealed off. There was a cop car and a van there. They've taken the jeep away.'

The scene of crime examinations would still be ongoing. They wouldn't let me in until they were finished, but I might be able to have an informal word with someone and find out a bit more about the timing of the killings. If Deek was truly innocent then it followed he must have an alibi. He couldn't have been in two places at the same time.

The big Civic Centre clock told me I was already way behind schedule. Malky would be going crazy.

'Robbie!' one of the court clerks called from the top of the stairs. 'Phone call from your office. It's urgent.'

I left Jake with assurances that I'd be in touch as soon as there was any news and went up to the Sheriff Clerk's office.

It was Grace-Mary. 'What do you think you're playing at?' she said. 'Your brother phoned looking for you. He said you were supposed to be back ages ago and he had to go to work.'

Work? Of course, it was Friday the day of Malky's weekly football phone-in. Surely he hadn't gone off and left Tina to fend for herself.

'Don't worry,' Grace-Mary said. 'She's here at the office, helping Joanna paint her fingernails.'

'Great. Keep her there. Tell Joanna if she runs out of fingers to start on her toes. I'll try and be back about five.'

'Try?'

'I'll do my best. If I'm not back you can stay on and make up for your half-day yesterday.'

'It was only a couple of hours and I still had to go to the post office,' Grace-Mary said, and whether she went on to debate the point further I didn't know because by then I'd hung up.

17

It was a typical late autumn afternoon in Scotland, overcast with light drizzle, when I left the Civic Centre. I met Paul Sharp as I came out of the clerk's office and we walked together back to our cars.

'I hear I narrowly missed out on a murder cut-in,' Paul said. 'I met Joanna and she was telling me all about it. Tricky situation for you. What's going to happen if they come up with some evidence against Jake Turpie? He won't like it if you can't act for him and I can't see how you could jump ship from Deek to Jake's defence. Not if there was even the remotest chance of a conflict of interest. That's how you get yourself struck off.'

'It won't come to that,' I assured him.

'Joanna was also saying that if it does go to trial you're likely to be a defence witness. Can't you find someone more credible?' He laughed. 'Who's going to believe a lawyer's word on anything?'

'Like I say, I don't see the prosecution going that far. There's not enough evidence.'

'What have they got?'

'The three of us at the locus, several days after the actual murders.'

'Who saw you there?'

'No one.'

'Well, how do the cops even know you were there?'

I thought about it. 'Because I told them.'

'Careless,' Paul said.

What did he think I should have done, arriving at a police station with a distressed child who'd been living alone in a house full of dead people for probably the best part of a week? 'The cops asked for a witness statement and I gave them one. I never thought for a moment that they'd actually arrest Jake and Deek.'

'And presumably you advised them not to answer any questions?' Paul continued as we crossed the bridge over the Almond to the car park at Livingston FC's stadium. The water below us was running in full spate and I could hardly hear Paul above it. 'Are you sure you've thought this through?'

'What do you mean?'

'Well, if there is only you putting your clients at the scene, that makes you more of a prosecution witness than a defence witness. Doesn't it?' I hadn't thought about it that way. 'And,' Paul said, warming to his theory on everything, 'if they've served Deek Pudney with a petition, and not Turpie, then they've obviously got something else on him. What does the summary of evidence say?'

I had absolutely no idea. I'd not bothered to look at it yet, more interested in getting out of court and back to Tina. More interested in being a father than a lawyer.

'That information is confidential at the moment,' I said. 'You understand.'

'Of course I do,' Paul said, in a tone that suggested of course he didn't. 'But watch out. These guys will sell you down the river if it means them spending one minute less in jail. Anyway, how did the holiday go? I didn't expect to see you back at work so soon.'

'I'm still on it and it's not a holiday,' I said. 'It's

childminding. Just like work, only a lot harder. Ask Mrs Sharp.'

Paul laughed. 'I'm joking. Anyway, I do my share of looking after the kids.' He set his key-phaser to stun and pointed it at a row of parked cars fifty metres away. Through the gathering gloom a set of indicator lights blinked orange. 'How is Tina? Got you Munro boys whipped into shape yet? I hope you're managing to keep Barry Munn sober long enough to do the paperwork.' He made it sound like Barry was helping me take out finance on a second-hand car, not fighting for custody of my daughter.

'Tina's had my dad and Malky wrapped around her pinky since day one,' I said. 'I'm still putting up a fight. I didn't realise that being a dad also meant being a spoil-sport a lot of the time.'

'It's called responsibility. Get used to it.'

We reached Paul's car. 'This being a parent – it's tricky, isn't it?' I said.

'Hard work's not easy. You're not having second thoughts, are you?'

When I first met Paul he was young, free and single. A man whose unexplained fascination for the music of the Sixties had extended not only to his clothes, but to a lovingly restored Triumph Spitfire. These days, married with a couple of kids, he drove a Ford saloon and the retro suits came out only on special occasions.

'Of course not. It's just that sometimes I wonder if I'm doing the right thing trying to run a law firm and raise a child at the same time,' I said.

Paul opened his car door. 'It's going to be difficult for you as a single parent. Just remember that at the end of the day a job is just a job, but family is everything.' He clamped a hand on my shoulder. 'And if you do decide to pack in the law, feel free to send me your clients.' He sat down and looked up at me through the open door. 'Seriously, Robbie. I know you. You've got what it takes to do what it takes. You'll be fine.'

I watched him drive away before setting off to find my own car further down the same row of vehicles. Once inside I took the rolled-up petition from my pocket and studied it under the dim glow of the courtesy light. What could they possibly have on Deek that they didn't have on Jake? It didn't take me long to find out. Fingerprints. Lots of them, and one in prize position; right there on the handle of the murder weapon. I'd told the big idiot to touch nothing and yet he'd obviously been wandering around that farmhouse kitchen slapping his dabs on every available surface. He deserved to be in jail just for being stupid. Still, the presence of those fingerprints did put my mind slightly at ease. It wasn't only my statement that had put Deek at the murder scene and I could provide a perfectly innocent explanation for Deek's fingerprints being there. My own prints would be on the front door, on the banister and in the bedroom where I'd found the child. Jake would be the same. Wouldn't he? I recalled a set of driving gloves. Who wore driving gloves these days? To drive an Aston Martin, perhaps. But a battered Ford Transit van?

I had that sinking feeling you get when your wallet goes missing or your favourite indie band signs for Sony.

I switched off the courtesy light and sat back. Why had Jake asked me to go see Daisy Adams? A sudden stroke of chivalry, not wanting to upset the lady farmer? How likely was that? About as likely as him turning up unexpectedly to give me a wad of cash to buy a present for my daughter. Deek wasn't the stupid one. It was me. Robbie Munro, Deek's very own DIY defence.

I could see it all. Deek had been sent by Jake to put the frighteners on the woman, and some bloke had stepped in and ended up with a knife in his chest. Daisy was the only witness, a loose end that needed tying off. That's where I came in. How better to muddy the water than by a second visit, with your lawyer in tow and ready to explain away the countless fingerprints left behind the first time?

The more I thought about it, the more I had to grudgingly admit it wasn't such a bad defence. I'd have to withdraw from acting. Even Jake would have to realise that, though he wouldn't like it. On the bright side it would mean I could go back to looking after my daughter, instead of putting my custody claim in jeopardy by running around trying to have Deek acquitted of a crime he'd probably committed.

I put the key into the ignition and then slammed the steering wheel with the heels of my hands. Probably committed. Probably wasn't good enough. I was only guessing that I was part of some devious plan. An educated guess, but a guess nonetheless. How often had I told a jury that probability of guilt wasn't good enough? The test was proof beyond reasonable doubt. And it wasn't as simple a choice as ditching Deek for the sake of my custody claim. Who could reasonably say that it was in the best interests of Tina to live with her down-at-heel dad in a one-bedroom flat when she could live with her grandmother in the lap of luxury?

Working on legal aid rates that hadn't increased in all my time as a defence lawyer, the only way I was going to afford a better place to live was to cut my business overheads. My biggest outlay was the office rent and to wipe it out I needed to have Deek Pudney acquitted. I remembered Paul's departing words of encouragement. I know you, Robbie. You've got what it takes, to do what it takes.

Did I?

I turned the key and started the engine. I was about to find out.

18

The same bored-looking pony and shivering donkeys stood in the field adjacent to Sunnybrae Farmhouse as I trundled my way up the rough track. The animals had been joined by an equally bored and cold-looking police officer, standing guard at a front door that was now criss-crossed with yellow and black tape.

He crunched his way across the gravel courtyard to meet me as my car came to a halt alongside a couple of police vehicles.

'Can I help you, sir?' he asked, once I'd alighted, pleased, no doubt, to be doing something other than standing around, inhaling donkey-dung fumes and being drizzled on.

I flashed him a smile and my Law Society ID card. 'I'm here to see the scene of crime officer.'

'There's two of them. Who exactly is it you wish to see?' he asked, sounding suitably unimpressed.

'Either will do.'

'You haven't anything arranged then?'

'It's more of a general enquiry.'

'About what?'

'About the murder.' *You know the double one that took place in the house that you're standing directly in front of?* I would have added if I'd thought it might have helped. 'I'm acting for Mr Pudney.' The cop looked at me blankly. 'He's been charged with the murders. I've just come from the court.' Nothing. I held up my ID card again in case he'd missed it the first time. 'I'm his lawyer.'

'Sorry, sir, I've not to let anyone into the crime scene.'

I laughed at the apparent misunderstanding. 'Oh, that's all right. I don't need to go in. I'm happy to speak to someone out here.'

All I wanted was the low-down on what scientific evidence there was, if any, that linked Deek to the body of Daisy Adams. When my client came to court in a week's time, the Crown would need to be satisfied of a sufficiency of evidence to fully commit him for trial. At the moment they had a few fingerprints to tie Deek to the murder of the man on the kitchen table. If there was nothing connecting him to the dead woman, I might be able to go over Hugh Ogilvie's head and make representations to someone at Crown Office. If I explained how Deek's fingerprints got where they did, someone more reasonable and more senior to Ogilvie might make a more qualitative, less vindictive assessment of the evidence and order my client's release.

Admittedly, it was a long shot. If Deek's dabs were all over the dead woman too, he was in deep trouble, but there was nothing to lose and I might as well learn the worst now as later.

The cop looked to his left then his right, as though hoping someone would come and relieve him of having to make an executive decision. No one did. He pressed the radio attached to his tunic breast.

A crackly voice came back, 'Go ahead.'

'I have a . . . '

'Mr Munro,' I said.

'Mr Munro. Says he acts for one of the suspects and wants to speak to a SOCO.'

'Would that be a Mr Robbie Munro?' crackled the radio in a depressingly familiar tone. Dougie Fleming.

The cop looked at me. I held the ID card up yet again.

'Yes, Robert Alexander Mun—'

'Then kindly tell him,' the radio crackled, 'to Foxtrot, Uniform, Charlie . . . '

Trust Fleming to be all over this, keeping things tight, making sure that any evidential findings were released to the defence only when absolutely necessary.

The cop tapped the radio, after Fleming had completed my phonetic dismissal. 'Copy that.' He turned to me. 'Did you get that, sir?'

Anyone whose duty was to stand guard outside a building in the middle of nowhere was probably not on the fast track to Chief Constable, but the only plan B I could come up with was to engage him in conversation and see if he'd managed to glean anything about what was happening inside. He couldn't have been out here all day. He must have taken a break for lunch or coffee, and cops, like lawyers, liked to talk. A little information was better than none.

'Yes, I got it all right. Still, it's a terrible business,' I said, an ice-breaker to which the cop could hardly take issue. 'You'll be glad to get off duty. Any idea how much longer they're going to be in there? Must be nearly finished by now.' I nodded towards the building just as Dougie Fleming hove into view, wearing a black raincoat, arms folded. He must have exited by the side door. He came no further than the corner of the farmhouse and stood there, glowering through the dreichness of that late afternoon. I thought at first he'd come out especially to give me the evil eye until I realised he was looking past me, down the field to the road. I followed his line of sight to a set of headlights swinging onto the track and slowly making their way towards us.

'Anyway, I'll be off then.' I searched my pockets for my car keys, stalling for time until the vehicle, a black BMW, had come to rest a few yards from me. A uniformed WPC emerged from the driver's door and walked across the courtyard to meet Fleming. The passenger door opened and a woman about my own age, maybe younger, long dark hair, climbed out. My built-in radar told me she wasn't a cop. She walked over to me, smiled stiffly and offered a hand. I accepted.

'Vikki Stark,' she said.

My grip tightened involuntarily. Vikki Stark? This was her. The woman on whom my hopes of keeping Tina rested. What was she doing here? She obviously didn't recognise me. Why should she? Up until now I would just have been a name to her.

'And you are . . . ? she asked.

'Oh, just keeping an eye on things,' I said. No way was I going to try and explain why I wasn't at home with my daughter and instead twenty miles away at the scene of a murder. We'd meet again. By then I'd have thought up an excuse. I turned to the cop. 'Oh, well. Can't stand about here chatting. Keep up the good work. Nice meeting you, Mrs—'

'Miss.'

'Miss Stark.' I gave her a curt, professional and what I hoped was a cop-like, nod of the head and started towards my car.

'Have they said when Daisy's body will be released for burial, officer?' Vikki called to me.

I turned. 'Sorry, that's information only the officer in charge of the investigation will be able to divulge.'

I was about to take my leave before there were any more awkward moments and then it struck me, Daisy? She'd said Daisy, not Mrs Adams.

'Did you know the deceased?' I asked.

She stared at her shoes for a moment, then looked up and brushed a strand of hair from her eyes. 'I was allocated Daisy's case when she applied to adopt Molly. It was all going so well . . . '

'The other deceased individual. Did you know him too?'

Vikki shook her head. 'I've been shown the photographs. I've no idea who he is. Then again, I hadn't spoken to Daisy in a while.'

'Was there a man in her life? Anyone special?'

'I'm sorry,' Vikki said, turning up the collar of her raincoat. 'Am I being interviewed again? Because,' she tried to smile, 'if I am, I'd rather do it somewhere less damp, if you don't mind.'

The sound of crunching signalled Fleming and the female uniform fast approaching from my starboard side.

I stepped forward and we shook hands again. 'I'm afraid I'll have to go, but I'll leave you in the capable hands of Detective Inspector Fleming.'

I didn't actually sprint, but, in something of a Le Mans start, I made it to my car and away before Fleming had covered the twenty yards to where in the rear-view mirror I could see Vikki standing, staring after me.

19

Around noon on a Sunday, Radio Scotland transforms itself from an informative current affairs medium to a station hurling accordion music at the hard of hearing. I was in the kitchen making lunch. The preparation of meals had become a major part of my life. B.T., that is, Before Tina, I'd grabbed a snack wherever I could and eaten it in my car, at my desk or, more often than not, slumped in front of the TV. Not any more. Kids, so my dad told me, needed to learn to eat sitting at a table and at regular times. According to him, it was all about maintaining a set routine. Sometimes I feared for my daughter. If you'd dipped the well of wisdom and pooled my dad's knowledge of parenting with my own, you'd have ended up with at best a very small puddle.

Tina came through as I was scorching something under the grill. She tugged at my shirt.

'Can we go and feed the ducks?'

'Not today,' I said, rescuing two slices of roasted cheese and burning my fingers in the process. I hurled them onto a wooden chopping board where they continued to singe silently. Was burnt cheese carcinogenic or was that a myth? I decided to eat them and make more for Tina.

She followed me to the fridge and back. 'Why not?'

'Because it's raining.' In support of my submission, I

pointed to the rain-spattered kitchen window.

'But ducks like the rain.'

'I know, but I don't.'

'They'll be hungry.'

I stopped slicing cheese and stared down at the little fed-up face. I didn't like lying to my daughter, but found it the best way of winning arguments. 'It's Sunday. You don't need to feed the ducks today because they go to a special duck place at the far end of Linlithgow Loch and get all their favourite things to eat there.'

'Who gives it them?'

I was going to invent the Duck Man, a mysterious benefactor to all of duck-kind: Santa Claus with webbed feet, but he sounded incredibly creepy even to me, so instead I came up with, 'It's just all there waiting for them. All the things they like the best.'

'They like bread.'

'Oh, there's better stuff than that,' I said, geometrically arranging slices of cheese on to bread. 'There's cakes and biscuits and ... '

'Toasted cheese?'

She said toasted cheese, I said roasted cheese. We'd been down that route; neither of us was prepared to concede. 'Probably ... '

'Sausages?'

'No, ducks don't like sausages.'

'I like sausages.'

'Yes, but ducks don't eat meat.' Did they? 'Now, you go and watch the telly and I'll bring your lunch through to you. How's that sound?'

It sounded acceptable, but temporarily so, because Tina departed only to return as the next batch of cheese and bread was starting to melt.

'Me and Gramps saw a duck eating a worm once. It was in a puddle and was all gooey and horrible.'

'After lunch why don't we go to the new soft playroom?' I said. 'Have you been to a soft playroom before?'

But my daughter wasn't to be sidetracked from her line of questioning. 'Worms are meat, aren't they?'

'I suppose so,' I said, not taking my eyes from the grill.

'But you said ducks don't like meat and they do.'

'That was probably a silly duck that didn't know the worm was made of meat, and ate it by mistake.'

'How wouldn't it not know?'

'Well, ducks aren't very clever and worms don't have faces, do they?'

Tina gave me the look I'd seen hundreds of times before on the face of Sheriff Albert Brechin. The look that said, usually quite correctly, that I was drifting beyond my knowledge of the law, or, on this occasion, the diet of the Mallard duck.

'Sausages don't have faces,' she said.

I removed the toast, cut the slices into quarters and laid them onto a pink plastic plate with a Disney princess on it. 'No, but the animals sausages are made out of do.'

Tina paused to think about that. Did she know where sausages came from? Cows and pigs slaughtered, minced and stuffed into sausage skins. Her wee face screwed up. Had I broken the news too suddenly? Had I scarred her emotionally or, worse, created a vegetarian?

'What about BN biscuits?' she said. 'They've got faces. And so do Jelly Babies and fruit bears.'

I handed her the plate. 'Grandpa told me all about the new soft playroom. He says it's great fun. Would you like to go there after lunch? I bet they've got one of those pools filled with plastic balls,' I said with as much excitement as I could muster.

Tina took her lunch through to the living room, where fortunately her line of questioning moved on to the likelihood of there being a chute at the soft room and whether there would be other boys and girls there.

As it transpired there was indeed a chute. There were quite a few of them and lots and lots of boys and girls, conveniently fenced off from the café area where later that same afternoon I sat reading the Sunday paper, sipping a coffee, eating a pastry and thinking that this childminding lark wasn't so bad after all.

I'd finished the important stories on the back page and was flipping the newspaper over, when I felt a tap on my shoulder. The smile that I now knew belonged to Vikki Stark beamed down at me. She stood there, a small child clamped onto her leg, hiding its face.

'Fancy meeting you here,' she said, with a glance around at a café packed with parents and pushchairs. 'Would you mind if we shared your table?'

I could hardly object. Nor could I make an excuse and leave. Not while Tina was whooping it up somewhere in the depths of the plastic-padded arena.

Vikki sat down and began to coax the child to take off a woolly coat, hat and scarf. 'We met, yesterday,' she said, as I attempted to raise the newspaper between us. 'I didn't catch your name.'

There was nothing for it. I folded the newspaper. 'Robbie Munro,' I said, lighting the blue touchpaper and waiting.

Vikki stopped, leaving the child half in, half out of its coat. 'Robbie Munro? You're Robbie Munro? I didn't know you were a police officer. They told me—'

'That I was a lawyer? I am.'

'But yesterday . . . up at Sunnybrae . . . ?'

Why hadn't I gone to feed the ducks?

'I was there on business,' I said, and hoped that would be enough.

'And you are Tina's dad?'

'That's right.'

'But I thought you were on paternity leave? I've tried to visit you a couple of times to see how things are going, but . . . ' Vikki glanced from side to side. 'Is Tina here?' Two possible answers sprang immediately to mind. One was, no, I've popped in unaccompanied for a peaceful read of my Sunday paper amidst the hordes of screaming kids. The other was, duh. I deemed neither appropriate in the circumstances.

Perhaps Vikki realised the stupidity of her question for she added quickly, 'The kids love it here, don't they? Do you have much experience of children?'

'Well, I did go to school with them for many years,' I said. 'In fact, I used to be one.'

She smiled a non-smile. 'And, of course, some people never grow up, do they?' Once she had managed to divest the child of its outer garments, Vikki stood up and laid them on the seat she'd vacated. 'Could you watch that for me while I put Molly into the soft room?'

She took the girl by the hand and tugged her off in the direction of the multicoloured padded area. I returned to the newspaper, not reading, my mind racing, ready for what I expected to be a thorough interrogation upon Vikki's return. What kind of business had I been doing up at the farm? Why was I working when I was supposed to be looking after my daughter? What kind of care could I provide when I really was working if I couldn't look after Tina on my days off?

100

'Dad! Dad!' The words carried to me through the deafening din. It was Tina's voice and I, like a ewe, had distinguished the bleats of my little lamb from the rest of the flock. That said, my little lamb's bleats were a lot louder than most of the other little lambs and she was standing only ten feet away, on tiptoe, trying to peer over the top of a bright-yellow picket fence.

Tina was thirsty. Again. Problem was there were several notices scattered about stating that no food or drink was to enter the soft play area and Tina didn't want to leave as that would entail me signing her out, returning to our table for a drink and then queuing up to be signed back in again; a process invariably delayed by a steady stream of snotty-faced children wailing about some minor injury or other and wanting their mums. So to circumvent this rigmarole we'd developed our own system. Tina squeezed her face against the fence, I held a carton of apple juice between the slats and she sucked it through a straw. It was the playground equivalent of a Formula One pit stop, and carried out at a speed with which the McLaren team would have been pretty pleased.

Refuelled, Tina sped off and I returned to my table to find Vikki, still with a teary-eyed little girl at her side.

'What's wrong?' I asked.

'Molly doesn't want to go in.'

Molly? It was the girl I'd rescued from the farm. 'Hi, Molly?' I said. 'Do you remember me?' If she did she didn't say, just turned and pressed her face against Vikki's thigh. A metre further north, Vikki was looking puzzled.

'Wait there,' I said, and went off in search of Tina. After a few minutes hunting, one of the supervisors came to the gate with her. 'There's a wee girl here who's not sure what to do,' I said to my daughter. 'I want you to

101

take her hand and stay with her until she gets used to everything, okay?'

Tina was prepared to give it a shot and so, after some persuasion, was Molly.

'Thanks for that,' Vikki said, after we'd resumed our seats and she'd brought us over some coffees. 'Forgive me for asking, but how is it that you know Molly?'

'I found Molly up at the farm and took her to the police.' At least that part was true. 'That's why I was there yesterday; I was just wanting to know how she was getting on. I wasn't sure what had become of her.'

'It was you who found her? The police wouldn't tell me what happened. Obviously, I know about Daisy. Were you a friend of hers?'

'Not a friend. I was there to see her about some legal business. It was confidential. You'll understand?'

Fortunately for me, Vikki did. The conversation moved on to Molly for a while, but it wasn't long until I had us back on the topic of dead Daisy Adams.

'She moved through this way about a year ago,' Vikki said. 'But you'll probably know all about that.' She looked to me for confirmation, didn't receive any and continued. 'She had problems in her personal life. She wanted to adopt Molly, and there were a lot of obstacles in the way. I guided her through the process and prepared the report prior to the court granting the permanence order.' Vikki took a sip of coffee. 'We saw each other so often during the adoption process that we became friends. She didn't seem to have many of those. Kept herself very much to herself. I used to drop by now and again or we'd meet up for lunch or to take Molly somewhere. The last few weeks I'd been so busy it was text messages only.'

'What's going to happen to Molly?' I asked.

Vikki shrugged. 'Difficult to say. Daisy has no family, just an ex-husband prone to domestic violence. Molly calls me Aunt Vikki. For the moment I'm the nearest thing to family she has.'

'But there must be plenty of people out there looking to adopt?'

Vikki set down her coffee mug, shaking her head. 'Potential adopters want babies, not five-year-olds. And Molly has other problems than just her age. At first they thought she had foetal alcohol syndrome. It's not as bad as that, fortunately, but now they think she could have a mild form of autism. She's not what you'd call a catch. She's a young girl who might grow up to be a bit of a handful. She looked over her shoulder at the play area. 'How's Tina doing? Are you coping?'

Everyone wanted to know if I was coping. Did women who were single parents get asked the same question? Or because they were women, was the ability to cope implied? Was it all part of the gender bias Barry Munn had warned me about? Maybe I was reading too much into what was, after all, an innocent enough question – even if it did come from the woman who would eventually write the report recommending, or not, my suitability as Tina's full-time parent. Why hadn't I at least paid for the coffees?

'No bother. We're getting on great,' I said.

'Can't be easy. Single man, busy professional life. Paternity leave is a fairly new concept for some employers. How is yours taking it?'

'No problems there either,' I said. 'I'm on very friendly terms with the boss.'

'Good,' she said. Had she done no research on me at all? Hopefully not. 'Still, no matter how understanding your employer is, it won't be easy when you go back to work and have to deal with both a professional and a family life. You don't have a partner, do you?' Maybe she had done some background checking after all. Or perhaps she could just tell.

'That particular situation is vacant at the moment, but I can manage. In my line of work I'm used to juggling court cases. Being in two places at the same time is practically second nature.'

'And you'll just add Tina to all the things you have up in the air? Better watch you don't let something drop.' Vikki took another drink of coffee. 'But being in two places at one time?' She looked down at the dregs in her coffee mug. 'That's a useful skill to have.' She said something else. I didn't hear what because I wasn't listening. Suddenly I realised that she was smiling and I wasn't smiling back.

'Sorry,' I said, thumping the side of my head with the heel of my hand.

'I think you were somewhere else just now,' Vikki laughed. 'Miles away, in fact.'

'I think it's called being a parent,' I said. 'There's always something needing done. I'm still trying to get to grips with it.' I made a reasonable attempt at a light laugh. What was I doing? I should have been concentrating more on making a good impression, and yet, two places at the same time? Wasn't Deek in Glasgow being assaulted by Marty Sneddon one day a couple of weeks ago? When exactly was Daisy Adams murdered? I needed to find out. It was at times like those I wished I had a watch to look at, so I could say, 'Goodness, is that the time?' and make an escape.

The appearance of Tina's face at the yellow fence, a much happier Molly by her side, helped rescue me from the awkward moment. I thought she might be thirsty again and picked up the half-full apple juice carton, but Tina just waved and then they were off again.

'Those two seem to be getting on well,' Vikki said. 'How about me and Molly come back with you after this? The girls can play and, since I've had no luck catching up with you through the week, you can tell me all about yourself and how the father/daughter bonding is coming along.'

I hadn't had a lot of practice dissuading good-looking women from inviting themselves back to my place, but I feared this would be no social visit. I had a fleet of dirty dishes floating in my sink, a bedroom festooned with unwashed clothes and a mountain of ironing you could have planted a flag atop. I couldn't let myself be seduced into a spot check on my daughter's accommodation. I could almost see Vikki's court report now, featuring adjectives such as unhygienic, chaotic and war-torn.

'Sorry,' I said, 'can we make it some other time?'

'Of course.' Vikki broke off eye contact, sat back, picked up Molly's folded coat, opened it and, for no apparent reason, refolded it.

Had I misread the signals? Maybe she was just being friendly. Maybe it was just a social visit. Did there have to be an ulterior motive? Why did women always have to be so subtle about everything? Semaphore was tricky, but at least there was a manual to read.

'Tomorrow?' I blurted.

'Tomorrow's not good for me, I'm afraid.'

'What about Tuesday? Or Wednesday? I'm pretty much free all week.'

Vikki paused. 'I could perhaps do Wednesday.'

'Tina has nursery in the morning.'

'Then let's make it the afternoon. That'll give you time to collect Tina from nursery and get lunch out of the way.'

The girls were at the fence again, waving to us.

'Wednesday afternoon would be fine,' I said. It would probably take me until then to tidy up.

20

I'd forgotten that Edinburgh Zoo was built on the side of a hill. I couldn't have been much older than Tina on my last visit, and too excited to notice the steep incline.

Unhelpfully, my dad had told Tina all about the giant pandas and it was the pandas my daughter wanted to see. Trouble was, so did everyone else and I wasn't all that keen on forking out even more money to stand in line just to see a couple of bears with a custom paint job eating bamboo shoots. As things turned out, I was spared the extra expense because the Chinese immigrants were attempting procreation. They needed peace and quiet and so their enclosure was closed for several weeks, while the mood-lighting was installed and Barry White music piped in.

'What else does it do?' Tina asked, as she stared through the security glass at a lioness, sprawled on a rock and being annoyed by a gang of impertinent sparrows.

'Not all that much, really,' I said. 'Unless you go in there beside it.'

'What does it do then?'

I grabbed her and gave her a shake, snarling, 'It eats you up for its tea!'

Tina found that more amusing than the couple a few yards away, whose own children looked at us as though we were part of the exhibits. When the one in the pushchair began to cry, I took Tina's hand and led her away in search of more animal magic. There wasn't any. The giraffes had gone and a bronze statue of an elephant wasn't the same as the real thing. I explained to her that the sign beneath it said that being in a zoo made elephants unhappy and so they didn't keep them any more.

'Are the other animals unhappy too?' she asked.

I told her the other residents were generally pretty ecstatic about their surroundings, especially the penguins. Pre panda-mania, they had topped the bill at the Edinburgh Zoo. Armed with ice lollies, we joined the crowd lining the avenue from Penguin Rock and waited patiently for the daily parade. On the appointed hour the gate was opened. Four penguins, a King, a Gentoo and a couple of Rockhoppers emerged and waddled past, more, I suspected, out of a sense of duty than any *joie de vivre*.

'Why are the rest of them not coming out, Dad?' Tina asked. I was wondering the same thing until the keeper explained that under some sort of European Convention of Penguin Rights, the birds were no longer made or even encouraged to take part in the parade nowadays, and only went for a walk if they felt like it.

'I think it's a bit cold for some of them today,' the keeper laughed, and waddled after his dinner-suited charges in his wellies.

Things didn't improve after that. Many of the enclosures that had promised so much were empty, their occupants having decided either to take that October Monday as a duvet day or been given early release for good behaviour.

I thought the reptile house might cheer us up. It had been my favourite as a lad. Sadly, like my childhood, it had long gone and as we hadn't pre-booked a ticket for the half-hour lecture on snakes, we had to slither off in search of other exotic life forms. It was the lemurs who saved the day. Some might say it was stretching the truth for me to call them baby pandas, but surely that was down to a quirk of evolution and, judging by Tina's excitement at seeing them, one black and white furry animal was as good as another to someone who still believed in Santa Claus and the Tooth Fairy.

'Where are we going now?' she wanted to know as I strapped her into the car. She was clutching a panda key ring from the Zoo gift shop as if it was made of gold, and which, by the price tag, it should have been. 'Are we going home for tea?'

We weren't. Not just yet. I climbed aboard, started the engine and set off towards Edinburgh, the city that hates motorists.

'Where are we going then?'

'To see a man.'

'Why?'

'He's going to help Daddy with his work.'

'Does he put baddies in jail too?'

'Sometimes. But he's not a lawyer like me. He's a doctor,' I said, trying to remember the way to Professor Edward Bradley's house. I'd only been to it once before, but in a posh area like this I was certain his rusting Volvo estate would stick out a mile.

I took a left turn into a wide tree-lined street, not a lacrosse shot from St George's School for Girls. There had been a couple of former pupils in my year at uni. I'd gone out with one of them for a while until her parents decided we weren't right for each other.

I suddenly noticed that Tina was awfully quiet. I checked the rear-view mirror. She was sitting picking the fuzzy skin off her panda key ring.

'Don't waste it,' I said.

She looked up and our eyes met in the mirror. Hers looked watery. 'Are you not feeling well, Dad?'

'Me? No, I'm fine.'

'Why are you going to the doctor then?'

'He's not that kind of doctor.'

'What kind of doctor is he?'

'A special doctor. He looks at dead people and finds out what they died of,' I said.

Silence from the back seat. My explanation hadn't helped much. What was going through that little head. Memories of her mum? I forced a laugh. 'Wait until Gramps hears that you saw some baby pandas.'

There was a long pause and then, 'I liked their big long tails the best.' Soon Tina was blethering away happily on the subject of her trip to the zoo, and I realised that there was only one thing worse than Tina's incessant talking and that was her not talking. I kept the chat going until I spied a familiar clapped-out Volvo in the driveway of a big old sandstone house and pulled in behind it. I was unbuckling Tina from her child seat when the professor materialised amidst wreaths of pipe smoke.

'Robbie Munro, is that you?' Tina jumped out. 'And who's this you've brought with you?'

'This,' I said, Tina in front of me, my hands on her shoulders, 'is my daughter. Say hello to Professor Bradley, Tina.'

'You shouldn't smoke. It makes you die. And it smells horrible,' Tina said.

'And very nice to meet you too, young lady.' The professor gave Tina a cautious pat on the head as though she might be infectious.

'You're still smoking,' Tina said, in case the professor hadn't noticed.

Professor Bradley stared down at Tina who, in order to drive home her message, had screwed up her face and was pinching her nose. 'I didn't know you had a daughter, Robbie.'

'Came as a pleasant surprise to me too,' I said.

He took a couple of draws from his pipe and after blowing a cloud of blue smoke skywards, pointed the stem at the house and the open front door. 'Run inside, dear, and tell Mrs Bradley to put the kettle on. Sounds like you and her have a lot in common.'

'No, we'll not disturb you,' I said, keeping a grip on Tina's shoulders. 'It's just a flying visit.'

'Robbie, if this is to do with . . . the little lady and DNA or something, I'm afraid that's not really—'

'What?'

Tina started to cough loudly. 'Are you going to stop smoking or do you want to die?' she asked.

'I'm talking about your little anti-tobacco campaigner.' The Professor tried to ruffle Tina's hair but she pulled away. 'If you're looking for me to run some tests . . . '

I laughed. 'No, nothing like that. She's definitely mine.'

'Yes,' said the professor, 'I was beginning to detect a certain familial likeness. Is she always quite so . . . forthright?'

A grey squirrel ran down a tree and across our path. It stopped on the front lawn to gnaw at something.

'Go and see how close you can get to it,' I said. 'Be very quiet, you don't want to scare it.'

'Scare it as much as you want,' the professor said, through another blast of smoke. 'If I could get close enough, I'd throttle it. One of them chewed through the telephone cable. I had to use the wife's mobile for a week, stupid wee footery thing, buttons the size of pinheads and, when you do manage to get through to anyone, you can either put it to your ear or at your mouth, never both at the same time. Anyway,' he said, watching Tina run off and letting loose a rapid series of puffs, 'where's the girl's mother?'

'Dead,' I said.

'Oh. But that's not why you're here?'

'No, I want to speak to you about the deaths at Sunnybrae Farm. The PF tells me you carried out the post-mortems.'

The professor turned the bulb of his pipe upside down and banged it against the palm of his hand. Sparks and burning tobacco fell out on to the driveway and burst on impact like tiny bombs. He ground the smouldering ash with the sole of an ox-blood brogue. 'Robbie, this is highly irregular.'

'All I want to know is time of death.'

'And that's something you'll find out soon enough – once the prosecution authorities are ready to release that information to you.'

'Meanwhile my client has to rot in jail for a crime he didn't do?'

'Your clients never do anything, Robbie. When I think of all those poor innocent men and women picked on by the state and—'

'Listen, when my dad dies you can have his job. Until then what's so top secret about time of death?'

The professor sucked on the stem of his dead pipe and adopted a studious expression. 'Hmm, let me think. Ah.' He raised an index finger. 'I tell you time of death and, wallop, suddenly not only did your client not do it, but he has witnesses to say they were with him when he didn't do it.'

'Not all alibis are fabricated,' I said.

'No, but some of the best ones are, and I'm not going to be the person who gives your client the material to cobble one together. The Lord Advocate wouldn't like it and he's paying my wages.'

Over on the rolling lawn, Tina stalked the squirrel with all the gentle finesse of a dawn drugs' raid, the animal darting here and there, just enough to keep my daughter at bay, but not sufficiently far for her to give up the chase.

'Persistent, isn't she?' the professor said.

'The prosecution say the murder took place sometime during a seven-day window. It was me who discovered the body in the kitchen and even I could tell he wasn't exactly fresh. Go on, narrow it a little for me. I'm not asking for a down to the minute opinion, just the day it's most likely to have happened.'

But the professor seemed more interested in what my little squirrel hunter was up to for she had left the lawn and was now careering through an area filled with plants and shrubs.

'Tell her to be careful,' he gasped, recoiling as though in pain, 'I just planted those beds at the weekend.'

'Tina!' I shouted. 'You're standing on all the flowers. Come back here.'

'There's no flowers!' she called back, transgressing further into the flower border.

'Get back on the grass!'

She stopped, looked around at the neat rows of bedding plants, some now no longer quite so neat.

'Tina! I said get out of the flowers and back on the grass!'

'And I said, there's no flowers! There's only leafs!' she yelled, her hands-on-hips pose a direct challenge to my authority. What did I do now that shouting hadn't worked? I started forward. Tina ran off giggling, happy to change from chaser to chasee as she trampled more and more of the professor's precious vegetation. I had to give up to prevent further damage.

'The Wednesday the week before he was found,' Professor Bradley said hurriedly. 'Maybe the Thursday, possibly even the Friday. That's the best I can do. If you want anything more specific time-wise you'll need to speak to, what's-his-name, you know, the fly-man.'

The squirrel reappeared from under a bush. Tina squealed with joy and ran after it. Grimacing, Professor Bradley chewed on the stem of his pipe. I had a feeling Tina had moved above squirrels on his things-needing-throttled list.

'Now for the love of God, Robbie, will you get that child of yours out of my Sweet Williams?'

21

Coming back from Edinburgh we diverted through South Queensferry and ate fish and chips in a car park with a good view of the Forth Bridges. On the way home I'd intended to discuss Tina's behaviour, but my daughter was more interested in telling me all about baby pandas, squirrels and Professor Bradley's imminent death from pipe smoking. When, eventually, I did manage to raise the subject of why little girls should do what they were told, I thought she was listening very attentively, until I realised she was asleep.

She was still out for the count when we arrived back at my flat. Children, I'd begun to notice, were peculiar. They never went to sleep when you wanted them to, but when they wanted to sleep it was practically impossible to wake them up. Somehow I managed to take Tina to the toilet, put her pyjamas on and tuck her into bed all while she remained in some kind of somnambulistic limbo.

Afterwards, I sat down in front of the TV with a cup of coffee. Peace at last. The phone rang. My dad.

'I can't bring her to the phone, she's sound asleep,' I told him. 'I know you haven't seen her since Thursday. We've been busy. We were at the new soft play area yesterday and I took her to the zoo after nursery today. By the way, if Tina starts going on about the baby pandas, don't look surprised if she tells you that there were lots of them and that they were swinging through the branches on long bushy tails.'

'What have you got lined up for tomorrow?' he asked.

'Nothing,' I said, 'but Vikki is coming to see us on Wednesday and there's a lot of housework to be done before then.'

'Then why don't I come and take Tina out tomorrow afternoon? It'll let you get on. I'll give the bairn her lunch and then if it's nice we'll go down the Peel. She can run around there for a while and go to the swings.'

Linlithgow Peel is the name for the grounds and gardens surrounding the Palace. It's a local thing, but for some reason one goes 'up to the Palace', and, 'down to the Peel', never the other way around. Anyway, no matter his plans, I wasn't about to make things easy for the old man. Not after his quality-time talk. 'Hmm. I'm not sure. Don't you think Tina should be spending more time with me? You're just the granddad after all, you're only supposed to be flitting in and out of Tina's life and Thursday wasn't that long ago.'

I could sense knuckles whitening on the telephone receiver and almost hear the clenching of teeth. That was enough. Mission accomplished. I put him out of his misery and after lunch next day the two of them set off in the direction of Linlithgow Palace leaving me to turn my flat into a semblance of tidiness in time for Vikki's arrival the following day.

After they'd gone I spent five minutes putting away the hoover, brushes, dusters and other items that I'd dug out in support of my Cinderella story and another five minutes to change into my suit. Five minutes after that I was in my car, avoiding Linlithgow High Street, and en route to Haddington; site of many an English invasion,

116

the birthplace of John Knox and home to Doctor Alfred Wiltshire, entomologist, AKA the fly-man.

'He's not here,' his wife said when I arrived at the front door.

'But I phoned last night.'

'Oh, was that you? I'm so sorry, Alf's diary-keeping's hopeless. He must have forgotten that he was lecturing today. He's not long gone, actually. Edinburgh Uni. Kings Buildings. You'll catch him there if you go now. I don't think he's on until two o'clock.'

I pulled up in front of Kings Buildings at one thirty and had no sooner alighted than I was approached by a member of security who asked if he could help, and actually looked like he meant it.

'Doctor Wiltshire,' I said. 'There's a lecture—'

'I've a Doctor Wiltshire, for a lecture,' the security guard said into a walkie-talkie. I couldn't make out the response, but he obviously could. 'You're already here, Doctor. You booked in half an hour ago.'

I thought he was joking. His serious face told me he wasn't. Could he be that stupid and work at a university? Or did he simply assume that all scientists were absent-minded? Once I'd explained I wasn't the fly-man, but someone looking for the fly-man, I was directed to Ashworth Labs, an immense stone building with a short flight of steps to a landing and an enormous double door, above which was carved into the stone facade the word 'Zoology' and the year 1929. Inside, the place smelt musty like an old school gym hall. Straight ahead there was an impressive staircase and to my right a laboratory filled with white-coated students.

I veered left down a corridor and followed a sign to a lecture hall. It was empty. Row upon row of wooden fold-down seats stood to attention, ready to inflict pins and needles on the next batch of students. On the wall a huge, coloured chart displayed the geologic periods.

'Lost?'

From behind me an elderly woman in a blue lab coat appeared, carrying a bucket. She pointed to a corner of the high ceiling. 'Just had the roof fixed for the umpteenth time and it's still leaking.'

'I'm looking for Doctor Wiltshire,' I said. She frowned. 'The entomologist?' I added.

'Oh, you mean Alf? You'll probably find him in Immunology, talking mosquito mouthparts to the malaria lot,' she said, and went on to give directions that caused me to retrace my footsteps down the corridor to where I met an elderly man at the foot of a flight of stairs. On his head he wore some sort of battered hat from beneath which wisps of grey hair made a bid for freedom. The rest of him was clad in a shapeless tweed suit that he was frantically patting down.

'Doctor Wiltshire?'

'Bloody lecture starting in ten minutes and I've gone and left my notes in the car.'

'My name's Robbie Munro. I'm a lawyer. I was hoping to catch a few words with you about the murders.'

He stopped patting. 'Which ones?'

'Up at Sunnybrae Farm.'

'Not pleasant,' he said.

'I was hoping you could give me an idea as to time of death.'

'I can't do anything until I find my car keys,' he said. 'I'm absolutely positive they were in this pocket.' He rummaged around in the tweed suit some more and then shook his head. 'I simply don't understand it. I parked the car, got out and locked it.' He mimed each action as he spoke. 'I put the keys in my pocket, walked to the front door, up the steps, turned left and—'

'Alf!' A voice from the top of the stairs. 'You've forgotten your coat. Catch!'

A navy-blue raincoat dropped down the stairwell, weighted by something heavy in one of the pockets. I took a guess at what that might be.

'My report's not yet complete, you know,' Wiltshire grumbled, as we walked through the car park. He wanted me to wait until after the lecture, but I explained that as he was having to walk back to his car in any event, we could talk on the way. 'All I have are my notes. Lawyers. So impatient, the lot of you. Everything's got to be done in a rush.'

I was content to let him grumble on as much as he wanted. All I needed from him was the time of the deaths at Sunnybrae Farm. Something I'd otherwise have to wait weeks for. The doctor might know all about flies and mosquito mouthparts, but he had much to learn about the criminal justice system. Not all lawyers were in a hurry, and those at Crown Office in particular wouldn't be busting any guts to disclose important evidence to the defence before it was absolutely necessary. Doc Wiltshire was my fast track to an alibi for Deek Pudney. The prosecution would hate to think I was getting such vital information before them and from their own witness at that. The good thing was that Wiltshire didn't seem to know or care. But, then, to a man who'd devoted his life to the taxonomy of bugs, lawyers, Crown or defence, we were all the same species.

'Okay, let me see.' Wiltshire sat on the driver's seat, door open, briefcase on his lap, a sheaf of papers in his hand. 'Oh, yes, here we are. One male, one female . . . ' He scanned down the pencil-written page. 'Male . . . injury to the nose, stab wounds to the neck and thorax.' He glanced up at me. 'October's not the best month for flies. Happily the weather the week before the bodies were found was mild for the time of year, even milder if averaged out over the preceding twelve days, and being on a farm with plenty of animals and dung about the place there was always going to be calliphoridae vomitoria around somewhere. I see that I calculated the ADH . . . That's accumulated degree hours.' I was none the wiser. 'At . . . ' He turned to a graph sketched out on one side of A4 and drew his finger along it to where two lines intersected.

I leaned into the car and placed a hand on his shoulder. 'I don't want to keep you, Doctor Wiltshire. I know you have a lecture to deliver. If you could just give me your opinion on time of death, I'll er . . . buzz off.'

He stopped tracing the curve of the graph and glowered up at me. At first I thought I'd crossed some entomological line with my attempt at fly-humour, but it wasn't that or at any rate, not just that. 'I don't have a T.O.D., I have a PMI.' He certainly sounded like he had PM something. 'Post-Mortem Interval is the time between the first blowfly eggs being laid on the body and the date the body was discovered.'

Wiltshire then went on to explain things in some detail. What I understood of it was quite interesting, although I was glad I wasn't having to sit on a hard fold-down seat while he spoke or sit an exam at the end of it. From his mini-lecture I learned there were lots of different types of blowflies and that they were all the very dabs at detecting dead flesh and making a beeline for it. Wiltshire reckoned that with a partially open door in a rural setting, a recent stab victim would attract the delightfully named C. Vomitoria in under an hour.

'It could be more, or even slightly less,' he said. 'In July you'd be talking fifteen minutes but given the time of year, my ADH calculations suggest around about sixty minutes. After that, in a centrally heated building with the temperature not falling below sixteen point five degrees centigrade at any time . . . '

It all began to get a little hazy, he started to lose me when he moved onto larval and pupal transitions and I didn't even want to think about maggot mass temperatures.

'Which brings me to the zero point of my PMI, being the time of egg-laying, to sometime late evening on the Thursday the week before the body was found. Give or take.'

'Which means . . . '

'Which means that, assuming they hadn't been moved, and the scene was as it has been described to me, those poor people were most probably murdered around midnight on Thursday the 8th of October,' the doctor said.

It was amazing how his timing could be so precise, and even more amazing that Deek Pudney's liberty was about to be secured, not by anything the law had to say, but on the breeding habits of a few creepy-crawlies.

22

'How do you know all this?' Hugh Ogilvie asked.

Wednesday morning, Tina was at nursery with the other Little Ships. I, meantime, had sailed up to Livingston and press-ganged the Procurator Fiscal into discussing Deek Pudney and what I now saw as grounds for his inevitable and imminent release.

'I've had it straight from the horse's, or maybe that should be the horsefly's, mouth,' I said, injecting a little insect-humour.

Ogilvie appreciated it about as much as the fly-man had. He sat back in his chair. 'I hate it when you're this cheerful. It usually means some criminal is about to get off on a technicality.'

'No technicality here, Hugh, old son. Just a plain, good old-fashioned alibi.'

'Really? How unusual. One of Munro and Co.'s clients has come up with an alibi.'

True it wasn't that rare an occurrence. 'Except . . . ' I took a piece of paper from my jacket pocket, unfolded it and spread it flat on the desk in front of him. 'This could be the best one yet.'

My turn to sit back, while I let the PF study my timeline. According to Dr Wiltshire, the folk in the farm had been murdered around midnight on Thursday 8th October. Working on what I thought was a generous four-hour margin of error either side, I had set out in writing Deek Pudney's movements.

'Eight o'clock on the Thursday evening he's in a pub in Glasgow. One thirty a.m. on the Friday he's admitted to A & E at Glasgow Royal Infirmary. Three fifteen he's stitched up and three forty-five he's in the back of a taxi heading for Linlithgow. At no time is he ever within a twenty-mile radius of the murder scene during what your own insect expert reckons was the time of death.' I leaned forward and pointed to the foot of the page where I'd jotted down the name of the casualty nurse and the phone number of the taxi company, just in case my word wasn't good enough. 'Oh, and, of course, the *piece de resistance*. A petition at the instance of the Procurator Fiscal, Glasgow, complete with summary of evidence alleging that at around 12.30 a.m. on Friday 9th October, Martin Sneddon assaulted Derek William Pudney and struck him on the head with a knife, or similar instrument, all to his severe injury and permanent disfigurement.' I slapped the petition down on the desk like a Royal Flush in a high-stakes poker game.

Ogilvie picked it up, barely glancing at it before giving me a slitty-eyed stare. 'You know you can get into all sorts of bother interfering with Crown witnesses.'

'If by interfering you mean asking an independent expert witness like Doctor Wiltshire for his independent expert opinion on an important piece of evidence that might prove my client's innocence, then, no, I'm not sure how much trouble that would land me in. I mean, we're both stakeholders in the justice system, aren't we?'

'I know one of us is.' Ogilvie threw the petition down on the desk on top of my handwritten timeline. 'Okay, I'll give it some thought.' By which he meant, he'd mull it over and then do whatever the Crown Office Gestapo told him to do.

'Yes, you do that,' I said, unable to keep the smugness out of my voice. 'Give it a good think. It's Wednesday. The full committal isn't until Friday. You can do the honourable thing and let my client out before then, or—'

'Or what? Your client's section 23D'd. He's going nowhere except back on remand.'

'Seriously, Hugh. In the face of all this?' I picked up the papers and wafted them in front of his face. I hadn't enjoyed myself so much in ages. 'Even section 23D allows for bail in exceptional circumstances and while I agree Sheriff Brechin might not think that being in two places at the same time is sufficiently exceptional, I have a feeling the boys in the red jerseys up at Parliament House might think otherwise.'

Ogilvie stood. 'Your opinion on the appellate court is, as ever, invaluable,' he said, pointing to the door. 'But, if you don't mind, I've other things to do than waste time on one of your dodgy alibis.'

On the way to collect Tina, I dropped in at the office. Joanna was out at court. Grace-Mary heard me enter and came through from reception. 'Sometimes I think I see more of you now that you're on holiday than when you're actually working. You've been told to stay away.'

'I know, I know. I'm picking Tina up in five minutes and I've only come in to use the phone.'

'Well, don't go messing the place up.'

'You'll never know I was here.'

Grace-Mary remained in the doorway, arms folded.

'I'm not going to touch a thing apart from the phone. Honest,' I said. 'So why don't you go about your business – whatever that is. Just pretend I'm not here.'

My secretary grunted and left me alone. 'Looks like Marty Sneddon did Deek a favour,' I said, once I'd got through to Jake and told him the good news. 'Better a scar on the face than a life in the jail, eh?' Jake agreed, but wasn't able to talk about transferring the title of the office to me because something very important involving a crane was happening down at the yard. Whether that was true or just his way of getting rid of me, one thing was certain: I wasn't letting him out of our arrangement. When Deek officially walked, the office was mine. 'Grace-Mary!'

My secretary came through at the third yell. 'What's all the shouting about? I'm busy.'

'Are you going deaf or something?'

'My hearing's fine, thanks. So is my memory. You told me to pretend you weren't here and that's what I'm trying to do except you're not making it easy.'

'I've got big news.'

'You don't say?'

'I want you to order up the land certificate for this place.'

'What place?'

I waved my arms around. 'This place. The office. Get the land certificate and knock up a disposition from Jake Turpie to me.'

Grace-Mary looked around. 'You're not actually thinking about buying this dump, are you? How much is that crook wanting?'

'Nothing.'

'What? No, wait, I don't want to know. Just tell me the spurious reason I'm to put in for a consideration. The love, favour and affection that Jake Turpie has for you?'

I didn't think there was any need for quite so much sarcasm. At that precise moment I had only warm feelings for my soon-to-be ex-landlord and was confident he also held me in similarly high esteem. 'No,' I said. 'Put this down as a transfer of title based on certain good and onerous causes.'

23

Housework: a perfect example of the law on diminishing returns. Instead of having fun at the Fiscal's, I could have easily spent the time spring-cleaning, dusting and getting right into the corners. As it was, transforming my small flat from disaster zone to quite tidy, even with Tina's help after nursery, took only a couple of hours.

'Sorry about the state of the place,' I said at half past two on Wednesday afternoon, helping Vikki off with her coat. I glanced around a neater-than-ever living room, shaking my head in disgust. 'It's been all go and I've had no time for housework.'

'I was hoovering,' Tina said. 'My dad said we had to make everything nice or—'

'Why don't you take Molly's coat?' I said to Tina, while draping Vikki's coat over the folded camp bed that was propped against the wall under the window. In the daylight and momentarily seen through the eyes of a third party, it seemed more rusty and rickety than ever. I caught Vikki staring at it. 'My temporary sleeping arrangement,' I said. 'Actually, it's a lot less comfortable than it looks.'

'What's the long-term plan?' she asked.

'There isn't one. There is a short-term plan, though.' I'm going to buy a new place with at least two bedrooms.'

'How far have you got?'

'I've been surfing a few estate agent sites.'

127

'Noted interest in anything? Made any offers?'

'Not yet . . . '

'How many properties have you viewed so far?'

'Not that many.'

'How many?'

'Well . . . '

'Less than one?'

'Everything's happened so quickly.'

'Tina has been in Scotland for three months, the court case has been on the go for two. Did you not think that you might be a bit short of space?'

What could I say? For most of the time since discovering I was a father I'd been in a state of shock.

I allowed myself to be distracted by Tina who'd got in a tangle with her friend's coat. Molly was clutching onto the toy animal that I remembered from that horrific day at Sunnybrae Farm and Tina was trying to pull Molly's jacket sleeve over the top of the stuffed bird. As a result the disrobing was turning into a tug-of-war.

'Let me take your birdie, for a moment,' I said. I took the soft toy. What was it? A stork? No, more like a pelican. Whatever, it looked a lot cleaner and the loose wing was now firmly attached.

With a final almighty tug, Tina wrenched Molly's coat off and laid it over Vikki's on the camp bed.

'La-La!' Molly said. It was the first noise I'd heard her emit. She snatched the stuffed toy from my hand and clutched it tightly.

'Laa-Laa?' I said. 'Like the Teletubbie?' My dad had bought Tina an old *Teletubbies* DVD from a charity shop. I'd been forced to watch it several times before we returned it to the shop so that the other girls and boys could get a chance to see it. Up until then the only thing that had got me through those viewings was trying to work out in which order I'd kill the fat, annoying, multicoloured creatures and what my weapon of choice would be. If Laa-Laa was the red one, it was first for the chop with a blunt machete.

'Let's talk about something else,' Vikki said. 'Tina, how are you enjoying nursery?'

On the basis that Tina had mastered the art of saying what I least wanted her to say at precisely the time I didn't want her to say it, I intervened before Vikki was told the story of Zack, his burst nose and the rudiments of combination-punching. 'Tina loves nursery,' I said.

'Do you, Tina?' Vikki asked.

'She likes painting the best. Don't you, Tina?'

Tina nodded enthusiastically in confirmation.

'Yes, I can see that,' Vikki said, taking in the series of crinkly masterpieces Blu-Tacked on and all around the kitchen door. 'Molly likes drawing pictures too.'

I clapped my hands together. 'Great! Then why don't we get the paints out?'

Tina was all for it, Molly less so, but it was either that or play a game, and the last thing I wanted was Tina hustling us all at dominoes while recounting tales of her gramps, his special lemonade and the smelly shop where she'd first picked up the old ebony and ivories.

'They get on well together, don't they?' Vikki said, as we watched them from the safety of the living room. I'd set up paints and paper on the kitchen table and the two of them were busy at work, Tina churning out works of art at a rate of knots, Molly much more careful, drawing everything first and then colouring it in with neat little brushstrokes. 'They've got very different personalities, but one thing in common; they've both lost their mums.

Molly, doubly so. First her real mum and then Daisy.'

'What's the story there?' I asked, as Tina brought through the latest edition to her gallery. I told her how wonderful it was and balanced it on the windowsill to dry.

Vikki waited for Tina to scamper off and pick up her brush again. 'Molly's mums were very different people. Daisy lived quietly, kept herself to herself. Molly's natural mum was quite a character, from what I hear. She was American. Her name was La-La—'

'As in La-La the bird thing?'

'I don't know who gave it the name. Molly's had that toy as long as I've known her. When she was first taken into care it was her only possession.'

There was a break in the story while I went off to clear up a water spill.

'La-La was a drug addict,' Vikki said on my return. 'She died of a heroin overdose.'

Tina came through again. This time the picture consisted of just a few generous red brushstrokes in a sort of box shape and a squiggle beside it.

'What's that supposed to be?' I asked.

'It's the dead doctor's house and that's a flower. Even though there wasn't any flowers.'

We'd already had the flower debate on the way back from Professor Bradley's. Apparently, I'd lost.

'I think you're rushing your painting,' I told her. 'You've only used one colour. Look at Molly. She's taking her time and doing it properly.'

'I am doing it propply!' Tina grabbed the picture and stomped off through to the kitchen again.

Vikki picked up where she'd left off. Daisy had come from a good home, done well at school and looked all set for university. Then, during a gap year, she had hooked up with some older guy. Her parents hadn't approved and she'd moved out. There was a lot of drink and little or no studying. Sounded a bit like my law degree. The worry had killed Daisy's mother. 'Fortunately, if that's the right word to use, her father also died very recently, before ... '

Vikki tailed off as Tina returned to present me with the same picture, though now in an even soggier state, the red paint mostly obscured by black.

'What have you done to it?' I asked. 'What's with all the black swirls?'

'It's smoke,' she said and dropped it in my lap.

Vikki grimaced. 'Dead doctor? Smoke?'

'Not as exciting as it sounds,' I said. 'We were at the zoo on Monday and on the way back I dropped in to see a friend of mine. He's a doctor. He also smokes a pipe and because of that, Tina is fairly certain he's about to peg out any moment now. After that we went to South Queensferry for fish and chips.' I cupped my hands around my mouth and called through to the kitchen where my daughter was setting about another piece of paper, holding the brush like a dagger. 'Why don't you paint the Forth Bridge! That'll take you a while and you'll only need one colour!'

She didn't look up. Just paused for a moment and shouted. 'I'm not doing a bridge! I'm doing a squirrel!'

'This dead-doctor thing. You don't think she could have a death fixation, do you, after what happened to her mum?' I asked.

Vikki shook her head. 'Everyone thinks of death from time to time, even children. It just sounds to me like someone has rung home the message on the dangers of smoking, and that's no bad thing.'

I made the girls juice and us a cup of coffee. Soon we

were back onto the subject of Daisy Adams. Her parents had been right to disapprove of her choice of partner. A severe battering had knocked some sense into Daisy and she'd gone to the police. Her partner was jailed and by the time of his release Daisy had an interdict in place.

I offered a packet of BN biscuits to Vikki. 'I hope you're not a vegetarian,' I said, after she'd taken a bite from one that was winking a jammy eye at her. She gave me a quizzical look.

'Just a discussion I had with Tina about veggies not eating things that have faces.'

Vikki laughed. 'She's a bright girl. You're going to have your work cut out for you there.'

'If I get to keep her.'

Vikki wagged a finger at me before wiping a crumb from her lip. 'This is a social visit, remember?' I'd liked to have believed her. She continued with Molly's history. 'They found her one morning strapped into a pushchair, her mum half in, half out of bed and stone dead. Molly was just a baby. That's when did Daisy came forward and asked to adopt her.'

'Just like that?'

'It wasn't easy. La-La was living in a women's shelter. She and Daisy were friends. Fortunately, the charity that ran the shelter insisted women with kids made out a will specifying who they wanted to be guardian if anything happened. I think the idea was to try and make things more difficult for the kids' fathers, especially if they weren't married, which was usually the case. If a single mum, with no father on her child's birth certificate, names someone in her will as guardian, it gives that person auto-matic parental rights and responsibilities. It makes things a whole lot easier.'

I didn't know that, but then, when it came to civil law, every day was a school day for me.

Vikki crunched the rest of the biscuit. 'Daisy wasn't a clean tattie and the social work department wasn't keen, but Daisy wouldn't take no for an answer.' She chased the biscuit with a sip of coffee. 'I was passed the file, met her a few times and was satisfied that she had turned the corner. She'd dabbled in drugs, it was true, but she'd been clean for a good while and seemed genuinely determined to make a go of things. More importantly, her bond with Molly was strong. Some people thought I was going out on a limb when I recommended her to the adoption panel. I suppose they were right.'

Tina interrupted again. This time the picture was mostly muddy-brown, with some green and red splodges here and there. Based on her earlier remarks I complimented her on what I guessed was a squirrel up a tree, though it looked more like roadkill. 'And look, Vikki. Tina's written her name. How clever is that?'

Vikki agreed with me that it was immensely clever. All signs of sulkiness gone, Tina hugged my neck, still holding the painting, imprinting squirrel on my clean shirt.

'It's all about seeking approval,' Vikki said, as Tina ran off again to climb up and kneel on the chair next to Molly, peering over her shoulder. 'Tina's slapdash paintings just mean that she needs regular doses of praise. She wants to know that even when she doesn't do her best, like the dead-doctor painting, that you're still pleased with her. She's seeking unequivocal approval. It's the most important thing to a child, knowing that her parents are proud of her.'

I'd have felt a whole lot prouder if I didn't have splodges of paint all over my best shirt.

133

'Come on. I'll give it a wipe with a cloth.' Vikki stood up and pulled me to my feet. 'If it's poster paint, it'll wash off.'

I followed her through to the kitchen where she wet the corner of a tea towel, put one hand inside the front of my shirt and pressed the towel against it, sandwiching the paint-smeared shirt. Her head was close to mine. I breathed in. Tina was right, she did smell like flowers.

'You know how this is a purely social visit?' I said.

Vikki took the tea towel away and examined what was now just a faint outline of brown. She pressed the towel against it again. 'What about it?'

'I was wondering if we could do it some other time.'

'Don't see why not.' She ran the corner of the towel under the tap, wrung it out and applied it once more. 'Molly's at the Home waiting for foster placement. I could bring her out, let me see ... How about next—'

'I was thinking sooner than that.'

Vikki gave the almost-vanished mark a final brisk scrub. 'There, that should just about do it.'

'And with no kids. Just the two of us. Me and you,' I clarified. I moved closer, just a fraction, just enough to make my intentions obvious. Vikki looked up at me. I put my hand on her waist. The gentlest of touches. I thought she moved closer. If I was wrong, things were about to become very awkward. It was worth the risk. I moved in slowly, giving her the chance to pull away. She didn't. Her lips opened slightly, eyes began to close.

'Dad!' My daughter's timing had to be admired, if not appreciated. She synchronised the yell with a tug at the tail of my shirt. 'Look at Molly's picture.'

Tina dragged me over to the table with Vikki following. 'It's really good, Dad, isn't it?'

It really was. It wasn't a child's painting. It was the work of someone much older than Molly. I doubted if I could have produced such a neat, precise drawing. Vikki lifted it from the table and together we studied the artwork. In fact we found it hard to take our eyes off it, such was the use of colour and fine detail; right down to the fireplace, the dresser complete with white mugs and crockery and the figure lying on the big farmhouse table with an out of proportion knife sticking from its stomach and a bright-red puddle below.

'Shit,' Vikki said under her breath. She let go of the painting and let it float back to the table.

'It's really good, Molly,' Tina said to her wee pal. 'And it's really scary too.'

Molly said nothing, just sat at the table swirling her brush in the water-filled jam jar and humming to herself.

'You're right, Tina,' Vikki said, regaining her composure. 'It is scary. I think Molly must be getting ready for Halloween. That's when her birthday is. Did you know that, Robbie?' Vikki was obviously trying to divert attention away from the picture.

'No,' I said. 'I didn't know that.'

'Will she be having a birthday party?' Tina asked.

'We could have a party for Molly here,' I said.

'Good idea.' Vikki placed her hand on the offending image and inched it along the table towards me, making eyes as though to say, get rid of it.

Tina placed a hand on the painting just as I was about to discreetly whisk it away. 'That one looks like a monster,' she said, pointing to another character, a much larger one, standing beside the table, dressed in black and looking straight at us.

Vikki went over, put an arm around her ward and

135

squeezed. 'I think someone has been watching too many scary films on the telly.' She forced a laugh. 'What do you think, Robbie?'

Staring down at that monstrous figure, with the stripe of red running from its bald head, over one crazy white eye to a row of wide-spaced, crooked teeth, I could only agree. But only if those scary movies starred one Derek William Pudney.

24

Thursday morning and it was open doors and smiling faces all around as I was shown upstairs to Hugh Ogilvie's office.

No need to blag my way in on this occasion. The PF had phoned personally, first thing, asking to speak to me. This was an event so rare that even Grace-Mary thought she should mention it to me when, Tina having embarked on another three hours of fun at the Little Ships, I called in to talk to Joanna about Deek Pudney's upcoming, full committal hearing and why I thought it wouldn't be going ahead.

'I know what a stickler you are for the truth, Robbie,' Ogilvie said, pulling out a chair and bidding me sit. 'I also know the store you place on independent expert opinion, and so I have something here I'd like to show you.' He opened a red folder that, apart from a penholder, stapler and paper-punch, was the only item on his desk. He took out a sheaf of paper and pushed it towards me. I feigned lack of interest, not wishing to give him the satisfaction.

He dragged it back across the table. 'There are a lot of big words, so I'll summarise for you,' he said. 'It's a fingerprint and DNA analysis report. It shows traces of Pudney all over the crime scene.'

'Hugh, I've explained his fingerprints already.'

He held up a hand. 'What about his blood? Can you explain that? It's all over the kitchen floor.'

Not good, but not all that bad. 'He was in the farmhouse with me. I said so in my statement. He was wandering about the place and out of my sight for at least ten minutes, while I was talking to Molly.'

'Molly?'

'Daisy Adams' daughter.'

'I see,' Ogilvie said, in an Eureka moment sort of a way. 'It's all so clear now. While you were talking to the girl, your client took the opportunity to do a spot of personal grooming, cut himself shaving and dripped blood everywhere.' He feigned a frown. 'No, wait. It wouldn't explain this.'

He reached out, flicked over a few pages of the report and pushed it towards me. Under the heading, 'Knife', the report confirmed that there was a mixture of blood on the blade, and several distinct spots on the handle. These could be attributed to both Deek and the dead guy.

'Seems strange to me how your client's blood is on the knife along with that of the deceased. Unless, of course . . . ' The PF rubbed his chin. 'Yes, I see it now. The man on the table strangles Daisy Adams, then so filled with remorse is he that he goes through to the kitchen, lies on the table and stabs himself through the heart.' He smiled at me. I thought I had been smug at our last meeting. I realised now I was a mere novice in the presence of a master. 'No, that wouldn't explain your client's blood on the knife and all over the floor.' He snatched the report from under my nose and placed it back into the red folder. 'Would it?'

'But something else would,' I said.

'Really? What's that then?' Ogilvie's open-eyed fake

innocence was annoying and worrying in equal measures. Surely he couldn't have missed the obvious.

'Deek Pudney had a cut on his face,' I said.

'Did you see him bleeding from it at any time?'

'Like I say, I was busy rescuing a starving wee girl at the time, but he did have quite a nasty wound, held together by a few paper-strips. In fact when your colleagues in Glasgow charged the man who assaulted him, they described it as a severe injury. It could easily have opened. Come on, Hugh, you know what those forensic girls and boys are like. A little blood goes a long way with them. They find a molecule of DNA, and their reports make it sound like there's ladles full of the stuff sloshing around.'

'Ah, yes, the injury. The one your client received at the hands of Mr Sneddon while visiting a public house in Glasgow. I'd almost forgotten about that.' Ogilvie's tone suggested he very much hadn't. I had the horrible feeling I knew what was coming next. 'Turns out Sneddon didn't lay a finger on your client. Oh, wait, they're both your clients, aren't they? Derek Pudney and Marty Sneddon. Strange that. I'm not sure the two of them could come up with what day of the week it was if they put their heads together, but someone seems to have come up with a cunning plan to give Derek an alibi. Unfortunately for him, the CCTV outside Sneddon's local in Bo'ness, suggests that not only was he not assaulting anyone that night, he wasn't even in Glasgow. He was in the Lighthouse Bar. And guess what?' Ogilvie coughed up a short dry laugh. 'No sign of Mr Pudney. Especially not around the Post-Mortem Interval that Doctor Wiltshire refers to in his report. So the good news is that not only do I have one of your clients locked up on a double murder charge, I have both your clients looking at a charge of attempting to defeat the ends of justice too. It really couldn't have worked out better. Anyway, thanks for coming. It's been good to talk things through. After all, we're both part of the justice system, aren't we? By the way, I've given it some thought and decided to continue to oppose bail for Pudney, after all.' Ogilvie pushed his chair back and stood up. 'Will we be seeing you at the full committal this afternoon?'

I got to my feet mumbling something about having to look after Tina and that I'd be asking Joanna to cover the court appearance.

'Didn't think you'd manage.' The PF held the door open for me. 'Never mind. I'll maybe see you at the trial. Unless your client would rather just plead guilty and save us stakeholders in the criminal justice system all the bother.'

25

A wet Friday afternoon. I'd been sitting in my car for nearly an hour, trying to keep Tina amused by racing raindrops down the window and feeding her Starbursts, when Jake Turpie eventually rolled into his yard behind the wheel of a low-loader, half a dozen smashed cars at his back.

By the time he'd unbuckled and jumped from the cab, I was right by his side. 'You going to tell me what's happening?'

'Is this about Deek?' he said.

'Yes, it's about Deek – who do you think? And Marty Sneddon.' How had Jake got me to believe that drunken Marty could so much as look sideways at Deek, far less carve the big man up, and live to tell the tale? The same way, I supposed, that he'd persuaded me to go with him to speak to Daisy Adams about an unpaid debt. It was all fatherhood's fault. I'd never have been so gullible if my mind hadn't been on other more important matters.

For a moment Jake looked like he might keep up the pretence, then he scratched the back of his head with a grimy hand and looked around at the vehicles coming and going. 'Not here.'

'Why not?'

'Too many folk about.'

'Nobody's listening, Jake. This is urgent. I need to know what's going on.'

'My office.'

He jerked his head at the prefabricated hut on stilts that served as the HQ of Turpie International Salvage Limited; a firetrap accessed by a flight of shoogly wooden stairs and guarded by a sociopathic mutt that snarled as we approached. Jake gave the dog a boot. While it retreated I lifted Tina and carried her up the stairs and into Jake's office. 'Be good and watch telly for five minutes,' I said, plonking her down on a sofa that had once been orange, but was now predominantly black and stinking of diesel.

'It's smelly here,' Tina announced, once she had assessed her surroundings. She pointed at Jake in his oil-stained overalls. 'He's smelly too.'

'Don't be cheeky,' I said.

'But he is.'

'Well, it's not nice to say it out loud.'

'How else can I say it?'

I switched on the portable CRT television with the wire coat-hanger aerial and flicked through the channels until I found a kids' programme. The picture was snowy, but it would have to do. I turned the volume up and went down to the other end of the hut where Jake was at the sink, rolling up his sleeves.

'She didn't mean the smelly thing,' I told him. 'You know what kids are like.'

'I'll get over it.' Jake dug into an open tub of Swarfega, rubbing the green gel over his hands, scrubbing at the oil and grease under his nails. 'What's the problem with Deek? I thought you said he was getting out today?'

'The problem with Deek is that he's guilty,' I said.

'How d'ye mean?'

'I mean the PF knows that the Marty Sneddon alibi is

a huge pile of mince. Not only that, Deek went and left enough of his own blood at the murder scene to make a black pudding. Why did he do it? Tell me it wasn't over the price of a second-hand motor?'

The bright-green gel now a murky-grey colour, Jake rinsed his hands off under the sink's only tap and then undid most of the good work by drying them on a filthy towel fixed to the wall of the cabin by a six-inch nail.

'You want a beer?' He opened the fridge door and threw me an ice-cold can.

'Better not,' I said, and tossed the can back to him. He caught it, ripped it open and captured the resulting foam in his mouth in one flowing motion.

'Most of what I told you was sort of the truth,' he said, burping and wiping his mouth with the back of a hand. 'The woman owed me for the car and I sent Deek to get it off her. There was no answer at the front door so he went round the side. He knew she had to be in because the jeep was there. He booted open the door and some guy came at him with a knife.'

'You saying that's how he got injured?'

Jake nodded. He downed the rest of the can, crushed it and lobbed it at a cardboard box in the corner that was already full. It rolled off the top and fell onto the floor. If Jake noticed, he didn't do anything about it. 'When Deek gives you first hit, you've really got to make it count. Whoever that guy was, he didn't.'

'What about the woman?'

'She was already dead.'

'I don't understand.'

'The other guy must have done it. Don't ask me why.'

Was this the truth or another one of Jake's tall tales? 'If it was self-defence, why didn't Deek go to the police?'

Jake let loose another loud belch. 'Who'd have believed him?'

Tina giggled. Whether it was at something on the TV or Jake's release of excess gas I wasn't sure. There was a sudden blast of cold air on my legs and I turned to see her standing at the open door, peering down at Jake's guard dog. She said something to it. There was a growl in reply. I leapt across, and slammed the door shut. Jake laughed. 'It's all right, the dog's on a chain.'

'Maybe you should have kept Deek on one too,' I said. 'Then you wouldn't have had to involve me in your daft scheme.'

'Could've worked.'

'Could've, but didn't.' I swept Tina up into my arms.

Jake sauntered over. He reached out and pinched Tina's cheek, while staring me straight in the eye. 'Then you'll need to think up something better.'

I put Tina down and gave her a gentle shove in the direction of the dirty, orange sofa. So far I'd been prepared to overlook the fact that Jake had treated me like a mug by taking me to Sunnybrae Farm in the first place. I'd even chosen not to mention the fact that Hugh Ogilvie thought I was behind the attempt to fabricate Deek's now well and truly burst alibi; not that the PF's opinion of me could sink much lower than its already subterranean level, but that wasn't the point. There I was doing everything I possibly could to liberate his gormless minder, and here was Jake pinching my daughter's cheek and ordering me around. If he wanted to order me around there was a queue, with my dad and Grace-Mary at the front. My daughter's safety – that was very different.

'Is that some kind of a threat?' I asked.

Jake didn't say anything, just kept staring.

'You think it's all right to pinch my daughter's cheek and order me around? It's you who's landed Deek in it. Did you think that stupid plan with Marty the alky was ever going to work? All you've done is give the PF even more ammunition.'

The corner of Jake's lip rose to reveal an upper canine. They say people take after their dogs. With Jake and his mutt it was more likely to be the other way around.

'If somehow I get Deek off with this, you'd better be telling the truth about giving me the office,' I said.

Jake spat on the floor and wiped it into the stained carpet with a couple of scuffs of a steel toe-capped boot. 'You think you're the only lawyer in Scotland?'

'I'm the only one you trust.'

Jake looked from me to Tina to out of the window.

I took a step closer. 'And trust me, if you come near my daughter, I'll—'

Jake grabbed my face. 'What?' He let go, laughing. 'You just do your law stuff. Keep your end of the bargain ... ' He let go and gave the side of my face a gentle, but not too gentle, slap, 'and I'll keep mine.'

26

'Quiet!' Tina yelled. She was the only one in the room making any noise. 'Uncle Malky's on the radio.'

My dad turned up the volume. The presenter introduced himself and the ex-soccer-legend that was my brother Big Malky Munro. The two of them would laugh, joke and bounce off each other as for the next ninety minutes they discussed the weekend football fixtures and took calls from a series of Friday night football fans, some serious, some drunk, some seriously drunk.

'Your brother wasn't on the show last week,' my dad said, at the first commercial break. 'Never gave much of a reason. Girl trouble he told me.'

I shrugged. 'That's Malky for you. Only works one day a week and can't make it on time.'

'He's got his newspaper column too,' my dad said.

'You don't think he actually writes that crap, do you?'

'Oh, you said crap,' Tina butted in.

'Well, don't let me hear you say it,' my dad said.

'I won't,' his granddaughter assured him. 'It's too rude.'

My dad patted her leg. 'That's right. Good girl. What do you have to say for yourself, Robbie?'

By the time I'd thrown myself on the mercy of the court, Malky was back on air, telling a story about the time he'd been playing Elgin City and one of the home support had lobbed a turnip at him. When Malky had pointed it out to the ref, he'd been told that if his head had fallen off he'd have to leave the field of play for treatment.

It was one of the few tales from Malky's professional career suitable for a family audience. My dad, like most of the listeners, would have heard it told a hundred times before, but laughed anyway and Tina joined in, though she wouldn't have had a clue what was so funny.

At the next break I went through to the kitchen to make my dad a cup of tea, fetch Tina a glass of milk and a biscuit, but most of all to think. Thinking time was what I missed most about having a child. What had I done before Tina came along? I must have had endless hours to myself. Now all I wanted was ten minutes peace so I could think about Deek and the dead people at Sunnybrae Farm.

'Hurry up, Dad!' Tina shouted from the living room.

'Yeah, what are you doing, growing a tea bush and milking a cow?' my dad joined in.

More laughter from Tina. I'd have to go back. If it was just the radio, it wouldn't have been so bad. I'd had years of practice blanking out my brother's inane blethers. Tina was a different prospect all together. Given half a chance she'd have talked Malky under the table and, as for sitting still, she was the nearest thing to perpetual motion on the planet. I needed to concentrate, clear my head and start looking at things logically. I leaned over the sink and splashed my face with cold water. Jake Turpie was a liar, I knew that. What if, his earlier lies having failed so spectacularly, he was now telling the truth? Could it be that Deek had acted in self-defence? If so, then whoever he'd stabbed must have murdered Daisy Adams. Not that it would have taken a leap of imagination to look at things another way. Deek goes to put the squeeze on Daisy. She doesn't have the money. A visiting male, boyfriend or whatever, intervenes, Deek overreacts and next thing you know it's carnage.

If Deek was to claim self-defence, at the very least he'd have to show that the dead guy had some kind of motive for killing Daisy. A better motive than his own.

There were two things I had to establish: firstly, that the new and allegedly true version given to me by Jake was consistent with the findings at the scene, and, secondly, the identity of the dead guy; something the cops had been unable to do despite their DNA and fingerprint databases.

'It's for you.' My dad came into the kitchen with the phone. I'd been so deep in thought I hadn't heard it ring. 'Vikki,' he mouthed silently.

'It's about us,' she said, once I'd taken the phone and shooed my dad away. Was there an us? 'I've been thinking.' Not a good sign. Over the years a number of women had done a fair bit of thinking about me. It seldom ended well. 'I'm not sure if we should meet . . . socially. Not while I've still got professional duties to do with Tina. It wouldn't look good if I was thought to be dating the father of the child I was writing a report about. Not exactly independent.'

I didn't know what to say.

'I've no problem bringing Molly to see Tina again,' she said hurriedly. 'It was the first time the wee thing has looked like she was having any fun since Daisy died, but . . . '

'I understand.'

'Do you? Am I being too cautious?'

'You're being professional. You've got a job to do.'

'Too true,' she said. 'And not a pleasant one either. I've to go back to Sunnybrae to collect Molly's clothes and other belongings. They need me to do it while the crime scene people are still there so that they can supervise. I've said I'll go up to the farm tomorrow morning to get it over and done with. I'm not looking forward to it. That time when I met you, I thought I could do it, but I had to leave. It was too soon, too horrible to think that Daisy ... ' Something caught in her throat.

'Send someone else.'

'That wouldn't be fair.'

'Why not? Ask someone to go who didn't know her.'

'I couldn't do that. I feel like Molly's my responsibility.'

'If you want, I could go with you,' I said. Vikki hesitated, but she didn't say no. 'Why not? You couldn't call it a date, me escorting you to a crime scene. Even I can show a girl a better time than that.'

My dad was waiting for me in the living room. 'What did she say? How does she think we're doing? Is she happy with the arrangements? Did you tell her you were looking to buy a new place and—'

'Everything's fine, Dad.'

'Dad was trying to kiss Vikki,' Tina said, still looking at the radio as Malky wittered on about an upcoming Dundee derby and doing his best to make it sound remotely interesting.

My dad looked from Tina and back to me. I smiled.

'You and Vikki?' he said. He flung himself back in his seat and ran a hand over the top of his head. 'Oh no.'

'Calm yourself, Dad.'

'Calm myself?' He clambered to his feet. 'Calm myself? That woman is the only thing standing between you and custody of my granddaughter and all you can say is calm yourself?'

'I'm just helping her out.'

'How's you slobbering all over her helping out? At least wait until this thing with Tina is all sorted.'

Malky was signing off; another hard night's punditry over.

'What thing with me?' Tina asked.

'It's a surprise,' I said. 'I'll tell you later.'

'I like surprises,' she said.

'Yeah, well, I'll be very surprised if your dad doesn't mess this up,' my dad said. 'No, don't roll your eyes at me, Robbie. You know fine well what you're like with women. If they're not trying to kill you, they're throwing engagement rings in your face or emigrating to Aus . . . ' He caught himself just in time. That was a conversation I'd have with Tina another day.

'Look, Dad. Vikki has to go back to Sunnybrae Farm to get the wee girl's property, and wants someone there for moral support. I'm doing her a favour. What can go wrong?'

'I don't know.' My dad dropped his buttocks into an armchair, like a Lancaster dropping bombs over Leipzig. Tina came over and sat on his knee. He ran a hand through her hair. 'But I'm sure you'll think of something.'

27

Saturday morning, Vikki picked me up and drove us to Sunnybrae. For the first time the farm was trying to live up to its name, and a low October sun threatened to impart some warmth to the surroundings, its weak rays reflecting in the farmhouse windows, though making very little impact on the faded paintwork of a certain vintage Volvo parked in the courtyard.

The same cop was on guard duty. Somebody somewhere hated him. He took Vikki and me to the side entrance. The old damaged door had been completely removed and replaced by an aluminium and polythene structure. It was there that any hopes I had of entering the building for a look around were dashed. Only Vikki was to be allowed entry, and only after she had donned a paper boiler suit and plastic foot coverings.

'Will you be all right?' I asked, as she tucked her hair into a blue shower cap. She gave me a thin smile and nodded. 'I'll be right here waiting for you,' I called after her as she walked down the plastic tunnel and out of sight.

So much for that idea. Other than seeing Vikki again it had all been a waste of time. I'd be permitted a site inspection in due course once the police forensic work had been carried out, but what I'd come along for was a chance to speak to one or two of the SOCOs in case they let anything slip about how they viewed the cause of the two deaths.

For the next twenty minutes I paced up and down the courtyard, watching the tunnel. At one stage a scene of crime officer came out carrying some gardening tools sealed inside a large production bag. He placed the equipment into the rear of a police van and was away again before I had a chance to grab him. I was kicking one of the bigger pieces of gravel about when down the plastic corridor and into the late autumn sunshine came Professor Bradley.

'What are you doing here?' I asked him.

'I was going to ask you the same thing.'

'Well, I asked first.'

The professor removed his plastic foot coverings and dropped them into a black plastic bin. 'The police are just about finished and wanted me to take a look at some blood stains.'

'And what did you find?' I asked.

'Oh, you know. Check the average kitchen thoroughly enough and you'll find all sorts of gore, human and animal. I wouldn't like to put my kitchen units under a crime-lite after I've been cutting things up for soup.' It wasn't really an answer. He unzipped his paper suit and struggled to climb out of it. 'How do they expect anyone to get into one of these things,' he said, 'far less get out again?'

Perhaps the manufacturers hadn't expected them to be used by overweight pathologists in tweed suits. I took a grip of the collar at the back and yanked it down to waist height. 'What's the verdict on Daisy Adams?'

The professor momentarily ceased his struggling. 'She's dead.' He stripped off the remainder of the suit, one leg at a time, using me as a leaning post.

'That's why you're the expert,' I said. 'No, really, how was she killed?'

'You'll see my report all in good time.'

'Then why can't you tell me now?'

'Because I haven't written it yet and it's the Crown who are paying for it.' He tossed the suit into the bin. 'And, by the way, they pay a lot better than legal aid does.'

He took his pipe and a soft leather pouch out of his pocket and began to pack the bowl with shreds of tobacco.

'Don't let my daughter catch you doing that,' I said.

He pretended to glance around anxiously. 'She's not here, is she? No, she can't be. Some of the shrubbery is still intact.' He put the pipe in his mouth and was about to light up when a paper suit appeared at the entrance to the tunnel and asked him to move further away. He did. I followed.

'I heard she was strangled,' I said. 'That strike you as odd? One victim strangled, the other stabbed?'

The Professor puffed smoke in reply.

'All I want is the answers to a few questions and I'll leave you alone. Call it a precognition. You'll have to provide me with one sometime. What's wrong with now?'

He thought about that, shifting the pipe from one side of his mouth to the other. Finally, he rattled the stem against his teeth. 'What about my fee?'

'You know I need to get sanction from the Legal Aid Board first, they never pay anything retrospectively.'

'Then do that and give me a call.'

He was all set to commence the short march to his car until I stepped in front of him.

'All right. I'll get sanction. I'll just have to be imaginative when I put the actual date of this meeting on my attendance note.'

'Good. Then you were told right, she was strangled. Now, was there anything else? I've not had breakfast yet, just toast, not a proper Saturday breakfast.'

'Let me put a scenario to you,' I said.

He puffed, lowered his head and directed blue smoke at his brogues. 'Okay, but do it quickly.'

'Someone sneaks in the side door.'

'Smashes through it, you mean.'

'No, I don't. It's a Thursday evening in the boondocks. Why would the door be locked?'

'Go on.'

'He locks the door behind him, goes through to the front room where Daisy is watching TV or something, kills her and is about to leave when someone else—'

'Let me guess. Your client?'

' . . . crashes through the kitchen door, confronts the killer and kills him.'

'In self-defence, no doubt?' He was catching on fast.

'But not before he himself is slashed, and bleeds everywhere,' I said.

The professor pointed the stem of his pipe at me. 'You're starting to lose it.'

'Why? What's wrong with that as a possible version of events?'

'Why would your client—'

'Someone.'

'Okay, someone. Why would someone having done that not call the police?'

Someone with a long and well-documented history of violence, well known to the police? Was it all that unreasonable to assume that Deek Pudney would only have been interested in covering his tracks? I doubted if the concept of calling the police was one that he'd have even considered. He might have a big head, but there was a lot of room inside. His chief concern would have been to get out of there and report back to Jake.

'I'm precognoscing you because you're a pathologist,' I said. 'Just because you smoke a pipe doesn't make you Sherlock Holmes.'

The professor pulled up the sleeve of his jacket to reveal a leather-strapped watch. 'Robbie—'

'Forensically, is there anything wrong with the scenario I've suggested?'

'Probably not, no, but . . . '

'The woman was strangled. How?'

'A ligature. Could have been anything, an electric cord, something like that.'

'Any blood?'

'No. There was a struggle. She had skin under her fingernails, but no open wounds as such.'

'And the skin under the fingernails?'

'Tests are still being done . . . '

'But?'

'There are matching scratches on the backs of the hands of the other deceased.'

'You're in the witness box, right hand up. Who do you say killed Daisy? It's got to have been the dead guy. Am I right?'

'You know who killed Daisy?' Vikki had appeared carrying two white bin bags stuffed full.

'Not you too,' the Professor said. 'Are you buying Robbie's defence or do you have one of your own?' He stuck out a hand. 'Sorry, we haven't been introduced. Edward Bradley. Joanna isn't it?'

'No, it isn't,' Vikki said.

Time for me to step in. 'Professor Bradley, meet Vikki

Stark. 'She's Molly's . . . that is Daisy Adams' adopted daughter's, curator ad litem. She's here to pick up some of Molly's clothes and things.'

Professor Bradley withdrew the hand that remained unshaken. 'Yes, terrible, really terrible. Still, kids, they can be very resilient.'

Vikki whipped off her shower cap letting her hair tumble out. 'You were saying something about a defence. Whose defence? Not the person who killed Daisy?'

The professor pressed down the extinguished tobacco in the bowl of his pipe with a thumb and lit it again. 'That's what we're debating,' he said, after a few rapid puffs to get his lum reeking.

'But the police have got him, haven't they?' Vikki turned her puzzled expression from the professor to me.

'Robbie seems to think his client is innocent. There's a shock for you.' The professor laughed. 'Anyway, must go. Nice to meet you . . . '

'Vikki.'

'Of course.' He shook her hand and then slapped me on the back. 'Robbie, I'll send you my fee note in a few days. Give you time to work something out with the Legal Aid Board.'

'Get everything you came for?' I asked Vikki, as Prof Bradley marched off in the direction of his Volvo and a full Scottish breakfast.

She dropped the bin bags at her feet. 'What did he mean client? Are you acting for the person who killed Daisy?'

'Honestly?'

'Yes, please.'

'I don't think I am.'

'But other people do?'

'I suppose so.'

'Then why not just come out and say it?'

'Because I don't think the person charged with the murder did kill Daisy.'

Hands on her hips, eyebrows lowered, Vikki reminded me of someone else. Someone younger. 'Of course you don't. Not if you're his lawyer.'

'I don't think Professor Bradley does either,' I said.

Vikki unzipped the front of her paper suit in one flowing, if violent, motion and slipped her slim frame out of it in a fraction of the time it had taken the professor. 'And that's why you're really here, isn't it? To see him. Not to support me. To support your client.' She threw the white suit hard at the black bin and missed.

'It's not like that,' I said.

Vikki picked up the bin bags. 'Well, it looks bloody well like it to me.' And, by the time I'd picked up the paper suit and dropped it into the receptacle, she had birled on a Cuban heel and set off for her car.

28

After spending a fortune on a taxi back to civilisation, the rest of Saturday went by without much further event. When I collected Tina from my dad, I kept short the report on my meeting with Vikki and he didn't suspect anything.

Sunday afternoon, he invited us round for lunch. Steak pie, mashed potatoes and carrots. Malky was there, much to Tina's delight.

'So what's this I hear about you finding yourself a woman?' Malky stuffed the last piece of pie-crust into his mouth. 'What's her name? Vikki?'

'Dad was trying to kiss Vikki, Uncle Malky,' Tina piped up. 'Me and Molly were painting and he was trying to kiss her.'

'It was an accident. I may have misread the signals,' I said.

'What are you talking about?' my dad asked. 'What signals? I thought you said you and her were—'

'I never said anything.'

'So everything's fine between you?'

'I like Vikki. She smells like flowers,' Tina said.

'What kind of flowers? Cauliflowers?' Malky tickled her tummy and she giggled, spluttering mashed potatoes.

My dad grabbed Malky's arm. 'Are you trying to make the lassie choke to death?'

'Finished!' Tina said, pushing her plate away.

'No, you've not,' I said. 'You haven't touched your carrots.'

'Leave her alone,' Malky said, his own mound of carrots still intact.

'They're horrible and orange,' Tina said, her face screwed up.

'That's what they used to say about your Uncle Malky when he played for The Rangers,' I said. 'Come on now, Tina. Gramps makes the best carrots in the world and if you eat them up you'll be able to see in the dark.'

'I don't want to see in the dark. There might be a monster or something.'

'There's no such thing as monsters. Come on. Try one. How do you know you don't like them if you won't even taste them?'

'I don't like carrots and I don't like onions and I don't like tomatoes.'

I'm sure Tina intended her list of hated foodstuffs to end the conversation there and then, but this was one argument I was determined not to lose. 'You do like onions because that's what Gramps puts in the mince to make it taste nice and you like mince, don't you?'

Tina sat back, arms folded, a fork still in one hand, sticking prongs up.

'Well done,' my dad said. 'That'll be her off mince now.'

'And you like tomatoes too, because that's what they put in spaghetti hoops and on pizza to make them taste nice too.'

'I don't like lumpy tomatoes.'

'She's got a point,' Malky said. 'I don't like fresh tomatoes either. The insides give me the creeps. It's like some kind of alien embryo or something.'

Tina, with her uncanny ability to latch onto comments better left unlatched, would normally have been all over Malky's embryo remark and there would have followed a lot of awkward questioning. Fortunately, she was too much in the huff.

'Just one piece of carrot,' I said. Tina didn't flinch. 'Come on. You've only got six. One wee carrot and you can leave the table. If you're good maybe Gramps will give you some ice cream.'

If anything my daughter grew more resolute. She was still sitting there ten minutes later. My dad having cleared away, the only thing left on the table was her plate, home to a small colony of defiant orange batons.

'She's going to have to leave the table sometime,' my dad said from behind a Sunday paper, when I went through to the living room, after having washed up.

'Yeah, she's starting school in the summer, isn't she?' Malky added.

'Just wait. She'll come around.' I said, chucking Malky a dish towel.

He cast it aside. 'It's more hygienic to drip dry.'

My dad folded his newspaper and laid it on the arm of his chair. 'I'll do them.'

'This Vikki. Tell me about her,' Malky said, after the old man had left, dish towel in hand. 'Dad's practically got the two of you married off and Tina with a brand-new mum.'

Typical. No happy medium with my dad. He was either trying to talk me out of seeing Vikki in case I messed things up or he was hearing wedding bells.

'Things aren't so far advanced as Dad might have allowed you to think.'

I walked over and lifted the newspaper. Malky punched

160

my arm. 'Don't give me that. I heard what Tina was saying about you trying to kiss Vikki.'

'Trying being the operative word. Me trying and failing to kiss Vikki has been the extent of our love-making thus far,' I said. 'And believe me when I say it's not likely to extend any farther. Not after what happened yesterday.'

'I can't believe you've mucked this one up as well. Not already,' Malky said, after I'd given him a brief summary of the previous morning's events. 'That's got to be a new personal best.'

'What do you mean, mucked this one up as well?' I turned to Malky's column on the inside back page to see what his ghost-written opinion was this week.

Malky snorted. 'Let's face it, Robbie, when it comes to women you've been chucked more times than a big log at the Highland games.'

I tucked the newspaper under my arm. I didn't have to sit there and be insulted. I could do that anywhere. I walked through to the kitchen to see how Tina was doing.

'Are you going to be good and try one carrot?' I asked.

Tina's eyes began to fill with tears. 'I don't want to be good yet.'

I closed the door and retreated. What was I trying to do? Discover who, father or daughter, was the most stubborn?

'All you need to do is say you're sorry and buy this Vikki some flowers,' Malky said, on my return to the living room. He'd obviously been giving my predicament some thought. 'Trust me. Don't fight it. Put your hands up to whatever it is you've done, and she'll be fine.'

'But I've got nothing to say sorry about. She wanted me to chum her back to the farm.

'Would you stop making things difficult for yourself? She's a woman. It doesn't matter if you're actually in the wrong. If she thinks you're in the wrong then you're in the wrong. End of. It's like the ref blowing for a free kick.' Most of Malky's analogies ended up on the football pitch. 'You have to play-the-whistle, they never change their mind. And even if she doesn't think you've done anything wrong and you still apologise, she'll know you're only doing that to get back on her good side and women love it when you do that. I'm telling you, chuck in a bunch of flowers and you'll be right in there.'

I tossed the newspaper at him. It fluttered and landed at his feet. 'You're wasted as a football pundit,' I said. 'Never mind transfer news. You should have your own Dear Malky column. You could maybe even manage to write it yourself, seeing how you seem to know everything about everyone else's love life.'

Malky reached down and lifted the newspaper. 'Robbie, I don't really care about your pathetic love life, but if you screw things up and Tina is taken away by her gran . . . '

Before he could say any more, the kitchen door opened and Tina danced through, all red-puffy eyes, but smiling. My dad was behind her carrying a plate completely without trace of any root vegetables.

'Good girl!' I said, and she hugged me and Malky in turn and then skipped off to fetch the domino box.

'What are you two talking about,' my dad asked.

'My murder case,' I said, before Malky could land me in trouble. 'There's a good chance my client didn't murder the woman. No, really,' I added, spotting a wry expression forming on the old man's face. 'The forensics don't stack up.'

Tina arrived, opened the box and scattered the dominoes all over the table and onto the floor.

'Was she in a relationship?' my dad asked, sitting himself down on the sofa, and for once not rejecting the presumption that my client might be innocent.

'That's not clear yet. She was married before, though. He was violent.'

One by one my dad took the fallen dominoes from Tina as she picked them up off the floor.

'There you are then,' he said.

'There I am then, what?'

'The ex. When a woman is murdered it's usually by a man and it's usually by a man she's in or has been in a relationship with. It's a statistical fact.' He turned the dominoes face down and helped Tina swirl them around on the coffee table. 'That's where you should start looking. Never know what you'll find.'

'And if I look in your kitchen bucket, what will I find there?'

He patted Tina on the head. 'There are some places it's best not to look.'

29

After enquiries with the Fiscal's office, Grace-Mary obtained the information I needed to follow up my dad's advice. When she told me that Daisy Adams' ex-husband ran a florist's shop on Gorgie Road, not a goal kick from the home of Heart of Midlothian FC, I'd half expected him to come mincing out from behind the dahlias, droopy-hands and blousy-shirt, talking corsages and centrepieces. He didn't. Monday morning, standing behind the counter in a full-length leather apron, was a man unshaven and with the look of someone who'd been to bed late and got up early.

'What do you want?' He folded his arms across his chest, the links of a chunky watch tangled in the hairs on his broad wrist. Here was a man convicted of domestic violence. A man who used to let his fists do the talking, now saying it with flowers.

'It's about your ex-wife,' I said. 'Can we talk somewhere private?'

The shop was quiet, the only other occupant a girl who looked to be in her late teens, cramming bunches of blooms into plastic buckets filled with water.

'Here'll do.' His manner suggested that he didn't think this would take long.

'I take it you know about Daisy.' It was only when I said her name that I realised the irony of a florist marrying a woman called Daisy.

'The police took me in for questioning. Four hours straight. I suppose you want to know where I was during the second week in October too? New York. My fiftieth. The cops have all the details.'

A trip to the Big Apple. Handy. Just what you need between you and your ex-wife when she's being murdered: three thousand miles of North Atlantic. That was a proper alibi.

'I'm acting for the man accused of her murder,' I said.

'And you think I can help? How?' He looked past me. 'Mary, when's the pick-up for Interflora?'

'Half eleven,' the girl replied around a wad of gum. She lugged a bucket of blooms to the front window. 'I left the list beside the phone.'

'I was wondering if you knew anyone who might want to harm Daisy?' I said.

'The police have my statement.'

'Yes, but I don't.' I asked him again. 'Can you think of anyone who might want to harm her?'

He picked up a sheet of paper and stared at it for a couple of seconds. 'Other than your client? No.'

'You know my client?'

'The police have told me about him.'

'He denies killing Daisy.'

'Don't all murder suspects?' The florist came around the counter and selected some sprays from the buckets on the floor. When he returned, he started laying out the flowers neatly on the counter. 'I was told he does the collecting for a moneylender. It was all over payments for a car, wasn't it?' Clearly Dougie Fleming, or whoever had taken his witness statement, had filled him in fully on how the Crown saw things. 'Hell, I would have bought her a car if she'd asked me.'

'I didn't think the two of you would have kept in touch,' I said. 'Not after the divorce.'

He lifted the bunch of flowers, held it upright, gently tapping the base with the palm of his hand. When the stalks were even he snipped a few centimetres off the end with a large pair of scissors that were attached to the counter on a piece of hairy string. 'You mean, not after I broke her jaw?'

'It's why your marriage ended, isn't it?'

'Oh, yeah. Except it wasn't me who broke it.'

'Isn't that what all suspected wife beaters say?' I asked.

He smiled like a pair of secateurs.

'When was the last time you spoke to Daisy?'

He checked his work, holding the bouquet in one hand while unfurling a roll of shiny-red paper from a dispenser secured to the end of the counter. 'Don't remember. It would have been a phone call, though. Last time I actually set eyes on her was at my trial. She was in the witness box, behind a screen. A vulnerable witness they said. Too scared to even look at me. I had to watch her tell her lies on a TV screen.'

In my line of work a lot of people told me they were innocent. It wasn't my job to believe or disbelieve. They told me their story and, no matter how incredible it sounded, I did my best to present it in the most credible way possible. It wasn't my liberty at stake and if there was one thing a defence lawyer learned after a few years in the job it was that sometimes the most outrageous version of events turned out to be the truth – even if it did still result in a conviction. Deek Pudney said he wasn't guilty, which meant someone else had murdered Daisy and with his alibi gone, the-ex-husband-did-it was the best, the only, defence available, so far as I could see. And, yet, there was something about the florist's mannerisms, the careful way he put together the bouquet, wrapped it, set it aside and started on the next, selecting the blooms, laying them out in a careful, unhurried manner. He couldn't have murdered his ex-wife from the other side of an ocean. Could he have ordered her death and still be so at ease with himself?

'So who did break her jaw?' I asked, conscious of the fact that at any time he could show me the door. This wasn't a courtroom. He wasn't in a witness box and he didn't need to answer my questions.

'What difference does it make?'

'It might have made a difference at your trial.'

'Too late for that now. I've done my time. I just want to forget all about it and get on with my life.'

'Still, I'd be interested to know.'

'Really?' The florist ran the scissors across the wrapping paper in one clean swipe. 'Why's that?'

'You say you didn't assault Daisy. Well, people blamed for something they say they didn't do – it's my line of work. Like you might be interested in a nice bunch of . . . ' I pointed to a flower with pretty purple petals and a yellow button centre.

'Asters,' he said.

'Probably not a good idea for me to use flowers as an example. I don't know the names of that many.'

His smile was more genuine this time. 'I'm not saying I'm an angel.' At six foot four and bordering on twenty stones, I wasn't about to confuse him with one. 'I've done time. Even before I met Daisy.'

'What for?'

'Theft mainly. A lot of thefts, in fact, and a few robberies. But I've never touched drugs. Never.' He said

it like that one fact excused his other misdemeanours.
'And I've never hit a woman.'

So he said. A man like him would have no trouble
breaking a facial bone. One drunken backhander would
have done the job.

'Why did Daisy say that you did?' I asked.

He finished wrapping the flowers, stepped back from his
work and looked at me across the foliage-strewn counter.
'For a long time things weren't great between me and
Daisy. When we had money, and that wasn't very often,
I'd drink or gamble it. When we didn't, I'd go stealing.
When I got out of jail the last time, I promised her I'd go
legit. I'd promised before, but this time I really meant it.
I met a guy inside. He owned this place and said I could
have it until he got out and then he'd want it back or I'd
need to pay him rent. It was a total fresh start for me. For
the first time I was going to make Daisy proud. Even her
dad saw it. He started speaking to me, gave me money to
buy stock. Daisy worked here too. She knew a lot about
flowers, more than me anyway, which wasn't difficult.
She showed me what to do. For a while we were a real
team. Everything was the best it had ever been.'

'Broken jaw?' I reminded him.

His assistant had finished arranging the buckets in the
window and was sweeping up fallen leaves and petals.
Still chewing away on her gum, I could see her give us
an embarrassed, over-the-shoulder glance. The florist told
her to take a break.

'Daisy got depressed,' he said, once the girl had gone
next door for a coffee. 'She wanted to start a family and . . .
' he shrugged, 'she couldn't have kids. After a while I
noticed money going missing. She started acting strange.
I couldn't get her out of bed in the morning. She never

came to work, even when I was run off my feet. One day I closed the shop and followed her to a house in Leith. I thought at first she was seeing someone else. She wasn't. She was buying drugs. That was the start of it. I don't like drugs. I've done a lot of bad things, but—'

'You've never touched drugs.'

'That's right. I don't like them. I had a quiet word with the dealer, put him straight on what would happen if Daisy ever got any more smack off him and I thought that was that sorted. A week later Daisy nearly died of an overdose. I was all set to pay her dealer another visit, until some boys I knew told me to lay off. They said the guy was serious trouble, well connected, and I was still on licence. So I lifted the phone.' The florist looked down at the counter and shook his head. 'Only time I've ever ratted on anyone. I wish I had just done him in.' He looked at the list, walked over to the window display and began the selecting process all over again. 'That's when it happened.'

'What happened?'

'One night Daisy came home with the side of her jaw way out here.' With an open hand he indicated an area six inches from his face. 'I took her to hospital. Next thing I knew I was in custody, charged with assault. I heard later, when I was inside, that the cops had done a raid on Daisy's dealer. They got his stash. It was the haul of the year. The guy must have been supplying the whole of Leith. He took it out on Daisy and I got the blame. I swore I'd do him in the second I got out.' The florist's face knotted. He smashed a fist on the counter, squishing stray, snipped-stalks and fallen leaves.

'And?'

'He disappeared. I just hope that was because somebody wanted him dead even more than I did.'

I shuffled my feet, not sure what to say. I wasn't interested in some missing drug dealer. I wanted to establish a motive for the florist having his ex-wife killed. If he was saying that Daisy had lied and got him the jail, that was definitely helpful, a reason why he might want to exact revenge, but his wife's allegation, false or otherwise, would only have been one piece of evidence. Where was the corroboration?

'You don't believe me,' he said, swiftly wrapping the next bouquet. 'Well, you know what?' He picked up the pair of scissors and cut a length of gold tape from a reel. 'I don't really care.'

'Her word against yours? If that's all they had, it wouldn't have been enough to convict you,' I said.

'You're right, it wouldn't.' He drew the trailing ends of the gold tape across a scissor blade, curling them. 'But Daisy had a witness. Another liar. A woman who swore blind she'd seen everything.' He set the scissors down between us. 'I don't know where she found her. She should have been an actress. Maybe she was, she was pretty enough. By the time she'd given her evidence, I almost believed I *was* guilty. They took me down to the cells to give me a cup of tea while the jury were out deliberating. I'd hardly blown the steam off the top before they came back with a unanimous guilty verdict.'

He held up the two wrapped bouquets, one in each hand and, satisfied, set them aside in a bucket by the door.

'So you're saying Daisy fabricated everything? She found someone who was prepared to perjure themselves just to convict you?'

'Not a woman. A witch. An American witch. Lafayette Delgado. That's a name I won't forget. I don't know where Daisy found her or how she managed to talk her into it.'

'Or why?'

'Do you think I've never wondered that myself? Let me tell you, I've got several theories. I've also got four more bouquets to make up in the next fifteen minutes.'

'When you're finished,' I said, 'do you think you could manage one more?'

30

'Robbie, you shouldn't have.'

'I haven't.'

Barry Munn's chubby little face fell in mock disappointment. His eyes were bright and his complexion as ruby-red as I suspected had been his lunch.

'Where is she?' I asked.

Barry looked around his office as though someone might have concealed themselves without his noticing.

'Vikki,' I said. 'Is she here?'

'Vikki? Vikki Stark? Oh, no. Not the flowers. Listen, Robbie, I know you have your own way of doing things, but the woman is preparing your child welfare report. It's still bribery even if you do it with flowers.'

'These . . . ' I said, the posy had flattened slightly on the drive from Edinburgh and I tried to resuscitate the blooms with a little tug here and a tweak there, 'are not a bribe, but by way of an apology. Vikki and I had a slight misunderstanding and I was hoping to clear the air.'

'Well, she's not here.'

'Her office said—'

'I'm busy, Robbie.' He pulled a file from a bundle on his desk, opened it and began to read.

'What's the big problem? I only want to know where Vikki is so I can give her these flowers and say sorry.'

'Was there anything else? Because if not . . . '

'I hope you're not thinking of driving home after work.'

Barry rolled his eyes. 'I've had one small glass of shiraz.'

'I may be a miracle worker, but there's no way I can get you off next time. Believe me, it took a whole lot more than a bunch of flowers to make that last drink-driving charge go away.'

Barry covered his ears. 'I know, I know, and I am forever in your debt. I'd just rather not be privy to your methods.'

If Barry ever found out my methods amounted to sheer blind luck, I was in for trouble, or, even worse, a fee for his work on my custody case; however, until then, he felt obliged to put up with me.

I sat down at the desk opposite him. 'So why was Vikki here?'

'*If* Vikki was here, anything we may or may not have discussed remains confidential.'

'Come on, Barry. We're both solicitors.'

'Sometimes it's very hard to believe that.'

'Was she here to talk about Tina? Or are you saying it's all a big coincidence that we fall out and next thing she's up seeing my lawyer?'

'Yes, that's right, Robbie. It's all a big cover-up. Vikki was here and we were having a secret meeting about you and your daughter.'

'Sarcasm is often a way of covering up the truth,' I said.

'Is that just your opinion or do all the other conspiracy theorists think that too?' Barry shut the file, put it to the side and took another from the bundle. 'I do have other clients, you know. As does Vikki. I'm a family lawyer, she's a lawyer who works with families, our paths cross occasionally. We don't centre our entire professional lives on what's happening to Robbie Munro's little girl.'

'So she was here?'

Barry's secretary put her head around the door. 'Sorry to interrupt. Miss Stark thinks she left her mobile phone on your desk.'

There was a small black leather case on the desk by Barry's penholder. He reached for it, but not quickly enough.

'I'll see that she gets it,' I told him and, phone in one hand, flowers in the other, followed his secretary out of the door, to where Vikki was standing in the corridor.

'Thanks,' she said sharply, not making eye contact with me. She opened the case, checked the screen and then having dropped the phone into her bag, nodded at the flowers. 'Who are those for?' It was more of a threat than a question.

I gave the posy to Barry's secretary. 'Just a wee thank you for all the work you're putting in on my custody case,' I said to her. By the time she'd thanked me, Vikki was already off and, if not running, moving pretty quickly.

I caught up with her in the car park. 'I'm glad I bumped into you.'

She fumbled around in her handbag. 'I've nothing to say to you.'

'Saturday morning at Sunnybrae ... I know how it must have looked. I didn't know Professor Bradley was going to be there, and when I saw him I thought I'd take the opportunity to ask his opinion on something.'

After more rummaging, Vikki found her car key. 'It wasn't just something. You were asking him about Daisy. You never told me you were acting for the man who murdered her.'

I let the whole presumption of guilt thing slide. 'Would that have made a difference?'

'Of course it would have made a difference. For one thing she was my friend. For another . . . Well, that's the main one, and, there's also the fact that you are supposed to be on paternity leave, not investigating a murder case.' I'd really hoped she wouldn't bring that up. 'Where is Tina? Why isn't she with you?'

'She's with my dad. I only nipped up here to see Barry about something.'

'And to bring his secretary flowers?' She didn't wait for an answer. 'Why were you phoning my office? They sent me a text saying you wanted to know where I was.' She delved once more into her bag and brought out her phone, presumably, in case I demanded to see evidence.

'I wanted to apologise,' I said.

'Really? Why ever, when you haven't done anything wrong?'

'I think you're blowing this whole thing out of proportion,' I said. 'I'm a defence lawyer with a client who needs defending. Sorry if everyone is happy to convict him because they can't find anyone else to pin the blame on, but some of us take our jobs seriously.'

Vikki pulled open the car door, threw her bag onto the passenger seat and turned to face me full on. She looked angry. Really angry and really pretty. 'You don't think I take my job seriously?'

'That's not what I said.'

'I take my job very seriously, which is why I don't mind telling you that your job should be to look after and bond with your child.'

'That's what I'm trying to do, but I'm also looking to the long term and this case is important to my business.'

'Is it? Exactly how much are you being paid to abandon your daughter?'

'It's not like that.' Well, it wasn't too much like that. 'If the court grants me residence of Tina . . . '

'*If*.'

'I'm going to have to keep working. It would be a lie to pretend otherwise. How can you write a report based on an artificial set-up? By continuing to work – and by the way I'm concentrating only on one case at the moment, so it's not taking up all of my time – everyone can form a much better idea of how things will be if Tina stays with me permanently.' Vikki's ire began to subdue slightly. 'That said, I suppose I should have told you about my involvement in Daisy's case.'

'You lied to me. That first day at Sunnybrae. You weren't there because of Molly, you were there for the same reason you went with me on Saturday: to find out what you could in order to get your client off.'

'How is Molly?' I asked.

The change of subject wasn't seamless, but had the desired effect.

'It's hard to tell,' Vikki said. 'As you know, her communication skills are extremely underdeveloped.'

'She's welcome to come back and see Tina anytime. You are too.'

Vikki didn't discount the suggestion out of hand. 'Look, I'm sorry if I'm being hard on you. I'm a bit upset. I had a meeting with Barry earlier.'

'About Tina?'

She shook her head. 'No, not about Tina.' She looked like she was about to start crying. Now what was I supposed to do? Give her a hug? I patted her shoulder a couple of times. She sniffed and wiped a hand across her brow, flicking hair out of her face. 'I was seeing Barry about another case in which things haven't gone quite

176

to plan and . . . no, let's say in which Barry has totally botched up. I hope that man's got professional indemnity insurance because . . . ' She reached into the car and tugged a packet of paper hankies out of her bag along with a stuffed pelican. The toy rolled across the seat, out of the door and onto the ground. 'And before I can do anything else I've to get that stupid thing back to Molly.' Vikki gave the stuffed animal a gentle kick with the toe of her shoe, blowing her nose on a tissue at the same time. 'She left it when they took her to the dentist yesterday. I told the Home I'd pick it up when I was passing and they've been on to say that she's howling the place down for it.'

I bent and picked up La-La the pelican. The only memento Molly had of her real mother. What was Molly's mum's real name?' I asked. 'I don't suppose it was actually La-La?'

Vikki almost allowed herself a smile. She took the stuffed toy from me. 'Lafayette,' she said. 'Lafayette Delgado. Now you know why people called her La-La.'

31

Tuesday. No nursery and I had things to do. First was to drop off my dirty suit. I'd already given it a pretty thorough wipe down to remove any lasting reminders of my first meeting with Molly, but felt I needed the reassurance of a proper dry-clean.

I was almost out of the shop door when the dry-cleaning man called me back in.

'You want this cleaned too?' he asked, holding up a mobile phone. It wasn't mine; that was still in my secretary's safe keeping. It took me a few seconds to remember that it was the one I had taken from Molly at the farmhouse.

I took the phone and shoved it into my pocket. So far so good. Next up was food shopping. Starting at ten I'd reasonably estimated a time frame of one hour to visit both dry-cleaner and supermarket. No chance. A shopping trip with Tina involved returning more things to the shelf than actually ended up staying in the trolley, and then there was a major delay caused by the great biscuit debate of aisle 18 where, due to some stocktaking disaster there were no BN biscuits other than apricot ones which Tina didn't like the look of.

After the baked-goods equivalent of the Man Booker Prize selection process, the choice was whittled down to either Jammie Dodgers or Jaffa Cakes. I told Tina she could have one or other; learning to make decisions was an important part of growing up. Much soul-searching, some pleading and one near-tantrum later, Tina and a packet of Jammie Dodgers did eventually make the trip from biscuit aisle to check-out, where was found, to Tina's alleged amazement, a pack of Jaffa Cakes hiding under a box of Rice Krispies. Another important part of growing up: getting your own way. Tina was ahead of the learning curve on that one.

'You can't treat this place like a crèche,' Grace-Mary said, when we dropped in to my office around noon. My secretary liked to complain. I was pretty sure it was in her job description. I slipped through to my office and put Molly's mobile phone on to charge. Grace-Mary was still speaking on my return to reception. 'There are people trying to work here, you know?'

'Where's Joanna?' I asked.

'Court.'

'Then what's the problem? If she's not dictating, you're not typing.'

'I don't just type. We've just been sent a whole lot of disclosure in the Pudney case and I've got to print it all and sort it out.'

I took a quick look at the latest evidence to arrive by the Crown's secure email system. It was mainly photographs of the crime scene and surroundings, as well as before-and-after autopsy shots.

'Leave it,' I said. 'I'll look through them later and print off the ones I think are important.'

'It's not just these. I've other things to be doing as well,' Grace-Mary said.

'That's all right. Don't mind Tina.' I set down two carrier bags full of groceries on the reception desk. 'I'll only be half an hour. Make her some juice, throw a couple of Jammie Dodgers in her general direction and she'll sit and draw until I come back.'

'I like drawing,' Tina confirmed. 'But I like painting better.'

Grace-Mary took some sheets of A4 off the desk and selected a pen, pencil and yellow highlighter. 'You're drawing.' She took Tina by the hand. 'Let's go through to your dad's office and you can draw me a letter of resignation.' She stopped on the way out of reception. 'Was there anything else? I am available at weekends and for children's parties.'

'Lafayette Delgado,' I said.

'Who's she?'

'She was the natural mother of Molly, the girl I found at the farmhouse. She died a few years back, a drugs overdose in Edinburgh somewhere.'

'Molly's my friend,' Tina said. 'Her mum is in heaven too.' Grace-Mary let go her hand and she ran through to my office.

'And . . . ?' my secretary asked.

'I wondered if you could phone the Fiscal in Edinburgh and see what you can find out about her.'

'Like what?'

'Anything. Where she died, when she died—'

'Her shoe size?'

'Probably not strictly necessary, but you're getting the idea.'

'You really think the PF's office will release information over the phone? They'll want a letter and a good reason for the request. Even then, what chance is there of actually getting a reply?'

True. Writing to the PF was one of life's more futile

exercises. Like a beam of light at the edge of a galactic black hole, correspondence, it seemed, could enter the Crown Office & Procurator Fiscal Service but not escape.

There was a crash from next door. The perfect distraction. Father and daughter working as a team. Grace-Mary went through to assess the damage. I took the opportunity to leave.

An hour later I was back with more carrier bags full of stuff I'd never realised were even for sale until my daughter had come to stay. 'Took a bit longer than I expected,' I said, by way of apology. Grace-Mary was sitting at reception with Tina who was playing with the phones. 'Who are you phoning?' I asked.

'I'm phoning Granny Vera,' Tina said, phone to her ear, punching random numbers.

Grace-Mary held up the end of the phone line which she'd unplugged from the wall.

'What's she wanting to phone her granny for?' I whispered to Grace-Mary.

'She misses her. Nothing wrong with that.'

Tina had lived with Vera Reynolds for several weeks before she came to live with me. I knew I shouldn't feel threatened, except I did.

'I haven't had my lunch yet.' Grace-Mary handed me the end of the telephone cable. 'When Tina's finished speaking to her gran, plug it back in.' She came around the reception desk and unhooked her raincoat from the back of the door.

'I don't suppose you got around to phoning the PF about Lafayette Delgado?' I asked, helping my secretary struggle into her raincoat.

'Of course I did.' Grace-Mary tilted her head at Tina, now deep in an imaginary conversation. 'After all, I've

181

had nothing else to do.' Point made and raincoat on she went to the fax machine. 'I find that if you want to know information about a dead person the best place to start is the Registrar's Office. Here.' She handed me a sheet of paper. Lafayette Delgado's death certificate. 'Robbie, this business with the Sunnybrae murders and Jake Turpie. Don't you think it's getting in the way of more important things?' She tilted her head at Tina.

'I'm doing this for you-know-who,' I said. 'I win the case and I own this office. Less outlay, more income, bigger house, better chance of keeping my daughter. Also, less chance of future back problems for me if I don't have to sleep on that camp bed.'

Grace-Mary wrapped a scarf around her neck and tucked it inside her coat. She said goodbye to Tina and walked to the door. 'Sometimes I think if you lived in a mansion and had a four-poster bed you'd still be doing this. Honestly, it's not fair on the girl.'

I followed her into the corridor and halfway down the stairs on her way to the front door.

'Where are you going for lunch?' I asked.

'Never mind me. All Tina has had to eat is some biscuits. A growing girl can't survive on Jammie Dodgers and Jaffa Cakes. Why don't you close the office for an hour and take her for something nice to eat?'

I put my hand in my pocket, pulled out all the cash I had left over from my morning at the shops and shoved it at Grace-Mary. 'How about you do that?'

32

Lafayette Delgado had been pronounced dead one May morning nearly four years before. She'd been thirty-one. The cause of death: diamorphine overdose. The place of death: Cypress House, Leith, an anonymous red sandstone building down by the Firth of Forth. Four storeys high, it was divided into a few self-contained bedsits with a communal lounge, kitchen and laundry on the ground floor.

Men who turn up unannounced at a women's refuge can expect a less than warm reception, unless it's the heat of burning oil being poured from an upstairs window. Defence lawyers take their lives in their hands, which was why, with a transient flash of my Law Society ID card, I introduced myself as a lawyer investigating the death of Daisy Adams, keeping my actual role in proceedings as hazy as possible.

The caretaker was a short, solid woman of indeterminate age with a bleached blonde crew cut. She was wearing denim dungarees and the sleeves of her checked shirt were rolled up to reveal a series of ancient India-ink tattoos. She remembered Daisy and had seen reports about her on the news.

'I thought they'd got someone for the murder,' she said over her shoulder, leading me from the entrance, down the hallway and into a laundry room that was home to a

183

couple of industrial-sized washing machines, a spin drier and a herd of clothes horses. The damp had lifted the cracked lino in places to expose a stone floor. Drying racks draped with wet clothes were suspended from the ceiling, their pulley-ropes tied to wall hooks in horribly complicated knots. 'You thinking maybe it could have been someone else? What about her ex?'

'He's forming part of my enquiry,' I said, trying to sound official and prosecutorial.

'He's got a flower shop.' Bleach-blonde put her back against a washing machine, placed two hands on top, jumped up and sat crossed-legged. 'Down Gorgie Road. I was in there once, before I knew who he was. He seemed all right, but then they're all sweetness and light when they want to be.'

From which I inferred she was referring to those of us with a Y chromosome. Now wasn't the time to stick up for my sex. Bleach-blonde struck me as a woman not overly fond of men, in any capacity. 'What was Daisy like?' I asked. 'Did she have enemies?'

'Apart from the bastard who broke her jaw? No, Daisy was really lovely. Got on with everyone. She was here quite a wee while coz her husband was out on bail for his trial and it kept getting put off. For most of the girls this is just a temporary stop-off until they can get themselves sorted and back on their feet.'

'She had a friend, I think. Lafayette Delgado. She died here, didn't she?'

The sound of feet in the hall. A child's voice.

'What's that got to do with anything?'

'Daisy adopted her daughter. I'm trying to make a connection, see if there are other lines of investigation I should follow.'

'Like what?'

'I can't divulge anything at this stage, it's all part of the ongoing enquiry,' I said. 'I'm sure you understand.'

A woman entered the room carrying a white plastic pail full of dirty clothes in one hand and dragging a toddler along by the other. She eyed me suspiciously.

The caretaker jumped down from the washing machine, said something to the woman about fabric conditioner and then led me out and up several flights of creaky stairs to the top of the building and a converted attic with a coombed ceiling. There was an ironing board in the centre of the room surrounded by baskets of laundry. She pointed at a bed in the corner of the room. It had no covers or pillows and was piled high with bundles of neatly folded clothes. 'That's where they found her. Right there.'

'Had you known Lafayette for long?'

The caretaker smiled. 'Sorry, it's just that you keep saying Lafayette. I only ever knew her as La-La. We were at the same school. I was the year below, in her sister's class. That's probably when she started getting called La-La – a whole lot of five-year-olds trying to say Lafayette? Not happening, is it?' She walked over to a window set into the slope of the ceiling, and on tiptoes tried to look out. 'We all looked up to La-La, and I mean up. She'd have had no trouble seeing out of here. She was about your height, taller in her heels.'

I went over and stood beside her and gazed out over a strip of grey sea to an island in the hazy distance. It was a fine view, even on an overcast October afternoon.

'That's Inchkeith,' she said. 'They used to quarantine folk with syphilis there. That was back in the Middle Ages. Did the same when the plague hit town.' She laughed. 'I like history. I read a book on it once. Did you know that James the Fourth had the great idea of marooning a dumb mother and her two babies over there to see what language the kids would end up speaking?'

I could probably have gone through the rest of my life happily not knowing, but she told me anyway.

'He thought that with no one to teach them a language, they'd come back speaking the pure language of God, whatever that is. All he got after a few years was a couple of kids doing a whole lot of grunting.' She turned to look at me, jerked her head. 'Men, eh?'

I shrugged apologetically on behalf of my brethren, and she was off again on the island's history, this time about 'The Rough Wooing' and Mary Queen of Scots. The clock on the wall said half past one.

'Was it you who found La-La's body?' I asked, as the Seventeenth Century loomed.

'Yeah. Daisy heard crying and went to see what the matter was. The door was locked and she couldn't get any response from inside except for the bairn breaking its wee heart. Daisy loved that kid. I'm not surprised to hear that she adopted it. Anyway, she shouted for me, I broke in and found La-La, stiff and cold with a syringe sticking out from between her toes.'

'Why was La-La staying here?'

'The room was spare. The other rooms are properly fitted out. We really only used this for storage. I do the ironing here now. It's not part of my job, but I like it. I whack the radio on and off I go. The girls give me a few quid sometimes. It's peaceful.'

'Why take her in? Did she have man trouble?'

'Is there another kind?' She laughed. 'No, actually I don't think La-La ever had any man trouble. That was her problem; men were absolutely no trouble at all. At fifteen she looked twenty-one. When the rest of us were all greasy hair and plooks, she was strutting about, tall, slim and legs right down to the ground. She left Leith on the first bus out of town on her sixteenth birthday, went to London and became a model.'

'She was American, wasn't she?' I remembered the florist telling me that. 'Why London and not New York? What was she doing in Leith in the first place?'

'The only thing Yank about La-La and Estelle was their dad. And La-La's accent, when she could be bothered. She thought it made her sound sophisticated. I don't know the full story, you'd have to ask her sister, but their old man was in the US Navy. He used to visit their mum. Ship in and ship out, if you know what I mean.' The caretaker walked from the window to the bed and looked down at it as though La-La's body was still lying there. 'La-La leaving home destroyed Estelle. A lot of us were sorry to see her go, she was always the life and soul and Estelle worshipped her. When she was older Estelle tried to go down the same modelling route as her big sister. I heard she did all right for a while, but La-La . . . now she was something special.'

'How did she come to end up here?'

'Look, Mr . . . '

'Munro.'

'I was friendly enough with La-La but she was a big girl and what she did and why she did it was up to her. All I know is that apart from on the front cover of a magazine, I never saw La-La for . . . fifteen years? Something like that. Then one night she turfed up on the doorstep, homeless, skint and out to here.' The caretaker mimed an exaggerated bump in her stomach area. 'She wanted a room for the night and ended up staying here for, I don't know,

187

six months? A year? Could have been more. Having that baby was the most important thing to her. All she wanted was to be left alone and I made sure that she was. We have one rule at Cypress House. No one tells anyone on the outside who's staying on the inside. The minute someone breaks that rule, they're out on their arse, I don't care who they are. If word starts going about who's in the refuge, next thing you know we've got an army of angry men at the front door.' As though stage-managed, somewhere far off a bell rang.

'Did you know La-La was taking drugs?'

'I knew she drank a lot and might have smoked some blow.'

'She died of a heroin overdose.'

'I'm not here to run folks' lives for them.'

'What about Daisy? Her ex says smack was the reason they split up.'

'That his excuse for hitting her?'

The bell rang again.

The caretaker walked to the door. 'I'm coming!' she roared down the stairwell. 'Look, Mr . . . ' I let her hang. 'I'm going to have to get back to work.'

'Okay, just one more question.'

The caretaker commenced her descent, stopped, turned and stared up at me from two steps down. 'What is it?'

'If La-La had a sister, why didn't she look after Molly?'

'Molly? Oh, aye, I'd forgotten that was the bairn's name. Better than Lafayette, I suppose.'

'Why would she let her niece go into a children's home?'

'Estelle's got her own problems.'

'Do you know where I could find her?' I asked, as we recommenced the journey downstairs.

'I thought it was Daisy's murder you were investigating?'

'I told you, I'm following a number of leads.'

'You're a lawyer. Everything I tell you is confidential, right?'

'That's right,' I said, though a more accurate answer would have been 'that's wrong'.

'Then if I give you her address, don't tell her who you got it from. In fact don't even let on to Estelle that you've been here. I don't want her to think I've been helping the polis.'

Three more impatient blasts of the doorbell.

'Don't worry,' I said, as we reached the ground floor. 'Your secret's safe with me.'

33

La-La Delgado's sister ran an amusement arcade in Portobello, not three miles from Cypress House. On a summer's day the Promenade would have been mobbed with visitors, eating ice cream and trying to sunburn themselves, but on a cold, damp Tuesday in October, the sun on strike and a chill wind whipping in from the North Sea, apart from a few dog walkers and some kids careering about on bikes, the beachfront was deserted.

It was only after much searching and twice asking for directions that I eventually found The Lucky Dime, an amusement arcade down a side street. It wasn't that far from the strip, but too far to catch much passing trade. If the shopfront was designed to attract stray promenaders, then it was difficult to imagine a less attractive layout than the swathes of faded-navy velvet, decorated here and there by cheap tin trophies, plastic horseshoes, bouquets of silk flowers and the occasional desiccated insect.

Inside, under dimmed lighting, rows of outdated gaming machines blinked, flashed and bleeped a weak come-on. To my right, some noisy teenagers shot zombies with a plastic shotgun, and, as my eyes grew accustomed to the twilight, I saw an elderly woman, sitting on a stool in the centre aisle, dipping her hand into a shortbread tin full of pound coins, feeding a slot machine, uncaring of the end result. It beat me why anyone would rather gamble their hard-earned at a dump like this when they could throw it away in style in the more salubrious surroundings of the much bigger and flashier arcade just around the corner, slap bang on the centre of the promenade.

'Looking for someone?'

A woman approached from my left, tall and slim, untidy hair swept back and tied at the back, accentuating her slender neck and high cheekbones. If she was the less photogenic of the Delgado sisters, La-La must have been really something. One glance from her and the old lady climbed down from the stool and disappeared, taking her tin of coins with her.

'Estelle Delgado?'

'Who's asking?'

'Robbie Munro. I'm a lawyer. I was hoping to speak to you about your sister.'

'What about her?'

'I'd like to know more about her relationship with a woman called Daisy Adams.'

'Relationship? What do you mean relationship?'

'I'm told they were friends.'

'Daisy's dead, so is Lafayette. What are you really? Polis or the papers?'

Three of the zombie-shooters sauntered over. Even in the semi-darkness I could see the pallor of their skin, the hollow of their eyes. Protection came cheap at The Lucky Dime and in tenner bags.

'I've told you. I'm a lawyer. A defence lawyer. I'm acting for the man charged with murdering Daisy and I heard that your sister was a good friend of hers.'

'That was years ago.'

I came straight to the point. 'Your sister was a heroin addict. So was Daisy.'

'What's that got to do with me?'

'I thought they might have had the same dealer and that you'd know who that was.'

She took a step forward, pushing her face closer to mine. 'And how would I know that?'

Where to begin? For a start there was her presence in the world's shittiest amusement arcade. Then there was the bunch of junkies in the corner, not forgetting the resident hag pumping pound coins into a puggy before, no doubt, emptying it and doing the same at the next in the row and the one after that, clicking up the numbers to explain away the receipt of hundreds of pounds of weekly income from another source. This wasn't an amusement arcade; it was the second laundry I'd been in that afternoon and these weren't slot machines, they were washing machines.

I waited for one of the puggies to complete a series of dings and whistles as it went through its automated routine and then I took a more diplomatic route. 'She was your sister. She died of a heroin overdose. Were you not interested in who gave her the drugs that killed her?'

'What Lafayette did was her business. Not mine. Not yours. And I don't see what it's got to do with Daisy's death.'

A sudden change of tack was the best idea when dealing with a hostile witness. 'When did you last see your niece?'

I had expected the question to cut the tension slightly, not to bring about the sudden change in Estelle's demeanour that it did. She nearly smiled. 'Not in a very long time. How is she?'

'Not too good.'

'You lot, mind the store!' Estelle yelled to the zombie-killers. I followed her down the centre aisle, through a

192

doorway fringed by multicoloured plastic strips hanging from its lintel and into a back room that had a couple of ancient, but comfortable-looking chairs, a table, an overflowing dustbin and a sink full of dirty mugs. In one corner below a large framed print of the Bay of Naples stood the skeleton of a partially dismantled bandit, in another a change-machine, the latter with a stool in front of it. I imagined Estelle spent a lot of time here putting through bundles of cash, one tenner at a time. This room was the first part of the wash cycle. The arcade equipment was for rinsing the cash.

'I suppose they've put Molly back in that home?'

'I'm afraid so. Right now she's pretty much traumatised. She's going to need a lot of love and attention from somebody,' I said. 'Losing one mother was bad enough, but two—'

'Did he do it?' Estelle lifted a kettle from the table. 'Your client. Did he kill Molly's new mum?'

'He says he didn't.'

'And that's good enough for you, I suppose?'

'It's my business to believe people other people don't believe.'

Estelle held the kettle up to me. 'Cup of tea?' I declined. 'Well, are you going to tell me what my late sister has to do with your client killing Daisy?' she asked.

'Here's how it looks to me – if my client didn't kill her, somebody else did.'

'I can see why they made you a lawyer.'

'And people who kill other people usually have a motive.'

'So you're looking for somebody else to blame, but first you need to find a reason why they'd do it?' Estelle filled the kettle at the sink, switched it on, came back and sat on the edge of the table. Arms folded she stared at me. In the bright light of the kitchen I could see how pale she was. The facial features that seemed so refined when softened by the dim lighting of the arcade, were harsh and drawn, eyes deep-set and shadowed. 'You do know she had a husband? He used to beat her. He got the jail for it.' She shrugged. 'That's all I'm saying.'

'I've been to see him already. He was in New York when she died. And he says he never beat her. He says somebody else did.'

'Does anyone ever tell you they've done it?'

'Daisy's ex says that she was taking heroin. I'm wondering if she owed somebody money.' I cast my eye around. I wouldn't have had to look far in that kitchen for a bag of citric acid, some needles and a blackened spoon. 'You married? Have a partner?'

Estelle's face froze for an instant and then relaxed. 'Why, Mr Munro . . .' she said coyly, adopting a Southern drawl, pretending to fan herself.

'I heard Lafayette could put on a good American accent too.'

She stopped. Stared at me. 'You seem to know a lot about us.'

'Just what I've heard on the grapevine.'

'Would that grapevine be a wee, blonde bint from Leith with a big mouth?'

'As a matter of fact it was Daisy's ex-husband,' I said, remembering my promise to the caretaker.

'Oh, Mr Innocent. I should have known.'

'Lafayette testified against him in court. He thought she was American.'

Estelle smirked. 'She was. But only when she wanted to be.'

'Lafayette and Estelle. Exotic names for a couple of girls from Leith.'

'Our father was in the US Navy. He named us after towns in Louisiana. I never met him. He only came to Scotland twice on manoeuvres. He managed to manoeuvre my mum into bed both times. Told her he'd come back and take us all to America with him. My mum died waiting. Years ago I tried to track him down via the US Armed Services, but they had no sailor by the name of Delgado. Only a ship.'

'You never said if you had a partner.'

'That's because my personal life is my own business, and as I'm sure Mr Innocent will have told you, my partner is no longer around.'

The florist had said that the man who'd dealt drugs to Daisy had disappeared. He'd hope that was because somebody wanted him dead even more than the florist did. Could that somebody have been the person he owed money to after their drugs had been seized, thanks to a certain tip-off? Small-time dealers never bought for cash. They bought on tick, sold the drugs and settled their suppliers – suppliers who expected payment for their merchandise and didn't let a little thing like a police raid frustrate the contract.

The kettle boiled. Steam billowed about Estelle as she rinsed out one of the dirty mugs, dropped in a tea bag and poured on hot water.

'While you're looking for people to blame, did you stop and think that the two people who gave evidence against your Mr Innocent are both dead?' she said.

'You saying it was revenge?'

'It's a better reason for killing somebody than because they owe you money. The dead don't pay their debts.'

195

Estelle sloshed some milk into the mug and stirred the whole lot around with a teaspoon before squeezing the milky tea bag against the inside of the mug and dropping it into the sink. It wasn't the Japanese Tea Ceremony, but then again Estelle wasn't a Geisha. She was a debt-ridden junkie, laundering money for the mob.

'You know you're never going to be able to pay them off so long as you keep using,' I said.

She leaned her back against the sink and stared at me, no make-up, hair tied at the back with a red rubber band, sweatshirt and leggings. If there was ever a woman in need of a makeover it was her. Two weeks of rehab, a couple of spa treatments, a fancy frock and she could have been on the cover of a magazine too. 'I was given two options,' she said. 'Use my head for business or put my body to work. As you can see I run a business, and . . . ' She took a sip of tea. 'What I do in my spare time is my concern. Understand?' After another quick drink of tea she pushed herself off the sink and carrying her mug of tea, headed for the multicoloured plastic-fringe. Apparently, I was leaving.

As we re-entered her world of flashing lights, squawks and bleeps, the glassy eyes of the zombie-killers swivelled in our direction, faces gaunt and twisted, like the characters out of their own video game.

'I'll tell Molly you were asking for her,' I said, as we marched together down the aisle.

Estelle stopped when we reached the front door and stared down the long length of her leggings to her feet. 'Yes,' she said. 'You do that.'

34

Joanna captured me the minute I walked through the door to my office, shaking off the rain.

'You owe me,' she said.

I'd been held up in rush hour traffic leaving Edinburgh. Tina was curled up on my chair sound asleep, her lips plastered in what Joanna informed me was Hollywood Red by Bobbi Brown.

'Who's the nail varnish by?' I asked.

'Staedtler. It's highlighter pen. Don't worry, it will wash off. And it's not about the lippy . . . well, not just about the lippy, that stick cost me twenty quid. I didn't finish court until half four and wasn't back here until five, by which time Grace-Mary was off and running leaving me with Tina. It's after six now. She only fell asleep five minutes ago. I've not had a chance to return any calls, far less get my head around tomorrow's cases. Where the hell have you been?'

'Portobello.'

'Portobello? As in Portobello by the sea Portobello? While I've been slogging away in court and entertaining your daughter, you've been at the seaside?'

I led Joanna to the couch against the far wall and pushed her down onto it. 'Just listen a minute. I've been working on Deek Pudney's defence and I've got some interesting news.'

'Go on, then,' she said, 'astound me.'

I shoved some files aside and leaned against the corner of my desk. 'It was Deek who killed that man at Sunnybrae.'

'No, I said astound me.'

'But it wasn't murder, it was self-defence.'

Joanna rolled her eyes.

'Yes, he went to chin Daisy Adams about the debt, but she was dead when he got there. The murderer attacked him and Deek did what Deek is very good at.'

Joanna wrinkled her brow. 'And you learned all this from a trip to the seaside?'

'Daisy Adams was into heroin.'

'Does the toxicology report say that?'

'No. I'm talking about a few years ago. I think she and Molly's real mother were being supplied by a drug dealer in Portobello.'

'And?'

'Daisy's husband found out, didn't like it, confronted the dealer and, believe me, Daisy's husband is someone you don't want coming to your door unless he's bringing flowers.'

'Flowers? Robbie, what are you going on about?'

'Daisy's husband tipped off the cops, the dealer was raided and he took it out on Daisy. He broke her cheekbone and she framed her husband for the assault.'

'Why?'

'She must have been coerced. Anyway, her husband got the jail and he—'

'Revenge-killed Daisy on his release?'

'It's a dish best served cold.' I pushed myself off the desk, walked to the window and looked out at late autumn in Linlithgow; the season of mists and mellow fruitfulness. It was hammering down.

'Why did it take so long to identify Daisy's ex-husband as being the dead guy at the farm if he's got a record?'

'He's not the dead guy. He's very much alive and making bouquets down Gorgie way. Unfortunately, he was in New York at the time of the murder.'

'What are you saying? That he went to the Big Apple to give himself an alibi while he had someone else kill his ex-wife? Doesn't help Deek Pudney's defence much, does it?'

'What do you mean?'

'Well, who might he have paid to do the job? Who do we know who is paid to hurt people?' Joanna put a finger to the corner of her mouth, tilted her head, and gazed into the mid-distance.

'I've got another idea.'

'I really hope so.'

'We may not know who killed Daisy, but we know what killed Lafayette.'

'Who's she?'

'Molly's real mum. She OD'd on heroin. Heroin that I'm sure was given to her by her sister's partner.'

'This your latest theory? Go on, then,' Joanna said. 'Try me.'

'I thought you had work to do, calls to return, trials to prepare for.'

'I need a wee-wee,' said a sleepy voice. Tina uncurled, sat up and yawned.

'Then let's go to the little girls' room.' Joanna said. 'We can clean your face while we're there.' She went around the desk, took Tina's hand and helped her hop down from the chair.

'I'm hungry too.'

Joanna crouched down beside her, hands on my

daughter's shoulders. 'Good, because so am I. And do you know what? Your dad's taking us both out for our tea.'

It's difficult to say which was more difficult, eating with chopsticks or discussing a murder defence over a banquet-for-three with an inquisitive four-year-old listening in on every word of the conversation.

'Put yourself in Estelle's shoes. Her supermodel sister, the girl she's admired all her life, leaves home. Naturally, she's devastated. Then one day La-La . . . '

Tina looked up from her lemon chicken. 'La-La's the name of Molly's birdie.'

I patted her head. 'That's right. Now eat up.' I scooped a mixture of sugary lemon sauce and rice with a prawn cracker and pushed it at her. She bit hard, sending cracker shrapnel flying.

Joanna brushed crumbs from her blouse. 'You were saying?'

'So, La-La's back from the smoke, pregnant and nowhere to go. She ends up at the women's refuge where she makes friends with Daisy the drug addict. Estelle is delighted—'

'Who's Estelle again?'

'La . . . ' I glanced down at Tina who, chopstick in either hand, was stubbornly trying to transfer a slippery slice of chicken from plate to mouth. 'You-know-who's sister, overjoyed by her long-lost sister's return, and then . . . ' I drew a finger across my throat.

'I thought you-know-who OD'd?' Joanna said.

'She did. That was me miming it.'

'No, that was you miming someone getting their throat slit. Stop confusing things. This . . . ' Joanna pretended to

200

inject herself in the arm and slumped in her chair, tongue sticking out the side of her mouth, 'is how you mime an overdose.'

'Whatever.' I said, 'She's no longer with us and so who do you think Estelle blames for that?'

Joanna, now recovered from her death throes, skilfully dipped a button mushroom in a dish of sweet chilli sauce and held it up in front of her face, neatly trapped between chopsticks. 'It would be a bit hypocritical, wouldn't it? Estelle killing Daisy for giving smack to her sister when, according to you, it was probably Estelle's partner who was La-La's dealer.'

'This is where it gets more complicated,' I said.

'I'm not sure if that's possible.' Joanna said, popping the mushroom into her mouth.

Tina was staring quizzically at a prawn. I really didn't want to have the food-with-faces discussion all over again, and so continued, 'Estelle's partner. The dealer. He's also posted missing. Could be Daisy's ex-husband has been tying off a few loose ends.'

'In that case ... ' Joanna prodded around in the sauce for more non-meat items, 'who's the guy on the kitchen table who Deek dealt with so efficiently in self-defence? A hired killer? If you're going to incriminate the florist, you'll have to establish a link.'

Tina had given up on the chopsticks and was cramming the piece of chicken into her mouth using fluorescent-tipped fingers.

Joanna caught her before she could wipe her hands on her T-shirt. 'It would have to have been a hit man with a clean record, otherwise the cops would have identified him from fingerprints or the DNA database,' she said, wiping Tina's hands with a red paper napkin, bits of it peeling off, adhering to my daughter's sticky little fingers. 'How likely is that?'

It was a good point, but then, ex-PF that she was, Joanna was trained to poke pins into defence balloons. I was still thinking of a way to patch up the hole in my theory after we'd waved her off and returned to my office to collect the bags of groceries from my earlier shopping trip. We were met by the sound of whistling made all the creepier by my darkened office.

Tina clung to my leg. 'Dad, what's that noise?'

It was coming from my room.

'Wait here,' I whispered.

'No,' Tina whimpered, voice shaking, clinging even more tightly to my leg.

Another whistle. Then another. The sound wasn't human. I laughed with relief when I remembered. 'It's okay, Tina. It's just my new phone beeping to say it's fully charged.'

My daughter didn't seem all that convinced, so switching on every light in the vicinity, I took her by the hand and together we went through to my room where I unplugged the mobile phone from the wall.

Whose phone was this? Molly's? What was a five-year-old child with learning difficulties doing with a nice new phone? I pressed the contacts icon. There was only one: Z.

Was this Daisy Adams' phone? Vikki said that she and Daisy had kept in touch via text messages. There was nothing to suggest this phone had ever been used to send a message or even make a call. So, if not Daisy's phone – whose? The dead guy's? I should have handed it into the police, and yet I couldn't help but be intrigued by that one and only contact number. I highlighted the initial and

202

pressed the little green phone. Would anyone answer?

They did. Immediately. A male voice, abrupt and yet I detected a nervous note. 'Who is this?'

A hundred different possible replies flew through my mind in an instant. 'Who do you think it is?'

The phone went dead.

Seconds later it buzzed with a text message.

35

The text contained a postcode, a number and a time.

The postcode took me to Hillington, an industrial estate between Glasgow and Paisley. I'd managed to rearrange Tina's usual Wednesday nursery appointment and booked her into the Little Ships for the noon cruise. My daughter had not been too pleased when she discovered her usual shipmates weren't aboard, and I'd been forced to shove her off with a strange crew for the afternoon. Still, it meant that by a quarter to one, a good fifteen minutes ahead of schedule, I was already in place and parked alongside scores of other cars on the perimeter of a central loading bay that served a number of commercial outlets and warehouse type businesses.

Across the yards of concrete from me, one unit was closed for business, a 'To Let' sign partially obscuring the name of the previous occupiers, a number 14 stencilled in white paint on a huge, steel, roller-shutter door drawn down over the front of the building.

I sat watching the minutes tick by. Lorries and vans came and went, were loaded and unloaded, but still no sign of life from number 14.

The one o'clock news came on the radio. The appointed hour. I waited five more minutes. Still nothing. Keeping it casual, I alighted and wandered over, not sure what to do when I arrived.

'Follow me.'

I turned to see a man, a good bit younger than me or perhaps just better preserved. His gelled hair was swept back, his shave a near-miss, his eyes concealed behind the tinted lenses of a pair of heavy-framed sunglasses. He was tall, wearing a navy-blue suit offset by a pale-blue shirt and contrasting mustard tie, the ensemble made complete by a three-quarter length, double-breasted camel-hair coat with wide lapels. In the fashion stakes I wasn't so much handicapped as a cripple. 'After you.' He pointed a hand-held device at the front of the building and the steel shutter rose to reveal a glass door.

Inside the air was stale. The young man pressed a button on the wall and the steel shutter began to lower again. A press of another button and row upon row of fluorescent strips buzzed and flickered into life. We were in a warehouse fitted out with ranks of metal racks. Forklift trucks and pallet trolleys stood idly around, every piece of equipment, every fixture and fitting, covered by a thin layer of dust.

'Zed?' I said, trying to keep the uncertainty out of my voice. Something I was well practised at. In court a lot of the time it wasn't what you said, it was how you said it.

The tinted lenses turned again in my direction, but the smile had slipped from his face. 'Why are you here?' he asked. 'We're not supposed to meet.'

I'd spent a lot of time preparing myself for such an encounter, trying to anticipate what questions I might be asked and how best to answer them. 'Change of plan.'

'But it's done?' he asked.

I shrugged trying to remain nonchalant while thinking of a way to find out what was going on without tipping the young man off as to my ignorance.

'I suppose you've come for the rest of the money?' he said.

This was one question I hadn't expected, but the answer didn't require a great deal of thought.

'Wait there. I'll get it for you.'

There was something in the way he said that. I couldn't place my finger on it exactly. His face was hard to read, eyes obscured by the tinted lenses. Had his tone of voice changed ever so slightly? Was he less confident now, more nervy?

The young man walked across to a long counter beneath which were row upon row of drawers, all of different sizes and ideal for holding various tools or spare parts for machinery. Or for stashing a gun.

I had a flashback to another industrial building, a vehicle inspection pit and a man with a box of matches and a can of petrol.

'It's right here,' he said, bending down to one of the lower drawers.

I could almost smell the fumes. I didn't like it. I didn't like the man in the camel-hair coat, I didn't like the deserted unit with its steel shutters and I didn't like what might be in that drawer. Call it intuition, call it instinct; the primeval sense that connects civilised man to the wild. The feeling that something isn't quite right. For the deer in the forest, the snap of a twig or the rustle of leaves. For me, the over-friendly attitude of a young man happy to part with cash to a man he had never met before. A man he must have believed was somehow involved in the murders at Sunnybrae Farm.

He pulled open the drawer and reached inside. The deer runs. The deer is in a forest. It's fast and only has a few trees to dodge. I was inside an industrial unit with a lowered steel shutter. I slammed the sole of my shoe against the drawer, trapping the camel-haired arm at the wrist. The young man screamed in pain. He stopped when I hooked a fist into his face. He fell sideways, head banging against the hard floor, hand still jammed. I wrenched open the drawer. Inside was a slim white envelope.

Instinct? Okay, sometimes it is just the wind rustling the leaves.

'I'm really, really sorry about that,' I said.

All the man could do was groan. I unbuttoned his coat, reached inside his suit jacket, searching for a wallet that might contain some form of identification. Fumbling around, my right hand sore and throbbing from the blow, the only items I could find were a set of keys and a folded handkerchief that matched his mustard tie. I changed to my left hand; less painful, but slower. The young man stirred. Still stunned, his body suddenly slammed into some kind of self-protection gear. He thrashed around, moaning and groaning, wriggling on the ground, scuffing the heels of his brown Chelsea boots on the concrete floor as though having a fit.

I waited. Eventually the thrashing around stopped. He came to, scrambled away from me to a workbench and used it to haul himself to his feet.

'You've got your money,' he whimpered. His glasses had gone flying. It had been one of my better punches.

'Look, I'm sorry about hitting you,' I said.

He wasn't listening. 'That was the deal.' His breath came hard and fast. 'The Adams woman is dead. Nobody knows anything.' He wiped blood from his lip with the back of his hand. 'Just take the money and go.'

I didn't want to go. Not yet. I had too many questions. I took a step forward, hands up and open to show my good intentions.

Once bitten, twice terrified, the young man fumbled in his pocket, pulled out the remote control and dropped it. The plastic device smashed, a battery rolled across the floor towards me.

'Take it easy. It's just been a misunderstanding.' When I'd started the sentence we'd been face-to-face. By the time I'd finished I was talking to the back of a camel-hair coat that was heading at speed in the opposite direction.

'Come back!' I called to him. 'It's all right! I made a mistake!'

My words were drowned by fists on steel shutters.

Time to leave. The white envelope fitted snuggly into my back pocket. An illuminated green sign in the far away corner indicated a fire escape. Loud clanging reverberated throughout the hollowness of the building as I retreated to the rear of the unit. I pressed down on the metal bar, threw open the fire escape door and ran out to meet fresh air, freedom and the most gorgeous woman I'd ever seen in my life.

36

Could you call it abduction? If I'd charged out of that fire escape, bumped into a couple of heavies, been hurled into the back of a car and driven off at great speed to meet their boss – now that would have been an abduction. Allowing myself to be enticed into a red Ferrari, driven by the woman of my dreams, no, that was something entirely different. Different but just as effective.

I was being taken to see Dame Ursula Pentecost. My driver made it sound like the Queen had asked me to nip round for a bite of lunch. I'd never heard of the woman. I let what I thought was a respectable amount of motorway hurtle past before asking, 'Who is she?'

The gorgeous one's eyelashes fluttered as though she'd been pinched somewhere sensitive. 'Dame Ursula? Dame Ursula is the head of the House of Pentecost. It's one of the world's most renowned fashion houses.'

Perhaps, but word of it had yet to reach the House of Munro. Still, there I was, trapped in a sports car with one of the Dame's top models; not to make the most of it would have been a dereliction of duty. Like finding yourself locked in a pub and cracking open a Diet Coke.

'Then I take it you're her top talent scout.' I breathed in, expanded my chest, smoothed down an eyebrow. 'Well, I'll say one thing. You obviously recognise quality when you see it.'

The azure eyes under the long, black lashes gave me a sideways look, scanned me up and down, from scuffed shoes to jeans to T-shirt and bomber jacket before returning their exquisite gaze to the Tarmac.

Some would have been put off by that. I took her non-response as a challenge. A Polar explorer equipped with only an anorak, a pair of wellies and a packed lunch, I pressed onwards through a blizzard of indifference.

Now it has to be said, the Robbie Munro book of chat-up lines, though not critically acclaimed, is a fairly substantial and well-thumbed volume built up over a lifetime. Yet, as I chucked about some of my best material like a curtain salesman on a market stall, still the woman on my right managed to remain resolutely unimpressed, her very occasional response polite, but stilted.

After five miles my initial enthusiasm began to flag. By the time we came to the sign for the Erskine Bridge I was more or less ready to jump off. We took the next slip road and rode on in silence, passing Bishopton Parish Church and made a right turn up a mile-long, tree-lined road towards Mar Hall, latterly a hospital for limbless servicemen, now a five-star golf and spa resort, where the Ferrari drew to a halt in front of the great facade of a neo-Gothic building. To our right the emerald fairways of the championship golf course stretched down to the south bank of the River Clyde. I got out, opened the door for my driver and we walked together up the steps, through the entrance lobby and into the magnificent Grand Hall. Either side of the central avenue, bathed in light from towering windows, guests lounged on plush sofas and elegant armchairs. I should have felt uncomfortable, dressed so scruffily in such high-class surroundings, clumping my way down an endless oriental carpet. But nobody was looking at me.

They were looking at the woman floating by my side. How could anyone walk so quickly with such grace and poise? I felt like a bull being led to market by a ballerina.

When we at last reached the top of the hall a member of staff showed us to the lift and from there to the first floor, through a set of double doors and into a room which, in keeping with the rest of the building, was richly furnished with a high, elaborately corniced ceiling and tapestries on the wall. On the far side, standing by an enormous window, taking in the view across the golf course to the Clyde and the Kilpatrick Hills beyond, sat a woman in a wheelchair, her steel-grey hair piled high and spiked with a single pheasant feather. She carried out a slow three-point turn when she heard us enter.

'Dame Ursula,' my driver said to me, and was gone.

'So glad you agreed to come, Mr . . . ?'

'Munro,' I said. 'Robbie Munro.' If she wanted to see me, how come she didn't know my name?

The woman manoeuvred herself so that we were face on. 'Pleased to meet you, and also very pleased that you Scots voted to keep the UK together. Scotland is still my favourite place to be. I find the culture, the people, so inspirational.'

'I can see that by your dress,' I said.

She looked down at a frock of palest lilac. Fine iridescent threads ran through the material, catching the light to give the outfit the ghostly appearance of plaid. 'I'd like to take the credit, but it's one of Stephen's designs. She smoothed an arm of ethereal tartan. 'He was a Scot, of course, and a great golfer. Well, perhaps not that great,' she laughed. 'Enthusiastic. And he loved the national drink. Which was unfortunate for me.' She tapped the armrests of the wheelchair. 'And even more unfortunate for him.'

'Dame Ursula. I don't want to seem rude, but I have a daughter. She gets out of nursery in an hour and—'

'You want to know why you're here?'

'It would be nice.'

'Then sit.'

I sat.

'This house was formerly the seat of the Lords Blantyre,' she said. 'This was the Duke's Room.' She tilted the pheasant feather at the window. 'Do you see that building across the river?'

It was hard to miss the white house, nestled at the foot of the hills.

'The Duke, I can't remember which number in the line he was, but whichever one, sometime in the eighteenth century he built that splendid house for his mistress. The story goes that when his wife retired to her room of an evening the Duke would place a lamp in the window and, if answered by a light across the water, would send a man in a boat to collect his mistress. She'd stay the night and be rowed back across come dawn.'

An interesting enough story; not one that took me much further in knowing why I'd been summoned.

Dame Ursula smiled at me. 'The Duke's wife turned a blind eye to the whole affair. No doubt she felt it more dignified than facing up to reality. Me? I'm the complete opposite. I don't care if it is a lamp in the window or a phone call or a secret rendezvous in a deserted warehouse. Deceit is deceit and I won't stand for it. I know Zander far too well not to keep him on a short leash.'

She had to be referring to the man in the camel-hair coat. Two Zeds in one day was too much of a coincidence.

She wheeled herself over to the Italian marble fireplace

and pressed a bell-button set into the wall by the side of it. 'I'm having tea.'

I had no time to start mucking about with cups of tea. I had a wee girl to pick up from nursery. According to the porcelain face of the gilt mantel clock it was a quarter to three, and I was thirty miles away from the Little Ships Nursery. Even with a following wind I was never going to make it on time. I took Molly's phone from my pocket and got through to Grace-Mary.

'I'm going to be late for the nursery,' I told her.

'Robbie, you're hours late. It's nearly three o'clock!'

'Not the morning session. Tina's in for the afternoon. It finishes at four. Do me a favour, pick her up and take her back to the office. I'll be back before five.'

'Robbie—'

'Can't talk right now. I'm doing something important.'

'It always is,' Grace-Mary said, before I hung up on her and turned again to the woman in the wheelchair.

'Tea?' she asked.

'No, thanks. Now do you mind if we stop the cat and mouse? I'm in a hurry.'

'That call just now. Your wife?' Dame Ursula asked.

'My secretary.'

'You're a single parent?'

'I'm single, but not yet a parent. Not officially. My ex-partner died and I'm hoping to be awarded custody of my daughter.'

'How's that going?'

'Not too well. My work and my gender seem to keep getting in the way.'

'Were you working when you met with Zander today?'

'I thought I was.'

'Who's your employer?'

'You're looking at him.'

She wrinkled her eyes. 'Your little meeting with Zander, it was about our latest designs, I take it. How much did you offer him?'

'Fashion is not my line of business,' I said. Something she seemed to accept quite readily.

'Then it's about La-La. Now that Stephen's dead the vultures of the press have stopped circling and are coming in to peck over the dead body.'

I didn't know what I'd been expecting to hear, but mention of La-La certainly wasn't it. I hesitated. 'Are you talking about La-La Delgado?' I asked, as though the world was full of La-Las.

'You don't deny it then? You don't deny that you've been snooping around trying to find out more on Stephen's affair with La-La? More sordid information so that you can smear his name without fear of reprisal now that he's dead. No doubt you'll be hoping for information that he raped her or was a paedophile or—'

I hated to interrupt while she was mid-accusation, but felt there was something I had to tell her. 'Dame Ursula, not only have I never heard of Stephen, but before today I'd never heard of Zander or . . . you.'

If I'd ripped off her pheasant-feathered hat and slapped her about the face with it, it would not have resulted in a greater expression of shock.

For a moment or two Dame Ursula was silent, then she smiled primly. 'Have it your way. You've never heard of Sir Stephen Pentecost, myself, the House of Pentecost, La-La Delgado or—'

'No, I have heard of La-La Delgado.'

'Really? And what have you heard? That she had a fling with Stephen? Oh no, wait. How could you? You've never

214

heard of Stephen.' She gave the bell another long press. 'Come off it. Every rag in the country covered the story, but I'm not the Duke's wife. I didn't turn a blind eye. It doesn't matter how deep you dig or what that little snake tells you about Stephen. La-La was a one-off. I forgave Stephen. He was a man. He made a mistake. A mistake I made sure La-La regretted for the rest of her life. After I'd put out the word on her she couldn't get a job lying across bonnets in a used car showroom.'

'That's not what I know about La-La,' I said. 'The only information I have on her is that she was a girl from Leith who left home to be a model, returned to Scotland and died of a heroin overdose.'

A purple sleeve reached out and rapped me on the knee. 'Anything else?'

'She has a sister.'

Dame Ursula nodded, thinking. 'Ah, yes. Stella, wasn't it?'

'Estelle. She runs a tacky amusement arcade and, I'd guess, is also a junkie.'

'I remember her. She came to London hoping to follow in her sister's footsteps. La-La insisted that Stephen and I meet her. Sadly, she didn't quite have what her sister had.'

'What was that?'

'Who can say? One only knows it when one sees it.' She wafted a hand at an antique oak sideboard up against the far wall. I crossed the room to it. The centrepiece was a glass drinks cabinet, home to a fine selection of single malts. Between a crystal fruit bowl and a vase full of fresh cut flowers was a cellphone. I picked it up.

'Do you know what that is?' she asked.

I brought it back to my seat and inspected it. A phone seemed too obvious an answer.

'It's a clone. Whenever Zander makes a call, whenever he sends or receives a text message, I know about it. Everything he does, I see. Everything he says, I hear. Everywhere he goes, I have him followed. I know his family, his friends, his lovers.'

I could take a hint. She didn't trust this Zander guy. If he was the young man I'd met in the warehouse this afternoon, I didn't trust him either and he sure as hell had good cause not to trust me. I placed the phone into her outstretched hand. 'I don't know what Zander has told you.'

'I haven't spoken to Zander yet. But I will. For the moment I know he received a call from an unknown phone yesterday. He replied with a cryptic text and I had him followed. The two of you met this afternoon at the industrial estate where we are about to shoot the promo for our new Urban Zealot range. That meeting was either for the purpose of industrial espionage, which I wouldn't put past Zander, or in order to try and smear Stephen's name. If it's the latter then I think you should know that whatever Zander may be, he would never utter a single word against Stephen, no matter how much money you offer him.'

'I'm not offering to pay him anything,' I said, almost extracting the envelope from my back pocket to prove my point.

'Then why did you arrange to meet with him?' Dame Ursula reversed the wheelchair a foot or two and studied me carefully, finger on her chin, as though I was the pattern for a new dress design she wasn't sure whether to risk on the Milan catwalk. 'Who are you?'

'I've already told you. My name is Robbie Munro.'

'What are you?'

'I'm a lawyer.'

'And what were you doing communicating secretly with the House of Pentecost's operations manager?'

'Most communications with lawyers are by their nature secret, but your man Zander is no client of mine. My client is a man charged with the murder of a woman called Daisy Adams. He says he didn't do it. I'm trying to find out who did. There was a phone found by me at the locus. I called a number on it and got Zander. The only reason I know about Lafayette Delgado is because she was a friend of the murdered woman.'

Dame Ursula's tea arrived on a rosewood tray while she was absorbing that news.

'Are you sure you won't have any?' she asked, composing herself.

Being whisked off to a luxurious destination by a super-model had long been on the Robbie Munro to-do list, but the whole experience wasn't living up to my expectations.

'All I want,' I said, 'is a little information and then a lift back to my car.'

37

'Of course there's way too many laws nowadays. The government's trying to give everyone a criminal record. Put us all in jail. Save a fortune on building new houses.'

The trip back to my car turned out to be a lot more conversation-filled than the outward journey: more chat, but equally one-sided. This time the person doing all the talking wasn't me, but the driver of a local limousine company. He'd started off on football, a safe enough topic of conversation, I thought. He remembered Malky, had seen him play a few times and, like every taxi-driver I'd ever met, had the answers to all the problems in Scottish football. When he'd finished sharing them he changed to politics and then the law after I made the mistake of telling him I was a solicitor.

'Take me, for example. When I started off in this game nobody wore a seat belt. Now they throw you in jail if you don't. Us cabbies can't even keep a wee chib under the seat. No, it's true,' he said, as though I'd tried to contradict him. 'The neds can rob you, but suddenly it's against their human rights if you hit them. You must know that. You lawyers will be raking in all that legal aid money. I mean, you've got Scottish nationalists running the country, banging on about Bannockburn and singing Flower of Scotland and sending the English home to think again, but slag off an Englishman in a pub and they lock you up for being a racist. You couldn't make it up. And what about the Romanian gypsies? Coming over here, nicking everything that's not nailed down. And don't get me started on the Muslims.' I didn't intend to, except it didn't seem that my input was all that necessary. 'Not that I've got anything against them.' I was sure Islam would be pleased to hear it. 'And then see those Blacks, or should I say, African Americans? Can't be doing with them. They're always harping on about roots and their ancestors being slaves. It was hundreds of years ago. Get over it. You don't hear me complaining that my great granddad had to leave school at nine and work down a mine, do you?'

'Did he?'

'No, but that's not the point. If it wasn't for slavery all them black Americans would be sitting in mud huts instead of cutting about Hollywood in gold necklaces and making that hip-hop racket that's never off the radio.'

I was going to suggest that he could always tune in to a different station, but by this time I knew that anything I said was only going to make things worse, so instead I tuned him out and thought back to my visit with Dame Ursula.

We'd parted on friendly enough terms, once, that is, I'd convinced her I wasn't a journalist looking for an exposé to damage the good name of her fashion house. It was too much to expect that she might disclose to me the very information that she'd originally thought I'd been prepared to buy from her allegedly traitorous operations manager, but she did provide some background details.

Stephen Pentecost and Miss Ursula Hattersfield had been children of the revolution: the fashion revolution, a revolution that never ends and which each generation claims as its own. Born in the late fifties they'd met in the seventies at St. Martin's College of Art and Design in London, and from there on had been the ones to watch. Immediately after graduating with distinction, Ursula was snapped up as buyer for a chain of female fashion stores, while Stephen, initially headhunted by a Japanese menswear monthly, went on to have a spell at *GQ* magazine before moving to Los Angeles where he made his name styling New Romantics and Post-Punk artists in the eighties. By the age of thirty, Stephen was poised to set up his own unisex brand and, needing a female perspective, sought out his old college chum, Ursula, by that time a clothing consultant to aristocrats across Europe. Together they became the House of Pentecost and since the mid-eighties there hadn't been an Oscar Night or royal wedding where a 'Pentecostal' design didn't grace the red carpet or curtsey to the Queen. Their marriage had sparked a bidding war between the celebrity photo-magazines and for the past twenty years they'd seldom been out of the fashion news. Which was probably why I'd never heard of either of them.

Ursula and Stephen Pentecost: a partnership made in fashion heaven and brought to a violent end on a windy stretch of road in the Highlands.

'It was Stephen's birthday and he was driving us to a fashion show at Balmoral,' Dame Ursula had told me earlier. 'Stephen could have hired a team of chauffeurs, and yet always insisted on driving us everywhere. "Why own a fleet of fast cars and let somebody else drive them for you?" he'd always say.'

I might have agreed more readily if I didn't keep thinking of my earlier driver. I'd happily have let her drive me anywhere.

There had been no other vehicle involved in the accident. Stephen had died many months later from head injuries sustained in the crash. Dame Ursula considered herself lucky to have crawled from the wreckage on knees so severely damaged that she was having to learn to walk again.

Out of action for the best part of a year, she'd had to rely on others to keep the business ticking over in her absence. Which had brought us back onto the subject of the mysterious Zander, a man Stephen had taken on as a gofer at the age of sixteen and who over the years had embroidered himself into the very fabric of the House of Pentecost. Stephen had treated him like the son he'd never had and Zander had treated Stephen like a god. Not a chocolate eclair was scoffed by one of the models, not a pin dropped in a Bangladeshi sweatshop, but Zander heard about it and reported back to his boss. Even when Stephen had lain in a coma for months, Zander was there to visit him every day. Devastated by Stephen's death, according to Dame Ursula, he'd been acting strangely ever since. She wanted to know why and hoped I could tell her. I couldn't. Other than that Zander had been prepared to hand over a wad of cash to me without any explanation and that the phone I'd used to contact him had probably belonged to a dead woman from a farm in Outer-West Lothian, I was as much in the dark as to his motives as she was. It had to be a case of mistaken identity. Zander and I had never met before our meeting in the warehouse. But then who did he think I was?

'Seen any of them?' the cabbie asked me, as we neared the industrial estate and my car.

I'd been so out of it I wasn't sure if we were still talking Romanians.

221

He cleared his throat, rolled down the window and spat. 'The models?' he said, as the window whirred back into place. 'They're up for a fashion show or something. Come here every year. Every day it's in and out to Glasgow to the shops. Money no object. Half of them are foreign. Can't understand a word they're saying. You'd think there were no British girls looking for jobs.'

I wondered. 'Have you come across a man called Zander?'

'Zander Skene? Oh, aye. He's the boss man now. Great tipper. I think he's probably a poof, but an all right one. Most of the guys in fashion are into all that gay stuff. I suppose you have to be if you need to know about under-wear and dresses and that.'

'Better watch what you're saying,' I said.

'How's that then?'

'Calling people poofs. For all you know, I could be gay. If I was, you'd be waving goodbye to a tip, maybe your job.'

'But you're not.'

'But I could be.'

He glanced again at me in his mirror. 'Naw, son. I know one when I see one.'

He sounded like Dame Ursula. She was able to spot modelling talent; my driver was some kind of gay-finder general.

'You ever meet Stephen Pentecost?' I asked.

'Sir Stephen?' He chuckled. 'Nothing poofy about him. And what a job he had. Surrounded by fashion models all day and paid millions for it.' He winked at me in his rear-view mirror. 'They could have me do it for half the price. I mean, what's so difficult? When you've seen one you've seen them all. Tall, lanky, no boobs. You'd need

222

to take one out for a fish supper before you could get a squeeze.'

'I heard he'd had an affair once with a model called Lafayette Delgado. Some people called her La-La?'

The cabbie shook his head. 'Scandal, was it? You're asking the wrong person. My missus will probably know all about it. Still, no big surprise. I mean, surrounded by top-class totty all day? It would be like working on the Pick 'n' Mix and never stealing a handful of cola cubes. Shame what happened to him. Although he did get every chance. If he'd been on the NHS they'd have unplugged him long before they did. I'm telling you, son, if you've got the money, go private. Mad not to. Think about it. Sick people cost the NHS money. Those GPs are all on budgets. The more they spend, the less money they get. Now, the private hospitals get their money from insurance companies. The more they treat you, the more money they get, which means the longer you live, the richer they get. Who's going to try and keep you breathing the longest? It's obvious.'

With those final words of wisdom ringing in my ears I was dropped off at my car and, as good as my word, I was climbing to my office with five minutes to spare before close of business.

Grace-Mary and Joanna were waiting for me at the top of the stairs.

'Where's Tina?' I asked.

'There's nothing to worry about,' Joanna said, in the way people say it when there's usually a great deal to worry about. 'But Tina's gone.'

Gone? What did she mean gone?

'Robbie,' Grace-Mary said. 'I think you'd better give your dad a call.'

38

My dad was pacing up and down beside the big hedge at the front of his cottage, killing nettles with mighty swishes of the ancient sand wedge he kept handy for beating the encroaching vegetation to death. 'They're waiting for you,' was all he could bring himself to say as I walked past him, down the side of the building to the back door and into the kitchen where I was intercepted by Vikki.

'Where is she?' I asked.

'Dad!' I heard Tina squeal from behind the closed living room door. I was ready to break it down to get to her.

Vikki stepped in front, barring the way. 'Don't.' She pulled out a chair from the kitchen table. I didn't want to sit down. I wanted to see my daughter. 'You will see her. In a moment. Getting angry is only going to make matters worse,' she said. 'Sit and let's have a chat.'

By chat I was sure she meant, let's go over where you went so tremendously wrong in the attempt to look after your child. Let's recap on how you failed so dismally in such a short space of time. I didn't need the lecture. I told her so.

'Dad!' Tina's voice was louder. I sensed a note of concern in it, heard an adult female voice uttering soft assurances.

'Be right there, sweetheart,' I called back.

Vikki pointed to the chair. 'Please, Robbie. Let's not make this any more difficult than it has to be.'

Why had I let myself be enticed into that Ferrari? More importantly, why hadn't I checked the time the Little Ships Nursery closed? I could have sworn it was four o'clock, not half past three. By the time Grace-Mary had gone down to collect Tina, she was already thirty minutes late. The nursery had tried to call me at home. I wasn't there. They'd phoned the next number on their list, my dad. He'd been out too. Then Malky, who was also otherwise engaged. I'd only put Tina's grandmother's details down on the contact list because there was a space for a fourth person. I'd never thought it would be required unless Malky, my dad and I were all killed in some kind of common calamity.

'Who's in there with Tina?' I asked.

'Mrs Reynold's lawyer.'

'That was quick.'

'Mrs Reynolds says she'll be here as soon as possible.'

'So Grandma's calling the shots, is she?'

'It's nothing to do with me, Robbie. I got a call from Mrs Reynold's lawyer. The only reason Tina isn't already winging her way to Oban right now is because I asked for a meeting to discuss things – civilly, and so that an accurate record can be kept.'

'For the court?'

'I've a job to do. So has Mrs Reynold's lawyer. Remember that when we go in there.'

So, there it was. Grace-Mary had been right; wasn't she always? It had been a trap. I could imagine Tina's lawyer planning the whole thing. How easy it would be to set me up to fail. Give him the kid on short notice, sit back and wait. There was probably an office sweepstake.

225

Four weeks until he screws up? Crazy, I'll stick a tenner on a fortnight.

Mrs Reynolds arrived within the hour. The four of us, Vikki, Tina's grandmother, her lawyer and myself sat in the living room while my dad played with Tina in the garden.

Mrs Reynolds remained silent, letting her lawyer, a small woman with lots of frizzy hair, do all the talking.

'It was a worthwhile exercise. It just didn't work out,' she said matter-of-factly. 'I think we've all learned something valuable from the experience. Now it's time to look at things in a more practical way and with a view to the longer term.'

I'd learned some valuable things all right. I'd learned that I wanted what was best for Tina. I'd also learned that I wanted her to live with me permanently. Did the two have to be mutually exclusive?

'It's not like you won't ever see Tina again,' Vikki said. Up until then she hadn't spoken, preferring to remain neutral. Now she was talking like it was a done deal.

Mrs Reynolds nodded. 'You're welcome to visit whenever you like.'

'Though it would be preferable to put something written in place,' her lawyer, the veteran of a thousand disputed custody cases, interjected, 'just so that everyone is reading from the same page. We could start with a couple of hours once a fortnight and see how it goes from there.' She looked to her client.

Mrs Reynolds nodded in confirmation. Just like that, we'd gone from whenever I liked to once every two weeks. Time to involve my own lawyer. Grace-Mary had already been on to Barry Munn and he was expecting my call.

'Not much I can do,' he said. 'It's Tina's Aunt Chloe

who has the say on matters for the moment. She was granted a guardianship order by an Australian court which allowed her to bring Tina to Scotland. That order is recognised here until such time as the Scottish courts make a final decision on custody.'

'So it's all down to Chloe?'

'For the time being,' Barry said.

Then why wasn't she here? She knew it was Zoë's last wish that I take care of our daughter. She'd told me so. Now when it came to the crunch she was nowhere to be seen. Could I rely on her to favour me against her mother's wishes? Water against blood?

'What's Chloe's view on all this?' I asked, after I'd replaced the receiver.

Mrs Reynolds looked to her lawyer.

'Tina's Aunt Chloe obviously has a say in the immediate placement of Tina,' Frizzy-head said. 'However, as she doesn't intend on applying for residency, permanent residence is a matter for the sheriff.' She smiled a professional smile. 'As guided by the child welfare report, of course.'

All eyes turned on Vikki. There was a long pause before she spoke. 'It's not your fault, Robbie. But you have to face it, today wasn't the first time you've not been there for Tina. Your decision to work on through paternity leave has meant that your father, your brother, even your staff have had to pitch in and help when you weren't available.'

'Isn't that a good thing? That I've got people able to support me when I need help?'

'It's a good thing if those people can be relied on,' Mrs Reynolds' lawyer butted in, 'and if formal arrangements are in place.'

Mrs Reynolds wanted her say too. 'Robbie, from what

I'm told, you've been fire-fighting, putting other people into very difficult positions. That sort of thing can't go on indefinitely.'

Vikki agreed. 'Eventually, you'd have to decide what it was you cared most about.' She looked away from me. 'Tina or your work.' She stood up. 'It's not easy for me to say this. I know how much you care about . . . '

Right on cue, the door opened. Tina ran in and hugged me.

'It was getting cold out there,' my dad said from the doorway.

Tina released me. Vikki knelt down beside my daughter and took her little hands between her own. 'Guess what, Tina. You're going to stay with your Granny Vera tonight.'

Tina looked confused. My dad didn't. He was ready to rip the head off somebody's shoulders and was leaving me in no doubt as to who topped that particular list.

'Dad, could you take Tina into the kitchen for a moment?' I asked, and when he'd gone I turned to the others. 'Just a couple of more days. I promise, I'll not let her out of my sight the whole time. No visits by me to the office, nothing.'

If Mrs Reynolds wavered, her lawyer was a rock. 'There is no point dragging this out.' She rose to her feet, briefcase in hand. Mrs Reynolds and then Vikki followed suit. I was the only person still seated.

'What about Molly's birthday party?' I blurted. 'Tina will be disappointed and it would be a terrible shame for Molly after everything she's been through.' Any straw was worth clutching at.

'Who's Molly?' Mrs Reynolds asked Vikki.

'A girl in my care. Her mother was murdered. She may have witnessed the killing and is completely traumatised.

228

She has some learning difficulties too and Tina . . . well, Tina is really her only friend.'

Mrs Reynolds frowned. 'And she has a birthday coming up?'

'This Saturday,' Vikki confirmed.

'We were going to have a party at my place,' I said.

'There's no reason why we can't still have the party,' Mrs Reynolds said. Her final words almost cloaked by the clearing of her lawyer's throat. 'Everyone can come down to my place for the day. There's plenty of room. We'll have a lovely time.'

Tina came crashing through again. She ran over and took Vera's hand. 'Hurry up, Granny. When are we going to your house?'

Mrs Reynolds smiled down at her and patted her hand. 'Soon, dear. I was just saying, wouldn't it be nice if your friend Molly came to see us? We could have a party with a cake and Aunt Chloe and your cousins could maybe come up. I know a man who will bring us a big bouncy castle for the garden. How does that sound?'

It sounded great if Tina's cheers and bouncing up and down were anything to go by. Still holding her grandmother's hand she grabbed hold of mine. 'Let's go, then!'

'No, dear,' Mrs Reynolds said, 'your dad isn't coming with us today.'

'Why not?' Tina demanded.

'Because,' Mrs Reynolds' frizzy-haired lawyer said, gently freeing my daughter's hand from mine, 'your daddy has lots of more important things to do.'

39

As a defence lawyer, the weak side of the argument was my stock in trade, and yet after all the pleas in mitigation of sentence I'd done in my time, all the jury speeches I'd spouted, I couldn't find a single word to say in my own defence and, even if I had, my dad wouldn't have listened anyway.

I arrived back at my flat around eight o'clock with no memory of the journey from my dad's cottage. There was an envelope in my pocket that, from a swift inspection, had to contain at least twenty thousand pounds, and for all that I cared could have contained my laundry list. All I could think of was my wee girl in the back of a car heading for Oban and out of my life.

Someone who was heading into my life at that precise moment was Malky. His car was parked where I normally parked mine and he'd used my not so cunningly concealed spare key to let himself in. I entered the living room to find him sprawled on the sofa, playing a football game on the PlayStation. 'What are you doing here?'

'It's Wednesday night. I always come to see my favourite niece on a Wednesday night. Where is she?'

'Has Dad not spoken to you?' I asked.

'What about?'

Malky hadn't heard yet. Good. I couldn't bear the thought of repeating the whole heart-breaking saga.

'Nothing.'

'Realistic, this, isn't it?' One of his pixel-players tried a long range strike at goal that sailed high over the bar.

'Very. That could have been one of your efforts.'

He wasn't listening. The hands holding the controller twisted and turned this way and that. At a particularly exciting moment his right foot shot out as though trying to block a strike at goal or intercept a loose pass.

'So where's Tina?' he asked again, once the electronic whistle had blown for full-time.

'Gone to stay with her gran for a few days.'

Malky threw the controller to the side and stood up, a broad smile stretched across his face. 'Giving yourself some breathing space, eh?' He punched my arm. 'You dog. You better make the most of it because, let me tell you, you are in the deepest of doo-doo.'

Most of my brother's chat, the little I actually listened to, was a stream of consciousness rather than anything remotely informative. What was he on about now? And why so pleased about it?

'Wee Gus told me,' he said, thinking he was making things clearer.

'Who?'

'I don't know if he's got a second name. Must have, I suppose. But you know who I mean. You've met him. Gus's been the Scotland team kit man forever. He still gets me tickets for the games.'

I did vaguely recall being introduced to a grumpy wee man at a sportsman's dinner once and though I thought that might be who Malky was referring to, I didn't care sufficiently enough to waste the electricity on a synapse between the relevant brain cells to make the connection. 'Oh, yeah, Gus. What did he tell you?'

'That he saw you today. Except he thought it was me. That's why he phoned.'

I walked through to the kitchen for a glass of water, hoping in doing so I might shake off Malky and his mad ramblings. It didn't work. He followed me into the kitchen.

'I said, it definitely wasn't me, Gus. I was in a radio studio doing a voice-over twenty miles away. It must have been my brother, even though he looks nothing like me, for a start he's fatter—'

'Bigger-built.' I filled a glass from the tap.

'And a short-arse.'

'I'm five eleven. That's above-average height. You're the only freak in the room.'

'And he said he could have sworn it was me, and—'

'Malky. Could you shut up? I'm tired and I'd really quite like to hit someone.' I drank the water in one go. 'And how come – if I look nothing like you – you told him it must have been me he saw?'

Malky thought about that for a moment. 'Okay, I'll admit there is a vague family resemblance, but, you know, seriously . . . ' He wagged an index finger between our respective faces a few times. 'What was the man thinking?'

I rinsed out the glass and left it turned upside down on the draining board, thinking it would be dry by the time Malky reached the end of his story. 'Listen, Malky. I've had a really hard day.'

'I bet you have.' He caught his reflection in the kitchen window and swept his hair back either side. 'Us Munro boys. It's not fair. Women can't help themselves.' He punched my arm again.

'I really wish you'd stop doing that.'

He laughed. 'You'll get a lot worse if Joey gets his mitts on you.'

'Joey who?'

'Joey Di Rollo.'

'The Spurs player?'

'Once upon a time. He's a coaching assistant these days. Went to Brighton after Spurs, that's how I know him. From my time down there. You know before Cat . . . before . . . ' Before he killed his former partner in a car crash he meant. 'Before she died.'

'Sorry, Malky,' I said. 'You're going to have to explain what on earth it is you're talking about.'

'Not me, kiddo. It's you who's got the explaining to do.' He pinched my cheek and gave it a shake. 'Nicking off to a fancy hotel with Joey's bird for a nooner? Let's see you put up a defence to that one. Guilty as charged, M'lud.'

From which I reasonably inferred that Joey and my glamorous chauffeur from earlier that day were romantically linked.

'She was giving me a lift,' I said, batting his hand away.

'I know what she was giving you.'

'Could you stop sounding like someone out of a *Carry On* movie for a minute? The girl gave me a lift to Mar Hall. I had an appointment to see Ursula Pentecost. It was to do with work. Nothing happened between me and—'

'You met Ursula? How is she? Did she know you were my brother?'

'Why would she know that and how do you even know who she is?'

'I used to see her all the time,' Malky said. 'She was always wearing something stupid. Not a woman who's scared of bright colours, is she?'

'Let's get this straight. You know Dame Ursula Pentecost?'

Malky wrinkled his nose. 'Nah, not really. Not to talk to. It was Stephen I dealt with most of the time.'

233

'Stephen Pentecost? Sir Stephen Pentecost? You knew him?'

'Do you know what the cost of living is down South? How do you think I managed to live in Brighton for three years?'

'Your radio show? After-dinners?'

Malky straightened his shoulders and breathed in. 'And a spot of modelling work.' He breathed out again and slapped his stomach. 'Okay, I've let myself go a wee bit, but me and some of the other boys used to model all sorts of stuff. Once Stephen had us modelling a range of leisurewear. What was it called? Half-time ... no, Full-time Fashion, I think it was. He was trying to move out of all the boutique stuff and go more ... '

'Downmarket?'

'High Street, was what Stephen called it. Anyway, the money was great and I got to keep the clothes. Well, I did if I sneaked them out in my holdall.'

We wandered back to the living room and plonked ourselves down on the sofa. Malky picked up the PlayStation controllers. 'So nothing happened between you and Joey's girl? Shame, next time I saw him I was going to wind him up about my ugly wee brother stealing his bird.'

'How many times did you meet him?'

'Joey? Hundreds of times. Last time I was in London we—'

'Not Joey, Stephen Pentecost.'

'Oh, tons of times. He was very hands-on. Especially with some of the models. We all were.'

Malky sorted his next game on the PlayStation. Scotland v England. I noticed he'd introduced a new player to the present Scotland line-up. 'I see you've got a certain Malky Munro playing centre-forward.'

'Yeah, found myself in the Scotland Legends team. On the bench. Can you believe it? Anyway, I beefed up my stats a bit and knocked in three against Argentina in the last round. Two headers and a thirty-yarder. But like I say, some of Stephen's models were definitely up for the cup. I mean, you know what models are like, right? Most of them are extremely ambitious.' Malky paused to make a few last minute alterations to his starting line-up. 'Not all of them can make it, so what you're left with is all these really good-looking girls whose legs aren't long enough or who want to eat food like normal folk,' he went on, apparently satisfied with his tactical set-up. 'There's hundreds of them. They try, they fail, they go on the prowl for rich guys.' That would normally have won the award for politically incorrect-statement-of-the-day, but for my earlier taxi ride. 'They just sort of assume all footballers are rich. By the time most of them found out I was skint, it was too late.'

He pressed the X button a couple of times and was transported to Barcelona and the Camp Nou, where he had arranged for the match to be played in snowy conditions because he thought his team of digital Scottish players would be more used to the cold weather.

'You'd think it would just be called the Camp nowadays,' he said. 'It's not exactly all that *nou*, is it? It's been around for years. They should call it the ... what's Spanish for old?'

'It's Barcelona so it wouldn't be Spanish. It would be in the Basque language.' That shut him up for a few seconds and allowed me to ask, 'Did you ever come across someone called Lafayette Delgado?'

'Might have. Who'd he play for?'

'I'm talking about your modelling career. Did you ever

meet a woman called Lafayette or maybe you knew her as La-La?'

'La-La? No, I think I'd have remembered a name like La-La. When it comes to models, I've got a good head for names as well as figures.'

Malky's game kicked off. There would be no talking to him for at least the next ten minutes. I went off in search of Barry Munn's home number and was about to dial directory enquiries when the phone rang.

'Malky, will you answer that? If it's Dad, tell him I'm not in.'

Malky paused the game and with much huffing and puffing picked up the phone, said hello and then without another word handed the receiver to me.

It was Jake Turpie. 'What's happening?' he asked.

I took him to be referring to Deek's defence, in which case not a lot was happening, if you excluded a lot of half-baked theories and the possibility that, thanks to him, I might be facing an attempt to defeat the ends of justice rap.

'Then I've got something that might help,' he said.

Right about then, I thought Jake butting out and letting me do my job was the only assistance I required from him. 'Really? Like what?'

'Like the man who killed Daisy Adams.'

40

I left Malky and his virtual teammates to battle it out with the Auld Enemy in snowy Catalonia. Half an hour later I was strolling with Jake Turpie down a canyon piled high either side with scrap cars, arc-lights casting our shadows huge across the uneven terrain as we stepped around water-filled potholes and over chunks that had fallen from the mountains of rusting metal.

'I've been doing some thinking,' Jake said – seldom a good sign. 'I went to see Deek and there was something he said about that guy he killed. The one up at the farm,' he added, for the avoidance of doubt.

I'd yet to formally take Deek's side of things from him. Other than tell him to keep his mouth shut during police interrogation, the only communication I'd had with my client had been through his boss. Prison visiting was an over-rated pastime and, if the big man preferred that I deal through the medium of Jake, I was happy not to serve time with an overly large man in an unduly small visit room.

'I told you not to visit Deek,' I said.

'Nobody was listening in to us.'

'Okay. What did he tell you?'

'That the dead guy was Russian, or Polish or Lithuanian or something.'

'And how did he know that?'

'Because he spoke in a funny language and he looked like a Russian.'

'Did he have on one of those wee furry hats and a pair of knee-length boots? I must have missed that.'

Jake stopped, one steel toe-capped boot in a puddle, one out. 'You trying to be smart?'

'No, I'm trying to stop you making things worse,' I said, broaching the subject of Jake's earlier attempt at concocting a defence for Deek Pudney. An alibi that had well and truly deflated long before there had been any chance to float it past a jury. 'First of all, you tell me Deek wasn't there, then you tell me he was there, but he was attacked and had to defend himself, now you're saying he stopped for a chat?'

The headlights of a five-ton diesel forklift rounded the corner coming our way, out-sized front tyres splashing through puddles, gouging deeper ruts in the shale surface. Jake waited for it to trundle by. 'Maybe I haven't been totally straight with you.' He grunted as though telling the truth was painful. 'You see, there wasn't just one guy up at the farm. There was two of them.'

'What?'

'Aye, well, don't blame me.'

'Who should I blame?'

'Come on. You should know that nobody ever does a hit single-handed. You're always going to need someone to watch your back.'

'How long have you known this?'

Jake shrugged, from which I took it that he'd always known.

'Why didn't you tell me?'

'Deek thought if he said he'd killed this other guy too it wouldn't look so good.'

238

'He killed someone else!'

'Keep your voice down.'

Where's the body?'

'That's what I'm trying to tell you.'

'Then you're making a very bad job of it.' I kicked a piece of shale and watched it bounce down the track in front of us until it eventually took a skip and nose-dived into a puddle. 'Just tell me what Deek is saying happened. Not half of what happened, the whole lot. Everything. Leave nothing out. Just tell me—'

'All right, all right. Deek goes to chin the Adams woman about the car. He chaps the door. Nothing. He chaps again. He knows she must be in because the motor's there. He hears screaming inside. He smashes through the back door and there's a guy in the kitchen with a big knife. He says something to Deek. Deek doesn't understand what he's saying. The guy slashes Deek, and ends up dead. The screaming stops. Deek goes to the door leading to the hall. He opens it and someone comes charging through and tries to jook past him. Deek trips him up, but this new guy manages to get to the back door. Deek goes after him. The guy's too fast. Just by the back door there's a grape stuck in the ground.

'A grape? You mean a garden fork?'

'Aye. Deek chucks it at him. It hits. According to Deek it really hits. But the guy somehow manages to keep going and runs off into the woods. Deek doesn't know what to do so he comes back here.'

And the rest, as they say, was history; the history of a botched-up, fabricated attempt at an alibi defence using yours truly as a stooge.

'And so you decided that, to be on the safe side, you'd make up the world's worst alibi defence involving Marty

Sneddon, and rope me in with a visit to the farm?' I said.

'Aye, to explain Deek's fingerprints and that.'

I recalled seeing a garden fork when I'd been up at the farm with Vikki to collect Molly's belongings. It had been in a plastic production bag and placed into the van the scene of crime officers had been using. If the cops had the garden fork, they'd find the new guy's blood and Deek's prints on it. 'So why are you telling me all this now? Killing the guy in the kitchen, okay, we could possibly work out a defence, but this other guy . . . '

'That's what I'm saying. He's maybe not dead. They'd have found his body by now if he was, in the woods or down the road or something, but they've been searching all over the place up there and nothing's come up so far, has it?'

Not that I'd heard.

'So . . . ' Jake paused to wave furiously at an oncoming low-loader, sending it off in another direction, 'I've been carrying out some investigations of my own.'

If there was one thing more likely to be detrimental to a successful defence than Jake thinking, it was him actually acting on some of those thoughts.

'Please tell me you haven't done anything stupid.'

'It's all perfectly legal. You know Sammy Veitch the lawyer?'

I knew Sammy Veitch all right. Anyone in Central Scotland who had ever tripped over a paving slab, slipped in a supermarket or been bumped in a car knew slip 'n' trip Sammy Veitch. Some of those people hadn't even known they'd been injured until they'd met Sammy. Jake and Sammy had an arrangement. If one of Jake's recovery vehicles was called out to a smash, he'd notify Sammy if there were any injured parties. Ambulance-chaser? Sammy could give an ambulance a five-minute head start and still beat it to A & E. If Sammy got any business as a result of the tip-off, Jake got his share. Sammy had a similar relationship with various members of the emergency services and primary care teams. On this occasion Jake had asked Sammy to use his contacts at the local hospitals to find out if anyone had sought treatment for garden-fork type injuries around the time of Daisy Adams' murder. There had been one: a man with infected wounds who'd been admitted to the Forth Valley Royal Hospital ten miles away in Falkirk. The history as presented to the triage nurse was that he'd slipped and fallen on a garden rake. Jake had other ideas.

'It's got to be the guy that Deek speared. Sammy's not been able to get a name. All they'd tell him was that the guy was foreign and couldn't speak English.'

We walked back to Jake's dilapidated HQ, him stopping every now and again to bark orders at the backshift, me deep in thought. I had to admit that on this occasion Jake's own thinking had been quite lucid. If we could identify the forkman we would not only have Daisy's killer, we might also find out why she'd been killed in the first place. With a bit of work Deek could actually have a defence.

41

'I heard about Tina.' Grace-Mary dropped the letter she was reading, removed her glasses and let them dangle on the gold chain about her neck.

I could tell she was torn between saying I told you so and sympathising.

'It's not over,' I said.

She grunted. 'I suppose you're expecting to come back to work?'

That was the intention. My being responsible for the Munro in Munro & Co., I'd always felt I should have a major say in the running of the business, something Grace-Mary had never fully conceded. 'Might as well,' I said, it'll keep you from sitting twiddling your thumbs and knocking off early. So here's three things for you to be getting on with: first, someone was admitted to Forth Valley Hospital a few weeks ago with wounds to his back, allegedly caused by a garden rake. He's foreign, possibly Russian. Find out everything you can about him. Second, make me an appointment with Barry Munn. It doesn't matter when as long as it's immediately. And, third . . . ' I held out my hand to Grace-Mary, 'my phone please.'

Joanna must have heard my voice. She walked into reception and gave me a hug.

'Robbie's come back to work,' Grace-Mary said, managing to keep the excitement out of her voice.

Joanna released me. 'If you want more time to try and sort things out, it's no problem. Everything's going fine here. Isn't it, Grace-Mary?'

'I was thinking that I'd break myself in gently,' I said. 'Can you help out for a few more days, Joanna, while I try and figure what to do about Tina and maybe look into Deek Pudney's case a bit more?'

'It's looking into that big eejit's case that's landed you in this mess with Tina,' Grace-Mary said.

Joanna scowled at her and turned to me again. 'You take your time, Robbie. This thing with Tina . . . it must be terrible for you.'

'Well, he can't say I never told him.' Grace-Mary had decided not to plump for the sympathetic approach. 'From day one I said it was a trap. How he thought he could—'

'Okay, I get it,' I said.

Joanna came in on my side. 'Give him a break. He was bound to—'

'Fail?' my secretary enquired.

'To find it more difficult to cope with a child than a woman would.' It was kind of Joanna to say so. In a sexist sort of a way. 'Listen, Robbie, seriously, if there's anything I can do to help.'

'There is,' Grace-Mary said. She handed Joanna a scrap of paper. 'There's a Russian bloke up at Forth Valley Hospital. Fell on a rake or something. Robbie wants you to find out all about him.'

Joanna looked at me. 'Robbie?'

'If you wouldn't mind,' I said. 'And Grace-Mary . . . ' I lifted her handbag from the floor beside the reception desk and fished out my mobile phone. 'I expect to be sitting across a desk from Barry Munn – today.'

And I was. Somehow Grace-Mary talked Barry into

giving me a lunchtime appointment, and at one thirty that same Thursday afternoon I was looking at him across a stack of case files, while he stared back at me through a pair of red-rimmed eyes. By the side of the desk there was a cardboard box, the name of a wine club stencilled on the side.

'I know what you're thinking,' he said, 'and, yes, I have had one tiny drink. I find a small glass of wine at lunch helps recharge my mental batteries for the afternoon ahead.'

'You can't do a proper job and drink at the same time,' I said.

Barry scoffed at my naiveté. 'Winston Churchill never made an important decision without a couple of brandies under his belt.'

'Yes, but he was only fighting World War Two. This is my daughter we're talking about.'

Barry leaned across the desk at me, arms folded. Whatever he'd been drinking it must have given him Dutch courage because he'd brought his fat face well within slapping range. 'If we're going to start . . . ' He had trouble with the word criticising and downgraded it to blaming folk. 'It's you who has made a mess of things. I gave you a shot at getting custody of Tina. It was you who blew it, not me. I can take a horse to water, but I can't make it drink.'

'Water?' I said. 'You should try drinking it yourself sometime – it's that stuff that looks like Pinot Grigio.'

Barry leaned back in his big black leather chair. 'If you want to talk rationally, I'll listen. If you've only come here to give me abuse, I'd rather you just got it out of your system and then left.' He extricated a file from the bundle and lobbed it on top of the pile on his desk. 'Go on. There's your file. Feel free to take it with you and find some other mug to take it on.'

Should I? Who else would I go to? I was a criminal defence solicitor. In the field of family law, I was a man with a fork in a world of soup. How could I find out who was the best family lawyer around? And, if I did find out, how long would I have to wait for an appointment? The good ones were bound to be busy. I bet old Frizzy-hair didn't do lunchtime appointments.

'All right then.' Barry seemed to take my silence and lack of movement as indication enough that he remained instructed. He placed my file on top of the bundle. 'As you're aware, the final hearing is fixed three weeks from now. You need to know your options, but before I tell you them I am going to have a very small refreshment just to keep my brain cells ticking over.' He swivelled in his chair, lifted a wine glass from the windowsill and then reached into the cardboard box to remove a half-full bottle of Spanish red. In what was clearly a well-practised manoeuvre, carried out at speed, he poured himself the largest very small glass of wine I'd ever seen and drank most of it in one go.

'You've got three,' he said, setting the glass down on a coaster by his phone. 'Option one: game over. Gran keeps Tina.' He held up the flat of a hand. 'Before you say anything, it isn't so bad. Think about it. This time three months ago you didn't even know you had a daughter. If it hadn't been for an unkind twist of fate you never would. You can always keep in touch by post: Christmas and birthday cards, that sort of thing.' He looked at me expectantly for a moment. 'Okay. Not option one. Option two: Tina stays with her gran, we set up contact for you once a fortnight to start off with, moving onto weekly if things pan out okay and maybe a weekend stay-over now and again, not to mention a couple of days at either Christmas or New Year. We should also be able to negotiate a week in the summer.'

'Option three?'

'I quite liked option two,' Barry said.

I didn't.

Option three required another swig of wine. 'You go balls-out for a full residence order.'

'Option three it is then,' I said.

'Then you'd have to call witnesses. People who could, honestly, say what a great dad you are. Tina's a bit young to sway any decisions, though the sheriff would probably speak to her in chambers to take her view on things.'

'Is that it?'

'No. You'd have to show that you had the necessary accommodation all set up, if not immediately, certainly in the foreseeable future and you'd also need to convince the sheriff that plans were in place for caring for Tina if you were ever not available for business reasons. That means people who you can rely on for support.'

At mention of my dad and Malky, Barry's glass became in sudden need of a top-up.

'Anything else?' I asked.

'Yes, the most important thing. A good report from Vikki Stark. She's an experienced professional and it doesn't matter who the sheriff is, they'll attach a lot of weight to whatever she says.'

Was Vikki on my side? Was she even talking to me? She'd seemed quite sympathetic at my dad's the night before, though not sufficiently so to stop Vera taking Tina away.

'And,' Barry took a glug of wine, smacked his lips,

'it's going to take more than a bunch of flowers to swing Vikki back in your favour. I'm telling you, Robbie. Let me negotiate a deal. Don't let this go to proof and have Bert Brechin throw you a couple of hours contact once a month until Tina's sixteen.'

This was how it worked. Family law, the seamy underbelly of the legal profession. It was the murky pool in which civil lawyers like Barry swam every day. I was a fish out of water, flapping on the bank, gasping for oxygen.

'Okay, tell me more about option two,' I said.

42

If I'd learned one thing about Procurators Fiscal over the years, it was their need for regular caffeine stimulation, and that the frequency of these restorative breaks, as well as their length, varied in direct proportion to seniority.

I'd been waiting outside Hugh Ogilvie's favourite coffee shop for less than half an hour when he entered the mall, approaching like a junkie homing in on his first tenner-bag of the day.

'What do you want?' He wandered over to a refrigerated unit and studied some cakes individually wrapped in cellophane.

I followed. 'All I want is a quick word about Derek Pudney's case.'

Ogilvie looked around frantically as though I was about to spout state secrets in the middle of Costa Coffee, took me by the lapel and led me outside. 'This is not the time and it's definitely not the place.'

'When then? I'm happy to come over to your office right now and we can discuss it over coffee and a bun,' I said, aware that the last thing the PF would want was me spoiling his mid-afternoon break.

'If this is about your latest defence,' Ogilvie hissed, 'don't bother. Professor Bradley has told me all about it. Apparently, someone else killed Daisy Adams and then your client killed that person while he himself was being attacked. That about sum it up? So, let me see, now that the original alibi has crashed and burned, we've moved onto incrimination and self-defence. You do realise that if they don't work, you're fast running out of special defences. Only two left: coercion and insanity. Nobody's ever successfully argued a coercion defence and insanity . . . ? Unfortunately, that doesn't apply to choice of legal representative.'

'Seeing how you think you know everything,' I said, freeing his grip on my jacket, 'how about I tell you something you don't know?'

Ogilvie gave me a nailed-on smile behind which I knew was the strong and sudden desire to scream. 'Like what?'

'Like the fact that the man on the kitchen table – the one with a knife sticking out from where it shouldn't be sticking – was foreign; Polish or Russian or something.'

'Italian, actually.' The PF made as though to move away.

I stepped in front of him.

'You know?'

'International police co-operation is quite the thing these days. For the moment at least, it's all part of our great European community. They've got computers and everything.'

'But not co-operation between the prosecution and defence in Scotland because otherwise this information would already have been disclosed to me,' I said.

'It will be. When I'm ready. More importantly . . . ' Ogilvie seemed in less of a rush to get way. 'How did you know he was foreign?'

It was too early to start revealing dubious pieces of information concerning my client's latest defence, like the possible existence of a man with fork holes in his back.

Even if Jake's story was true, it was all very well for Deek to defend himself against a knife-wielding Italian, less so to hurl garden forks at folk who were running away and claim self-defence. This wasn't America or South Africa where the law allowed you to kill and ask questions later. To coin one of my dad's phrases, when dealing with representatives of the Crown office and Procurator Fiscal Service, the less they knew the more the better.

'All in good time,' I said. 'The fact is that you've now gone from a dead innocent bystander to a dead Italian who, if Interpol has been helping out, must have a criminal record or at least fingerprints on a police database. It can't hurt an incrimination defence.'

'What?' Ogilvie sneered. 'You're going to attack his character? With a record like Pudney's?'

The PF had a point. Bringing up the dead man's past crimes in the course of the trial would only open the door for Deek's record to be placed before the jury. The last time they printed the big man's previous convictions they had to chop a tree down first.

'What was your Italian doing on a farm in the wilds of West Lothian?' I asked.

Ogilvie checked his watch. 'Apart from being murdered by your client, you mean?'

I was going to get nothing out of him. I'd hoped that by tipping him off that the dead guy was foreign he might have extended his enquiries, but he already had; he just hadn't let me know the results and wasn't going to any time soon. What could I do?

My hesitation gave Ogilvie the chance to escape and he shimmied off in the direction of a vanilla mocha and a Belgian teacake.

What was Daisy Adams doing entertaining Italians? It

250

could all have been perfectly innocent, of course. A couple of economic migrants working casual on a farm; nothing unusual about that. Along comes Deek, starts pushing Daisy around and demanding money. The chivalrous Italians weigh in on her behalf and suddenly it's slaughter at Sunnybrae Farm.

Only four people knew the truth. Two were dead. One was in prison. Where was the other?

'He's still in hospital,' Joanna told me when I phoned the office on the way to my car. 'I'm just back from there.'

'Did you get a name?'

'Lorenc Bizi. He has a punctured kidney. The injury wasn't all that bad until it became infected. It was touch-and-go for a while. The doctor I spoke to made it sound like our man's spent the last few weeks peeing into a bag and being pumped full of antibiotics.'

I didn't bother to ask how Joanna had managed to glean this information. I could imagine her cornering a young male registrar and him putting up all the resistance of aspirin to a dose of Dengue fever.

'They expect him to get out early next week,' she said. 'Do you want me to do anything else or can it keep until Monday?'

I told her to leave things for now. She'd played her part. If Mr Bizi had anything to hide and knew that someone had been asking questions about him, he'd discharge himself early and disappear. Anyone who could suffer a punctured kidney for a few days before seeking treatment, wasn't going to hang around hospital a minute longer than he had to if he thought the authorities were onto him.

I phoned Jake with the news and he sent one of his men over to the hospital to keep an eye on things.

I drove back to Linlithgow, washed the few clothes Tina had left behind and hung them over the drying rack, each wee T-shirt or pair of tiny dungarees, a sad reminder of my loss and my own stupidity. After lunch I called Mrs Reynolds. Tina couldn't come to the phone. She was taking a nap. I'd tried that once. We'd crashed out on the couch one afternoon after a prolonged duck-feeding expedition and slept for four hours. When I woke up I had a stiff neck and a headache. Tina had been as bright as a button and stayed that way until two in the morning.

'I'll call later,' I said.

'We're going out later,' Mrs Reynolds replied. 'There's a children's show on in the town hall and we'll probably go for tea afterwards. Tina's bound to be tired by the time we get back.'

'Tomorrow then.'

'I'm not sure what we're doing tomorrow. Tina needs some new clothes.'

'Saturday.'

'Saturday's Molly's party, and—'

Enough. I hung up and called Barry Munn's office. His secretary told me he was engaged with a client and couldn't be interrupted. I tried his mobile and got his answering machine. I wondered about paying him a visit, except that would have involved more attempts by Barry to talk me out of what I had wanted to do all along. Tina was my daughter. So what, it was by chance that I'd learned of her existence? I didn't know why her mother had never told me about her. Perhaps she would have one day. You heard of people who discover some distant relative from overseas has died and left them a fortune. Well, Zoë had left me a daughter, and, now that I'd learned of my inheritance, I wasn't about to squander it. I needed to send Barry a message. One that was clear and simple. One that he'd understand, even through a Thursday afternoon Rioja-mist. I took my mobile and entered his number again. Seven characters one space. That's all it took to signal my intent. It was all or nothing. It was: Option 3.

43

Thursday evening. I hadn't seen or heard from my dad since Wednesday afternoon. Like the Italian with the punctured kidney, the longer I put things off, the longer the wound would fester. I rolled up outside his cottage around seven o'clock to find he already had a visitor.

'Oh, it's you, is it?' he said, as I walked into the living room to find him and Vikki pinning cut-out pictures of pumpkins, witches and bats all around the room.

'For the party,' Vikki said, by way of explanation.

'You're having a Halloween party?'

My dad ignored the question. He was holding a paper silhouette of a black cat and staring at it. Tina's name was printed along the cat's tail in silver pen. I went over and tried to take it from him. He wouldn't let go. I gave up.

'More tea, Vikki?' he asked, after the cat was duly stuck to the wall with a dod of Blu-Tack.

Vikki shook her head and pointed to a mug on the mantelpiece.

'Well, I'm making another,' my dad said, without any offer to me.

I intercepted him at the kitchen door. 'I'll make the tea. You keep going with the decorations.'

'I'll make my own tea, thanks.' He pushed past and shut the kitchen door firmly behind him.

'That,' I said to Vikki, jerking a thumb after my dad,

'I expected. You being here, I didn't.' I went over to the black paper cat on the wall. 'You see this? The nursery cut cat-silhouettes out for all the kids. They were supposed to adapt them, draw faces and whiskers, collars and what have you. The nursery pinned them by the door for the parents to see. When I went to collect Tina, one of the assistants told me that Tina hadn't been joining in. She wanted to paint a cat. She didn't want to make a 'silly-wet' and was dead stubborn about it. There had even been a short trip to the naughty corner. I asked Tina why she hadn't given her cat a face or decorated it like the ones the other boys and girls had done. I was all set to give her a lecture about not always getting her own way and doing what she was told.' I had to pause. Even now, weeks later, despite everything that had happened, it still made me laugh. 'I was expecting an argument, but Tina just looked up at me all sweetness and light and said, "Dad, you can't see my cat's face 'cos she's got her back to us." And that was that.' I pressed the cat cut-out more firmly to the wall. 'My dad loves that story.'

'She's a smart girl,' Vikki said.

'Good on her feet.'

'Like her dad.'

It was a nice attempt to butter me up, but Vikki must have expected what was coming next.

'What do I have to do to keep her?'

'Robbie . . . '

There were some noises from the kitchen, but nothing to indicate that my dad was returning soon. Was he giving me time to work on Vikki?

'If an ex-drug user like Daisy can adopt someone else's child, why can't I get to keep mine?'

Vikki put a hand on my arm. 'Because you never had

her to start with, Robbie. You didn't even know you had a daughter until Tina's mum died. Daisy Adams knew Molly practically from birth, but more importantly La-La wanted Daisy to be Molly's guardian if anything happened to her.

'Zoë wanted me to have Tina. Ask her sister.'

'But Zoë never left a will. 'Without La-La's will, Daisy wouldn't have stood a chance of adopting Molly. Not even with me on her side.'

'My lawyer gave me three options, forget about Tina, go for contact or try for full residence,' I said.

'And which option did your lawyer recommend?'

'Option two.'

Vikki shrugged. 'I'd be happy to go along with that recommendation in my report.'

'I'm going for option three.'

Vikki sat down on the couch and patted the cushion next to her. 'Think with your head, not your heart,' she said, when I'd joined her on the sofa. 'Are you sure you're not like a little boy who wants a puppy for Christmas? By Easter his mum's having to feed it and his dad's taking it for walks.'

'I know what I want and I think I know what is best for Tina,' I said.

'Good, because that's what it all boils down to: the best interests of the child. Let's look at the negatives. You're a single man with a business to run. You don't keep regular hours, you—'

'We've been through all my negatives before. What about Tina's gran? What age is she? Can she go running after her? Play football with her?' I added in case my dad was eavesdropping. 'What happens if Mrs Reynolds gets sick?'

'Anyone can get sick, Robbie. Think of Tina's mum – a young woman.'

'What has Vera got that I haven't got? She's female. Is that what really counts?'

'No, it's not. What really counts is that she's a female with nothing to do all day but care for her grandchild. A female who can give Tina all the attention she deserves. A female who'll always be there for her and who won't forget to collect her from nursery because she's too busy with a client. A female with a lovely big house who can give Tina her own room and a garden to play in.' Vikki stood. 'Look, I'm sorry to have to say these things, but there's no point in me sugar-coating it. All other things being equal, you being Tina's father, there would be no problem with you having custody. But all things aren't equal. Face it, Robbie. Looking after a child takes careful planning and . . . well, from what I hear, you have enough difficulty planning your own life without a four-year-old daughter tagging along.'

Enter my dad, stage left, not bearing a cup of tea, but a claw hammer and a face that should have carried a Government health warning. 'Let's get these decorations finished and you can get away, Vikki.' He took some panel pins from his pocket and, using the hammer, began to tack a string of crescent moon bunting to the wall.

'What's all this in favour of, anyway?' I asked. 'Apart, obviously, from the fact that it's Halloween on Saturday.'

My dad busied himself trying to find the end of a roll of sticky tape.

'Molly's birthday,' Vikki said.

'I thought she was having it at Vera's lovely big house?'

'That was the idea until I realised that taking Molly all the way to Oban was a long way to go,' Vikki said, not rising to my sarcasm. 'She's still very vulnerable and I wasn't sure if I should take her out of the local authority's jurisdiction.' Vikki set out a row of cheap ceramic pumpkin-lantern tea light holders, spacing them along the mantelpiece. 'After all the promises I'd made to Molly about having a birthday party with Tina, I didn't want to call it off, so Mrs Reynolds phoned your dad and he volunteered. She said she'd tried to mention it to you when you called, but . . . '

'I hung up on her?'

Vikki nodded. 'You're not doing yourself any favours. Vera's a good woman. You think you know what's best for Tina – so does she.'

My dad taped the last string of black and orange bunting to the wall and dusted his hands off. 'That's that then.'

'Great,' Vikki said. She collected her handbag and waited for my dad to bring her jacket. 'How about I bring Molly along, say, four o'clock Saturday afternoon and maybe stay until around seven? The Home don't like it if I keep her out late.'

'That'd be fine,' my dad said. 'It's good of you to do this. I'm sure there's plenty other things you could be doing with your time on a Saturday evening.'

Vikki dismissed his words of appreciation with a wave of her hand. 'Now is there anything else you're going to need to get this party started? What about food and drink?'

'I've got everything bought in already,' my dad said. 'Don't you worry, I'll throw the wee lassie a birthday party she won't forget.' He walked Vikki to the door and opened it for her. After the final farewells had been made I noticed that the door remained open, my dad gripping the handle and staring at the floor.

'Dad . . . '

His stare swept from floor to ceiling, never for an instant landing on me. Well, if he wanted to stay in the huff we'd see how long that lasted. I walked past him. He caught my arm as I reached the threshold. 'I don't think you should come on Saturday,' he said.

I turned. 'She's my daughter.'

He moved his bulk closer, his face in my face. 'You should have realised that before you let them take her away.'

There would be no talking to him. Not tonight. I caught up with Vikki as she was opening the door of her car and laying her handbag on the passenger seat. 'Sorry,' she said. 'I didn't know your dad hadn't told you about the change of venue. It was all very last minute.'

'You don't have to stick up for him.'

'He's upset about Tina.'

'And blaming me.'

'It's understandable.'

'Which? Being upset or blaming me?'

Vikki put a hand on my shoulder. 'Tina's going to stay the night at your dad's. Vera's coming too and booking into a hotel. She'll take Tina home sometime on Sunday afternoon. There will be plenty of time for you to see her.' She forced a laugh. 'You can even come to the party and dook for apples.'

'About that,' I said. 'Halloween? I know it's Molly's birthday, but considering that her own mum is dead and her adopted mum was murdered . . . do you think it's appropriate, ghosts and witches and all that?'

Vikki hesitated.

'My dad?' I said.

'It was his idea. He went out and bought all the stuff

as soon as I told him. What could I say? He means well.'

'Hopeless, but means well. Like father like son?'

Vikki's tight smile made my question rhetorical. She walked around the other side of the car.

'I'm not giving up, you know.'

'I know,' she said. 'But sometimes it doesn't do any harm to take advice. Even if it comes from Barry Munn.'

'Barry's all right,' I said. 'If you can keep him away from the grape juice.' I formed the distinct impression that Vikki didn't agree. 'You've not forgiven him, then? Whatever it was you were so angry with him about. It still rankles, doesn't it?'

'I don't want to talk about it.' She opened the car door and climbed in behind the wheel. 'I'm sorry how things have turned out. Think about it this way. At least Tina has two people who care enough to battle for her. Think of Molly. How great would it be if someone actually wanted her and she didn't have to spend the rest of her childhood in care?' Vikki put the key in the ignition. 'So, will I maybe see you at the party?'

'I'm not on the guest list.'

'Let me work on your dad,' Vikki said. 'I'll talk him around. Don't go too far away Saturday afternoon and keep your phone switched on.'

44

Vikki's tail lights had no sooner rounded the corner and disappeared down the dark country road that meandered from my dad's cottage in the general direction of Linlithgow, than Jake Turpie called. The eagle hadn't so much landed as been snatched and bundled into the back of a Transit van.

Ten minutes later my own vehicle was trundling up a rough track to where Jake was waiting for me along with Tam, one of his regular workforce, a band of hard-living, hard-drinking men, whose names frequently graced the Sheriff Court's rolls of business. Tam had been elevated to the post of Deek's replacement. Something that Jake intended to be a temporary promotion. Personally, I thought it more likely to be a permanent appointment.

Between the two of them, legs stretched straight out in front, sitting on a car seat that had been ripped from some scrapped vehicle or other was what appeared to be a man, his head stuffed inside a grimy-yellow cloth bag secured by silver duct tape around his neck. The man's arms were wrapped either side of the seat, his wrists locked together at the back by an electrical cable-tie.

Jake took me aside. 'It's the Eyetie. I've got him. I had Tam stake out the hospital and grab him. So, what's the plan?'

'The plan? What are you talking about? I don't know

what your plan is. My plan is not to get involved in crazy stuff like this. You can't go about abducting folk off the street. You want us both to end up inside with Deek?'

As ever, Jake was having difficulty coming to terms with the fact that he wasn't a law unto himself. 'But this is him. This is the Tally that Deek speared. What was I supposed to do? Let him get away?'

'Yes, that's exactly what you should have done. Let him get away and have Tam follow him, find out where he lives. That way we maybe could have built up some sort of a case. Until we've got more evidence, all we've got is Deek's word for any of this. We've nothing to take to the cops. We can't even give a reason why your man here would want to murder Daisy Adams.'

For Jake the motive was obvious. 'Robbery gone wrong. We've all been there.'

'No, we haven't, Jake. And, anyway, what had Daisy Adams got that anyone would want to steal?'

'We'll soon find out,' Jake said. He turned, walked up the wooden steps to the door of Turpie International Salvage Ltd and rattled his fist on it. From inside came loud snarls and fierce barking. I'd wondered where his scrapyard mutt was hiding.

At the sound, the man in the seat struggled from side to side, straining his arms in his efforts to break free. With all the diplomacy of a wrecking-ball, Jake clumped back down, marched over and booted the back of the car seat. The man's thrashing around stopped. His breath came short and sharp, the cloth bag flattened to his face and then billowed out rapidly in quick succession.

'Would you stop that?' I had to shout at Jake to be heard over the racket his dog was making. 'And take that thing off his face. How's he supposed to talk if he can't breathe?'

262

Jake sagged his shoulders and, head cocked, looked sideways at me as though I was some sort of molly-coddler.

'And don't kick him again,' I said. If the man taped to the car seat was freshly discharged from hospital having sustained a punctured kidney, Jake's prescription of repeated steelies to the lumber region was not the therapeutic aftercare his medical team would have prescribed.

Jake whipped a knife out from a boiler suit pocket and proceeded to cut the tape around the man's neck. He ripped off the yellow bag to reveal a thin face, beneath a mop of curly dark hair all bunched up on top because of more silver tape wrapped around the man's forehead and over his eyes. Free from the bag, the man sucked in huge lungfuls of air, turned his head to the side and spat.

I hunkered down. 'Do you speak English?'

The man spat again. This time right in my face. I jumped to my feet, wiping the spit away.

'You want to try it my way now?' Jake asked.

With a face full of saliva, it was tempting to give Jake free rein. On the other hand, while I was all for preparing a successful defence for Deek Pudney, that did not extend to my being art and part in the torture of a potential witness. Instead, I took a couple of paces to where I thought I was safely out of spitting range, and asked again, 'English. Do you speak English?'

'English!' Jake shouted at him, adopting the kind of approach exercised by Sheriff Brechin towards those immigrant-accused unfortunate enough to find themselves in his court. Surely everyone understood English if the words were spoken clearly and loudly enough. 'Do you speak English!'

The man started to struggle again. I could sense Jake's pent-up anger. Hoping fear might have assisted the man's understanding of the language, I had another go. 'Just tell us what we want to know and no one's going to harm you.'

Nothing.

Jake climbed to his cabin again, opened the door and stood back. Like its owner, the dog wasn't big, but compact and solid and every inch as evil. It took a cautious step onto the landing, looked at us all through pale eyes and trotted down the stairs, growling every step of the way.

'Stay!' Jake roared, once it had reached the bottom of the flight. The dog froze. Jake disappeared into the cabin for a moment and returned with an open tin of dog food. 'Take his shirt off.' Without question, his assistant went over and with much ripping and pinging of buttons, tore the shirt from the man in the car seat.

Jake tramped down the steps, dug a hand into the can of dog food and smeared it across the man's bare chest. The terrified man's head swung from side to side as he strained on the electrical tie that kept him secured to the car seat. Jake said nothing. No words were necessary. Jake had the gift of universal language. He was saying in his own way, 'now would be a good time to remember that you speak English.'

A snap of his fingers and the dog was at Jake's side. He took it by the scruff of the neck and brought the snarling snout level with the man's ear.

'You can't do this!' I shouted.

Slitty-eyes fixed on the man in the car seat, Jake pushed the dog's face closer to the man's. 'You said we need him to tell us why that Daisy Adams woman was killed. He's going to tell us.' Jake let go of the dog's neck. It stood there, shivering in anticipation. Waiting for its master's voice. 'Trust me. If he knows anything, he's going to want to tell us it in about ten seconds. Nine, eight . . . '

The man might not speak English, but he knew a count-down when he heard one. By the count of five his struggles were so violent that the car seat toppled sideways.

Jake paused at three. His assistant righted the seat.

'Two . . . '

I jumped in between prisoner and dog. 'I'm warning you, Jake. I'm not letting this happen.'

Jake, all clenched teeth and fists, begged to differ.

'Whoah! Look at this!,' Tam yelled, and rubbed away some of the dog food to reveal a tattoo situated directly over the man's heart: a navy-blue, two-headed eagle.

A snap of Jake's fingers sent the dog back up the stairs and into the cabin. He shuffled forward and bent over for a closer look. 'What is it?'

'It's a gang tattoo,' Tam said. 'I was dubbed up with one of these guys when I was in Spanish jail. He's mafia. He'll never talk and if his mob find out we've got him, they'll kill the lot of us.'

'That's that then,' Jake said. He kicked a lever at the side of the chair and it reclined. Quickly. Jake was on him in an instant, sitting astride the man's chest, hammering in blow after blow. I grabbed hold of Jake and wrenched him back by the shoulders. 'Stop! You're going to kill him.'

Jake climbed off the man to confront me. 'What do you want me to do? Call him a taxi?' He pointed down at the man in the car seat who was now blowing bloody bubbles from a deformed nose. 'If we let him go what do you think he's going to do?'

Jake drew back a steel toe-capped boot. I shoved him, knocking him off balance. He spun around, face bright red, the deep furrows in his brow livid-white. Tam rushed forward as though his boss might need assistance. I squared up to the two of them. 'Would you listen to me? We need him alive. So what, he's got a tattoo? Big deal. He doesn't know who we are. How can he? His head's been in a bag for the last two hours. He doesn't know who we are or where he is. Thanks to you and Tam, we're in a dodgy situation already. Let's not make things any worse.'

'Oh, yeah? What do you suggest smart-arse?' Jake replied in response to the outlandish notion that we didn't beat the prisoner to death.

'What I suggest,' I said, 'is that we do this my way.'

'And that would be?'

'Have you any write-offs that are still driveable?'

Jake jerked a thumb at a row of bashed cars on the far side of the yard.

'Good,' I said. 'Put our friend in one and let's take him for a drive.'

45

'It's called stalking,' Hugh Ogilvie said, not looking around as I slipped into the queue behind him. 'They've brought in a whole new law about it. Section 39 of the Criminal Justice and Licensing (Scotland) Act Two thousand and something. You should read it sometime.'

'It's hardly stalking, Hugh. I like coffee, you like coffee. Why wouldn't we bump into each other now and again?'

'Two days in a row?'

'Purely coincidental. Mine's an Americano, by the way.'

Mine wasn't to be an Americano. At least not an Americano paid for by the Crown. If I'd stayed to buy my own, Ogilvie would have been off and safely behind the door of his office before I'd had a chance to count my change so, coffeeless, I tailed him out of the shop and along the mall walkway.

'I heard you've caught the man who stole one of my client's cars last night,' I said. 'They tell me he's Italian. Drink-driver, was he? What else have you got him on? Careless or dangerous, obviously. Did he stop at the scene?'

'Oh, he stopped all right,' Ogilvie said, as he came to the exit, lemon and poppy-seed muffin in one hand, cardboard cup of coffee in the other. He allowed me to pull open the big glass door for him. 'He was stopped right up against a wall the other side of a bus shelter.'

'Seat belt?'

'Doesn't seem like it, He's bashed-up and spent the night in hospital.'

'Thought as much, no seat belt. That's section fourteen. Drink-driving and dangerous driving, Sections 5 and 2. He won't have had insurance, 143. Stolen car? Has to be a 178 at least. What about a licence?' Ogilvie didn't reply, just speeded up his walk. 'There you are then. Lob in a Section 87 and that's bound to be the best RTA bingo card the Fiscal's office has had in a long time.'

Ogilvie stopped walking, turned and faced me. 'What do you want?'

'Yesterday you tell me that the man my client is supposed to have killed—'

'Murdered.'

'Okay, the man my client is supposed to have murdered – was Italian. Now you've got another Italian stealing cars and crashing into bus stops.'

'So?'

'So, I want to know who he is and, as you told me yesterday, you've got the Interpol connections to find out. While you're at it, you might want to check his DNA with the prongs of a garden fork Scene of Crime bagged and tagged up at Sunnybrae Farm.'

Ogilvie looked from me to his coffee, weighing up whether continuing the conversation was worth the risk of a cold cappuccino. Apparently it wasn't.

And while you're at it, check for any tattoos that might link him to an organised crime gang.'

'How do you know about that?'

Had I struck a nerve? It was worth a gamble just to see Ogilvie's reaction. 'The dead guy at Sunnybrae Farm. He had a tattoo, didn't he?'

Ogilvie pushed the cake into his pocket, pulled the lid off his coffee cup and had a sip. The foam stuck to his top lip. His silence was enough of an answer.

'It's nothing that wouldn't have been disclosed to me by the Crown, I'm sure,' I said. 'In the fullness of time.'

'Joanna Jordan,' he said.

'What about her?'

'It's her, isn't it? She's getting inside information from her old pals in my office.'

'No,' I said. 'She's definitely not. I haven't even seen her today.'

'Then how do you know about the Italian?'

'I have my sources.'

Ogilvie grunted, drank some more coffee.

'You know what this means, don't you?' I said.

'No.' He replaced the lid on his cup. 'But I have this horrible feeling you're going to tell me.'

'It was a hit. The mob didn't turn up at Daisy Adams' back door to ask if she needed a spot of weeding done.'

Ogilvie slapped his broad forehead with the hand not holding the coffee. 'Of course not. How stupid of me not to have realised this all along. The mafia had a contract out on Daisy the farmer. Seriously, Robbie, I liked your alibi defence better.'

'The alibi was just a misunderstanding. A mix-up over dates.'

'No, it wasn't. It was a lie. An attempt to pervert the course of justice.'

'Hugh, could you try and focus on what's important? And I don't mean your coffee and bun. Can't you see? The day Deek Pudney went to the farm he was there on legitimate business and found himself in a situation where he had to defend himself.'

'He's an enforcer. He's an employee of Jake Turpie and he was there to collect a debt for his boss.'

'And what would be the point of killing the debtor? How does Jake get paid then? Ask the person to leave the money in their will?'

'Killing non-payers sends a message to anyone else who thinks they might fall behind with instalments.' Ogilvie pulled the lid off his coffee again, had another mouthful. 'For all we know, the Italians were in on it with Pudney and they fell out over money or something.'

'Would you listen to yourself, Hugh? Deek Pudney doesn't need to take two gangsters with him to put the squeeze on a woman about late car payments. He was there on business, was attacked in the process and killed one of the people who'd murdered Daisy Adams. Summary justice, it saves you all the hassle of a trial and no expensive jail time either. I thought you'd appreciate it. You should be striking a medal, not prosecuting him.'

The PF wiped froth from his face. 'Oh, so he's a hero?'

'He might have been if he'd arrived earlier. It's just unfortunate he arrived too late to save Daisy.'

Ogilvie pressed the plastic lid back onto his coffee cup. 'I'll look forward to you leading that defence at trial. The jury should find it quite amusing. Especially considering that we don't know if this other Italian was even there.'

'Not yet we don't,' I said, 'but check the fork.'

46

'Option three?' Barry Munn pursed his lips and blew, scratching the back of his head like a builder who's just been asked to knock down a supporting wall. 'Tricky.'

I thought that while I was in Livingston I might as well drop in on my family lawyer and make sure he was giving my custody case the urgent attention it deserved. With superb timing I'd walked into his office just as he was showing a client out and he'd agreed to give me ten minutes of his precious time over lunch. He'd already poured it.

'I know it's not going to be easy, I just want to know what I've got to do to win?'

'These lunchtime visits are becoming something of a habit,' he said, 'and we've been over it all before. I still think you should go for option two. Regular contact, but with Mrs Reynolds having full residence. Even that's not certain to be agreed, but, if it is, you'll have the best of both worlds. You remain footloose and fancy-free and still see your daughter. Think of it. No homework, night-time toothache, laundry, no nagging her about what she's wearing, her choice of friends, no "what time do you call this to be coming in at?" None of that stuff. You're the guy who turns up at the weekend, takes Tina off to do something nice before returning her. It's like being a grandparent, but in reverse. Perfect for the single man.'

'Barry, listen to me. I want to be there for Tina when she's growing up. I want to help with her homework, nurse her toothache—'

'Do the laundry, ironing?'

'Girls get the hang of that sort of thing pretty quickly, don't they?'

Barry shook his head. 'You asked for ten minutes and if you wore a watch you'd know you've had half of them.' He took a restorative slug of wine. 'If you really want to go all out for custody then you either need to talk Mrs Reynolds around . . . ' that wasn't happening in a hurry, 'or have Vikki Stark write you the child welfare report of a lifetime. How are things between the two of you anyway?'

'Fine, and I mean that both professionally and extremely platonically. I saw her last night at my dad's. They're gearing up for the big party.'

'Why is Vikki arranging your dad's party?'

'It's not for my dad. It's for Tina's friend Molly. You know, Daisy Adams' daughter.'

Barry scowled. 'What's Vikki been saying about me?' He stood up, walked over to his window and looked out.

'Nothing.' I thought I'd leave it at that. Whatever his problems with Vikki, I didn't want to know. I had enough of my own. 'Right, I'll be off then. I'll catch up with Vikki, turn up the Robbie Munro charm full blast and talk her into a stoater of a report.'

'Do that,' Barry grumbled, still gazing out at the rain-drenched Scottish landscape and no doubt wishing it was the sun-drenched vineyards of La Mancha.

I walked to the door.

'When is it?' he asked.

'When's what?'

'The party.'

'Saturday afternoon. Halloween'

'At least it will be a chance for you to see Tina.'

'It would be if I was invited.'

'Vera Reynolds going?'

'It's BYOB,' I said. 'Bring your own broomstick.'

'Then I take it Vikki's going too?'

'She's bringing Molly.'

'How is the girl? She's autistic, isn't she? That business with Daisy . . . ' by which he meant the brutal slaying of Molly's mum-to-be, 'does she even understand what happened?'

'I think she understands a lot more than she lets on,' I said. 'And she'll be wondering what's going to happen to her now that Daisy's gone.' Being Molly's mum was a dangerous business. Could the wee girl dare hope for a third time lucky?

Barry walked across the room to see me out. 'Think carefully before you do anything rash,' he said. 'Vikki Stark is not someone who easily forgives and forgets. I should know. Remember, option two is still very much a goer. Don't do anything to spoil your chances. Get on the wrong side of Miss Stark and your only contact with your daughter will be swapping Christmas cards.'

47

It was hardly worth going back to the office. I returned home and spent the early part of Friday afternoon plittering about, always in the back of my mind the nagging thought that I had things I should be doing. When Tina was with me there had been juice spills to wipe up, meals to make, games to play and skint knees needing kissed. Now she was gone, I had nothing to do. Had it been like this before? So much time on my hands.

I sat down at the kitchen table. My dad had left an unfinished crossword puzzle. One question left unanswered. He'd be expecting to come back to it. He was probably turning the clue over in his brain right now, trying to figure it out. Five across, five letters, HIJKLMNO, beginning with W ending in R. What kind of a clue was that? I should crumple the newspaper and toss it in the bucket. That would really annoy him. But not as much as it would if I solved the answer for him. I gave the clue a few minutes' thought and gave up. I had my own puzzle to solve. Who killed Daisy Adams? I took up a pen and in the margin of the newspaper jotted down all the reasons I could think of why the woman would have been murdered. First up: revenge. Her ex-husband. The florist hadn't seemed like the vindictive type to me. Not a man you'd want to mess with, true, but he'd seemed genuinely at peace with himself. Then again, a lot of murderers were easy-going. Some of them because they had murdered the one person in their life who really bugged them.

Alcohol. In my experience murders were usually arguments that escalated; more often than not, after drink had been taken. And yet the toxicology results on Daisy and the dead man's body fluids were negative for ethanol. Rule out revenge and drink and what was left?

Money. Jake had thought it a robbery gone wrong. What did Daisy Adams have worth stealing if she was so skint she'd fallen behind in her payments for a second-hand car? Unless that was just another of my landlord's lies. If money was the motive, someone must have benefited financially from the lady farmer's death, but who? What had Daisy owned that was worth someone killing her? The farm that she'd bought both literally and metaphorically? It was nothing more than an old building, a few acres of scrubland and some geriatric livestock. The only actual money I could remotely connect her to was the wad of cash I'd received from the late Sir Stephen Pentecost's right-hand man and which was now resting comfortably in my office safe. Daisy Adams had been in possession of Zander's phone number. It was the only number on her phone and he'd been happy to hand over to me what turned out to be £25,000 in cash, no questions asked. Why? Who did he think I was? I remembered his words, 'We weren't supposed to meet.' Why not? Whoever he thought I was, why weren't we supposed to meet? If you hired a hit man did you need to meet the assassin? It could leave a trail and seriously complicate matters if you did, and there were other more secure ways of communicating than face-to-face. Like a mobile phone. Was it even Daisy's phone I'd found?

I got up from the table, pushing the newspaper and unfinished crossword aside. Zander wasn't the answer to my puzzle, but he was the best clue available. I had to find him.

I called Mar Hall. He wasn't taking calls. No one from the House of Pentecost was. Dame Ursula and her entourage were packed and all set to check out in the morning. Before that they'd be celebrating the end of their fortnight-long fashion-shoot with a party at a nightclub in Glasgow. The club was called Diamond Dave's. It was invitation only. I really needed to get in and there was only one man I knew who could open the door for me.

48

'Robbie, it's half past nine. I was working today and I'm just back from five-a-sides. I thought I'd have a quiet one.'

Which, translated, meant that he'd been blethering a lot of rubbish on his radio football phone-in for an hour or so, played a game of football with some of his pals, most of whom could hardly run the length of themselves unless it was last orders at the bar, and he was now wanting to crack open a few frosty ones and crash out in front of the telly.

I walked past him into the well-appointed Glasgow city centre apartment that his weekly sports punditry somehow managed to support. 'A quiet one? It's Friday night. What happened to my brother Malky the party animal?'

Invitation or not, Malky was welcome on any licensed premises in Glasgow. Well, perhaps not some in the east end that had shamrock motifs on the signage, but footballers were royalty in Glasgow, especially legends from the Old Firm and if anyone could blag our way into the Pentecost party it was my brother.

'What happened was that I turned forty last month and much more recently someone gave me a dead leg.' He rubbed a thigh. 'I can hardly walk.'

'You could hardly run, but it never stopped you being a footballer. Come on, Malky. This is really important. Do this and I'll definitely owe you one.'

'Has this got anything to do with your work?'

' . . . sort of.'

'Then definitely no.'

'Listen, it's about that murder case. The one up past East Riggburn. I'm acting for Jake Turpie and you know what he's like. He's never going to believe my investigations have been stymied because you refused to go out partying on a Friday night.'

Malky grunted. 'A murder in East Riggburn? Why bother? Even CSI Miami couldn't solve that. There's nobody up there with any dental records and their DNA's bound to all be about the same.'

I gave him my best laugh. 'Are you coming then?'

'Robbie . . . '

'It's going to be full of fashion models.'

' . . . Go on.'

'It's Ursula Pentecost's party. It's at somewhere called Diamond Dave's. It'll be swarming with girls dying to meet the great Malky Munro.' Was my brother big-headed enough to believe that? Of course he was. He'd have been thinking the exact same thing before I'd even said it.

He left the room, returning in a remarkably short time wearing a black silk shirt, a sharp shiny-grey suit and too much cologne.

'You going like that?' he asked, looking me up and down.

'What's wrong with jeans and a T-shirt?' I said. 'It's a timeless combination.'

He grabbed a trouser leg and pulled, almost toppling me over. 'Is that blood?'

I wrenched my leg away and studied what looked to be a splash of red paint from one of Tina's art sessions. 'It'll come off with a bit of a scrub.'

It didn't.

Luckily I owned a suit for every day of the week. I'd brought it with me in the car just in case Malky didn't approve of my preferred ensemble. I put it on over a borrowed white shirt, no tie. Malky still wasn't happy, but I was going to have to do.

'Leave this to me,' he said when we pitched up outside the door of the nightclub to be met by two men in formal evening wear and heavy black coats, one at the mouth of the silver canopy leading off the pavement, the other standing further back at the front door.

'Evening gents,' said the nearer of the two, a Cockney.

'Evening,' Malky said. 'Could you do me a favour?'

'What's that then?'

'Nip inside and tell them they can start the party. I've arrived.' Smiling, my brother stepped forward and immediately bumped into the flat of the bouncer's outstretched hand.

'Name?'

'Really?'

'Yeah,' said the bouncer. 'Really.'

Sensing there might be a problem, the other dinner-suit marched down to meet us. He stopped a few feet away and peered at my brother. Realisation dawned slowly. 'Ho, look who it is. Malky?' Glaswegian accent. 'Malky Munro, how's it going?'

'Better late than never, eh?' Malky said. He jerked a thumb over his shoulder at me. 'My agent. I was going to give it a miss, but he insisted I come along.'

'Listen, Malky,' said the Weegie bouncer. 'Your name's not on the door list. I woulda noticed.'

Malky laughed. 'That's all right, I can lend you a pen and you can write it in.'

The bouncer laughed too and then was serious. 'If it was down to me I would, but security is rock solid the night. This place is full of super-totty and celebs.'

'That thing work?' Malky pointed at the Bluetooth headset in bouncer's ear. 'Give one of the Pentecosts a shout on it.'

'You mean the one who ain't dead?' Cockney said. He gave Malky a shove. 'Go on, beat it.'

A red sports car pulled up at the kerb and its doors opened to an accompaniment of bright flashes.

'Where were the paparazzi when I arrived?' Malky wanted to know.

'Waiting for someone famous,' the Cockney bouncer said, trying to usher us out from beneath the canopy towards the pavement. 'Beat it. If your name's not on the sheet, you're out on the street.'

'How long did it take you to think that up, Shakespeare?' Malky sneered, standing his ground. 'Bet you've been waiting all night to use that line on someone.'

Cockney growled.

'Easy, easy,' the Weegie bouncer intervened, 'I'll check with Mr Skene. If he says Mr Munro's in, he's in. Okay? We all happy with that?'

Cockney gave a reluctant shrug and took a step back, not lifting his malevolent gaze from Malky.

Mr Skene? That was Zander. I didn't want him to know I was here. Not yet. I needed the element of surprise.

'Malky!'

My brother and I turned around to come face-to-face with Joey Di Rollo – like my brother, another has-been footballer. Unlike my brother, a very rich has-been foot-baller. Joey's career had spanned a good number of years and he'd been the subject of more transfers than an Airfix

Spitfire. Malky's professional career had been cut short by injury and he'd stayed with the same club the whole time. At the end of their respective playing days, both Joey and Malky had invested a lot of money in pubs and clubs, but while Joey had gone for bricks and mortar, Malky had been more interested in purchasing liquid stock. That was why Malky was out with his brother, while at Joey's side, looking more gorgeous than ever, if that were possible, was my former chauffeur, balanced on a pair of high heels, her lithe body encapsulated in a flimsy garment that was no protection from a cold October night.

'Who's this?' Joey asked, after he and Malky had shaken hands and slapped backs.

'The man with no fashion sense is my brother,' Malky said.

I put out a hand. None came in my direction.

'Oh, is that right?' Joey made a face like a fist and stepped right up to me. 'This your brother, is it?' We were about the same height. His forehead touched mine.

The cockney bouncer was straight in there. Hands like shovels pushed us apart.

'Hold on,' Malky said. 'If this is about Robbie and your girlfriend, that was all a mistake. You know what Wee Gus is like. They don't pay him to wash football kit because he's got a degree in rocket-surgery.'

Grudgingly, and with the assistance of the Cockney bouncer, Joey backed off, still glaring at me.

'I told you that, Joe,' said the gorgeous one. In a flap of diaphanous material she flounced past the door staff and into the club unhindered. If you looked like she did, no one bothered to check if your name was on a list.

'That's you on a yellow card,' I said to Joey. 'Make a change from all those straight reds you collected.'

It wasn't funny, it wasn't meant to be, and it didn't help matters a lot. Joey threw a punch that was intercepted by Cockney like a weak baseball pitch into a catcher's mitt. Unfortunately, in doing so, the bouncer's elbow caught Malky in the face. He doubled over and soon blood began trickling through the gaps in his fingers.

A flash of bright light.

'Now the buggers want to take my photo,' Malky muttered.

'Get them inside,' roared the Weegie, his SIA licence no doubt flashing before his eyes. He knew how this would look in the morning papers. Two famous ex-footballers battling it out on the very doorstep he'd been paid to guard.

Three seconds later Joey, Malky and I were being pushed up the steps and through the doors of Diamond Dave's into an overly warm foyer with silver walls, a silver ceiling and some kind of silver-laminated flooring. It was like being inside a microwave oven. I was expecting the floor to revolve at any second.

The bouncers presented us to another dinner-suited man who was standing at a chrome lectern. He was older, slimmer, face bronzed and moisturised, less Marine Corps more Diplomatic Corps. He nodded to the grunts and they returned to their stations without a word.

I gave Malky my hanky. 'I want to speak to whoever's in charge,' I said, before anyone else could say anything.

The man with the tan smiled a calming smile. Unlike Weegie and Cockney, he was there to handle not manhandle the punters. 'Let's all settle down, shall we?' He took a look at Malky, hanky pressed against his nose. 'Now, Sir, do you require medical treatment?'

Malky removed the hanky, dabbed it once or twice

against his face to check that the blood was drying up and then shook his head.

'Good. He turned to Joey Di Rollo. 'I don't think we need detain you further, Mr Di Rollo.'

'Eh?'

'You can join the party,' the doorman clarified.

With a slap to Malky's back and a sideways glower at me, the ex-footballer sauntered off in the direction of the thumping bass line of a techno track.

'Now then Mr . . . '

'Munro, Malky Munro.'

'Mr Munro, let me show you to a room where you can freshen up,' the doorman said, and he led us down a side corridor into a small dressing room. A large mirror faced us, LED lights around its perimeter and a shelf crowded by bottles of lotion and bags of cotton-balls. After he'd finished pointing out the sink and some white towels he made to leave.

'Not so fast,' I said. I pointed a finger at my brother's bloody nose. 'This man is a former employee and personal friend of Dame Ursula Pentecost. He invited me along and when I arrived, firstly, I was accosted by another guest while the door staff stood back and did nothing, then when my brother intervened on my behalf he got a bouncer's elbow in his face for his trouble. Correct me if I'm wrong, but after all that, you seem to think he should settle for a sink to bleed into?'

'Well . . . '

'I don't think so. Get the manager. No, in fact, I want to speak to Mr Skene. If he's organised this do, he should know what's happened and apologise in person.'

The doorman weighed up the situation for a moment and then left with a curt, 'Wait here.'

I waited a full ten minutes, trying to keep a lid on Malky who, face washed, was now raring to go. For him the bump on the nose was a small price to pay for entry. Voices in the corridor. I ducked behind the door as it opened and Zander was shown into the small room wearing a cream suit with wide lapels. The thick-framed sunglasses were missing.

'I am so terribly sorry for what's happened, Mr Munro,' he effused, having obviously been briefed en route. As he homed in on my brother, I stepped out and into the doorway, thanked the doorman and said we'd take things from here on, closing the door after him.

Still smiling, Zander turned to see who else was present in the room and in the instant it took for him to recognise me and his friendly expression to change to one of abject fear, I had a hand across his mouth and was forcing him up against a wall.

'Stop it,' Malky hissed. 'What do you think you're doing?'

'Shut it,' I said. 'I told you I was here on business. Now get outside that door and make sure I'm not disturbed.' He hesitated. 'Now!'

When Malky had gone, I manoeuvred Zander to the stool in front of the big mirror and forced him down onto it. 'I only want to talk, but one squeak from you and I'll . . . ' I looked around for some kind of weapon to threaten him with. Other than face cream and cotton wool there was nothing. 'Understand?'

Fortunately, it seemed he did. Slowly I withdrew my hand, ready to clamp it back over his mouth at the first sign of a cry for help. None came.

'Right,' I said, 'I'll make this quick.' A dark patch had developed in the groin area of the cream suit. 'Would you stop that? I'm not here to hurt you.' I realised how unlikely that must have sounded. I selected a big fluffy white towel and threw it in his lap.

Zander wiped tears from his eyes with the corner of the towel that he hadn't clamped to his groin. If this was the man who'd arranged for the murder of Daisy Adams, then he deserved all he got. By now Jake would have been feeding him light bulbs or squashing his fingers with a mash hammer. For the moment I had fear on my side. I had to use that and be quick. Soon enough someone would wonder where the host had got to.

'Do you know who I am?' I asked.

Zander had come to meet me at the warehouse with a wad of cash and handed it over assuming I was somebody I wasn't. If, for what reason I still had no idea, he had organised the hit on Daisy, he must have known that one of the assassins was dead – the murders at Sunnybrae Farm had been widely reported. That meant he would also know that one of the assassins was still at large. Did Zander think that was me?

Zander nodded, then shook his head, then nodded again.

I tried another tack. 'Who do you think I am?'

He sobbed and took in a big gulp of air, then another and another. He was starting to hyperventilate. I ran some cold water in the sink, cupped my hands under the flow and threw it in his face. It didn't compare with smearing dog food on his chest and threatening him with a hellhound, but then I wasn't dealing with an Italian gangster. Zander would probably have been just as terrified if he knew I was wearing navy-blue socks with my charcoal suit.

At the impact of the water, he sat bolt upright as though

I'd hurled acid, the scared look for a moment transforming into one of angry petulance.

'I paid you your money!' he shouted.

I clamped my hand over his mouth and pointed a finger at him. 'Keep the noise down. Understand?'

He stared at me for a second or two and then nodded. I took my hand away. 'Good. Then let's talk about the money. Why did you give it to me?'

Zander looked at me narrowly. The brain behind those teary eyes whirred. He had to wonder why I'd be asking such a stupid question.

I clenched a fist and held it right where he could see it. 'Tell me.'

For just a moment it looked as though he might, and then the door burst open. Into the room, crutches first, came Ursula Pentecost, all yellow taffeta and lace under-skirts. Behind her the tanned doorman and behind him Malky.

'Right then, I'll just away and leave you to sort things out,' my brother said to no one in particular. 'Nice to see you again ... Mrs ... Dame ... Ursula ... ' he tailed off and disappeared.

Ursula Pentecost leaned on one crutch, pointing the leg of the other directly in my face. 'Got you!' she said. 'Right, this time I want to know exactly what is going on.'

Zander's attempt at a protest was cut off when the crutch-leg swung in his direction and the rubber stopper planted itself in his chest.

'Not here,' Ursula said. She lowered the crutch, performed a clumsy pirouette and hobbled out again.

The doorman crooked a finger at us, and like a pair of naughty schoolboys we followed him, Zander still clutching the towel to his groin, out of the door and further along the same corridor to a much larger and more extravagantly furnished room; Diamond Dave's personal quarters I presumed, whoever and wherever he was.

At that moment I could have just left. What could anyone do if I insisted on leaving the party I'd gatecrashed? I hadn't broken any laws, unless throwing water in your host's face was a crime. But I decided to stay. I wanted to winkle out a lot more information from Zander and had a feeling that where I had failed Dame Ursula might succeed.

'Let me help you with those.' I caught Dame Ursula's crutches as she lowered herself onto a cream chaise-longue. Though there were other equally comfortable-looking seats in the room I had a feeling the rest of us were expected to stand.

Once she had flattened her frock and got herself settled, Dame Ursula dismissed the doorman with a regal wave of the hand.

'Zander, you have some explaining to do,' she said, once the man with the tan had left, closing the door behind him. 'First, you meet a strange man in an empty warehouse, now in a cupboard. Stephen's barely been dead a month and already you're putting some kind of plan into action. What is it? A takeover bid? Is it not enough that he left you one-quarter of the business? What scheme are you hatching?'

She turned an accusing eye in my direction.

'Don't look at me,' I said, 'I'd like to know what scheme he's hatching too.'

Dame Ursula leaned back, layers of lacy underskirts billowing her yellow dress about her. 'You can stop the innocent act now, Mr Munro. I know you're in on this. And to think you nearly had me believing all that murder investigation nonsense.'

Zander leapt back as though someone had plugged him into the mains. He dropped the towel. The dark stain remained in his groin and had spread south. 'I had nothing to do with any murder.'

'Is that right?' I said. 'You had nothing to do with a woman who was strangled to death in her own home? Her daughter left terrified and living in squalor for a week. You don't know anything about that?'

'Don't be ridiculous. That had absolutely nothing to do with me.'

'She had a mobile phone,' I said. 'It had only one number on it – yours.'

Zander didn't respond so I continued. 'I still have the phone.' I took it out of my suit pocket and tossed it into Dame Ursula's lap. 'I should have handed it over to the police, but I don't trust them to keep as open a mind about things as I do. They've got my client locked up and are unlikely to place much store in anything that doesn't point to his guilt. I, on the other hand, find it all very strange.'

Dame Ursula extricated the phone from the folds of bright-yellow fabric and examined it carefully. She tapped the screen and scrolled through the call logs. It didn't take long. One final tap and the strains of a musical ringtone could be heard emanating from Zander's suit pocket.

'Why are you doing this?' Zander asked me. 'We had a deal.'

I had to disagree. 'No, we didn't. You had a deal with someone, but it wasn't with me. I don't kill women and terrify children. I am a—'

'You're a lawyer!' Zander screamed, face crimson, a bright-blue blood vessel proud on his forehead. 'What happened was supposed to be done in the strictest confidence. You know fine well that was the arrangement. What is it?' he sneered. 'You've had your money and now you want more, so you're piecing together a story linking me with the murder of Daisy Adams in order to blackmail me?' He turned to the Dame. 'That's what this is, don't you see? This man is nothing but a shakedown artist.' If he was seeking support from his boss he wasn't finding any. 'You've got to believe me, Ursula. I've done nothing wrong. This man is making everything up. He wants money or he aims to blacken the name of the House of Pentecost.'

Dame Ursula reached out a hand to me and let me help her to her feet. She hobbled over to where her crutches were propped against the wall. 'I'd like to believe you, Zander,' she said, putting her hands through the grey plastic arm-supports. 'But there's just one tiny thing bothering me.' She walked up to the young man and stared him in the eye. 'I don't recall Mr Munro mentioning the name of the murdered woman. So how do you know it?'

Zander held his hands out by his sides to steady himself, like a man on his first day at surfing school. I thought for a moment he was going to faint. I grabbed him. He pushed me away. Beads of sweat had gathered in the roots of his hair. One or two ruptured and began to trickle down his broad and rapidly paling forehead. He wiped them away with the back of a hand. 'I need a drink,' he croaked.

'You need a fresh pair of trousers too,' Dame Ursula said, pushing past him and propelling herself towards a drinks cabinet in the corner of the room. Leaning on one crutch she filled a tall glass with ice, poured a shot of gin over it, added a dash of Angostura bitters and topped it up with tonic. 'Mr Munro? What'll you have?'

Seeing how she was asking, I walked over to view

what there was in the way of single-malt and settled for a Benromach ten-year-old; in my dad's humble opinion the best-value malt out there, and for him to say that about a spirit not distilled on his beloved Islay was praise indeed.

'I take it yours is a vodka martini?' she asked the man in the damp trousers, pushing the cork back into the neck of the whisky bottle. 'Sorry, we're out of olives.'

But the young man seemed to have lost his thirst. 'Munro . . . ' he said. 'Did you call him Munro? I thought his name was Munn. Barry Munn.'

49

The bottle of ten-year-old Highland malt was one hour older and a couple of inches shallower by the time Zander had finished his own drink, sent out for a change of clothes and finished putting things straight with his boss.

Dame Ursula had asked for the truth and had been given it, both barrels at close range. Her husband was a womaniser. The quickest way to get on the front cover of a fashion magazine was to go under the covers with Sir Stephen.

At first Dame Ursula wouldn't believe it. She knew all about La-La Delgado. The affair had threatened their marriage and nearly brought down the House of Pentecost. Stephen would never have dared run such a risk again.

Oh yes he would. I listened intently as strip by strip Zander peeled away the layers of intrigue and disguise that had been the clandestine love life of Stephen Pentecost, reeling off a list of names, each one a razor-slash to Dame Ursula's self-esteem. She might have thought her husband had trespassed just the one time; that was because she'd only managed to catch him once. The reason she was unaware of the scores of others was largely down to Zander, who for years had been tasked with concealing Sir Stephen's indiscretions from both the public and his wife. He'd bribed hotel staff, eased the pain of jilted lovers with jewellery and bought the silence of over-inquisitive journalists with extravagant nights out and trips to exotic locations.

Over a few drinks Dame Ursula's initial denial turned to disbelief and, eventually, acceptance. The woman in the bright-yellow gown who had earlier blazed at us like some kind of angry sun-goddess, now sat on the chaise-longue, a wilted daffodil.

'And where does Barry Munn fit into all this?' I asked.

Zander seemed much more relaxed in his recently delivered clothes, a dark grey suit and lilac shirt. He walked over to the drinks cabinet and poured his boss another stiff one. 'Most of Stephen's . . . well, most of them were one-night stands. Sometimes they'd last a week or two if we were off on a shoot. Usually, the girls knew the score. There was nothing permanent about the arrangements. Stephen never left them in any doubt about that. La-La was different. He became infatuated, careless. I couldn't buy off everyone who owned a camera. It was just a matter of time. The best I could do was leak the story the day after the General Election. It got some coverage. Nothing like it would have on a slow-news day.'

Zander mixed himself another drink and sat down beside his boss. 'You think it was you who drove La-La away?' he said, handing her a tall glass. 'It wasn't. It was me.'

'How could you?' she said. 'After all I've done for you. Why didn't you tell me this was going on?'

Zander's laugh was as dry as his martini. 'Honestly? I didn't think you'd want to know.'

'You didn't think I'd want to know that my husband

292

was cheating on me with the owners of every pair of legs that strutted our catwalk?'

'Your not knowing kept you and Stephen together, kept the House of Pentecost standing . . . and there was something else.' Suddenly the young man didn't look so young. 'La-La was going to have a baby.'

Dame Ursula's body went rigid at the news.

Zander put a comforting arm around her shoulders. 'Stephen didn't know. If he had, he would have encouraged La-La to have it. I booked her into a private and very discreet clinic in Switzerland.'

'She had the baby. You know that, don't you?' I said. 'A wee girl called Molly.'

Dame Ursula stared into her drink.

Zander tightened his arm around her. 'The minute the thing was born La-La tried to put the squeeze on Stephen. I intercepted her call. She thought she could blackmail him, screw him for money for herself and the child for evermore. I told her it would never work. The minute Stephen's name went on the birth certificate, he'd have had the lawyers onto it.'

You didn't need to be an expert in family law to guess how the case of Pentecost v Delgado would have gone. Rich Establishment Figure v Junkie Mum. Not so much a custody battle as a massacre.

Dame Ursula knocked back her drink in one go. 'How can you be so sure the child is his?'

Zander took the empty glass from her. 'I had tests carried out. Told Stephen we needed a blood sample to check on his cholesterol level. It's his all right. After that I explained to La-La in words of one syllable that if news got out, the child would be taken from her. She had a choice to make. She chose to keep the baby and to keep quiet about it. For her discretion, I kept her on the House of Pentecost payroll with a small monthly retainer.'

The more Zander explained, the more admiration I had for him. After the car crash in the Highlands Sir Stephen had lain in a coma for months while the doctors tried everything they could to save him. After a time it became apparent that no more could be done and it was just a matter of deciding when to turn off the life support, something his wife had tried to delay indefinitely. Dame Ursula had been a basket case throughout much of her husband's hospitalisation. Sir Stephen was dying, she couldn't walk and there was only Zander keeping their business alive. That was when the issue of Molly's parentage had arisen once again, though, by this time, La-La had been dead for a few years.

'I thought that when La-La died, the identity of the child's father had died with her.' Dame Ursula declined Zander's offer of a refill and let him continue. 'Then,' he said, 'during Stephen's last days, I received a call from the Adams woman to say that when he died, the child would have a claim on his estate.'

'Nonsense.' Dame Ursula was starting to pull herself together. 'Stephen left a will. I'm sure you're very familiar with its terms, Zander, since he left one-quarter of his share in the House of Pentecost to you.'

Zander looked at me invitingly.

'In Scots law there are such things as legal rights,' I said. 'They take priority over a will. I suppose the idea is to stop parents cutting their children out of an inheritance.'

Suddenly Dame Ursula seemed less distressed and a lot more alarmed. 'How much?'

'One-third of the moveables,' I said.

'And those are?'

'Cash, cars, insurance policies, savings, shares, anything not classed as heritable property, like land and buildings.'

Dame Ursula's condition had advanced from a state of alarm to one of shock. Zander set down her empty glass, took her hand and stroked it. 'Don't worry. I took care of things. Mr Munro will explain why, but once a person is adopted they no longer inherit from their natural parents, only from their adoptive ones.'

I remembered my conversation with Vikki the day of our almost kiss. How Daisy had sorted her life out and applied to adopt Molly. Though I didn't know much about the actual procedure, I assumed that was when Barry had entered the picture. La-La and Daisy were friends at the time of the baby's birth. La-La must have confided in Daisy and she had told Barry.

'So,' Zander said, 'you can appreciate how vital it was that the adoption went through before . . . before . . . '

Before they pulled the plug on Stephen, he meant, but didn't say. If it was all Barry's idea, it was a good one. Molly was being adopted anyway; why not make a few quid out of it?

From the look on Dame Ursula's face she was having great difficulty taking it all in. 'What does it mean for me . . . ?' She squeezed Zander's hand. 'For us?'

'It means Molly's out of the picture and Stephen's estate is all yours,' I said. 'Apart from Zander's quarter-share and what Barry Munn took for his troubles.'

'His demands weren't all that high,' Zander said lightly. 'A country property for his client and a cash sum for his legal services.'

'How big a cash sum?' I asked.

'Fifty. Half upfront. Half on completion.'

'You seem to have been acting fairly free with the Pentecost bank account,' Dame Ursula said.

'Would you have stopped me?'

'What about our meeting in the warehouse?' I asked.

Zander stood up. 'I've never actually met Munn, never even spoken to him. All my dealings were done through his client. Daisy said Munn was way too cautious to become personally involved. He just saw to the legal work. House of Pentecost purchased the farm for two hundred and fifty thousand and transferred title to Daisy. The first instalment of cash I delivered personally to her a couple of months ago.

It began to make sense. Sort of. When I'd phoned Zander he must have thought I was Barry who, in Daisy's absence, had come to collect the rest of the money.

'So you see, Mr Munro. Before you go accusing anyone of murder you should really get your facts straight. I had absolutely no reason to kill Daisy Adams. In fact, Daisy did Dame Ursula and me a great favour. Our shares in the House of Pentecost secured for a measly three hundred grand? That, I think you'll agree, was an excellent piece of business, and . . . ' Zander got to his feet and walked across the room, 'all perfectly legal.' He opened the door. 'Mr Munro is leaving,' he told the doorman. The man with the tan stepped into the room and politely gestured to the exit.

I looked down at Dame Ursula.

She didn't look up. 'Goodbye, Mr Munro.'

As I turned to leave, the side of my face met the flat of Zander's hand. It was a feeble blow. 'I take it you have the twenty-five thousand you stole from me?' he said. I felt the doorman's vice-like grip on my upper arms. It was pointless struggling and, anyway, I'd deserved it.

'Strangely enough not on me,' I said. 'But it's safe.'

'Then as per my arrangement I'll expect you to account to Mr Munn for it.'

'Don't worry,' I said. 'I'm going to.'

50

The suntanned doorman was decent enough to let me go off and find Malky, which I did, at a corner of the bar well away from the dance floor in a group that consisted of Joey Di Rollo and his charming girlfriend, three other inadequately clothed females and an older man wearing an ensemble not entirely dissimilar to my own intended attire until Malky had insisted I put on a suit.

'We'll need to bounce,' I yelled at Malky over the music. 'Something's come up.'

'Bounce? Are you kidding? The party's just getting started.' He gripped the back of my neck and turned me to face his companions. 'Everybody, this is my wee brother Robbie.'

Everybody shouted hi.

'What do you think of the place?' the man in jeans and jumper asked. I noticed he had a single diamond earring. This had to be Dave. He could dress like a scruff because it was his club. I glanced around at the fixtures and fittings. My mind had been so firmly on other things I'd scarcely had time to check out my surroundings. The floor was black marble embedded with flecks of crystal that caught and reflected every ray of light from the laser display. The bar was a long strip of chrome. There were no barstools, no tables or chairs, instead Perspex columns stretched

298

from ceiling to floor with circles of chrome at waist height on which to rest drinks. The dance floor, a distance away, was heaving with beautiful people gyrating in a strobing sea of colour.

'I like it,' I said, my voice raised. I could hardly tell my host anything else. 'It's very . . . uncluttered. Must help pack them in. Not much good if you want a seat, though.'

That was Joey's cue to butt in. He lunged forward, stepping on Diamond Dave's toes in the process. 'Who wants to sit down?' he shouted. 'You don't come to a place like this to sit on your arse. This is what it's about. Me and Dave use the same interior designer. I've done out all my clubs like this. It's called new-age min . . . minim . . . ' He made several attempts before his girlfriend helped him out.

'Minimalism,' she said.

I cupped a hand to her ear, so as to be heard over the music. 'Tell Joey I love minimalism. I can't get enough of it.'

She laughed. I'd spent an entire car journey trying to chat her up and she'd never cracked a light. Tonight I was Captain Hilarious.

'What are you two laughing about?' Joey roared at us.

The gorgeous one flapped a hand at him, still giggling.

'Listen,' I said to her. 'I hate to leave, but . . . ' I tilted my head at the doorman who was standing waiting patiently for me a few paces away, 'I am. It's just a case of me picking a window.'

I called out to Malky that I was going, but he was too busy rolling a cocktail olive down the forehead of one of the three unknown girls and seeing if she could catch it in her mouth.

My former chauffeur put a hand on my arm. 'If you're

having to leave because of what happened earlier outside, that was all Joey's fault. I can speak to Ursula and—'

Joey lunged forward, reached out, pulled her back by the shoulder, crunching another Diamond toe. 'What do you think you two are doing?'

'It's all right,' I said. 'I was just saying to . . . ' I realised that I didn't know the gorgeous one's name.

'Ellie,' she said.

'I was just telling Ellie I was leaving.'

For the second time that evening Joey pushed his face at me.

'Hey, Joey!' Malky took time off from rolling olives down the faces of young ladies to come over. He put a hand on Joey's shoulder. 'Leave it, will you?'

Joey shrugged Malky off. His forehead touched mine, pushing hard.

I'd seen Joey Di Rollo play many times. He was a doughty, mid-field-battler, a man without so much as a creative metatarsal, whose job it was to win the ball and give it to the skilful players. A water-carrier. Every team needed one, so they said. What they didn't need was a narky, complaining moaner who wanted to argue every decision with the ref. Joey had seen more cards held up than a conjuror's assistant and been given his marching orders more often than Napoleon's army. If chatting up a supermodel had been at the top of the Robbie Munro to-do list, giving Joey Di Rollo a slap wasn't far behind. Opportunities like this didn't come along every day, and hell, I was about to be ejected anyway.

Joey's forehead pressed harder. He snarled. Someone grabbed my clenched fist. It was Ellie. She stepped in between us, facing me, pushing me backwards. 'Let's go,' she said. Joey wasn't having any of it. He grabbed her by the wrist and wrenched. Ellie stumbled backwards, spinning around off balance. Joey gripped her delicate jawline between thumb and index finger, squashing her cheeks and shoving his face into hers. 'You're going nowhere.'

It was Diamond Dave's turn to intervene. 'You're right,' he said. 'She is going nowhere. You, on the other hand . . . '

Without a word or any noticeable gesture, Dave's wishes were transmitted to and received by the doorman. The man with the suntan snapped his fingers and before Joey had a chance to protest, his nose was rubbing up against Italian marble as London and Glasgow united to help him make a horizontal departure.

Malky drifted away with his three pretty companions in tow.

'Are you not going after Joey?' I asked Ellie.

'Not this time,' she said, taking a Martini glass down from the ledge, draining what little was left and leaving behind a spiral of orange peel.

'What was it? I'll get you another.'

The doorman materialised at my side. 'No, sir, you won't. You're still leaving.'

And I did leave, but, unlike Joey Di Rollo, I left vertically and with his girlfriend. A gin twist has one hundred and fifty calories. Mineral water with a spiral of orange peel has none. The red sports car was brought around front and we climbed in.

'Where to?' Ellie asked.

'Your place?'

'Try again.'

A starry night, a beautiful woman, a high-performance motor car – there was really only one place on my mind.

51

There are towns in West Lothian where on the way even the Sat Nav has to stop and ask for directions.

As the crow flew from Glasgow it was thirty-five miles to Barry Munn's home, situated somewhere on the road between the village of Kirknewton and Dalmahoy Country Club. We didn't have wings, but then crows don't have five hundred and sixty horses under the bonnet and a top speed of one hundred and ninety-six miles per hour.

Ellie was a lot more talkative on this trip. The first time we'd met she'd been under instructions from Dame Ursula not to speak to me. Now she was dying to find out what the big secret was. First of all, I wanted to know where she fitted into the Pentecost set-up, and, as she tried and failed to keep the Ferrari within the prevailing speed limits, she provided me with a potted history of herself.

Ellie had excelled at school and was midway through the first year of an English Literature degree when she was spotted by the Pentecosts who were sponsoring a charity fashion show at Bristol University. She'd never looked back. Thirty-two years of age, she'd spent the past dozen or so of those travelling the world with the House of Pentecost as one of its retained stable of elegant clothes horses.

'You'll have known La-La Delgado, then,' I said, as we took a particularly tight corner at a speed it had no right to be taken at.

'Ah, so that's what it's all about. The affair.'

'Sort of,' I said.

'Ancient history, though, isn't it?'

'You knew about it?'

'Of course. And Stephen's other affairs. Just about everyone did. Except Ursula. Zander made sure of that and, anyway, she's not the sort of person who takes bad news well. Talk about shooting the messenger? Ursula would have machine-gunned anyone who came to her with tales of Stephen's infidelity. I knew from the start that La-La was trouble. She wanted Stephen for herself. Worse than that, she wanted the world to know. Big mistake. There was no way Zander would let the House of Pentecost collapse over one of Stephen's little flings.'

'I heard it was more serious than a fling,' I said.

'Perhaps.' Ellie hurled us into and out of an S-bend. 'Whatever, the Delgados nearly drove Zander crazy. First of all, La-La's sister came down to London and threw herself at Stephen . . . '

'Are you talking about Estelle?'

'Yeah. Half as pretty and twice as smart.'

'What happened?'

'What always happened when the latest young thing threw herself at Stephen. He caught her. Usually he let them go again pretty soon, but Estelle kept hanging in there and eventually Zander had to step in big time. He was the only person Stephen ever listened to. Together Stephen and Ursula might have been the creative brain behind the House of Pentecost, but Zander was the business head. He sold Estelle's contract to a model agency abroad and told her that if she so much as dropped Stephen an email she'd never work again.'

'Dame Ursula told me that Estelle didn't have what it took to be a model.'

'She probably thinks that. Zander would have put the idea in her head to explain why he thought they should let Estelle go. Otherwise it would never have happened.'

'How did La-La feel about her sister being sent away?'

'Are you kidding? I'm pretty sure it was La-La that alerted Zander to the situation because no sooner was Estelle out of the way than La-La made her own move on Stephen. Creepy, if you ask me.'

'But logical,' I said. 'Why have the ugly sister when you can have Cinderella?'

Ellie laughed, shifted down a gear and accelerated through the next corner. 'La-La actually thought it would work, that Stephen would leave Ursula for her. She even tried to force his hand by threatening to go to the press. It was arrogant and stupid. Playing it low-key would have been the smart thing to do.'

'She was smart enough to have his baby,' I said.

Ellie braked sharply reducing our speed down from potentially dangerous to unreasonably fast. 'No way. Really?'

It was a long story to cram into what was fast becoming a short journey. I did what I could to summarise before the Ferrari pulled into the driveway of a new-build bungalow set back from the road and surrounded by a neat, well-kept garden that contrasted sharply with the wildness of the countryside beyond its manicured borders.

I thanked Ellie for the lift, told her that there was no need to wait as I thought I might be some time, and walked to a front door that was already opening as I approached.

'Robbie Munro in a Ferrari California?' Barry Munn's partner, Neil, was the perfect example of how opposites attract, if you ignored the fact that they were both of the same sex. Barry was short, plump and not bonny. Neil was tall, lean and handsome. Barry was a civil lawyer scraping a living from legal aid, Neil was a plasterer and, with the construction business on the rise again, more work on his books than he could shake a trowel at. Holding the door open, he shouted over his shoulder. 'Hey, Barry! I thought you said crime didn't pay!'

'Who is it?' Barry called back, immediately before Neil dragged me into the house by the front of my shirt and pushed me aside for a better look at Ellie who was fiddling with an eyelash by the glow of an illuminated courtesy mirror.

'It's Robbie Munro and . . . ' He looked out at Ellie for a few more seconds, closed his eyes tight for a few more, opened them again and then looked at me. 'Get that woman in here this minute,' he said, placing a hand on my back and shoving me towards the car.

It took some persuasion, but soon Ellie was sitting next to me on a pale-blue leather sofa, while Barry watched a sci-fi film on an enormous plasma screen and Neil ran around plumping cushions and rearranging ornaments.

'Okay, what do you want?' Barry asked, eyes still fixed on the TV screen, even though Neil had switched it off.

'I hope we're not disturbing your evening,' Ellie said.

'Don't be stupid,' Neil pushed his partner's feet off the coffee table where they had rested by a bottle of red and an empty wine glass. 'Ignore Grumpy. Ever since he bought that monstrosity all he does is sit drinking wine and watching aliens or anything with Mark Wahlberg taking his shirt off. These days the buckets go out more than we do.'

305

'Alien v Predator is a classic,' Barry said. 'And everyone remains fully clothed throughout.'

'Yeah, unless they're being eviscerated,' Neil said. 'Now, sit up and say hello to the Ellie Swan.'

Barry grunted. 'Hello, Ellie. Thanks for coming. I mean it. It's clearly made Neil's day, if not his year, but, Robbie, if you've come here to talk about Toni—'

'Tina.'

'Then my office is closed until Monday morning.'

'I'm not here about Tina,' I said. 'I'm here about you.'

Barry leaned forward, reached for the wine glass and sighed. 'What do you want?'

'What our guests want is a refreshment,' Neil said, trying to read my face and the situation. 'Come on, Ellie. We'll leave these two alone for a moment, but . . . ' He fixed Barry with a stare like a laser-sight and tapped the top of the wine bottle with a finger. 'This better not be about what I think it's about.' Taking Ellie's hands in his, he pulled her up off the sofa. 'Robbie's great, isn't he?' I heard him say as the two of them left the room. 'I broke a mirror once and he got me off with only three years bad luck.'

Once they were gone, Barry poured himself a glass of wine. 'Okay, talk to me.' He returned his feet to the coffee table. 'And when Neil comes back I want you to make it very clear that this visit is all about showing off your new girlfriend and nothing to do with me drink-driving. Understand?'

It was nice of Barry to think there was any way I could pull someone like Ellie, and, I suppose, I should have put him right on the subject, but it wouldn't do my reputation any harm if word got out that I was dating supermodels. There was also the time element to consider. How long would it take Neil to rustle up a beer for me and a mineral

306

water for Ellie, even if he had to peel the skin off an orange?

'I know about your little arrangement with Zander Skene and how you relieved the House of Pentecost of twenty-five grand.'

Barry just managed to stop himself from doing a Jackson Pollock on the ivory carpet with a mouthful of claret. He sat up, set the wine glass down and dabbed at his shirtfront with a tissue.

'It was kind of you to set Daisy up with Sunnybrae Farm, and I see your fee helped to buy a few little luxuries.' I nodded at the enormous TV.

Barry composed himself, crumpled the wine-stained tissue and chucked it onto the coffee table. 'Robbie, Robbie, Robbie. I can tell you've been drinking, but drugs too? Tut-tut.'

'No need to start getting all defensive,' I said. 'In fact, well done. Just don't bother to deny it. I've spoken to Zander and everything's okay, only he and I know about it and your secret is safe with us. All I want you to tell me is—'

'A bottle of Peroni okay for you, Robbie?' Neil yelled through from the kitchen, and I shouted back in confirmation.

Meantime Barry had started to shake with laughter. Not the reaction I'd expected.

'Robbie,' he tore another tissue from the box and wiped a single tear from the corner of his eye. 'The plot of *Alien v Predator* is making more sense than you are. Seriously, what is going on? You turn up in a Ferrari with a smoking-hot girl, obviously drunk or full of drugs, or both and start accusing me of . . . of what, exactly?'

'Taking advantage of a situation,' I said. 'Daisy Adams came to you for an adoption—'

307

'Do you even know the legal procedure for an adoption, Robbie?'

Ignorance of the law was no excuse and hadn't hurt my legal career thus far, so I wasn't going to be distracted by it. 'Daisy came to you for an adoption, she told you who Molly's father was, you knew he was rich and, more importantly, on his deathbed. You made a deal with the operations manager of the House of Pentecost to rush through the adoption. You were just doing the best for your client.'

Ellie entered the room with a tall glass, sucking some kind of pink liquid through a straw. Neil wasn't far behind with two bottles of Italian lager. He gave one to me, took a swig of the other and said, 'All right, you two, that's enough shop talk for one night.'

'We're not talking shop,' Barry said. 'Robbie has invited himself here because he wants to accuse me of something.'

'What's Barry done now?' Neil asked. 'Is he going to get banned again?'

Barry's face was growing redder by the second. 'I've not done anything!'

Neil ignored his partner's protests. 'Robbie?'

'It's confidential,' I said.

A gay man working in the construction business has to develop a certain degree of assertiveness. 'Nothing he does . . . ' Neil pointed a finger at Barry and then a thumb at himself, 'is confidential from me. That is right, isn't it, Barry?'

Barry shrugged and took a slug of wine.

'I'm glad that's settled,' Neil said. 'Now, come on, Robbie. Spill.'

'I'm not sure if it's something I should talk about in the present company,' I said, turning away from Neil's steely gaze to look at Ellie who had once again taken up position on the sofa.

'Has this got anything to do with La-La and the baby?' she asked, absently prodding a piece of fruit at the bottom of the pink concoction with her straw. The drink was probably the biggest meal of her day. 'What you were talking about on the way through? If it is, don't worry, my lips are sealed.'

Suddenly all eyes were on me and the surrealism of the moment hit home. Here I was dropping in late at night and unannounced to publicly accuse a fellow solicitor of . . . what? Doing his job and making a reasonable, well . . . more than reasonable fee out of it in the process? It was nothing I wouldn't have done given half a chance. Even if it was true, if Barry had rushed through Molly's adoption, so what? Daisy wanted to adopt the wee girl and the House of Pentecost wanted the child out of the way for inheritance purposes. Daisy got a daughter, Molly a new mum and they both got a farm to live on with their very own donkeys. For his input, Barry received enough money to buy a whacking great telly and a lifetime subscription to the Sunday Times Wine Club. It was hard to see how it could add up to a motive for murder. But it was the only clue I had to solve the puzzle of Daisy's untimely death and, like one of my dad's crosswords puzzles, the clue had to be solved one piece at a time. Nothing made sense until you put the parts together.

Ellie sensed my reluctance to speak. 'Perhaps I should go,' she said. 'It isn't really any of my business.'

Neil put a hand out. 'Stay right where you are. It's none of my business either, but I think we'd all like to know what Barry's been getting up to.'

So I revealed to all those gathered what I knew about

Barry's involvement with the House of Pentecost. How, in exchange for Sunnybrae Farm for his client and a whopping great cash fee for himself, he'd agreed to rush through Molly's adoption before they disconnected Sir Stephen from the mains.

When I'd finished, Barry, who'd sat quietly sipping a glass of wine, leaned forward to pour another and stopped. He looked over at Neil who was standing arms folded, legs crossed in the doorway. 'You know?' he said, 'I think I'll leave the wine and have a bottle of whatever Robbie's drinking. It seems to get you drunk a lot quicker.'

Neil wasn't impressed by his partner's light-hearted reaction to the allegation. 'Is it true?' he asked me. 'Is Barry in some kind of trouble? Again?' he added, transferring his gaze to his partner. 'Because if he is—'

Barry stood up, walked over to Neil, led him to where he himself had been sitting and pushed him into the seat. 'I've listened very carefully to what Robbie has to say,' he said, pacing the room. 'It's certainly an interesting theory; however, I have detected one flaw, legally speaking, that is.' He stopped directly in front of where I was sitting and stared down at me. 'Stop me if I'm getting too technical,' he said, his volume control going up a notch with every word. 'But isn't what you've just said actually a load of old bollocks?'

'So it's just a coincidence that this adoption Robbie's talking about gets rushed through and suddenly we have the world's biggest telly?' Neil said.

'Two flaws in that argument,' Barry replied, getting into his stride. 'One: check our credit card statement and you'll see that we haven't paid for the TV yet and, two, the adoption never went through. I thought his girlfriend, his other girlfriend, would have told you that?'

'Robbie's other girlfriend?' Neil said. 'It's not Robbie who's drunk, it's you. That's Ellie Swan sitting there. Why would he want another girlfriend?'

'I'm not his girlfriend,' Ellie seemed keen to point out. 'Well . . . we are friends, I think . . . sort of and . . . obviously, I am a girl . . . '

'More than obviously,' Neil said.

Barry looked at him. 'I'm beginning to wonder about you.'

'Are you talking about Vikki?' I asked. The range of remotely possible incumbents for the role of girlfriend to Robbie Munro was one that didn't require too much narrowing down.

'You saw how angry she was with me that day you met her at my office,' Barry said. 'Why do you think that was?'

I had no idea.

'Because she thinks I mucked up Molly's adoption, that's why.'

Now I was really confused. 'In what way?'

'By not having it completed before Daisy's death.'

'What does that mean?' Neil asked.

'It means that Molly won't inherit Sunnybrae Farm because unless the adoption was finalised, Daisy and Molly were strictly speaking not related to one another for inheritance purposes.'

Neil was even more confused than I was. 'So you did muck up?'

'Muck up? No. Did my job properly? Yes,' Barry said.

'So if you didn't make a mess of things why is Vikki so angry with you?' I said.

'Do you know what a permanence order is?' Barry asked me. 'Oops, sorry, of course you don't. For a minute there I thought I was talking to a lawyer.'

'Play nice,' Neil said, which was kind of him, but, reluctantly, I had to admit that I'd absolutely no idea what Barry was talking about.

Barry enlightened me. 'A permanence order from the court officially frees a child for adoption. That's not my job. That's for the Local Authority lawyers to do before an adoption even comes my length.' He finished his drink and smacked his lips. 'Council solicitors. Flexi-time arseholes,' he muttered, banging the glass down on the coffee table.

'So whose fault was it the adoption didn't go through?' I asked.

'The Council's legal department didn't intimate the original application to all the relevant people. The whole thing was just begging for an appeal to be lodged if someone came forward later to object because they hadn't been notified. And who do you think had to sort out their mess for them? Yes, there was a slight delay, a very slight delay, but it had to be done. Vikki knows that fine well. Not that it's stopped her bad-mouthing me to everyone.'

She hadn't mentioned anything to me.

'I hope you know what he's talking about, Robbie,' Neil said. He glared at Barry. 'Are you telling this man the truth?'

'Of course I'm telling the truth.' Barry refilled his glass, splashing some wine over the side. Neil left the room, I presumed to fetch a cloth to wipe up the spill.

'Next time you see Vikki, you tell her I'm sorry my psychic powers weren't fully functioning.' Barry pressed a podgy index finger against either temple. 'I suppose I should have known that your client was going to strangle mine.'

I could tell Ellie was growing more uncomfortable by

312

the second, and yet not quite so uncomfortable as Barry when Neil returned, not with a strip of kitchen roll but with an envelope. The end had been torn away to reveal the purple edge of a wad of hundred pound notes. I had an envelope just like it, but a good deal thicker, stuffed inside a pair of shoes in a box under my bed.

'So you're telling the truth?' Neil said. He tossed the package at Barry. 'I found this weeks ago in your sock drawer and never said anything. Ten grand. Care to explain?'

Barry's next sip of wine seemed to turn to vinegar. Neil came over and swiped the wine glass from him. 'Not another drop until you tell me and Robbie everything.'

As torture methods went, wine-deprivation wasn't up there with thumbscrews or the Judas Cradle, but it was enough for Barry.

Daisy Adams had asked him to do the legal work for her adoption of Molly and wanted it done quickly. Barry didn't know what the big rush was, only that where the Scottish Legal Aid Board was involved nothing was ever particularly rapid and Molly would probably be having kids of her own by the time civil legal aid was granted. That was when he'd been told that money wasn't a problem. For a lawyer, money-is-not-a-problem is about as believable as it's-not-the-money,-it's-the-principle-of-the-thing; however, on this occasion it had been true. For a rubberstamp adoption that would have paid Barry a few hundred on legal aid rates, the ten thousand pounds in that envelope was a fortune. What had happened to the other fifteen, I wondered?

'I've had the money for months now,' he confessed. 'Silly, really, holding onto it, not doing anything with it. I just kept remembering the tough time we had a few years back when you had no work, Neil. You know what my own business has been like. It's was nice knowing the money was there.'

After that, Neil's accusatory stance weakened. He even refilled Barry's wineglass. Surprisingly, though, for a man working in a trade where cash was king, he was keen for Barry to give it back. There lay madness. If Barry started refunding money to the House of Pentecost they might have the crazy idea that I should too.

'Barry, you've earned that fee,' I told him. 'Make up an invoice, pay VAT if you really must and put it through the books. What's the big problem? It's not your fault the client agreed to pay over the odds. I spoke with Zander Skene just an hour or so ago and he seemed delighted with your services.'

Ellie stood up still clutching her pink drink. 'I don't know if I should listen to any more of this.'

Barry ignored her. 'Who's Zander Skene?' he asked, his face a mask of florid confusion. You keep going on about Zander. Zander who?'

'The guy who gave you the money,' I said.

'I keep telling you, I don't know any Zander. Daisy gave me the money and I'm not putting through my client account a late payment in cash from a woman who's since been murdered. How do I explain that to the Law Society on their next inspection – or to the police?'

Daisy gave him the money? There I'd been thinking that Barry was some kind of legal mastermind when it had all been Daisy's idea. She knew who Molly's father was and had approached Zander asking for Sunnybrae Farm and a lump sum. Given Sir Stephen's wealth, she should have asked for a lot more. Maybe she had. Who knows what had been discussed? Running an international fashion

314

house, Zander was, I suspected, a businessman who could drive a hard bargain. What chance would Daisy have had negotiating with someone like him? Perhaps he'd threatened to take Molly away. To raise a claim to the child on behalf of Sir Stephen's widow. Her own wee slice of Scotland probably felt like a good enough deal to Daisy and no doubt Zander had only agreed on fifty thousand to cover legal fees because he was used to dealing with magic-circle London lawyers who charged like the Light Brigade. It was part of the puzzle I felt sure I'd never solve. Only two people knew the truth: Zander and Daisy. One wouldn't talk to me and the other couldn't.

Now that it was all off Barry's chest and the legitimacy of his nest egg confirmed to everyone's satisfaction, the mood lightened. Stern words and accusations made way for laughing and joking, beer, red wine and pink concoctions for Ellie.

Where did it all take me in the search for Deek Pudney's missing defence? Right back to the House of Pentecost. If Molly wasn't legally adopted then she was still due to inherit a chunk of Sir Stephen's estate.

'Maybe the fact that young Molly's an heiress will finally shut Vikki up,' Barry said, popping another bottle. 'And it's all thanks to me and my professional thoroughness.'

I smiled and along with everyone raised a glass to Barry. I had a lot more questions about how it all tied in with Daisy's death, but none, I was sure, that my wine-bibbing lawyer could answer. For the moment it was enough to have solved part of the puzzle.

'I can't wait to tell her,' Barry said. 'You better believe it. First thing Monday morning, I'll be on the phone to little Miss Stark with Mr Munn's very own recipe for humble pie.'

But by first thing Monday he'd be too late. If anyone was going to impart the good news to Miss Stark it was Mr Munro. She'd been critical of me for working on Deek Pudney's defence to the detriment of relations with my daughter. What would she say when she found out that it had been those same efforts that had discovered her poor wee Molly was poor no longer, and that the girl whom nobody wanted would soon be recognised as heir to a major shareholding in one of Europe's foremost fashion houses?

If that didn't put me in pole position in the race for Tina, nothing would.

52

Saturday morning, I was wakened by a newspaper being thrown in my face accompanied by a familiar and very angry voice.

'What happened last night?'

What time was it? I vaguely recalled sitting down on my sofa to take off my shoes. It had been dark then and my dad wasn't there. Now it was light and he was. I fought my way out from under the newspaper, swung my legs around and sat up.

My dad grabbed the newspaper and folded it to a photograph on one of the inside pages. 'Your brother gets attacked and you just stand back admiring the scenery?'

I tried to focus on the page, the effort threatening to tear my brain apart. Under the headline: Late Night Tackle, was a picture of Joey Di Rollo's twisted features, a doorman's outstretched arm, Malky bent double holding his nose and me performing a hapless photobomb in the background.

I managed to mumble something about Malky, a party and my immediate need of caffeine, before navigating my way through to the kitchen. Painkillers, a cold shower and coffee then, just maybe, I could face my dad. Why was he even here? Had he forgotten he wasn't talking to me?

'And drugs aren't the answer,' he shouted after me, as

I limped my way from kitchen to bathroom, crunching a couple of aspirin tablets. 'Just look at the state of you. You're a disgrace. Have you been to bed?'

I hadn't. But as I stood under a life-restoring stream of freezing water, sleep was fast receding as a priority. I had to find Vikki.

'Where's my coffee?' I asked when I returned to the living room, barefoot and drying my hair with a towel.

My dad looked up from his newspaper, pen in hand. 'Make your own coffee. I'm busy.'

'Did you even fill the kettle? You only had to pour hot water on top of some coffee. The cafetière was right there on the sink,' I said.

'Cafetière? Would you listen to yourself? Cafetière? If you'd spent less time mucking about with cafetières and more time looking after your daughter we wouldn't be in this mess. Anyway, that's why I'm here. About Tina.'

I found a pair of socks and pulled them on. 'I know, Dad. Don't worry, it's all in hand.' I looked around for my shoes. 'I'm going to see Vikki. Right after I've had a cup of coffee.'

'Do you know where she lives?'

'No, but I've got her number.'

'Then why not just phone her?'

'I want to meet her face-to-face. She lives in Edinburgh somewhere. I thought I could take her out for lunch or something.'

'You never learn, do you? It's no good trying to influence her by wining and dining. She can read you like a book and she knows that you've been neglecting Tina.'

He made it sound like I'd thrown my daughter out on the streets.

'I've been doing my job, Dad. I don't remember you

missing too many shifts when Malky and me were boys.'

'That was different. You had each other.'

'When Tina wasn't with me, she was with you or Malky. What's wrong with that? I love Tina, but my life can't come to a grinding halt because of her.'

'Robbie, you forgot to pick the girl up from nursery school. Before that you left her with the staff at your office, and all that was when you weren't even supposed to be working. Do you really think you can sort everything out by taking Vikki out for a pizza?'

'Yes, I think I can,' I said. 'When she hears what I have to tell her I think she'll see things very differently.'

I went through to the kitchen and put the kettle on. The way I saw it panning out was me and Vikki in a nice restaurant: 'I know you think I've been neglecting Tina, but there's been a reason I've not been able to give her my full attention. Right from the moment that I rescued Molly from the farmhouse I've been thinking about what I could do to help.' Vikki would be sceptical at first, it was only natural, and then I'd hit her with the news. 'I know you were upset to learn that Molly won't inherit Sunnybrae Farm, or the donkeys . . . ' No, I'd leave the donkeys out of it. 'But thanks to my efforts she's now one of the richest wee girls in Scotland. Perhaps I should have ignored her plight and let her rot in that children's home so that I could spend more time with my own daughter, but, hey, that's the kind of guy I am.' That last part needed more work. I'd give it some thought on the way through to Edinburgh, but try writing a bad report about yours truly after that.

The kettle boiled.

'I'll have a cup of tea if you're making one,' my dad called through to me.

319

I tipped some coffee into the cafetière, picked up the kettle and poured. Some of the hot water hit the glass rim and splashed down onto the draining board, spattering my dad's old newspaper and the crossword with the one remaining clue: HIJKLMNO. I'd be lucky if there was enough water left to make my dad's tea. Water. Of course. That was the answer. Water. Fortunately there was just enough H_2O in the kettle.

'And what's this important news you have for Vikki that can't wait?'

'I suppose I could wait and see her at the party,' I said, handing him his cup of tea on a saucer. 'That's if I'm invited.'

He sniffed noncommittally and took a sip of tea.

'Look, Dad, I'm coming to the party whether I'm invited or not, but I don't want to speak to Vikki there, not when Tina's Gran is around. So it's best if I go see her now which means I'll need a lift. I had way too much to drink last night.'

'You don't say.'

'So how about it?'

'You're getting no lift from me. I'm playing in the medal and teeing off at ten o'clock.'

'Oh, well, if a golf game is more important to you than your granddaughter . . . ' I drifted back through to the kitchen to collect my coffee.

'I'm not your chauffeur. And it's not my fault if you can't drink sensibly,' he yelled through to me.

'How about this? You give me a lift to Vikki's and I make my own way back. That'll still give you time to get to the golf, and—'

'No. I don't think you seeing Vikki is a good idea. Leave her to me. I'll have a quiet word this afternoon at the party.'

'And say what?'

He drank some tea and started looking about the place as though he'd never been there before.

'Dad?'

'I'll take that camp bed back seeing you've no use for it anymore,' he said, 'and you can give me the rest of the wean's clothes.'

'Dad. What are you going to speak to Vikki about?'

'Vera Reynolds is retired, has a big house and a decent pension.'

Whose side was he on? 'I'm well aware of that,' I said. 'In fact, people won't stop telling me. Just like they're very keen to point out that I'm not retired, live in a shoebox and have a pension plan that's dependent on my accurately predicting six numbers. The fact is I'm still Tina's father.'

'And I'm her grandfather.'

'Obviously.'

'Well, I'm retired too. I have a nice wee cottage with a spare room and a decent police pension.'

That remark woke me up quicker than my cold shower. 'You're going to apply for custody of Tina?'

'Why not? Ex-polis, impeccable character . . . '

'High blood pressure and an over-fondness for the falling down water.'

'You got a better idea?' he asked.

'Yes. Take me to Vikki's.'

'No.'

I ducked into the kitchen and came out with the old newspaper. 'I'll tell you the answer to the crossword clue you're stuck on if you do.'

He said nothing, just took another drink of tea.

'You know the one. HIJKLMNO,' I said.

My dad set the cup down on the saucer that was

balanced on an arm of the sofa. He wiped his moustache with a finger. 'You think you know the answer, do you?'

I tapped my forehead. 'The legally trained mind is an awesome weapon.'

'I thought you were no good at crosswords?'

'Do you want to know the answer or not?'

'If I wanted to know the answers I'd look them up in the paper the next day. The whole point of a crossword is the satisfaction of beating the crossword-setter by myself. One to one. Getting help would be like turning up at a square go mob-handed. So you can just keep your legally trained mind to yourself.'

Why did he have to make everything so difficult?

'Am I getting a lift from you or not?'

'No.'

'Water.'

'What?'

'Water. HIJKLMNO. It's H to O. Get it?'

My dad clambered to his feet, upsetting the cup. It toppled, spilling tea into the saucer, over the arm of the sofa and onto his newspaper. 'Don't dare show your face at that party,' he growled. 'I mean it. If I so much as see one hair on your head, I'll . . . I'll . . . '

'You'll what? Tell Tina that the reason she can't see her dad is because he's better at crossword puzzles than you?'

He stood there glowering at me for a moment, then picked up his soggy newspaper, ripped it into pieces and threw it into the air.

'You think you're good at puzzles?' he said. 'Put that lot together again.'

53

Vikki wasn't answering her phone. I left a message asking her to contact me urgently. Worst-case scenario I'd have to try and head her off at the pass on her way to the party. It was set to start around about four o'clock and she would be collecting Molly from the children's home shortly before then. I could wait for her there. It wasn't ideal, but I really wanted to give her the good news about Molly so that I could impart my own spin on it before Barry took all the credit.

With nothing to do but drink coffee, watch Saturday morning TV and let my blood alcohol level fall below the legal limit, I turned my mind to the question of Deek Pudney. The dead guy I'd found on the table at Sunnybrae Farm must have been acting along with the Italian Jake had tried to turn into dog food. The two of them had murdered Daisy Adams. Deek had been in the wrong place at the wrong time, and, too late to save Daisy, had acted in self-defence, killing one and injuring the other.

Obviously, I'd have felt a lot happier if I had an idea why the Italians would want to kill Daisy. That was the part of the puzzle I couldn't work out for the life of me. Still there was no doubt it was Deek's best line of defence, and it depended on two things: securing the attendance of the living Italian as a hostile witness and confirming the presence of his DNA on the prongs of the fork.

There was nothing for it. I picked up the phone again.

'You? It's Saturday morning, can you not give me peace?' the voice on the other end of the line croaked, in response to my friendly good-morning.

Some time before, Hugh Ogilvie had made the mistake of giving me his mobile number. Well, he didn't actually give it to me, he phoned me about something and I'd saved his number for times such as these.

I heard the sound of fumbling in the background as the PF reached for a watch or alarm clock. 'It's not even nine o'clock. What do you want?'

'That Eyetie. How did his blood test results compare with the fork?'

'What?'

'We spoke about it yesterday. The Italian the cops lifted for drink-driving. The one that was taken to hospital. I asked you to run blood tests on him and the garden fork that Scene of Crime took from Sunnybrae Farm.'

'I'm ending this call,' Ogilvie said. 'Speak to me on Monday morning – if you can find me.'

'Do not hang up, Hugh. This is really important.'

'Important to who? Your client? Having failed dismally with one defence, you're now starting off on another, or is it another? You know, you should really write a book. You could call it the *Robbie Munro Bumper Book of Really Shit Defences*.'

'Please, Hugh. All I'm asking is that the Crown does its job properly.'

'I'm hanging up now.'

'Do this for me and I'll lose your number.'

A sigh. 'You said that the last time.'

'Yeah, but I mean it this time. Just get forensics to speed up the testing on the garden fork. The cops will have fingerprinted and DNA'd the Italian when he was arrested.'

'They didn't. Because of his injuries he was taken straight to hospital.'

'All the better.'

'You've got it all worked out, haven't you?'

'Hugh, I'm trying to find out who murdered Daisy Adams. Who really murdered her, not just the first handy suspect that comes along that Dougie Fleming thinks will fit a frame. If the scene of crime officers took away that garden fork they must have placed some importance on it.'

'The SOCOs took everything away from Sunnybrae Farm but the kitchen sink. In fact, for all I know, they took that too.'

'Hugh, for once can you accept that I might know something you don't? Do what I ask and you can take all the credit when you catch the real culprit. All you need to do is phone whoever it is that needs to be phoned and tell them to test the blood on the fork and compare it with the Italian's. After that, you can go back to sleep and I'll never phone you out of hours again. Simple, isn't it?'

'I've got to say,' Ogilvie said, yawning, 'you do make it sound very tempting. Especially the part where you never phone me again, but, unfortunately, while we may still have the garden fork, we no longer have the Italian to go with it. You might say he's forked off,' Ogilvie sniggered. The man was as funny as he was handsome.

'He's escaped?'

'Not exactly. It seems like he was a very fast healer and discharged himself yesterday afternoon with a prescription for paracetamol and a head injury advice sheet.'

'How do you know this?'

'Because, though it may surprise you, I did ask for those tests to be run, if for no other reason than I thought it might stop you ambushing me during coffee breaks.'

'But how could you just let him go? He must have broken more road traffic laws than Mad Max.'

'None that we could prove,' Ogilvie said. 'It's not easy pinning road traffic charges on a person who's sitting bruised and battered in the passenger seat of a crashed car he doesn't own, with the keys nowhere to be seen and his fingerprints missing from the steering wheel. Vandalism by bleeding on the upholstery, I suppose, but it seemed churlish, given his injuries.'

Tam, Jake's replacement minder. The big numpty had botched the fit-up. All he had to do was park the car at the side of the road and leave the Italian in the driver's seat with the keys in his pocket while I made the anonymous call to the cops. Instead he'd wrecked a bus shelter and taken the keys away with him. No wonder Jake wanted Deek out and about. It seemed you just couldn't get the help these days.

By the time I'd stopped hitting myself over the head with the receiver, the PF was gone and the chances of him accepting any more calls from me were about the same as me finding the tattooed Italian walking down Linlithgow High Street. By now he'd probably be sitting in the shadow of the Trevi Fountain sucking down a Sambuca. My only hope was that the hospital had a sample of his blood and we could match it with the fork and find him on the Interpol database. None of that was going to happen quickly or without a series of court orders. I had a lot of work to do.

To try and cheer myself up I phoned Tina. Her gran's number rang out. Vera Reynolds had said something

326

about going shopping for new clothes. I left a message to say I'd called, and spent the rest of the morning nursing my hangover and generally moping about. Just when I thought my day couldn't get any worse, Malky arrived.

'I'm in hiding,' he said, before I could ask him why.

'Can you not hide somewhere else?'

'No, because I'm hiding from Dad. He'll want to know all about last night and I know he's fallen out with you, so this is the last place he'll look.'

'As a matter of fact, he's already been and gone.'

Malky strolled through to the kitchen to examine the contents of my fridge. An unedifying experience normally, but during Tina's stay the appliance had become home to an array of strange foodstuffs. Having considered, and wisely rejected, the slices of Billy Bear cold meat and a packet of cheese-strings, he chose a carton of yoghurt, took a teaspoon from the drawer, came back through to the living room and flopped onto the sofa. 'So I'm safe for the moment?' He lifted a piece of the torn newspaper that was scattered about and let it fall to the floor. 'I take it you saw my picture in the paper?'

'According to the old man, it was all my fault.'

My brother brightened somewhat at the news. 'Did he?' He peeled off the foil lid from the yoghurt carton and licked it. 'How come?'

'Because, Malky, everything you do wrong is somehow my fault. Like when you went hillwalking last year with what's-her-name.'

'Jenny. No, Jenna.'

'Apparently the reason you got lost and had to be rescued was all down to me forgetting to let you borrow the compass that I'd forgotten I even had and you never asked for.'

'She was all right, Gemma.' Malky said, tipping some chocolate-covered raisins from the dry side of the carton into the wet. 'Great legs. All that climbing, I suppose. Never saw the attraction in it, myself. It would be okay if they had a bar at the top, but when you actually get there it's very much like the bottom, only a bit higher.'

If only the human popsicles that littered the route to the summit of Everest had taken the time to have a word with my brother before setting off from base camp.

'Any big plans today?' he asked, stirring the yoghurt pot and setting about it.

'I'm meeting someone.'

'Not Ellie?'

'No, not Ellie.'

'Didn't think so, but I did hear that you two sloped off together last night. How'd that go for you?'

'Fine.'

He winked. 'How fine?'

'Not that fine.'

'Did you get her number?'

I'd had a lot to drink, but not so much as to forget to do that.

'You tried calling it?' Malky asked, giving me a big yoghurty grin.

'Not yet. Why?'

'Because I'm guessing all the right numbers will be there, just not necessarily in the right order.'

I pulled out my phone. 'Do you want me to put your theory to the test?'

'Don't embarrass yourself,' he said. 'Let me explain. Beauty-wise, on a scale of one to ten where would you put Ellie?'

'Ten, I suppose.'

'Probably nearer eleven. What about you?' he asked, through a mouthful of yoghurt and chocolate raisins. 'How do you rate yourself?'

'I don't know . . . an eight?'

Malky laughed at my self-assessment. 'Six and a half, maybe seven with the light behind you. I'm probably only a solid nine myself.'

'But you've got other good points,' I said. 'Like your modesty.'

He dismissed the compliment with a wave of his teaspoon. 'So there you go. Clattering into the first hurdle.'

'How many hurdles are there?'

'Two. And you hit them both bang on.'

'What's the second?'

Malky stopped mining the bottom of the yoghurt carton to look at me as though I were some sort of imbecile. 'Money, of course. Where women are concerned you either have to be better looking than them, a lot better looking in your case, or richer. Sorry,' he said, shrugging and sucking the last of the yoghurt from the spoon. 'I don't make the rules.' He rescued a chocolate raisin that had jumped overboard and landed on his shirt.

I was casually stuffing my phone back in my pocket when it rang. Vikki.

'You called and said it was urgent.'

'It is. I've got some great news,' I said.

'Really?' She didn't sound convinced. 'About what?'

'I'd rather tell you face-to-face.'

'Robbie . . . '

'There's no need to be suspicious. What are you doing for lunch?'

'Getting my hair done.'

'Getting your hair done as in getting your hair done, or

getting your hair done as in I'm sorry I can't go out with you, getting my hair done?'

'It's not an excuse. I booked the appointment weeks ago. Unlike a man, I can't simply walk in off the street and ask for a gauge two all-over, so you'll either have to tell me now or wait until the party tonight.'

'It's too long a story to tell over the phone and the party . . . well . . . it's not looking too good.'

'Your dad's not changed his mind then?'

'No, and I think I helped reinforce his decision during a discussion we had this morning.'

'Okay,' she said, 'let's meet up. I'm collecting Molly at half three and taking her to your dad's for four. I suppose I could escape for half an hour. Why don't we go for a coffee, have a chat and then we can gatecrash the party? Where would you recommend?'

It wasn't exactly how I'd imagined it, still . . . 'Do you know Sandy's, I mean, Bistro Alessandro on Linlithgow High Street?'

'No, but I'll find it. See you there about four thirty? And, Robbie, I'm bringing some good news with me too.' She laughed. 'The trouble is I think I may owe Barry Munn an apology.'

'Who was that?' Malky asked, after Vikki had rung off.

'Vikki. I'm meeting her later.'

'The Vikki that you tried to kiss?'

'She's going to smuggle me into the party at Dad's so that I can see Tina.'

'The party? Is that today? Listen, will you tell Tina from me, sorry I can't make it, but . . . well, think of an excuse for me. That's your job isn't it – making up excuses for folk? Tell her I'll drive down and see her at her gran's next week.' Malky flicked off his shoes, stretched out on

330

the sofa and, finding the remote control down the side of one of the cushions, pointed it at the TV. 'And this Vikki,' he said. 'If she's more than a seven and you don't want to be disappointed I'd lie about how much you earn before you try and kiss her again.'

54

I walked to Sandy's, breathing in the cold fresh air and planning my upcoming meeting with Vikki. How could I salvage a good conduct report from the shambles of my childminding efforts, especially as it sounded like Barry Munn had spiked my guns and taken all the credit for Molly's windfall? Even at a stroll, it took me less time than I'd thought and I was first to arrive. At twenty past four on a Saturday there was no trouble finding my usual seat in the far corner.

'Pretty quiet in here, is it not?' I said, when Sandy came over to give the surface a wipe.

'Eye of the storm. It's been going like a funfair all day,' he replied. 'Every shopper in Linlithgow has been in for coffee, there's not a scone left in the place.' He gave the table a last swish with his damp cloth and stood back to make sure he hadn't missed a bit. 'Then there was the usual stampede for paninis at lunchtime and—'

'A coffee will do me just now,' I said. Sandy seemed to be having difficulty distinguishing between an off-the-cuff greeting and a request for a blow-by-blow account of his business day. 'I'll probably be wanting some food later when my guest arrives.'

'Guest? Robbie, you know I don't like it when you meet your clients here. Can you not take them to the Red Corner Bar? I had Jake Turpie looking for you earlier. I

332

had to keep the door open for half an hour after he'd left just to get rid of the diesel-stink.'

Jake had probably been wanting an update on Deek's defence. Something that his new minder had managed to demolish single-handedly. How difficult would it have been to lift the battered Italian into the driver's seat and leave the keys behind?

'It's okay,' I said, 'it's not a client. I'm meeting a woman.'

Sandy smiled. 'Why didn't you say?' He left me for a moment and came back with a small glass vase of plastic snowdrops that had been gathering dust on the window-sill. 'I take it you've left Tina with her grand-père?' he asked.

'Grand-père's French. You're supposed to be Italian, remember?'

'So what? I'm multilingual. I'm just saying that it's nice of her . . . '

'Nonno?'

'Gramps, to look after her while you go off to find her a new mum.' He placed the vase in the middle of the table, turning it until he found its best position, giving me a nudge with his elbow at the same time.

'It's not like that. It's business.'

Sandy picked up the vase again, clearly not happy with it. 'I think I'll just give these a quick run under the tap.'

While he was doing so, Vikki came in, dumped her handbag on the floor and sat down opposite me. It was only a couple of minutes past the half hour, but she apolo-gised anyway. 'Sorry if I'm late. I've been rushed off my feet today.'

'I like your hair.' It's important to at least pretend to notice when a woman's had her hair done. 'Is it shorter?' Again, another safe line because, although it's difficult to get hair cut longer, it still sounds as though you were paying attention to the state the hair was in previously.

'It's exactly the same,' Vikki said. 'I never made the hairdresser's, I was way too busy.'

'Still,' I said lamely. 'I like it.'

Sandy came back, set the snowdrops in between us and added Vikki's request for a latte to my order.

'So Barry told you?' I said. 'About Molly?'

Vikki smiled and rubbed one of the plastic snowdrops leaves between her fingers. 'Can you believe it, after the way I treated him? It looks like he may have saved the day. Saved Molly from a life in a children's home anyway.'

How entirely predictable of Barry to take all the credit for my work.

'Not that he knew what he was doing,' I said. 'He didn't know anything about it until I told him last night.' There was no way to say it modestly. 'If anyone's saved Molly, it's me.'

Vikki sat back abruptly almost bumping into Sandy who'd arrived with my coffee. 'You, saved Molly?'

'Of course me.'

Vikki didn't seem to be taking me seriously.

'What did you do?' she asked, smiling expectantly as though waiting for me to deliver a humorous punchline.

'What do you think I've been doing these past few weeks?' I said. 'Obviously, I've been looking after Tina, but, in any spare time I've had, I've been making enquiries. Enquiries that I'm pleased to say have been to Molly's benefit. So, you see, if I've been in any way remiss in not giving my daughter my full attention, it's only because I've been trying to help out another wee girl. A more disadvantaged wee girl.'

Vikki hadn't moved since I began my little speech.

334

Sandy arrived with her latte. She picked it up, brought it to within six inches of her lips and then set it back down on the table.

'Let me get this straight. You've been spending the last few weeks trying to find Molly a new mum?'

'Yes . . . what? No.'

'That's what Barry just might have done.'

If I'd had a mirror I might have been able to work out which of us looked the more confused. 'When did you last speak to Barry?' I asked, after a drink of coffee, hoping the injection of caffeine might assist my thinking process.

Vikki pouted and frowned. 'Couple of weeks ago. He probably doesn't know what he's done yet. Which is good, because it will give me some time to think up an apology.'

Now I was completely lost.

Vikki lifted her latte glass. 'In case you didn't know, I was furious with Barry,' she said, taking a sip of hot coffee through the froth. 'I'm still a bit annoyed. His delaying Molly's adoption means she won't inherit Sunnybrae Farm and it will end up going to some long-lost relative, a laughing heir in Canada or somewhere or, if there are no takers, to the Queen's and Lord Treasurer's Remembrancer.' Vikki drank some more milky coffee. 'Now it looks like thanks to Barry insisting that intimation of the adoption be made to certain relevant people the Local Authority thought irrelevant, Molly may have a possible contender for Mum. I didn't even know she had an aunt in Portobello. I took Molly to see her yesterday afternoon, we had a good long chat and . . .' Vikki checked her watch. 'I'm expecting her to arrive any minute, so . . . ' She held up a hand, fingers crossed.

Over Vikki's left shoulder, I could see Sandy at the counter, winking at me and signalling his approval by placing a hand on a bicep and raising a straight forearm.

'Now then. What's your good news?' Vikki asked, oblivious to the café owner's gestures.

I'd been planning what to say most of the afternoon. I wanted to take my time, lay out my investigations in detail, demonstrate how much work I'd done and why it could only be expected that, in turning Molly into a very rich young woman, I may have on occasion had to leave Tina in the care of others. Instead I blurted, 'Molly is the love child of Sir Stephen Pentecost and heir to part of his fortune.'

It took a few minutes for Sandy to clean up the spilled latte that had turned the little vase into an island and bring Vikki another.

'I can't believe it,' she said, after I'd summarised my discussions with Zander and Dame Ursula from the night before. 'And you found this out when you were . . . ' Vikki pushed her new glass of latte aside, leaned forward and, both her hands planted on the table, eyes narrowed, stared at me over the plastic snowdrops. 'You weren't making investigations on Molly's behalf. You were investigating Daisy's death in order to save your client.'

I was hoping she wouldn't have managed to join the dots quite so easily.

'Don't give me all that . . . ' Vikki put on a squeaky voice that I took to be her imitation of my own, 'I was neglecting my own child for the sake of another.' She pointed a finger straight at me, a sneer stretched across her face. It was amazing how quickly you could go off people. Even really pretty people. 'The only person you were looking out for was your murdering client. You were . . . ' Vikki tailed off and sat back, no longer staring accusingly at me, but at something that seemed to be fixed to the wall behind me and three feet above my head. 'This guy Zander . . . '

'Yeah?'

Her eyes lowered to meet mine. 'It was him. He killed Daisy,' she said, when at last her eyes lowered again to meet mine. 'He killed her because the adoption didn't go through in time and he didn't want anyone to know about Molly.'

It was nice to be out of the firing line for a minute and kind of her to think that my client might actually be innocent, but I'd already ruled Zander out of the who-killed-Daisy-Adams equation.

'There are three good reasons why it wasn't Zander,' I said. 'Firstly, he would be scared he broke a fingernail in the process.'

'That's not a reason. He could have paid someone to do it.' Which, to be fair, did tie in with Deek's story of the two Italian hit men.

I ploughed on. 'Okay, not my best point, but, secondly, there was no need for him to kill Daisy. He thought the adoption *had* gone through.' After all, wasn't that why he'd given me the cash – thinking I was Barry Munn come to collect the other half of Daisy's money? It was a part of the story I hadn't thought it necessary to share with Vikki.

'That's what he'd have you believe,' Vikki said. 'What if he knew it hadn't? All it would have taken to find out the truth was a phone call to the Sheriff Clerk.'

Vikki was swatting away my reasons not to suspect the House of Pentecost's operations manager like they were flies coming in to land on the foamy head of her vanilla latte.

'And thirdly, and most importantly,' I said. 'He had nothing to lose. Sir Stephen made a will years ago leaving

Zander one-quarter of the business. Molly will have legal rights to a third of the moveables,' I said, showing off my knowledge of inheritance law, 'but that will only affect Dame Ursula's widow's share, not Zander's 25 per cent.'

'Robbie . . . ' Was that pity in her eyes? 'You're a criminal defence lawyer. It's not your fault,' she said, without waiting for me to apologise for my chosen career. 'These days everyone has to specialise. To learn more and more about less and less.'

'Tell me about it,' I said. 'Pretty soon I'm going to know everything there is to know about nothing.'

But my attempt to lighten the mood wasn't going to slow Vikki down. 'You're off to a good start then, because you certainly don't seem to know much about wills and the laws of succession,' she said.

Which was harsh, if not far from the truth. All I knew about wills was that executry lawyers liked people to make homemade ones, copied from books or downloaded from the internet, because there was more money to be made sorting out the mess later than there was doing it properly before the person died.

'Remind me,' I said.

'The birth of a child revokes a will. If Sir Stephen bequeathed a quarter-share to Zander before Molly's birth, or even if he did it after, without knowing he had a child, all bets are off so far as Zander is concerned. He gets zilch and even his widow would only be entitled to her prior rights. Molly would scoop by far the largest part of the estate.'

The woman was wasted in civil law. Or maybe it was a career in that murky world that had made her so cynical; whichever, my instincts had been right all along. From the minute I'd met Zander in that deserted warehouse I

338

knew there was something not quite right about him, and it hadn't been just his fashion sense. He'd put on quite an act for me and Dame Ursula. In fact, for all I knew, she was in on it too.

I asked Vikki to excuse me while I went to the toilet, as much to give me time to think as to expel my recent Americano. Was Daisy Adams the only one who knew the truth? Who else might La-La have confided in? The chances were that a lot more people knew the identity of Molly's father than just dead Daisy. Were those people's lives also in danger? I was one of them. So now, thanks to me, was Vikki, not to mention Barry, Neil and Ellie. Zander couldn't have us all killed.

I washed my hands and ran out of the toilet wiping them on my jeans. 'Vikki, who's with Molly just now?'

'Vera, your dad and Tina. I think they're expecting your brother too. He wasn't there when I dropped her off. I thought we'd give it an hour and then I'd try and smuggle you in.'

By the time she'd finished the sentence I was already phoning my dad's house. Tina answered. 'Hi, Dad. Are you okay? Can you still come to the party?'

'Yes, I'm fine,' I said. 'Me and Vikki are coming along in a wee while. Put Gramps on.'

The line went silent for a moment and then Vera's voice. 'Is that you, Robbie? Are you okay?'

Why was everyone asking if I was okay? 'Yes,' I said, 'I'm fine.'

'Your dad's on the way to the hospital. He's taken my car. He'll not be long.'

'What's happened?' Had the thought of losing his granddaughter been too much? It was all Vera's fault. 'Is he all right?' I yelled down the phone at her.

'Robbie, don't shout. It's you who's not all right. A nurse from the hospital called. She said you'd been involved in an accident . . . haven't you?'

Not that I knew of. Why would the hospital phone my dad? Was it a mistake? Had they meant Malky? No, he was hiding out at my house. He wasn't going anywhere in a hurry. 'Vera, get off the line right now and call the police.'

'But . . . '

'Do it!' I reached down, grabbed Vikki's handbag and emptied out the contents. 'I'm sorry, but I'm taking your car,' I said, simultaneously snatching the keys and sliding my mobile phone across the tabletop at her. 'Phone the cops,' I said, breathing heavily, trying to remain calm. 'Tell them it's an emergency and to get someone to my dad's house right now!'

55

A supermodel in a super-expensive sports car is all very well; however, if you really want to break some speed limits, you need to put a dad in a reasonably priced hatchback and tell him his child is in danger. In fact the only thing moving faster than Vikki's car on the twisting three miles to my dad's cottage was my brain. What would I do when I got there? Screech to a halt, horn blaring and headlights blazing?

I slowed to take the final bend. Through the gloaming I could see the high hedge at the front of my dad's cottage and the dark shape of a motor car beyond. Whose was it? Apparently my dad was away in Vera's, rushing to see his son in hospital. I braked, switched off my headlights and, foot on the clutch, coasted silently along the short driveway for a better look. I didn't recognise the vehicle. Fear took hold, paralysing me. A voice in my head told me to wait. The cops were on their way. Yeah, the same cops who hadn't noticed me breaking a new land-speed record and who, since the closure of the local police station, were based half an hour away. On a late Saturday afternoon in October, I'd be lucky if there was a mobile unit within a ten-mile radius.

As quietly as possible, I alighted from the car and crept along the front of the cottage trying to peer in the window. A shadow skipped past a crack in the curtains that had already been drawn. Whoever it was, they were too fast. Pressing my ear against the glass I held my breath and listened. The sound of Tina's happy voice sent a wave of relief washing over me. I might have a lot of explaining to do when the cops eventually did arrive. I really hoped so. I walked around the side of the cottage to the back door and was letting myself in when I felt something blocking my entry.

'I'll get that,' a woman's voice called out cheerfully. I gave the door another push and it opened to reveal Vera Reynolds struggling to shift a basin full of water in which a fleet of red apples dipped and bobbed. 'Robbie, it's you,' she said when I'd stepped inside. 'What's going on?'

'Did you call the police?' I asked.

'Don't be silly, and if your way of getting in here to see Tina is by sending your father on a wild goose chase, then—'

'Whose is the other car outside?'

'The door from the living room opened and a man came in giving Tina a piggyback. He was smartly dressed in a black suit and open-necked white shirt.

'Hi,' he said, allowing Tina to clamber down, come over and give me a hug.

'Hello,' I said, taking a grip of Tina's upper arm so she wouldn't wander off.

'Don't worry. I've been getting that reaction a lot recently.' He pointed to his battered face. 'Car accident,' he shrugged and then, smiling, wagged a finger at Tina. 'Always remember to wear your seat belt, young lady.'

His English had improved remarkably over the space of only a couple of days, but I'd heard enough of Sandy's bad Italian accent over the years to recognise the real thing. Did he know who I was? Did he recognise my voice? Did he know I'd been there when Jake Turpie had done that to his face and tried to feed him to the dog? Did he know I'd saved his life? Most important of all, did he know that I knew he was the person who'd strangled Daisy Adams?

'Get out,' I told him.

'Robbie, that's not very nice,' Vera said. 'This young man's come to collect Molly. There's a problem up at the children's home and she has to go back, isn't that right, Mr . . . '

'That's right,' said the man, no longer smiling, looking me hard in the eyes.

Vera reached out for Tina's hand. 'Come on, help me find Molly. I think she's hiding.'

I tugged Tina away from her. 'She's going nowhere and neither is Molly.' Not taking my eyes off the man in the dark suit, I sidestepped and lifted my dad's claw hammer that was lying on the kitchen worktop next to the bread bin. 'Now, I'm telling you for the last time . . . ' I said, hammer at my side, 'to get out.'

'And I'm telling you, you're making a big mistake, threatening a local authority official,' he said.

'Why don't we give the Home a call, Robbie? Sort this all out with them?' Vera said.

'Be quiet and take Tina and Molly away,' I said. Eyes still on the man, I gave the hammer a threatening jerk. 'Out!'

With a shrug, the man turned around and walked into the living room. If he'd come in by the front door and wanted to leave the same way, that was fine by me. I just wanted him gone. As soon as he re-entered the living room I could hear screaming. Molly. Other than her wails on the first day I'd come across her, I didn't think I'd ever heard the wee girl make a sound. Now she was screaming

343

and shrieking at the top of her lungs. I followed the man the length of the room, keeping my distance, still gripping the hammer with one hand and trying to shake off a clingy Tina with the other. Mrs Reynolds ran around me to try and console Molly who was hiding behind my dad's favourite armchair next to the fire, hugging her stuffed pelican.

The man came to a halt at the door to the hallway.

'Keep walking,' I said.

He gave Vera an apologetic over-the-shoulder glance. 'My coat?'

Vera left the screaming child and unhooked a black overcoat from the back of the armchair. Frowning, lips pursed, she shoved past me and handed it to the man who accepted it with a little grunt of thanks and stepped into the hall. Just a few more paces. Once he was gone I'd lock the doors, phone the cops and wait.

The man stopped in the porch to put his coat on, taking his time, doing up the buttons, one by one. Vera appeared at my side pressing buttons on a mobile phone.

'Have you called the cops yet?' I asked, not taking my eyes off the man in front of me as he walked unhurriedly to the door. His back was to me. One skelp with the hammer. That's all it would take. I'd have him. But who would I have? A dead or seriously injured Italian. How much would Dougie Fleming and Hugh Ogilvie enjoy that? Yes, Mr Munro, we've examined the garden fork from Sunnybrae Farm and found no blood, just some dried soil. We have, however, found blood on a dirty big, claw hammer from your father's home and also a good deal of hair and scalp tissue belonging to one of the workers at the local Children's Home. What actual evidence did I have against this guy? The word of Jake Turpie? My gut

344

feeling that Zander Skene was behind him? I knew how reliable my instincts were.

'I'm not phoning the police, I'm phoning the children's home to apologise,' Vera said, phone to her ear.

'Do that,' I said. 'Tell them Mr Bizi came to collect Molly and see what they have to say.'

The man opened the door, stopped on the threshold and breathed a stream of white into the cold October dusk.

Tina tugged at my arm. 'I don't like this,' she said softly. I glanced down at her little scared face; only for a second. Too long. When I looked up again the man was facing me, something dark and square in his hand. It was barely visible against the blackness of his overcoat that merged with the shadows of the motor car and the roadside hedge at his back. In that instant I knew there would be no negotiating. No talking my way out of this one. This man had come to take Molly away and kill her. Me and my big mouth. If I hadn't said his name, would he have gone? Now I was a witness. Just as Daisy Adams had been. He couldn't let me live. He couldn't let any of us live. I let go of Tina's hand. 'Run,' I said. She didn't move. 'Run!' I screamed and this time she ran.

The man raised his arm. Suddenly the hammer felt very heavy. If I went for him, I'd be dead before I covered the two metres between us. If I tried to turn and run, the end result would be the same. I was scared, terrified and yet with that fear came the realisation that my death was a price worth paying for my daughter's life. Better to stay right where I was. It might only be a matter of seconds, but the police were on the way; weren't they? The longer I stood there, a physical barrier between this man and my daughter, the better Tina's chances. The pistol pointed straight at me. 'I only want the kid. Give me her to me and I'll go.' The man brought his other hand up to steady his aim. I could still hear Molly crying in the living room, then the sound of scampering feet and the back door opening. I squared myself to the gun and closed my eyes. The next sound I'd hear would be my last, the roar of the gun a millisecond before a bullet tore into my chest.

But it wasn't. There was another sound. A sickening crack, then the sound of something heavy falling at my feet and a handgun clattering its way across the hard wooden floor towards me. I opened my eyes to see the prone body of a battered Italian face down, and the tall, slim, elegant figure of Estelle Delgado standing on my dad's welcome mat, a rusty old sand wedge gripped tightly in both hands.

56

I stood up to stretch my back. The bolted down seats of the police interview room were hard and unyielding and I'd been sitting on one across a table from Estelle Delgado for over an hour while the cops worked out what to do with us.

I'd already been interviewed on the immediate events leading up to Lorenc Bizi's hospitalisation with a serious head wound. Even thinking about it – the gun at my chest, Molly and my daughter running for their lives – made me break out in a sweat. I hadn't been able to stop my hand from shaking as I'd given my statement, sipping at a plastic cup of scalding coffee.

Estelle was in a very different situation. Yes, she was a witness, but she'd also carried out an assault on a man with a weapon. An attack that was likely to have caused severe injury, permanent disfigurement and endangerment to life. At least, that's what the indictment would say if one was ever served. But one wouldn't be. Not when the person Estelle had banjo'd had been about to shoot me and then an old lady and a couple of kids.

To keep the formalities in order, Estelle had been officially detained as a suspect and because of that was entitled to the services of a solicitor. Step forward Robbie Munro. If Dougie Fleming had been there he might have come up with a reason to prevent me, a witness, serving as Estelle's legal counsel, but the inspector on duty that evening seemed unconcerned. Perhaps, if the facts had been less obvious, she might have objected. As it was, while I'd been filling one policewoman's notebook with my own account, Vera Reynolds, plied with gallons of sweet tea, had been giving a similar version of events putting everyone but Lorenc Bizi well in the clear.

It was the work of a minute to give Estelle the same advice I'd give any suspect before a police interview: say nothing and sign nothing. When it came to her interview with me, however, I wanted to learn everything there was to know about Lorenc Bizi. Why he'd murdered Daisy Adams and why he'd been prepared to put a bullet in me.

Sitting there with me in that room, Estelle had the look of a woman wrung dry of all emotion. She put up no resistance to my questions, asked none of her own and talked slowly and quietly, as though in a trance.

Estelle Delgado had never forgiven her sister's treachery in ending the brief but torrid affair with Sir Stephen Pentecost that had led to her eviction from the House of Pentecost. From there she had worked freelance for a pan-European model agency, moving across the continent from one crummy job to another, and it was during those wilderness years that she'd met her future partner.

The handsome Lorenc Bizi had drifted easily in and out of the Naples fashion scene, usually drifting into the scene with drugs, drifting out having sold them, shortly before drifting back in again with some more. It was said he could have been a model himself, if he hadn't found his true vocation as a drug dealer, a vocation Estelle supported him in after their move to Scotland: Lorenc motivated by the interests of the Neapolitan mafia, Estelle by a raging heroin habit.

For a time, life back in Edinburgh was good. Lorenc was clever. He ran a string of foreign mules who imported the drugs and a team of local dealers who attended to distribution. His stock was always stashed in other people's houses and his home kept as clean as the money in his bank account, thanks to his amusement arcade laundrette.

The least clever thing Lorenc ever did was to supply Daisy Adams with heroin. Estelle knew that Daisy and La-La were friends and saw no reason to help her sister out, even if there was a profit in it. Lorenc didn't care. To him a sale was a sale. Then one night Daisy's ex-con of a husband called the cops, and the resulting drugs raid on the home of one of Lorenc's dealers was inconveniently timed to coincide with the arrival of a new shipment. It was sheer blind luck on the part of the drug squad. Ten kilos of smack was seized and Lorenc's business gone with it.

Lorenc had worked with the mob long enough to know that their unwritten terms and conditions stated clearly that drugs duly delivered must be paid for. You dropped the stash down a drain? Pay the money. An eagle swooped down from the sky and carried it off? Pay the money. The cops took it? Pay the money. Lorenc was left owing the best part of a quarter of a million pounds he didn't have or just wasn't prepared to hand over. So he disappeared, leaving Estelle to work it off.

'Lorenc hasn't been running from the law these last three years,' Estelle said, joining me to stretch her legs. 'The cops had nothing on him. The dealer kept quiet, was convicted and got eight years. He's still inside. Lorenc's running from the Camorra.'

349

'When did you find out about Molly?' I asked, moving onto Estelle's relationship, or, rather, non-relationship with her niece.

'I knew La-La had a kid. I didn't know or care who the father was. When La-La died I didn't even go to the funeral. Then, a month or so back, I got a lawyer's letter saying that I was a relevant person, whatever the hell that is. It said that La-La's bairn was up for adoption and did I have any objections. I was going to bin the letter until I saw the name of the person wanting to adopt her was Daisy Adams.'

'So?' I said.

'Her address was a farm. Last time I'd heard, Daisy was a junkie living in a women's refuge. Three years later she owned a farm? I told Lorenc about it next time he phoned me. I thought we could put pressure on her for a few quid, say I'd object to the adoption if she didn't pay up. Lorenc spoke to his cousin in Naples about it. He knew a lawyer out there who checked and found that the farm was sold in a back-to-back transaction, first to Pentecost Holdings Limited and then onto Daisy for nothing. There was only one possible link between Daisy and the Pentecosts I could think of and that was La-La's bairn.'

The inspector knocked on the door and asked me if she could have a word. Outside in the corridor I was told that a decision had been made not to charge Estelle, but to use her as a witness against Lorenc Bizi. On that basis my services as a solicitor would no longer be required and they'd like to speak to her as soon as possible.

I asked for a few minutes so I could explain to my client her change of status. In the short time I had left, I discovered that Lorenc's cousin had done a bit more digging and

350

realised that come Stephen Pentecost's imminent death Molly would inherit everything.

Estelle resumed her seat, elbows on the table, hands either side of her face, propping up her chin. 'The first I knew about any inheritance was the night Lorenc arrived at my door injured, stabbed in the back. He told me Daisy was dead and so was his cousin. He stayed the night for the first time in years. We talked and I said I'd tell the social work that I'd be interested in looking after La-La's bairn. After that I didn't hear from him for a while.'

'Her name's Molly,' I said.

Estelle sat back, leaning against the hard backrest of the metal chair. 'The social work weren't keen. They said that if I cleaned myself up, they'd maybe consider letting me visit Molly at the children's home. Take things slowly. See how they went from there. I did my best. That day you saw me I'd been off the kit for four days and was feeling like shite. Two weeks later and, hey.' She threw her arms out to her side and smiled tightly. There certainly was a big difference in her appearance since our first meeting, her face fuller, with more natural colour, hair worn long, no longer a greasy tangle tied with a rubber band but shiny and as black as rocks in a riverbed.

'You were supposed to be meeting Vikki Stark this afternoon,' I put to her.

She hesitated before replying. 'My car broke down . . . I . . . '

'You're lying,' I said. 'You'd spoken with Vikki. You knew about the party, you knew that Vikki and I would be sitting at the café waiting for you and you phoned my dad and told him I was in hospital. You were clearing the path for Lorenc.'

Estelle turned her head to face the stark, white wall of

351

the interview room. That one gesture told me everything. Lorenc had gone to my dad's cottage to kill Molly. Daisy Adams had only dabbled in heroin for a while and even with Vikki's backing, it had still taken years for her to be declared a fit and proper person to adopt a child. Supposing Estelle had got her act together, she must have known how doubtful it was she'd ever be assessed as a suitable parent for a vulnerable wee girl like Molly. At best it would have taken several years. By then Molly's ancestry would have come to light and her inheritance placed in a trust, well out of Estelle and Lorenc's grasp.

It didn't take a finely tuned legal mind to puzzle out the quickest and surest way to Sir Stephen Pentecost's fortune. On the fashion guru's death the lion's share of his estate would have vested in Molly. Upon the wee girl's death it would fall to her next of kin. Her only living relative: Aunt Estelle.

'Molly was the target all along,' I said.

Estelle sat, hands on the table, studying her chewed fingernails.

'The whole thing was nothing personal. Strictly business,' I said. 'Daisy Adams got in the way. Just like I was in the way today.'

Head bowed even lower, hair falling across her face, Estelle began to sob.

'You did the right thing stopping him,' I said quietly. 'Better late than never, but don't think that there's anything you can say to the cops now that can save both yourself and him. You try to make up some story to say that he wasn't involved in Daisy's murder and I'll stick you in so fast—'

'I didn't want him to do it!' Estelle screamed, grabbing her hair with both hands and throwing her head forward

352

so that her face almost touched the table. She rocked back and forth. 'I didn't want it! I didn't want it!' Now the tears came.

There was a knock on the door. It opened. The inspector and another policewoman were standing there. 'Are you going to be much longer?' the inspector asked.

'Just a couple more minutes,' I said. 'My client is upset. Do you think she could have a glass of water?'

The inspector looked at her colleague. I closed the door again, walked over to Estelle and stood beside her. 'No one needs to know about the phone call from the hospital. No one needs to know anything about your involvement. But Lorenc's going down for what happened tonight and he's going down for the murder of Daisy Adams too. You need to decide whether you want to help or whether you want to spend the rest of your life in prison.'

I'd asked for two minutes. I'd been allowed one. Without a knock this time the door opened and the two police officers entered, one carrying a ridged white plastic cup of water and a box of paper tissues.

'The witness is all yours,' I said.

Estelle composed herself, wiped each eye with the heel of a hand and looked up. She held my stare until it became too uncomfortable, and then turned her head to the wall.

'Do the right thing,' I said, as I walked past her out of the door, leaving her in the custody of the two female police officers. 'For yourself if for nobody else.'

57

Estelle did do the right thing. So did Dame Ursula Pentecost.

One week later, whether it was because Molly was, after all, a reminder of Stephen or whether it was a means to keep the Pentecost fortune intact, the fashion designer came forward and expressed an interest in adopting her late husband's love child. Under Dame Ursula's wing and guided by the wrongly maligned, by me at any rate, Zander Skene, there was no telling how far the child's undoubted aptitude for art might take her.

Although I felt bad about taking the twenty-five grand from Zander, and the manner in which it was taken, I didn't feel sufficiently bad to give it back to him. He may not have been paying off a hit man as I'd originally thought, but he'd still been trying to deprive Molly of her rightful inheritance. Instead I gave the money to Grace-Mary and told her to find a children's charity that might find it useful and make an anonymous donation.

Two weeks later Deek Pudney was uprooted from prison, granted immunity and, along with Estelle, planted atop the Prosecution's witness list in the case of HMA v Lorenc Bizi

The Crown wanted to convict the murderer of Daisy Adams, and, to be sure of that, needed the evidence of the man who had killed Lorenc Bizi's accomplice in self-defence.

Two weeks five minutes later, I had Jake Turpie sign a disposition transferring title to the office, and to celebrate my promotion from tenant to owner I ordered a new sign to supplement the little brass plate at the front door.

Three weeks later I was sitting at a table in Sandy's cafe along with my dad, Malky, Grace-Mary and Joanna. The custody hearing had started at nine thirty that day. First thing, Vikki and Tina had gone into Sheriff Brechin's chambers for a private chat. Hopefully, there'd been no mention of the events of Halloween which I'd later sold to Tina as all being a big scary joke, and with my sincere promise that I would never arrange anything like that ever again. The Sheriff was presented with a copy of Vikki's final report, which Barry assured me left things fairly evenly balanced.

After that, in open court, the evidence of Vera Reynolds and Tina's aunt Chloe was taken, followed by my own.

I'd been to court hundreds of times. It was my place of work where daily I haggled and bartered my clients out of, and sometimes into, prison. The place where a favourable plea bargain depended on whether the Fiscal had had a good lunch or a bad headache and an accused's guilt or innocence, liberty or freedom, hung on the whim of a Sheriff. That morning I'd been forced to stand in the witness box, a stranger in my own land, while the family lawyers asked me questions and I tried to answer them in a way that would persuade the court it was in the best interests of my daughter to remain with her father. It was the most nerve-wracking court appearance of my life.

Shortly after noon, a poker-faced Bert Brechin adjourned for an early lunch. Come two fifteen it would be the turn of my supporting cast. I drove back to Linlithgow to meet with them and carry out a final rehearsal before we all set off for court.

'Okay, let's go over this one more time.' I ignored the groans. 'Dad, it's Monday . . . '

'No, it's not.'

'Shut up and listen. Hypothetically, it's Monday. Grace-Mary has picked Tina up from school at three and brought her back to the office. Now it's five o'clock and I've been held up at court. What do you do?'

My dad sighed hugely. 'I receive a phone call from Grace-Mary to let me know.'

'On what?' My dad dug into his pocket and held up his mobile phone, until now the most immobile, mobile phone on the planet. 'Which . . . ?'

'Which I always have on my person with the volume turned full up,' he said.

'And?'

'I come and collect Tina, take her to your place and give her tea.'

'Good, don't fluff your lines. Trust me, giving evidence isn't as easy as you think.'

'You don't need to tell me how to give evidence,' my dad said. 'I'm a cop. I've been in the witness box hundreds of times.'

'Yeah, but this time you're going to be telling the truth.' I turned from him to my secretary. 'Grace-Mary. Same scenario, except you can't get hold of my dad because he's lost his phone or for some reason can't make it.'

'I wait with Tina or I ask Joanna to wait with her until you get back.'

'If you can't stay on and Joanna's not in the office?'

'I phone her.'

356

My assistant was next up to bat. 'Joanna?'

'Are you keeping me on for my legal or childminding capabilities?' she asked.

'Joanna we've got forty-five minutes until the hearing restarts.'

'I wait with Tina or . . . ' she said, anticipating my next question, 'if I'm not available I phone Malky.'

My brother was staring out of the big window at a pair of legs walking past on the opposite side of the road.

'You still got Ellie Swan's number?' he asked.

I didn't. I never had, though I did seem to have acquired the emergency number of a joiner in Bolton. 'Never mind that,' I said, giving him a shove. 'Come on, you're up.'

'Is it Friday yet? Cos if it is I've already told you I need to be at the radio station for two at the latest.'

'Would you pay attention, Malky? We're still on Monday.'

'It's going to be a long week,' I heard my dad mutter.

He was right. What was I doing? All these arrangements to fit around my own hectic lifestyle weren't fair on my friends and family, and more importantly weren't fair on my daughter. What kind of life would she have with me? Shoved from pillar to post. No two days the same. Kids needed routine. Tina's grandmother could provide that and had the money to make sure that the routine was a very comfortable one.

I got up from the table, walked out onto the High Street and punched a number into my mobile. It took Vera Reynolds a while to answer.

'Is that you, Robbie?' she asked hesitantly.

I took a deep breath. 'For what I've got to say, I thought it best if I phoned you direct, rather than go through your lawyer.'

'All right . . . Though I'm not sure if—'

'I'm sorry things have come this far,' I blurted. 'I've been giving matters a lot of thought and have decided it would definitely be better if Tina went to live with you.'

'I see.'

'You were right, I would make a hopeless father.'

'I never said that.'

'But you must have thought it and it's true. I can see that now. Tina needs stability in her life and you can give her that. Life with me is too . . . I don't know.'

'Exciting?'

'Uncertain. It's no way to bring up a child. I'm having to assemble a team of family and friends together just to make sure there's a plan in place to have Tina's tea on the table every night.'

'Well, if it's really what you want, Robbie . . . '

'It's not what I want that's important. It's what's best for Tina. I need to stop thinking of myself so much. I see that now.'

'You weren't thinking of yourself when you were ready to let yourself be shot to save Molly from that mad man.'

'Another reason why Tina is better with you,' I said. 'Less chance of armed men turning up at the door.' I tried a light laugh. It came out as more of a croak.

'And here was me thinking that was something of a one-off especially for Halloween.' I could hear the smile in her voice. My opinion of her had never changed despite the civil dispute. Vera Reynolds was a good woman, a strong woman. Like her daughter had been. Like her granddaughter would be.

'Tell your lawyer it's over,' I said. 'I'm not coming back to court today. Take care of Tina. Tell her I'll visit as often as possible. I'll bring her gramps down to visit too. It'll be fine. We'll work something out.' I could hear Frizzy-hair's inquiring voice in the background. I didn't want to speak to her. Not when I was fighting off the tears, and, anyway, she didn't need me to tell her she'd won. She'd know that already. She would always have known her plan would be a success. I'd been given a month to show the world I could be a good parent and only managed to prove what a complete failure I was.

I hung up and returned to Sandy's to let the others know. One by one they drifted away, leaving me staring into the darkness of a coffee cup, an untouched bacon roll on a plate by my elbow.

I don't know how long I'd been sitting there, when I became aware of a shadow falling over me, followed by a rap on the window. I turned and looked out to see the rotund and florid face of Barry Munn, smiling like he'd just found a case of Château Latour 1928 in the bargain bin at Tesco.

'Grace-Mary said I'd find you here,' he said, when I met him on the pavement. 'Don't you ever answer your mobile?'

My cellphone was always on silent to avoid musical moments in court and, anyway, for the last hour or so I doubted if the Scottish Philharmonic could have attracted my attention.

Barry put a hand on my shoulder. 'I'll come straight to the point. Remember how I was forever in your debt? Well, no longer.' Barry continued. 'Mrs Reynold's lawyer approached me before the case recalled after lunch. She's agreed to go for option two.'

At least that was something. 'How often?' I asked.

'Nothing's written in stone, but I expect she'll want to see Tina at least once a month, perhaps more often than that. And then there will be holidays to think about. Tina will be starting school soon. You may have to let Mrs Reynolds take her for a day or two over Christmas and a couple of weeks in the summer.'

'What are you talking about?'

'Are you not listening? Mrs Reynolds is settling for contact with Tina. She's agreed that the residence order should be made in your favour. Robbie, do you hear me?'

I could hear him. It was just that his words seemed to be coming at me through a tunnel, a long way off and taking forever to arrive.

'B . . . but . . . why?' I managed to stammer.

'She said any man who's prepared to take a bullet to save someone else's child and loves his own daughter enough to give her away because he believes it will be in her best interests, doesn't need to prove any more to her that he's got what it takes to be an excellent father.'

At some kind of prearranged signal, Vikki alighted from her car parked further down the High Street and started to walk towards us holding Tina by the hand.

'What's the matter?' Barry slapped my back. 'Go to her. Tina's yours.'

He may have said a lot more. He probably did. I didn't hear it. I was running down the High Street towards Tina who had stopped to look at a wasp in a shop window. I picked her up, kissed her head and blew a raspberry on her cheek.

My eyes filled with tears. I'd won a lot of court cases in my time. This was by far the most important. I kissed her again. Tina pushed me away, laughing.

'Do I get one of those?' Vikki asked.

I put Tina down. 'If at first you don't succeed . . . ' I said, and we kissed. We might have kissed some more if

Tina hadn't dragged me off to where the sign-maker was fitting the last bronze, well ... plastic-bronze, letter to the wall above the door to the close.

'What's it say?' she asked.

'Can you read it? Try.'

'Rrrr, Ah,'

'That's right. R for Robert ... '

'Robert who?'

'I'm Robert.'

'No, you're Robbie.'

'Robbie's just for short.'

Tina started to count the letters on her fingers and gave up. 'Ah ... '

'For Alexander ... ' I said. 'The next one's easy.'

'Munro,' she squealed. 'What's the squiggly thing?'

'That's an ampersand. It means *and*.'

Grace-Mary and Joanna emerged from the close, laughing, calling to Tina.

Oblivious, she kept reading. 'Robbie, Alexander, Munro and ... and ... '

'And Co,' I said. 'R. A. Munro and Co.'

Tina looked puzzled. 'Who's Co?'

I hunkered down, took both my daughter's hands in mine and looked her straight in the eye. 'You are,' I said. 'You are.'

Turn the page to read the first chapter of *Present Tense*, the next great title in the Best Defence series.

1

Clients. They tend to fall into one of three categories: sad, mad or bad. Some people said Billy Paris's time in the military had left him clinically depressed, others that he had a personality disorder bordering on the psychotic. Personally, I'd always thought him the kind of client who'd stick a blade in you for the price of a pint. Friday afternoon he was in my office, chewing gum and carrying a cardboard box all at the same time. The box said Famous Grouse on the outside. I didn't hear the clink of whisky bottles as he thudded it onto my desk.

'Look after this for me, will you, Robbie?' he said. No 'how's it going?' No small talk. Nothing. Just a request that sounded more like a demand.

A number of questions sprang immediately to mind. First up, 'What's in the box?'

With an index finger the size of a premium pork sausage, Billy tapped the side of a nose that was deviated considerably to the left.

'You either tell me what's in it or you and the box can leave now,' I said.

Chomping on an enormous wad of gum, Billy walked to the window and stared out at a dreich December afternoon.

'Billy...?'

The big man clumped his way back over to my desk,

1

wedged himself into the seat opposite and sighed. 'Just for a few days, maybe a week, two tops. Definitely no longer than a month.'

The box was well secured with brown tape. I shoved it across the desk at him. He shoved it back.

'What's the problem?' He tried to blow a bubble with his gum, failed and started chewing again.

'For a start I don't know what's in it.'

'It's just stuff.'

'What kind of stuff?'

'You know. Stuff. It's not drugs or nothing.' Billy seemed to think I wanted to know what wasn't in the box rather than what was.

'Stuff? What, like guns?'

'When did I ever use a gun...?'

'All those Iraqis shoot themselves did they?'

'I was in Afghanistan, and I'm a sparky. I was in the REME. I didn't shoot anybody. I fixed the guns so that other folk could do the shooting.'

The Royal Electrical and Mechanical Engineers was a fine body of men whose recruiting officer must have been having a duvet-day when William Paris took the Queen's shilling. It had taken seventeen years and a commissioned officer's fractured nose for Her Majesty to come to her senses and discharge Billy dishonourably from further service.

'Knives, then?'

Billy rolled his eyes. 'That was ages ago *and* I never got done for it. You should know, you were there. Not proven. Same thing as not guilty.'

It was the end of another hard week, and I'd promised my dad I'd be home to make Tina's tea. 'Listen, Billy. Stop wasting my time and tell me what's in it.'

Billy held up a hand, as though swearing an oath. 'No

2

guns, no blades, no drugs. And nothing stolen,' he added, reading my mind. 'It's just some personal things I can't keep at my place.'

'You've got a *place*?' It turned out he had: a homeless hostel in Dunfermline.

'It's temporary. I like to keep on the move and I can't leave anything lying about up there. The place is full of junkies. They'd steal the steam off your pish.'

I wasn't buying any of it. Even a light-fingered Fifer rattling for his next fix wasn't going to take the chance of being caught nicking from Big Billy. Not unless they fancied making the headlines next morning.

He sighed again. Hugely. 'A hundred. I'll give you it when I come back for the box.'

I gave one of the cardboard sides a prod with my finger. One hundred pounds to warehouse a box of personal belongings? If he'd offered me twenty I might have believed him. But a hundred? No, there was more to it than that. This was Billy Paris. I'd have to be as mad as he was not to think there was something extremely dodgy going on.

There was a knock on the door and Grace-Mary, my secretary, came in wearing her coat. She stared disapprovingly over the top of her specs at Billy and his box and asked me if she could have a quick word.

'That's me away home,' she said after I'd followed her through to reception. 'I'm minding my granddaughter tonight and need to leave sharp,' she added, as though she wasn't off and running at the stroke of five every night.

'Then let me be the first to wish you bon voyage and God speed.'

'You might not want to look quite so happy about everything,' Grace-Mary said.

Why not? I was one client away from the weekend.

'I've just had SLAB on the phone about last week's inspection.' Suddenly that Friday feeling evaporated. 'They want to go over a few files with you.'

'Files? Which ones?'

The Scottish Legal Aid Board's compliance and audit inspectors carried out regular inspections of those lawyers registered to provide Criminal Legal Aid. Fraud was practically non-existent, but the inspectors had to justify their existence someway or other and were famed for their strict adherence to a set of regulations which, unlike the legal aid hourly rate, changed frequently and with little warning.

'You know how they sent us an advance list of files they wanted to examine?'

I did. I'd spent much of the previous weekend going through those files, turning each one into a SLAB auditor's dream, stuffed full of attendance notes fully time-recorded and in duplicate.

Grace-Mary winced. 'When the lady from SLAB turned up on Monday you were out at court, or otherwise making yourself scarce.'

'And?'

'She gave me another list.'

Another list? I didn't understand.

'A different list,' Grace-Mary clarified.

I didn't like the way this was going. 'But you wouldn't have given her the files on that different list. Not before I'd had a chance to look them over.' Which was to say pad them out with all the bits of paper the SLAB boys and girls wanted to see.

She sniffed and fumbled in her raincoat pocket for a scarf.

'No, Grace-Mary, you would have told the witch-woman from SLAB that those other files she wanted were

4

out of the office, in storage, destroyed by flood or fire, orbiting the moon or something. You wouldn't have—'

'I couldn't stop her.' Grace-Mary stiffened, buttoned up her coat. 'I went out of the room for a moment and when I came back she was raking around in the filing cabinets, hauling out files.'

'You left her alone in my office?'

'I was making her a cup of tea—'

Tea? For SLAB compliance? That was like Anne Frank's mum handing round the schnapps before showing the Gestapo up to the attic.

'Yes, I made her tea. Why not? I make tea for all your thieves, murderers, robbers and goodness knows who else.' Grace-Mary, my dad and Sheriff Albert Brechin shared similar views when it came to the presumption of innocence.

'Firstly, Grace-Mary, those thieves, murderers and robbers you refer to are *alleged* thieves, murderers and robbers. There's nothing alleged about SLAB compliance. Everyone knows they're a shower of bastards. And, secondly, those thieves, murderers and robbers are keeping me *in* not trying to put me *out* of business.

Grace-Mary said nothing, just looked down at her desk and the small green tin box sitting on it. By the time her eyes were fixed on mine again I already had a one pound coin in my hand.

'Why didn't you tell me this before now?' I asked, dropping the money into the swear box. It didn't have far to fall.

'I was hoping the files would be okay.'

'Okay? Why would they be okay? You know I don't have time to do a double-entry attendance note every time I meet a client for five minutes or make a trip to the bog!'

'Well, if you're going to start raising your voice...'

Grace-Mary yanked a woolly scarf from her coat pocket and whipped it around her neck, almost taking my eye out with the corner. 'I've put the appointment in your diary. See you Monday.' She strode off down the corridor performing an about-turn after only a couple of steps. 'And I've put a bring-back in as well so you'll remember that Vikki Stark comes back from the States a week on Monday.'

A seven day bring-back to remind me of my own girl-friend's return from a trip abroad? As if I needed it. Vikki, legal adviser for a private adoption agency, was off on a two-week lecture tour of America. She and I were now officially an item. Our relationship hadn't exactly been torrid thus far, our times together infrequent, interrupted by work commitments or with Tina there or thereabouts, cramping what little style I had. The last few months had been hectic for me. First discovering that I was a father and then having to try and act like one. Keeping a romance going on top of that wasn't easy. So we'd been taking it slow.

Once Grace-Mary had bustled off, I returned to my room to find Billy Paris standing on my desk fiddling with the fluorescent light strip. It had been flickering for ages so I'd been making do with an arthritic, angle-poise lamp.

'Problems?' Billy asked, when I returned to my office.

'Nothing I can't handle,' I said, wishing I believed that. 'By the way, what do you think you're doing?'

He jumped down and went over to the light switch on the wall. After a couple of practice blinks the fluorescent light came on and stayed on. 'Your starter's knackered,' he said. 'I've sorted it with a piece of chewing gum wrapper, but there's nothing for it - you're going to have to splash out fifty-pence on a new one.'

'Thanks,' I said, 'and talking of money, I think you were saying something about *two* hundred pounds.'

The big man winked at me and his features carved out a grin, revealing teeth, most of them molars. At least he'd disposed of his wad of gum. 'You're a good man, Robbie,' he said. 'You'll not regret it.'

That's when I knew to say no thanks. If Big Billy Paris was ready to shell out two hundred quid for me to babysit a cardboard box, whatever was inside had to be extremely valuable. Extremely valuable and/or extremely illegal.

I showed him the flat of my hand. 'But I'll need the cash up front.'

The Best Defence Series

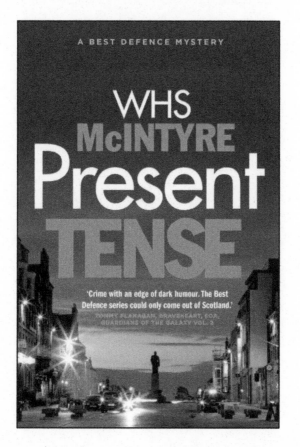

A BEST DEFENCE MYSTERY

WHS McINTYRE

Present TENSE

'Crime with an edge of dark humour. The Best Defence series could only come out of Scotland.'
TOMMY FLANAGAN, BRAVEHEART, SOA, GUARDIANS OF THE GALAXY VOL. 2

Robbie Munro is back home, living with his dad and his new-found daughter when one of his more dubious clients leaves him a mysterious box. The contents will change his life forever...

'Clear and crisp writing... a fresh take for the Tartan Noir scene.'
Louise Fairbairn, *The Scotsman*

The Best Defence Series

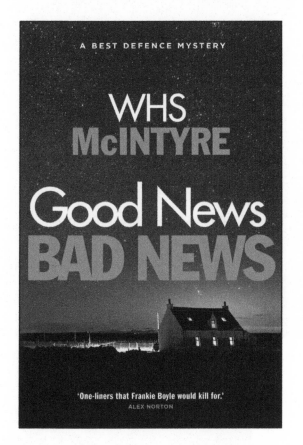

A BEST DEFENCE MYSTERY

WHS McINTYRE

Good News BAD NEWS

'One-liners that Frankie Boyle would kill for.'
ALEX NORTON

Robbie takes on a new client, only to find she's the granddaughter of a Sheriff who hates him.
His old clients are causing a few problems too, not to mention his shady former landlord. The more Robbie tries to fix things, the more trouble he's in.

'A page-turner of the highest quality.' **Alex Norton**

www.sandstonepress.com

 facebook.com/SandstonePress/

 @SandstonePress

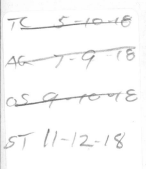